I0662227

Chloe

Chloe

BETWEEN THE CRACKS
BOOK FOUR

P.D. WORKMAN

 PD WORKMAN

Copyright © 2016 by P.D. Workman

All rights reserved.

No part of this book may be reproduced in any form or by any electronic or mechanical means, including information storage and retrieval systems, without written permission from the author, except for the use of brief quotations in a book review.

ISBN: 9781988390505 (IS Hardcover)

ISBN: 9781988390499 (IS Paperback)

ISBN: 9781774688298 (KDP Paperback 2 ed)

ISBN: 9781774688304 (KDP Hardcover)

ISBN: 9781988390468 (Kindle)

ISBN: 9781988390475 (ePub)

ISBN: 9781774688311 (Lulu Paperback 2 ed)

ISBN: 9781774685334 (accessible audiobook)

Also by P.D. Workman

FIND MORE BOOKS AT PDWORKMAN.COM

YOUNG ADULT FICTION:

Medical Kidnap Files:

YA Suspense

Mito

EDS

Proxy

Toxo

Pain

Fail

Pulse

Between the Cracks:

Gritty Contemporary YA Family Saga

Ruby

June and Justin

Michelle

Chloe

Ronnie

June, Into the Light

Tamara's Teardrops:

Gritty Contemporary YA

Tattooed Teardrops

Two Teardrops

Tortured Teardrops

Vanishing Teardrops

AND MORE AT PDWORKMAN.COM

That those who care for others may always triumph

Prologue

S HE HAD BEEN AWARE that there were two Chloes for a long time. The one who experienced and the one who watched. When she was a child, there had only been the one who experienced. Life had been experienced in full color, full of sound, taste, smell, and touch. Immersive. But over the years, the one who watched had become more and more prominent. She watched from a distance, where it was safe. Anything negative was minimized so she didn't have to feel it. The distance pulled her back from the sound, taste, smell, and touch—and from the emotion.

And that had been a good thing. So many things in life were hurtful, and it was better if Chloe could avoid them, and just watch from far away.

CHAPTER

One

Chloe was dragged out of sleep by shouting and by someone shaking her violently. Her head and shoulders flopped around, out of control, and she tried to go back to sleep instead of having to wake up and face whatever was going on. She thought maybe it was a family fight. She was no stranger to yelling in the middle of the night, to fights between her parents or between her mother and one of the other kids.

But the shaking and the shouting didn't stop. Even when they fought at night, they didn't come and shake her awake. She was supposed to be asleep in her bed. She didn't get up in the night. It was against the rules. And Chloe always followed the rules, no matter how unreasonable they might seem.

"Wake up!" a harsh voice yelled. "You need to wake up! Right now!"

He pulled the blankets off of her and dragged her to the edge of the bed. Chloe put her feet on the floor, her head so foggy and thick that she still couldn't force her eyes open enough to see what was going on.

The thick, strong fingers pulled her upright. Chloe's knees sagged, refusing to take her weight. Why wouldn't they just let her sleep? She was supposed to be sleeping. She wasn't supposed to be getting out of bed. He continued to shake her and hold her upright while Chloe tried to find her feet and give her legs the command to hold her up.

"Come on. Open your eyes now," the voice yelled in her ear. Chloe turned her head away from him, but he let go of one arm and grasped her chin, forcing her head to turn back, shaking it, slapping her lightly on the cheeks. "Open your eyes. You need to wake up. You need to get up now!"

Chloe blinked sluggishly. The bedroom light was on. The window was still dark. It was the middle of the night. The man holding her wasn't her father. She had known that, but she hadn't stopped to wonder who he was. Now as she blinked, she saw it was some kind of policeman. A dark blue uniform. Gold decorations. A heavy utility belt with a gun holster on one side and a baton on the other.

"Wha—?" Chloe's tongue was clumsy, and she couldn't slur out the question. "What's...?"

"You need to come with me now. Can you walk?"

Chloe looked down at her feet. They were on the floor now, and apparently holding her weight. She concentrated on getting them to move. On getting her right foot to slide forward so that she could take a step.

The policeman put an arm around her waist, dragging her arm around his shoulder to support her. With him taking most of her weight, he took a step toward the door of the bedroom. Chloe stumbled along with him. Her feet were moving, but her steps were the wrong length or timed wrong because nothing felt natural and right. There were other voices yelling back and forth. Too many people in the house. Why had the police come? Was there a fire? A fight? Why would they be taking Chloe out of her room?

He kept encouraging her, dragging her along by force and acting as if she was walking of her own volition. "Come on... that's right... keep going..."

He walked her through the living room, which was swarming with people. When Chloe turned her head groggily to look around at them, the cop turned her head back the other direction, away from the living room, toward the kitchen.

But Chloe had already seen, and as the policeman walked her out the front door, her brain was trying to process it. Trying to assemble the pieces of what she had seen in the living room, the fragments of voices, all the strange things going on, to try to understand what had happened.

4

He took her right out the front door, and Chloe was distracted momentarily by the frigid concrete under her bare feet. It helped to wake her up a little, and she suddenly wondered why she was still wearing her nightgown and had nothing on her feet. Why hadn't she changed before going outside? Why hadn't she gotten on her socks and shoes, at least? And a sweater. It was cold outside.

She was blinded by flashing, strobing lights. Red and blue. And more people outside. Chloe could finally hear her mother's voice as she screamed and railed at someone. She and Chloe's father must have gotten into a fight. The police had come to break it up. Her father was still in the house, in the living room, and her mother, Mim, was outside complaining to the police about the whole thing.

She could hear Justin's and June's voices too. June crying and screaming. Justin's voice calm and even. But all the noise and activity broke everything up and made it impossible for Chloe to understand. There were more sirens, cops yelling back and forth, an ambulance driving up to the house, siren screaming away. Chloe swayed on her feet with a wave of vertigo. But the policeman still held onto her firmly and she didn't fall down.

"It's okay," the policeman assured her. "Everything is going to be okay. We will take you somewhere safe, and everything will be fine."

"I want…" Chloe was still struggling to tame her sluggish tongue. "Want to go to bed. What's… what's going on?"

"There's been an accident. We'll explain more to you when we get somewhere quiet. Let's get you somewhere you can sit down."

He walked her through the cold, wet grass with no regard to her bare feet. He was wearing socks and shoes; why would he notice how damp the grass was? He took her to one of the police cars pulled in front of the house at random angles and opened the front door. He lowered her gently into the front passenger seat. Chloe pulled her feet into the car and placed them on the warm, dry carpet. It was gritty with gravel, but at least it was dry. She closed her eyes.

"When can I go home?"

"Don't worry about that right now, okay? Everything will be taken care of. They'll take you somewhere safe tonight."

"Who will? You?"

"No, it won't be me." Chloe looked up at his face and blinked, trying to adjust to all of the flashing lights and force away the afterimages. Why was she trying to memorize his face when he said he wouldn't be the one that would take her somewhere safe? He had other things to do. She would never see him again.

Chloe closed her eyes again. "So sleepy."

"Try to stay awake. There are going to be questions for you to answer."

He stood there for a moment longer, not saying anything, but not leaving her alone. Then she heard his footsteps as he retreated. Or at least she imagined she did. Probably she couldn't, over all the chaos raging around her. Chloe tried to just retreat into sleep again. Maybe when she woke up, she would find that it had all just been a dream. A very realistic dream.

She couldn't remember whether she had fallen back asleep in the police car, or whether she had just sat there, watching all of the police running back and forth outside. She wasn't sure whether hours had passed or only minutes. Everything seemed out of step. It had to be a dream. That would explain why it didn't make any sense.

A cop got into the driver's seat beside her, introduced himself, and talked all the way to wherever they were going. But Chloe didn't hear a single word he said. She didn't look at him. Didn't ask him to repeat his name, and didn't introduce herself. She didn't know whether he asked her any questions, or if he just chattered on to fill the silence without expecting any answer from her. They got to the police station. Chloe was pretty sure it was the police station. Red brick, set low to the ground; it looked like a police station. The cop pulled into the parking lot and got out of the car, then went around to Chloe's side and opened her door.

"Come on, sweetheart," he encouraged, putting a hand under her elbow and easing her out of the car. Chloe swung her feet out of the car and stepped on gravel atop concrete. She winced. It was as bad as stepping on Lego bricks when she had to get up to go to the bathroom.

The policeman said something to her, and Chloe directed her gaze at his face, wondering what he had asked. He was obviously waiting for some kind of answer.

"Is that how they took you out of the house?" he asked, shaking his head. "In your nightgown? Don't you have any other clothes?"

Chloe shook her head. He led her through the parking lot, stepping gingerly over the sharp gravel and onto the smooth tile of the police station hallways. Chloe rubbed her arms, trying to rub away the goosebumps.

A few minutes later, they were at a counter with another cop.

"Chloe Simpson," the officer who was escorting her said. "Age twelve or so? They'll be bringing in the mom and the brother."

"Thirteen," Chloe said. "I'm thirteen."

She rubbed her eyes with her fists, trying to focus on what was going on. But her brain was still too fuzzy to pull everything together.

"Where's...? What's...? What's going on?"

"All your questions will be answered soon," her escort assured her.

He stuck a red-bordered 'visitor' label with her name on it to the front of her nightgown. Then he was guiding her through the hallways again.

Chloe was taken to a bare conference room, with just a table and a few chairs. He nudged her into one of the chairs.

"Have a seat, please, Chloe."

She was happy to get off her feet again, but the metal of the chair was cold enough to feel through the nightgown. Chloe hugged herself tightly, trying to stop the shaking that started deep down in her stomach.

"What can you tell me about what happened tonight?" the policeman asked her.

Chloe studied him for a moment and then closed her eyes, wanting to go back to sleep and not have to think about anything. What had happened tonight? She'd been pulled out of bed because her parents had gotten into a fight. That was all. It was nothing to do with her. Nothing to do with any of the children.

"Chloe."

She ignored him. As uncomfortable as she was, she was going to go back to sleep sitting in the cold chair. Block him and anyone else out. Not think of anything.

"Chloe."

7

His hand closed around her arm to get her attention, then released her abruptly. "You're cold as ice!" The backs of his fingers brushed her cheek. "Wake up. You have to stay awake, Chloe. Come on."

Chloe opened her eyes again and blinked at him. The shaking inside was getting worse and so was the desire to just shut everything out. The cop moved across to the door of the conference room. Chloe heard him call to someone, and they had a muttered conversation.

"All she's wearing is a thin nightgown…" one of them growled. "…blankets, clothes… going to need a social worker…"

Chloe roused herself, rubbing her eyes. "No social worker," she insisted. "I don't need any social worker."

They ignored her. Within a few minutes, the officer was wrapping a dark wool blanket around her. It was scratchy like a camp blanket, but at least it provided a little warmth. Chloe lifted her feet off the floor to her chair, pulling her knees up to her chest so that she could enclose her whole body in the warm cocoon.

"Wait, are you hurt?"

Chloe followed his gaze to the floor where her feet had been. There was a smudge of dirt and what looked like blood. Chloe rubbed her feet.

"Maybe I cut them on the gravel," she suggested.

More dirt and blood transferred to her hands and she rubbed it away with the blanket. The cop bent over her and used the blanket to wipe her feet, examining them for cuts from the gravel. Maybe there had even been broken glass in the gravel. Where in the city could you walk through loose gravel uncontaminated by bits of broken glass?

"I don't think it's your blood," he said.

Then whose blood was it?

"There was blood in the living room." Chloe pinned down one of the fragmented impressions from walking through the house. "Why was there blood? Who got hurt?"

Her mother and June and Justin had all been outside, seemingly well. But Chloe remembered the ambulance and June crying.

The policeman let her feet be and wrapped the blanket back around her.

"You can't go back to sleep," he told her. "I know you're too young for coffee, but do you want a cola? A little bit of caffeine to help wake you up?"

8

"I drink coffee," Chloe said. She remembered how she used to criticize Ruby for drinking coffee when she was a young teen—while secretly envying her for being so daring. It hadn't been very long before coffee had replaced Chloe's customary juice and dry cereal breakfast.

"You want a cup? That would help you to be more alert."

"I was sleeping," Chloe said defensively. She looked around the room, but there were no windows or clocks. "It's the middle of the night."

"I know. You want to be able to sleep. And you will be able to when we're done. But right now, I need you to be awake and answer some questions."

Chloe rubbed her temples. "I drink it black," she announced. She wasn't a little kid, diluting it with milk and cutting the bitterness with spoonfuls of sugar. She drank it straight, like a grown-up.

"Okay. Give me a minute to get you some."

Chloe nodded her heavy head. She clutched the edge of the table, the movement of her head making her dizzy and causing a moment of stomach-dropping vertigo. The policeman noticed nothing amiss and went back to the door to ask someone to bring a couple of cups of coffee, black. In a few minutes, he was seated across from Chloe, a steaming mug in front of each of them. It was too hot to drink, but even just the smell perked Chloe up a little. Her heart sped in anticipation of the stimulant.

"Who got hurt?" she asked. "Was it June?"

"June is going to be okay. All of you kids are going to be just fine," he assured her.

Chloe shook her head at the answer. "But whose blood was it? What happened?" She rubbed her arms. "Why did you bring me here?"

"Chloe... I'm sorry to have to tell you this, but there has been an accident. Your father has been killed."

Chloe stared at the depths of the black coffee, trying to process this. There was no immediate pang of regret or sadness. Just a blank, unfeeling sense of unreality.

"My dad? How? I don't understand." She tried to think of how it might have happened. An accident? Did he fall? Maybe someone pushed him. He tripped over something and hit his head. The blood had leaked from his head into a pool...

But she knew from the fragmented memories of walking through the living room that the blood hadn't pooled anywhere. It had been spattered over everything. Small droplets. She watched enough TV to know that that didn't happen when someone fell and hit their head. Maybe if they were hit over the head repeatedly. Bludgeoned. Or stabbed, hitting an artery that pulsed and sprayed.

An accident?

"What happened?" she asked numbly.

"I'm afraid that what it looks like right now is... Justin shot him."

Another whirl of images and memories that made Chloe dizzy with their rapidity. Justin's and June's childish faces. They were eight. How could Justin possibly have shot anyone? It didn't make any sense.

Chloe took a sip of the coffee. It was still too hot to drink, but she had to get it down somehow or she was going to faint. She wished now that she had told him to put sugar in it. Maybe sugar would help to keep her from blacking out.

"Are you okay, Chloe?" the cop asked in a sympathetic tone.

"I'm... no... what...?"

"Did you know that there were problems between Justin and your father?"

"No."

"Did they fight?"

Chloe rubbed at her eyes and took another drink of the coffee. "Fight...? No... Justin talked back sometimes, maybe got—uh—spanked for it, but they didn't... fight... He's only eight!"

"It's pretty hard to comprehend, isn't it? I'm sorry, I know this must be a shock. How about your mom? Did Justin fight with her?"

Chloe shook her head.

"Was there any other trouble? There have been calls to your house in the past."

"No. Nothing. What do you mean?"

"Disturbance calls. Possible domestic violence. Your sister, a couple of years ago, being admitted to the emergency room."

"Ruby?" Chloe said blankly. Then she remembered. "Oh, Ronnie. Before she... when she went to that foster family."

He nodded. "Do you want to talk about it?"

Chloe's head whirled. "About what?"

"About the situation at home. It sounds like things have been pretty rough."

"No." Chloe shook her head and took another drink, trying to counteract the dizziness. "It wasn't. Things are just normal. There wasn't any trouble."

"You didn't see any problems cropping up between June and Justin and your father?"

"No."

"There hasn't been any increased tension? Unusual behavior from Justin?"

"No." She concentrated. "He acts like he's older than he is. Admires the boys in the gangs and wants to be grown up like them. That must be it. He just wanted people to think he's grown up. Doing something that would make them think he wasn't just a little kid."

"That seems like an unlikely reason to shoot his father."

"You just don't get how it is. He just wanted to look grown up."

The cop didn't say anything for a few minutes. The coffee was starting to do its job. Chloe didn't feel like falling asleep again as soon as he went quiet. She rubbed the back of her neck. Her head hurt.

"Justin says that your father was molesting June."

Chloe's jaw dropped. She sat there staring at the cop. It was even more unbelievable than the news that Justin had killed their father. Their father molesting June? She couldn't even conceive of the possibility. He wouldn't ever touch June. He couldn't. The idea was so unbelievable that Chloe couldn't even wrap her mind around it.

"No. That never happened."

"You never saw anything... that didn't seem appropriate between the two of them?"

"No!"

"No touching or kissing that might not have been as innocent as it looked?"

"No! No, he wouldn't ever do that."

"Did he ever do anything... that made you feel uncomfortable? Sort of icky inside?"

Chloe shook her head, tears escaping the corners of her eyes. He was talking to her like a child. Like she didn't know what molesting meant. And she could see by his kind, compassionate gaze that he didn't believe a word she said. They were automatically taking Justin at his word. Why would they believe an eight-year-old over a thirteen-year-old? Chloe was old enough to be responsible for the twins. She took care of them every day, supervised their comings and goings. She knew everything that went on in the house. It was impossible to even conceive of what the cop had said.

"You can't believe Justin," she said. "He's just making it up."

"Okay. I'm sorry to upset you. How have things been with June and Justin lately? Generally speaking?"

"Where's my mom?" Chloe looked at the closed door. "I want my mom. I want to see her."

"Someone else is talking to your mom right now. You'll see her later."

Chloe pulled the blanket more tightly around her, a shudder running through her body.

"Please. I want to see her."

There were tears running down Chloe's cheeks. She wasn't playing a game; they were real tears. She wanted to make sure that her mother was okay. Mim would be upset, crushed at her husband's demise. Chloe wanted her mother to tell her what to do. She didn't know what she should say to the cop. Maybe she had already said things that she shouldn't.

"I'm sorry, you can't see her right now, Chloe. There will be a social worker here in a few minutes to sit with you."

"I don't want any social workers! I don't need a social worker. I'm going to be with my mom. She didn't do anything wrong! I didn't do anything wrong! We're going to go home."

"You won't be able to go back to the house today, or in the near future."

"I'm going to be with my mom. Not with a social worker or foster family."

"You may need respite care for a day or two—"

"No!" Chloe insisted, her voice breaking. "I'm not! I'm not going to anyone else!"

"Tell me about June," the cop said, changing the subject. "What is June like?"

Chloe sniffled. "I dunno. She's eight. She's got dark hair like

Daddy and Justin." Chloe raked her fingers through her own thick, dirty-blond mane. "She's in grade three." She wiped her nose with the back of her hand. "She's not doing so good at school."

"No? Why not?"

"I don't know. She's been skipping a lot."

"Skipping school?"

"She doesn't feel good in the morning, so she thinks she doesn't have to go to school. I feel sick some mornings too, but I still go to school."

"She's been sick how?"

"Just her stomach. Mom says it's nothing, she's just putting it on. So I make her go to school."

"It's good that you help to look after the younger kids."

Chloe nodded. "Someone has to be responsible. I always look after them if Mom's not home."

"I'm sure she appreciates your help. How about Justin? What's he like?"

Chloe wrinkled her nose. There were a lot of words that she could use to describe Justin, none of which she would use in polite company. "He's a brat. Doesn't want to listen. Wants to be a hood. He and June…"

The policeman raised his eyebrows. "Yes…?"

"Well, they're twins," Chloe offered. "So they're really close. Always together, even a lot of the time at school. Eat lunch together and walk home together and stuff. Justin's always looking after her. Protective," Chloe finished lamely. She bit her lip. Had she said too much? Mim always said that family business stayed in the family. They weren't supposed to talk about family stuff to others.

Chloe needed to watch herself. Cops and social workers were dangerous. They broke up families. Chloe had seen it over and over again. Cops and social workers couldn't be trusted.

She recognized the social worker who was eventually shown into the little conference room. He was Ruby's and Ronnie's social worker. The last year or two. Chloe had seen him a couple of times when he came to the house to talk to her parents about something to do with one of the girls. But they didn't like to talk to him. They said he didn't need to come to the house to deal with Ruby's and Ronnie's cases. The girls didn't live there anymore; their parents didn't have anything to do with their lives.

When he walked in, Chloe gave him no sign of recognition. She just slouched back in her chair as much as the straight-backed seat would allow and pulled the blanket tightly around herself, arms wrapped protectively around her body.

"Hi, Chloe," the social worker greeted gravely. "I don't know if you remember me. My name is Mr. Clive."

Chloe just raised her eyebrows.

"How are you doing? This must all have been a big shock to you."

She didn't say anything. Mr. Clive looked her over.

"Are you okay?" he persisted.

"I'm fine."

"You need warm clothes and sleep. I'm here to make sure that you're being treated okay, and I'm working on getting you a place to move into for now until everything gets straightened out."

"I'm not going to some foster home," Chloe snapped. "I'm staying with my mom."

"Your mom is tied up right now. It might be a few days before she can really give you the attention that you need."

"If it was Justin that shot my daddy, then why are they holding Mom? They can't arrest her when he's the one that did it."

"She hasn't been arrested. But she is a witness. Both to the shooting… and to the events that led up to it. It's going to take a few days for the police to sort that out."

"They can't keep her here if she isn't arrested," Chloe said stubbornly. "They have to let her go, and I'm going with her."

Clive considered this, studying Chloe with slightly lowered lids.

"Social Services would like to take a few days to make sure that you are going to be safe going back to her," he said finally.

This, at least, was more honest. It wasn't the police. It was Social Services. They wanted to apprehend Chloe. The family had already lost two girls, and Chloe wasn't going to be the third.

"I'm not going. If Social Services takes me out, they're never going to let me go back." He opened his mouth to object, and Chloe continued, speaking over him. "Ruby and Ronnie never came back."

"Ruby's and Ronnie's cases are different. We just want to make sure you're safe."

"Safe from what? What has Mom done?"

"Possibly she allowed abuse to go on under her own roof. Allowed children access to firearms. She may have been a participant in the abuse, for all we know."

"She didn't do any of that. You can't take me away. Just because Justin's making stupid accusations about my dad, that doesn't make it true. And even if it was, he's not there anymore. What's going to happen?"

"I'd really appreciate your cooperation, Chloe. Let's work this out together. Sort out a solution."

"I'm not going to respite. I'm not going to a foster home. If you put me in one... I'm going to run away. I'm not going to be like Ronnie, a little sheep going wherever you say."

"You know why Ronnie is in foster care. She was hurt pretty badly."

"And no one ever proved it was Daddy who hurt her. He was never charged with anything. But you kept Ronnie, even though there was no proof. That's not going to happen to me. You're not going to take me away."

"It's not up to you, Chloe."

"I've got two feet."

Clive knew Ruby's history. Knew that they hadn't been able to do anything to keep her from running away. He knew that no matter what he said about who was in charge, Chloe could run the first chance she got, just like her sister. They couldn't physically force her to stay. They couldn't put her in detention for her own good. Not until she had done something other than threaten to run away.

He looked at his watch. "I still have to see the others. I'm not sure what we're going to do with you... I'll have to make some phone calls."

"I'm not going to foster care," Chloe maintained.

He gave a little grimace and got up. He snapped a business card down on the table in front of her.

"If you need to reach me, for anything—"

Chloe swiped the business card off the table, and it fluttered to the floor. Clive didn't pick it back up. He just walked out of the room.

CHAPTER
Two

I t was morning before they wrapped everything up. Chloe knew it was morning, not because she could see the daylight out a window or could accurately calculate the passage of time, but because they brought her breakfast. Chloe had shifted between groggy and wakeful states in turn, sometimes falling asleep in the chair and other times so uncomfortable she could hardly sit still. It had been a weird, disrupted night, and she felt a little like she was hallucinating the whole thing.

A policeman brought her a plate of food. She didn't know whether it was the same cop who had brought her in. She supposed he had since clocked out and gone home. But their faces were all a blur. She couldn't keep track of which cops had come and gone throughout the night, and hadn't heard any of their names.

The meal consisted of scrambled eggs, two slices of white toast, and two strips of oily bacon. Chloe's stomach twisted, and she didn't know whether the smell of the food made her hungry or nauseated. She poked at it with the fork, not sure what to do.

"I brought you some clothes, too," the cop said, depositing a white plastic shopping bag on one of the other chairs.

Chloe looked at it, then prodded with a finger to look at the contents. "Whose are those?"

"They are for you."

"Yeah, I get it, but... whose were they before? Somebody else wore them."

"They are clean. You can eat and get changed, and then I'm sure you'll be feeling much better."

"Where's my mom?"

"She is still being questioned."

"How come it takes so long when she didn't do anything? It was Justin that shot my daddy."

"These things take time."

Chloe looked at the clothes. "Are they from some dead person? Or the lost and found? Where did they come from?"

"I don't know," he said in a firm, measured tone.

Chloe looked back at her food.

"Can I have coffee? And I gotta pee."

"I'll take you to the restroom. You can change in there," he offered.

"I don't want to wear someone else's clothes."

"Well, you can't go back to your house to get your own clothes, and neither can I. You can't walk around here or leave here wearing just a nightgown. You can't go to the store to buy new clothes looking like that. So you may as well put them on."

He picked up the bag and handed it to her. Chloe stood up, keeping the blanket wrapped around her, and took the bag. He was right about that. She couldn't go anywhere in her nightgown, no matter how gross it was to wear someone else's clothes. And better to change in the bathroom than in the conference room with its surveillance cameras and a window in the door.

People looked at Chloe curiously as she was escorted through the halls to a restroom. Chloe felt her face flush in embarrassment.

"It's okay," the policeman told her. "Don't worry about anyone else. We've all seen some pretty bizarre things. A girl in her pajamas is pretty normal."

That just made her feel more awkward. The cop gestured to the bathroom door. Chloe hesitated, then gave him the blanket. "Uh— here, I guess."

He took it.

In the bathroom, Chloe looked at herself in the mirror. What a mess. She'd been dragged out of bed in the middle of the night, and her hair looked like it. It was a tangled rat's nest of stringy blond hair. There were dark shadows under her eyes. The nightgown was practically see-through. Chloe quickly pulled on the stranger's clothes. The pants were tight around her butt and baggy everywhere else. The t-shirt pulled tight across her bust, and not in a flattering way. Chloe tugged at the clothes to try to make them look better, but she didn't have much to work with. She washed her face with cold water and finger-combed her hair, which didn't make it look much better. Eventually, she stepped back into the hallway to meet her escort.

"Are you going to take me to see my mom now?" she demanded.

Chloe thought it was just before noon when they finally took her back to Mim.

"Mommy!" Chloe ran to her mother and threw her arms around her. "Mom, are you okay? Did they hurt you? Did they give you something to eat?"

Mim thumped her on the back and pushed her away.

"What they call breakfast around here," she complained. "They certainly don't know how to feed a body properly."

She indicated her ample body as if it had somehow been desecrated by the trash food. Chloe grabbed her arm and snuggled close.

"Can we go now, Mom? Where are we going to stay?"

Mim looked at the policemen. "They said we can't go back to the house. I don't know where we can go. A hotel, I guess, for today. Then after that… I don't know. We'll have to find something. There's not much money in the bank."

Chloe cuddled against her mother. Mim pushed her away in irritation.

"Don't do that. You're a big girl, not a baby. Come on, then."

Things were tense. Chloe's mother was obviously upset and still tense over everything. A policeman had dropped them at the house to allow them to pick up the car, but there was yellow tape all around the house and sealing the door and they were not allowed to go in, even to retrieve personal items or important papers. The policeman stayed there watching them until Chloe and Mim got into the car and drove away. Chloe watched out the back window until the police car was out of sight.

"Are you okay, Mom?" she asked worriedly. "Everything will be all right, won't it?"

"Does it look like everything is all right?" Mim demanded. "My whole family is gone! I have no home, nowhere to go. I need to find somewhere to lay down. I need to sleep." She blinked her eyes and rubbed her forehead. "I didn't sleep all night. They kept me up, questioning me, the whole time. Like this was my fault! I'm not the one who shot him. There's something wrong with that boy. How could he do such a thing? There must be something wrong with his head."

Chloe nodded. She knew it wasn't time to ask questions. As confused as she was by everything, there was a time and a place, and she was good at recognizing what her mother needed and when it was okay to ask questions. They had to find somewhere to sleep first.

"How about... the motel over by the dentist's office?" she suggested. "That one doesn't look too expensive."

"It's a rat trap! Of course it doesn't look expensive. It's a wonder they haven't shut that place down."

"Oh." Chloe nodded her understanding. "What about... the one that your friend stayed at, when she came to visit?"

"The Palisade?" Mim considered this, her red-lipsticked lips pursed. "Yes, that might do the trick. Not too upscale, but it's not a fleabag. I don't want to stay somewhere with bedbugs!"

"No," Chloe agreed with a shudder.

"I don't need your approval, miss."

Chloe closed her mouth. It only took a few minutes to get to the motel. Green, with a red roof. Chloe stayed in the car while her mother went in to the reception desk. Mim didn't look at her or say a word, acting as if Chloe wasn't even there. Chloe watched her through the glass doorway, though she couldn't see much with the reflection. Mim didn't turn to look at her. Maybe it cost extra to check in with a kid, and she didn't tell the manager that she had one.

When she finished registering and got the key, Mim marched out of the lobby and headed for her room. Chloe scrambled to get out, locked the car, and ran to catch up with her. Mim didn't look at Chloe or say anything to her. She opened the door of room fifteen with the key and went in. Chloe caught the door and entered behind her. Mim did not flip the light on, and Chloe left it alone. There was one bed: a double, not a queen. There was no couch or cot. Mim groaned, pulling off her shoes, and stretched out on the bed with a noisy sigh. Chloe moved slowly, using her toes to remove the flimsy tennis shoes. She crept over to the bed as silently as she could. Mim took up most of the space with her bulk. Chloe carefully slid into the remaining space.

"Do you want me to rub your back, Mom?"

Chloe knew that Mim's back hurt most of the time. It would be worse after staying up all night at the police station. The hard chair had hurt Chloe's tailbone and back, and she was young and flexible. Her mother didn't say anything. Chloe took it as a yes. If it were no, Mim would have snapped at Chloe. Told her not to touch her. Chloe touched Mim's back tentatively. There was no objection. Chloe started to rub, very gently at first, and then harder, focusing on Mim's neck, the small of her back, and the bottom near her tailbone. Mim groaned a few times when she hit a tender place, but she didn't say anything to stop Chloe. Eventually, she started to snore.

Chloe cuddled up behind her, giving her mother a hug and closing her eyes, soaking up the warmth of Mim's body. They were safe. She was with her mother, and they were safe together. Everything was going to be okay.

It was growing dark when Mim started to stir. Chloe had been awake for a while, but lay very still, not wanting to disturb her mother's sleep. It wasn't like there was anything to do. She couldn't turn on the TV, or it would wake Mim up. She didn't have a book to read, or the inclination to read even if she had. For a while she was hungry, but she just lay there cuddled up to her mother until the hunger eventually died away again.

Mim groaned. "What time is it?" she demanded.

Chloe pulled away from her slightly to turn around and look at the clock.

"It's seven."

"Seven o'clock?" Mim stretched and sat up, rubbing her eyes and twisting her neck while grimacing. "I can't believe I slept that long. We need to get something to eat."

Chloe's stomach growled. "Yeah, I'm hungry."

"I'll bet you are. You kids are always hungry."

There was no more 'you kids.' There was only Chloe.

"What's going to happen to Justin and June?"

"They'll go to jail. That's what happens to murderers."

"June too? She didn't do anything."

"Spreading lies like that! They'll have to put her somewhere. You can't have a kid like that just running around, making accusations about good, decent people. They'll have to put her away."

Chloe tried to picture the kind of place that they would put an eight-year-old murderer and a little girl who spread lies. Would it be like a jail? With bars instead of walls? Or would it be like a boarding school? Would they really lock June away somewhere or would they just put her in a foster home? Chloe decided it was best not to pursue it yet. Certainly not while Mim was hungry. It was bad to ask her questions while she was hungry. And she looked like she had a headache from sleeping all afternoon too, kneading her forehead with her knuckles.

"Do you need a pill, mom? I'll get you a glass of water," Chloe offered.

"Yes. Yes, get me a pill," Mim agreed.

Chloe took a cup out of its paper wrapping and went into the dingy, stained bathroom, where she ran the water for a few minutes to make sure it was nice and cold and wouldn't taste of rust. She rifled Mim's purse to find the pill container and took out two for her. Chloe presented the pills and glass of water to her mother solicitously.

"Here, Mom. These will help you feel better."

Mim took them and gulped down the water without a word of thanks.

"We'll go find something to eat," she said. "And stop by the store for a few things." Her eyes went over Chloe, brows drawn down. "What are you wearing?"

"They gave me clothes at the police station. Because all I had was a nightgown." Chloe tried to readjust the shirt so it wasn't so tight around her bust. "It doesn't fit real well."

"No. You look like you've been stuffed into a sausage casing."

Chloe didn't know whether to be hurt or to laugh at the image. She *felt* like she'd been stuffed into a sausage casing.

～

When they returned from eating supper and shopping, with everything charged on the credit card, Chloe judged that Mim was in as good a mood as she was going to get. Mim turned on the TV and was surfing through channels, looking for something good.

"Mom..."

"Mmm-hmm?"

"Why... why did Justin do it?"

Mim flashed a glare at Chloe and then turned her eyes back to the TV to continue looking for a program to watch.

"I told you. He must be wrong in the head. What kind of an eight-year-old shoots his father?"

"Was it an accident? Maybe he didn't mean to."

"It wasn't an accident," Mim maintained.

"Then... why did he do it? Did he really think that..." Chloe lowered her voice and tried to think of how to word the question. "Did he think that Daddy would... hurt June?"

"He's crazy. Don't ask me what he thinks."

"But Daddy wouldn't hurt June. He wouldn't do anything like that to her. Would he?"

"Of course not," Mim snapped.

Chloe hesitated to go on. She knew she shouldn't press Mim too hard. She should just back off and let Mim watch TV. But the questions burned inside of Chloe. Whenever she thought about it, there was a heavy, ten-pound knot in her stomach. She insisted to herself, over and over again, that there was no way that her father would ever do such a thing. But other thoughts, unwanted thoughts, kept cropping up, pressing their way into her consciousness.

"What about Ronnie?" Chloe asked. "She got hurt, and they thought it was Daddy."

Mim turned her head and looked at Chloe, her face flushing an angry red. "What did you say?"

"I just thought... something *did* happen to Ronnie. You took her to the hospital. I remember. But that... that wasn't Daddy. Daddy wouldn't hurt any of us."

Mim slapped her. The impact cracked like a whip and Chloe's head snapped back, hurting her neck. Chloe put her hand over the burning skin.

"Mom! Mommy, I didn't say he did it. I said he *wouldn't* do that!"

Mim was up on her feet, the TV forgotten. She looked around the little hotel room, her eyes afire. "You little minx! We've always done everything for you. Protected you and took care of you, and you have the gall to ask questions like that? You cast aspersions on your father? On me?"

"No, no!" Chloe protested, tears starting in her eyes. "No, Mommy!"

Mim thrust her hand into the narrow closet and came out with several thin wire coat-hangers. Grabbing Chloe by the hair with her other hand, Mim wrenched her around and pushed her face-down into the bed.

"No, I'm sorry," Chloe begged. "Please..."

The coat hangers whistled through the air and landed on Chloe's backside, almost making her shout with the pain of the impact. She pressed her face into the pillow, strangling her cries, willing herself to be silent. The coat hangers struck several more times, and then Mim, apparently not satisfied with the severity of the punishment, grabbed Chloe's pants and yanked them down so that she could strike bare skin. Chloe cried out into the pillow. As the blows continued to fall, she tried to protect her bottom, and the hot, stinging stripes burned her hands instead. Chloe jerked them back out of the way, putting her fingers into her mouth; until it hurt too much and she again had to block the blows with her hands to get relief from the repeated lashes.

All throughout, she choked back her cries. The walls of the motel were paper-thin, and she didn't have any desire to bring the cops down on them yet again. She muffled the screams that she couldn't keep inside with the pillow and pressed her hand over her mouth or bit her fingers, willing herself to be quiet.

When she couldn't take the pain anymore, she felt herself leaving her body, and she was floating up at the ceiling of the motel room instead, watching Mim whip the girl on the bed, feeling nothing but pity for both of them.

Finally, Mim flung away the hangers. Back in her body again, Chloe heard them all clatter to the floor. Then Mim sat down on the bed, picked up the TV remote, and started thumbing through the channels again.

"I'm sorry, Mommy," Chloe sobbed. "I'm sorry."

"Move your fat butt out of the way. You're taking up the whole bed."

Chloe pulled her pants back up over her hips and moved to the far side of the bed, squeezing herself onto the edge.

"I'm sorry," she sobbed again.

"You're usually such a good girl," Mim growled. "I don't know what's come over you. Why are you such an ungrateful little witch?"

"I was just mixed up. I'm sorry, Mom. I'll be better. I'm sorry. I didn't mean to be bad."

"See that you are," Mim snapped.

Then she said nothing more, watching the TV.

CHAPTER
Three

C hloe looked in the mirror in the bathroom while she carefully covered the bruise on her face with makeup to camouflage it. Her hands hurt, but were not too obviously bruised. Not unless you looked at them carefully under a good light. The real damage was hidden from sight. She would have to be careful not to wince when she sat down. No one could know what had happened.

"Why do we have to see Clive again?" she had asked Mim, who was wolfing down her breakfast while sitting on the bed.

"Some nonsense about making sure that you are in a safe environment. I don't think he has any right to insist on an interview. He doesn't have any evidence that you're not safe. But..." Mim sighed heavily. "Sometimes it's just easier to meet with them for a few minutes than it is to protest and try to talk to someone further up the line. It's a pain in the rear, but it's easier to just see him for a few minutes than to waste time arguing about it."

"Okay. So... it's just a few minutes, right? And I don't have to go with him. He can't take me away with him."

"He has no reason to take you away. June and Justin can tell all the stories they want; there's no evidence that you are in any danger or ever were."

"Okay."

Chloe examined her face, turning this way and that in the light to see if she could spot any sign of the bruise where Mim had slapped her. Finally satisfied, she turned off the bathroom light and went back into the hotel room. Mim was finishing her breakfast. Chloe picked up a slice of orange abandoned on the side of one of the plates and sucked on it.

"Stop that disgusting sound."

"Sorry." Chloe tossed it into the garbage can and it bounced back out. Bending down to retrieve it, Chloe saw a coat hanger under the edge of the bed. She picked it up and hung it back in the closet where it belonged and put the orange peel into the garbage. She eyed Mim's mug. "Do you want any more coffee, Mom?"

"No, any more and I'm going to float away. I'll be peeing all morning."

Chloe poured the rest of the coffee into her own empty mug.

There was a knock on the door. Chloe looked at the clock. It was ten on the dot. She opened the door to Clive.

"Chloe," he greeted with a nod. He reached out his hand to shake with her, but Chloe just folded her arms in front of her and looked at him. He could think it was defiance if he liked. But she knew she couldn't shake hands with him without a grimace of pain from the whipping she'd taken. "You're looking better," Clive observed.

She couldn't look much worse than she had, bedhead, in shock, lost in confusion over what had just happened. Now her hair was combed, make-up perfect, and she was wearing one of the outfits that they had purchased the previous day, neat and clean.

"Come on in," Chloe said.

There was nowhere for him to sit, unless he wanted to sit on the bed with Mim. He didn't. Chloe did, though, easing carefully onto the bed next to Mim and snuggling up against her, resting her head on her mother's well-padded shoulder. Mr. Clive entered, shut the door, and leaned against the wall. He tried to look casual but was obviously uncomfortable standing there.

"How are things going Mrs. Simpson? I realize that the two of you have been through a terrible ordeal."

"Oh, you realize that, do you? Not to mention being grilled by the police. Grilled, after my husband was killed in front of my eyes! Treating me like a criminal. Making horrible, hurtful accusations. Is that how you treat innocent victims of tragedy?"

"I'm sorry. That was the police, not me. I'm not here to interrogate you or to accuse you of anything. I truly just want to know how you are getting along. I'm here to help."

"How are you going to help? Are you going to get me my house back? Clear my good name? Change the past? There's nothing you can do to help me."

"I could take Chloe off of your hands for a few days. Put her into respite. Give you a break to get yourself back together again."

Chloe shook her head but didn't dare argue with Clive in front of her mother. If she embarrassed the family in front of Mim, she'd live to regret it.

"You are not going to take Chloe away from me. The girl is all I've got left!"

"I'm not threatening anything. I'm offering to help."

"We don't need that kind of help. You can see everything is fine. Chloe is dressed and fed. We have somewhere to sleep for a few days. How long is it going to be before we can go back home again?"

"It will be a while. It is still a crime scene and there is more investigation to be done. When you do go back..." Clive shook his head, looking at Chloe. "Are you going to want to live there? Where this awful thing happened? I imagine you'll want to move. Start fresh somewhere else. Without all those memories."

Mim's mouth was a grim, straight line. "You're probably right," she admitted. "But moving... isn't that simple. We don't own the house. I don't have money for a damage deposit somewhere else."

"Yes, that makes it difficult. There are programs. We can help you to find a place if you like. Cover the first month."

Mim's eyes glinted. "Maybe," she agreed.

"Was..." Clive hesitated, his mouth twisting as he considered his question. "Did your husband have any insurance?"

"We never bought any."

"Maybe through his work?"

She nodded slowly. "There might have been something through his work benefits. Who would I talk to about that? His boss? Just go down to his job site?"

"I'm sure his boss could point you in the right direction, anyway. If he does have insurance through work, then it might be enough to help you move somewhere more suitable. Maybe put down a deposit on a house of your own."

"Our own house?" Chloe whispered.

They had always, in her memory, rented. There were always strictures against changing anything, putting nail holes in walls, fights over who was to fix the plumbing or deal with electrical wiring problems. There were always landlords who didn't like kids, neighbors who complained, sometimes upstairs or downstairs neighbors who yelled about every noise they made. To have a house of their own, where they could paint rooms whatever color they pleased and put pictures up wherever they wanted to... it was like a dream.

Mim glared at her. Chloe closed her mouth and was careful to keep her expression neutral. Mr. Clive might be there to see Chloe, but Chloe did not have permission to speak and should not say anything without Mim's approval.

"And schooling...?" Clive suggested.

"She'll get to school once we're settled somewhere. She can't exactly go while we're moving around, homeless."

"You have a car and could get her to school. Or I could arrange for transportation."

"You will not. I will take her to school when I decide the time is right. Do you know how she'll be treated if I take her back to her old school now? When we're settled I'll figure it out. I'm not subjecting her to being bullied by the other students who have been told all out about our private lives. No."

"I'll go to school whenever you say," Chloe promised her mother. "I don't care what the other kids say to me."

Mim glared at her. Chloe swallowed and ducked her head, looking down at her hands. Clive shifted, looking around the tiny motel room.

"This won't do for long. Chloe needs a bed of her own and you will need a fridge and stove. You don't want to live on fast food."

"It's only temporary." Mim pointed out the obvious. "I can't afford to stay here for more than a few days. I'll find out about that insurance thing."

≈

Things were disrupted for a long time. There was insurance, but it was going to be a while before they could get their hands on it. There were a couple more motels, each one rougher than the last, and then sleeping on couches and floors at the houses of friends and people who were almost strangers.

They were allowed to go back to the house just in time to clear everything out before they were evicted. They had a day to go through everything they owned. Not just Chloe's and her mother's possessions, but June's, Justin's, and their father's. There was no way to keep anything. Chloe managed to save a necklace her father had given her, a couple of her favorite pieces of clothing, and a spare pair of shoes. Mim threw everything else out with no sign of regret. But Chloe noticed that Mim's bag of rescued clothing was bigger and heavier than Chloe's.

They spent way too much time meeting with the prosecutor who was building the case against Justin. Chloe listened carefully to every instruction the tall, silver-haired lawyer gave. What Justin had done could never be forgiven. His slander of the family was an even worse sin than the murder.

When the police released the body for burial, Chloe went with Mim to help with the arrangements. Chloe went everywhere with Mim. She wasn't going back to school yet and her mother needed her help to deal with all the new challenges that life was throwing at her. At the funeral home, they looked together through the books of caskets to find the cheapest ones. Mim started to cry.

Chloe rubbed her shoulder. "It's okay, Mom. It will be okay."

Mim sniffled. "I can't even afford a decent casket. It might be months before we can get the insurance money. In the meantime... we're maxing out the cards. All I can afford is... a box."

Even the simplest caskets were out of their budget.

"We'll just have to try, and hope the card goes through..." Mim sobbed.

"Look. Daddy would like this one. Don't you think he would? It's very professional looking."

Mim looked at the glossy black casket that Chloe pointed to. "Yes," she agreed, "I guess he would like that one."

"No one will know it's a cheap one. It looks good."

Mim nodded, wiping her eyes.

"We'll need some flowers," Chloe said.

They moved onto the flower catalog and pored through it to find an acceptable arrangement. They talked to the somber-looking funeral director about a church that would host the funeral for free, and the other little bits and pieces they needed to make decisions about. Mostly Mim sobbed and sniffled her way through the interview and Chloe made the suggestions or decisions.

"Would you like to view the body?" the director asked. "And do you want to dress him, or do you want us to do that?"

Chloe looked at Mim. Her mother had retrieved his one suit from the house when they went through it and she had brought it in a white grocery bag. Mim had been mortified to discover that she hadn't thought to keep any of his underwear or socks, and was not comforted when Chloe pointed out that no one would know the difference. Mim was shaking her head, looking white and frightened.

"Do you want to see him, Mom?"

"Yes. Yes, I want to see him."

"But you don't want to dress him?"

Mim thrust the bag at Chloe.

"You want them to do it?"

Mim nodded. Chloe passed the bag to the man, handling it as delicately as a bomb. The last thing Chloe wanted to do was to see the body. But her mother wanted to see and they couldn't be separated. Her mother needed her for this. Chloe had to be there to give her strength. The funeral director led them to a viewing room. It wasn't like the morgue on TV, with long refrigerated body drawers or a black body bag. It was like someone's living room, and the body was decently covered as if he was only asleep. Mim started crying immediately.

Chloe had not cried over her father's death. It all seemed so unreal. But when she forced herself to think about it, when she tried to comprehend that it was true, and he was gone forever, she felt no sadness and regret. She was almost devoid of feeling. There was something, some emotion that she felt when she looked at the body and tried to impress upon her mind that this was death. This was final. He was gone. She felt just a twinge of relief.

Mim pulled the drape back, baring the upper torso of the body. Chloe was embarrassed. She had certainly seen her father's bare chest before. But it seemed indecent there. She looked quickly away, but her brain ticked away, cataloging what it had noted. Flaccid chest muscles, not rippling with power as they always had in the past. A bit of a paunchy belly. The curly hair of his chest starting to gray.

And the bullet holes and Y-incision that had been sewn back up.

Mim touched the bullet holes with her fingertips, choking sobs bursting from her.

"How could he do that? Oh, look at you... how could he do that?" she mourned. She laid her cheek on his chest. She turned her head and kissed the bullet holes as if they were boo-boos that a mama could kiss away.

Chloe was sick. She turned and fled from the room. There was no time to ask the funeral home staff where to go. She had seen one restroom on their way in and she bee-lined for it. She made it to the toilet, where she lost what was left of her breakfast of coffee and hash browns.

She retched and heaved long after her stomach was empty.

No one interrupted her, but when she was done and washing up at the sink, one of the female staff solicitously brought her a glass of water to rinse her mouth and an ice pack to put on the back of her neck.

"It's okay," the woman crooned. "It's nothing to be embarrassed about. Everybody reacts differently. This is a difficult time."

Chloe nodded, not knowing how to explain what she was feeling. The woman put her arm around Chloe to comfort her. The first hug Chloe had had since it happened. The first warm, human touch since she had been wrenched out of bed in the middle of the night. Chloe buried her head against the woman's shoulder, trying to catch her breath. She wasn't crying. There were no tears, but she desperately needed the comfort.

Eventually, she went back to the viewing room. She didn't go in, but waited outside for Mim to finish her goodbyes. Eventually, her mother came out. Chloe grasped Mim's fleshy arm and hugged it to her.

"Where did you go?" Mim demanded.

"I thought... you should be alone," Chloe lied.

Mim seemed to accept this. She shook free of Chloe's grasp.

"We need to go buy socks."

31

"Okay."

As they browsed through the rack of men's socks at the department store, Chloe thought about the funeral arrangements.

"Who will be at the funeral? Will it just be you and me?"

"We'll make some phone calls. People will come to say goodbye."

Chloe nodded. She hoped she didn't have to make too many of those phone calls herself, while Mim sobbed in the background.

"The other children will be there. Mr. Clive has been asking when it will be, so that the others can be there."

"Ruby and Ronnie? It will be nice to see them," Chloe suggested.

"*All* of his children will be there."

Chloe pressed a hand to her stomach, willing it to stay quiet and still. She wasn't going to throw up again.

"All of them? June and Justin?"

Mim nodded.

"But they... they can't come! They're in jail, aren't they? They can't come when Justin's the one who killed him!"

"Mr. Clive said we have to let them come. The lawyer said it would look bad if we kept them away. People would feel more sympathy for them, and that wouldn't be good for our case."

Chloe shook her head. Mim took down a pair of argyle socks in dark colors.

"What do you think of those?"

Chloe shook her head. "He'd hate them. You know he hated socks with patterns on them."

"Yes," Mim agreed fondly, gazing at the socks. "It would be sort of funny to dress him in those for his funeral."

"You wouldn't do that, would you?"

Mim bought the argyle socks and a pair of plain, black, wool socks. They went back to the funeral home. Mim gave the plain socks to one of the women funeral workers. She kept the argyle socks and sat in the car with them in her ample lap, stroking them like a kitten.

Chloe hoped that June and Justin wouldn't come to the funeral. It would make it too hard. Couldn't they come early, before the funeral, and say their goodbyes, and leave the rest of the family to mourn at the funeral undistracted?

Chloe stood with Mim at the front of the room with the casket as people came into the viewing to look at Chloe's father one more time before the casket was shut. Chloe wished that they had decided on a closed casket. She could see the morbid curiosity in people's eyes as they walked past the casket, searching for some sign of the bullet wounds they knew were there.

Everyone had kind words and hugs for Mim and Chloe. Mim broke down and cried every few people, then wiped at her tears and was brave for a few more minutes. Chloe didn't cry. She put her arm around her mother occasionally, trying to comfort her in her grief.

June and Justin were escorted in by a woman Chloe assumed was a social worker, and by a uniformed police officer. Justin was in hand-cuffs. June was not. June was dressed in a snug red dress that was off one shoulder and emphasized the fact that she had no figure. Justin was in blue jeans.

Chloe had on a yellow cotton dress purchased just for the occa-sion. She didn't know when she would ever wear it again. The social worker and cop escorted the twins right up to the front to stand next to Chloe and Mim like they were still part of the family and were there for support. Chloe knew the only reason they were there was to look good. They wouldn't look good if they didn't show up at their own father's funeral. Justin—or his lawyer—had to be concerned about how that would look to the jury. The shooting was still all over the papers and Chloe had seen a couple of reporters with big cameras and boom mikes outside the chapel. They would be sure to report whether Justin was in attendance or not.

Chloe and Mim didn't look at, smile at, or acknowledge the pres-ence of June and Justin. The room went deadly quiet at their entrance. But gradually, whispered conversations started up again.

When Ronnie arrived, she didn't join the receiving line, but went through it, giving Chloe an awkward hug and Mim a little peck on the cheek. She looked uncertain and anxious and kept glancing back at her foster family as if she was afraid of being criticized for doing the wrong thing. Ronnie was ten now. Still flat-chested. Still in pigtails. Chloe hadn't seen her since she had gone to the emergency room two years ago. They used to be close. Chloe wished they could have a few minutes to talk, but Ronnie kept moving through the line, going on to greet June and Justin. Chloe was grimly pleased to see the policeman prevent Ronnie from hugging Justin.

Ruby never came in. When the family moved from the viewing room to the chapel, Chloe looked around and spotted her tucked into the back row. Ruby looked so grown up. Blond like Chloe, in a white t-shirt and jeans with her hair pulled back into a tidy ponytail. Chloe saw Ruby's crutches and remembered the news that Clive had relayed. Ruby had gotten into a fight in juvie and got a clot in her brain, causing a stroke. Her speech and mobility were both impaired, though Clive indicated that she was improving. Chloe wondered whether Ruby had been able to put on her own lipstick, or if someone had helped her with that.

Mim sobbed through the preacher's sermon. Chloe wasn't sure why. They had never been religious. Her father was barely even mentioned. It could have been anyone's funeral. Just a generic speech. Chloe put her arm around Mim and rubbed her neck and shoulders.

With the funeral out of the way, the focus turned back to the murder trial. It was a number of months out, but the preparation time passed quickly. Sometimes Chloe wondered why they were trying to convict Justin. Was he even old enough to understand what he had done? He didn't deny what he had done. He made no attempt to hide what he had done and continued to justify it with the assertion that he had been protecting June. He was so young; Chloe couldn't see a jury ever convicting him. They would look at him and see a child, not a murderer.

It was up to Chloe and Mim to make everyone see the kind of person that he really was. Justin had always been bright, quick to pick up on things. He did well at his school work despite the days he missed when June was sick. June's grades had plummeted, but Justin's had remained high. He had also always been defiant and oppositional. He wanted to be a gang banger right from the time he was in kindergarten and saw the kind of power and lifestyle that the older gang boys had. He was a rule breaker.

Chloe had always followed the rules. She was always obedient and did everything she was told. If she was ever scolded for doing something the wrong way, she never did it that way again. She was mortified any time she was criticized. She was the good daughter. The perfect, responsible, obedient one.

The trial opened with shocking testimony from June and Justin. Chloe listened to them in disbelief. She had heard about implanted memories. The prosecutor had told them that the children might believe what they were saying, even if it wasn't true. And they obviously did. June's raw emotion as she did her best to describe the abuse and answer the prosecutor's questions was almost palpable. She believed what she was saying. Justin looked like he was ready to jump over the table and physically attack the opposing lawyer if he said anything to hurt June. Justin's testimony had been matter-of-fact and was all the more shocking for his candor and transparency. The prosecutor didn't have a lot of questions for either one. Justin's lawyer, Thorne, didn't cross-examine them. Chloe looked over at the jury. Several of them were in tears. And then Ronnie was called up. Her voice was so quiet they had to ask her several times to speak up, and they readjusted the mike to pick up her words a little more clearly.

Chloe knew from Clive and fragments of memory over the past few years that Ronnie had never accused their father. She had never said that he was the one who had hurt her. In fact, she had denied it repeatedly. Had Clive and Thorne talked her into echoing June's testimony for a better impact on the jury? Or had they implanted memories with Ronnie too? Her voice was flat and robotic. Just reciting memorized testimony. But the jury and spectators appeared to hang on every word as if they believed it absolutely. Chloe wished she could go over and smack Ronnie. Wake her up to realize what she was doing. She couldn't lie and slander their father just to keep Justin out of jail.

Chloe rubbed Mim's back, as much to soothe herself as to comfort her mother. When Ronnie's testimony was finally done, it was time for lunch. The prosecutor treated Mim and Chloe. Just sandwiches and a tray of fruits and vegetables, but it was a welcome break from greasy fast food.

"I'm going to be calling you after lunch," he warned, looking from Mim to Chloe and back again. "There won't be any surprises. We've gone over the questions that I will be asking you. Thorne will do his best to discredit your testimony, but you just need to stick to the testimony that we've discussed. Don't get emotional. Don't answer if he hasn't asked a question. If you're not sure what you're being asked, ask for clarification. Okay?"

Mim nodded. Chloe shifted, suddenly not hungry anymore. Right after lunch, she was going to have to get up there as the younger kids had done and call them liars. To open herself up for attack by Thorne. She was just thirteen, how was she supposed to know all the right things to say? What if he tried to trap her somehow? What if something Chloe said was taken the wrong way and people thought that her father had been a child molester? That Justin had been justified in what he had done?

"Chloe...?" the prosecutor prodded gently.

Chloe nodded in agreement. She tried to remember his name. He had introduced himself the first time, but she had always thought of him by his role. The Prosecutor. It made her feel like she was safe and protected and on the right side.

"What's your name again?"

Mim had just taken a big bite of her sandwich and sent Chloe a glare, her mouth too full to say anything. The prosecutor frowned at her.

"You know who I am, Chloe," he said in an encouraging voice. "Come on, don't crack up on me here." He gave a little chuckle, but his eyes were worried.

"I know who you are. I was just trying to remember your last name." She said it like she remembered his first name, which of course she didn't.

"Voychuk," he told her in a precise voice. "I know it's a weird name and not easy to remember. Elya Voychuk."

"Oh," Chloe said. "Oh, yeah."

"Are you with me, Chloe? All you have to do is tell the truth. Your father never touched you in an intimate way. He never touched June or the others, to your knowledge. We don't know why Justin did what he did. Maybe he had a nightmare and thought it was real. Maybe he was angry for another reason. We don't have to know why he did it. We only have to tell the truth. That the sexual abuse never happened."

"I'm scared."

"I know it's scary. But you can do it. Look at June and Justin and Ronnie. They were scared too, and they're just little, but they did it. You're older. You can too."

"Okay."

Voychuk smiled encouragingly. "I know it's scary. But in a couple of hours, it will all be over, and you won't ever have to do it again. It will all be behind you."

"Yeah."

"And Mrs. Simpson?"

"I'm ready," Mim said sharply.

"Good. Remember, now. No emotional outbursts. No matter how angry you are, you can't say anything to the children, and you can't argue with me or Thorne. You just answer questions as briefly and politely as you can. No yelling, no tears if you can help it. Just be calm and clear."

"I know. We've gone over this a hundred times."

"Well, I guess we don't have time for a hundred more, so that will have to do."

He gave them each a warm smile.

"Chloe? Not hungry?"

Chloe shook her head, looking over the food that she had put on her plate. As much as she wanted the nice fresh food, she knew her stomach couldn't take it.

"No."

"Are you sure you don't want a little? We don't want you fainting on the stand, you know."

"Don't want me barfing, either."

"No." He chuckled. "No, I don't think that would impress the jury."

Mim was on the stand first thing after lunch. Chloe watched her critically. She did well, speaking exactly as Voychuk had said, giving the answers that they had rehearsed ahead of time, but without sounding like they were memorized. Mim's eyes were snapping whenever she looked at Justin or his attorney. If she'd had the ability, she would have vaporized them on the spot. Justin watched her with interest, apparently unconcerned by her glare. Chloe would have been. Chloe knew every shade of her mother's expressions, and if Mim had been looking at Chloe like that, she would have been down on her knees begging for forgiveness.

Eventually, both lawyers had finished questioning her, and Mim was released to sit back down. Chloe knew that she was next. She walked slowly up to the stand when her name was called out and sat down. The chair was uncomfortable. Chloe fiddled with the mike and reminded herself to speak up when she was asked questions. She wanted everybody to be able to hear her clearly, and she didn't want to have to repeat anything.

Voychuk started off with Chloe's name and age and confirming that she lived at home with her parents and the twins prior to the shooting. Then they got to the important stuff.

"Chloe, did your father ever touch you in an inappropriate way?"

"No!"

Voychuk blinked at her. Too loud. Chloe pressed her lips together and gave a tiny nod of understanding.

"He didn't ever touch you in a way that made you uncomfortable?"

"No."

"Did he ever hug you or kiss you?"

"Yes. But not in a bad way."

"Not in a way that ever made you feel uncomfortable," Voychuk clarified.

"No."

"Did he ever spank you?"

Chloe hesitated. She knew what the right answer was. They had practiced it. But it made her feel ashamed. The jury and the spectators would wonder what she had been punished for. What she had done that was wrong.

Voychuk waited, not repeating the question. He had told them that he wouldn't repeat questions. It would make it sound adversarial, and they were on the same side. She could ask to have a question repeated, but he wouldn't do it without prompting. Instead, he just stood there, waiting.

"Yes," Chloe admitted. "When I was little. And not very often!"

"That's all right, Chloe. Just answer the question, you don't need to add anything. Nobody here thinks that you are a bad person. Everybody makes mistakes from time to time."

Chloe nodded, her face burning.

"But you didn't feel like you were disciplined in an abusive way?"

"No."

"Did your father ever spank Justin?"

"Yes." Chloe shot Justin a look.

"Did he spank him the day before the shooting?"

"Yes."

"And Justin was angry about it, wasn't he?"

Chloe nodded emphatically. "Yes." She looked at Justin again. *That* was why Justin had done what he did. Not because of real abuse.

"Did your father ever touch June in an intimate way?"

"No!"

"You never saw anything inappropriate happen between them?"

"No."

"You were never awakened in the night when he came and got June out of bed."

"No."

"You never heard your mother running the tub in the middle of the night."

"No. Maybe once," Chloe amended. "When June threw up."

"Just one time?"

"Yes."

"And June slept in the same room as you, so you would have woken up if anything was going on."

"Yes. And I never did."

Voychuk nodded thoughtfully.

"Do you remember when Ronnie lived with you?"

"Yes."

"And did you ever see or suspect any intimate contact between your father and Ronnie?"

"No."

"Did Ronnie ever, any time in the past three years, say that it was your father who hurt her?"

"No."

"Did she ever hint that it was your father?"

"No."

"Do you believe that it was your father?"

"No."

Chloe looked again at Justin. This was on him. He had shot their father for no reason at all. The whole notion that their father had done such a thing was unthinkable.

Voychuk finished his questions and returned to his seat, motioning for Thorne to cross-examine Chloe. Thorne had been ruthless with his questions to Mim, and Chloe was terrified about what he was going to say to her.

"Hi, Chloe," he said with a warm smile.

Chloe darted a glance at Voychuk. *Don't offer anything if Thorne doesn't ask a direct question.* Thorne hadn't asked a question. She kept silent.

"How are you doing, Chloe?"

Chloe shifted. "Okay."

"Can I get you a glass of water or anything before we go on?"

Chloe shook her head, confused by his approach. She looked at Voychuk again, hoping for some guidance.

"You've done a good job answering questions so far. You just keep it up, okay?"

Chloe waited for Thorne to begin the cross-examination.

"Did you love your dad, Chloe?"

"Yes. Of course I did."

"Yes. And things have not been easy for you and your mother since the shooting."

Chloe glanced at Mim. No. Not easy. Justin had turned their lives completely upside-down.

"How do you sleep, Chloe?"

She frowned and looked at Voychuk, who raised his eyebrows. Chloe looked back at Thorne. "What?"

"We know *where* you sleep," Thorne said, walking over to an easel that showed the floor plan of the house. He pointed. "You are in the corner bedroom, with Justin's room on one side, and the bathroom on the other side. Correct?"

"Yes."

"You testified that you never heard your mother running the bath in the middle of the night, like Justin said she did."

Chloe scowled in Justin's direction.

"Except for once. When June had thrown up." Thorne gave her a smile.

Chloe looked at her mother, hoping that she understood Chloe would never say anything against her. Mim didn't have to worry about what Chloe would say. About what traps Thorne would set for her. Because Chloe wouldn't say anything about her mother.

"You also testified that you would have woken up if your father came and got June in the night, or there were other comings and goings."

Voychuk had told Chloe not to say anything unless she was asked a direct question. She nodded impatiently, anxious for Thorne to ask what he was going to and get it all over with.

"That's why I asked you how you sleep. Are you a heavy sleeper? A light sleeper? Are you restless? Do you wake up a lot of times in the night? Make a trip to the bathroom at midnight? Tell us about how you sleep."

Chloe set her jaw. "I sleep pretty light," she said. "I would wake up if someone came into the room. I don't get up at night. Kids aren't supposed to get up in the night. You should go to the bathroom before you go to bed and then be able to hold it until morning. I don't get up at night."

"You weren't allowed to get up."

"Allowed?" Chloe challenged the word. "They didn't make me stay in bed if I was gonna wet myself. I *could* go to the bathroom."

"But you weren't supposed to."

Chloe considered the question. "No," she agreed grudgingly.

"How did your parents react if you got up in the night?"

Chloe looked at Mim. "They'd just tell me to go back to bed."

"Would you be punished if you got up?"

Chloe folded her arms across her chest. "No." Even though Justin had already testified that he'd been threatened with a whipping when he got out of bed. It had been a long time since Chloe had been punished for getting out of bed. Thorne didn't say anything for a few minutes. Chloe shifted uncomfortably in the hard chair. A couple of times she opened her mouth to protest further, but remembering her instructions not to talk unless asked a direct question, she kept clamping it shut again, and waited.

"Do you ever take sleeping pills?"

Chloe swallowed. She looked over at Justin. He had never seen her take a sleeping pill. Neither had June. The only one who knew that she took them was Mim, and she wasn't going to admit it.

"No."

"No?" Thorne raised his eyebrows, his voice rising a couple of tones in surprise. "You've never taken a sleeping pill?"

Chloe wrapped a long lock of hair around her finger and shook her head, trying to look Thorne in the eye as if she was telling him the truth.

"Did you take a sleeping pill the night of the shooting?"

"No."

"The police report made that night says that you were very difficult to waken. You were confused and couldn't walk on your own. Several officers indicated that you were groggy and acted as if you were drugged. There was talk of taking you to the hospital and of having your blood tested."

Chloe swallowed and maintained her silence.

"If I call some of those police officers as witnesses, they're going to say that you were on something," Thorne said.

"I was just tired!" Chloe snapped. "It was the middle of the night!"

"It wasn't that late. What time did you go to sleep?"

Chloe tried to remember and tried to consider all the angles. Should she say it was later to explain why she was so tired?

"I don't know... nine," she suggested.

"Then why were you so groggy less than an hour later?"

"I just... was really tired."

"So you're not such a light sleeper."

"I... sometimes I am..."

"But you weren't that night. You slept through the gunshots and screaming and sirens. The police couldn't wake you up. So *sometimes*, you sleep pretty heavily. And you wouldn't wake up to someone drawing the bath or walking into the bedroom."

Chloe looked at Voychuk. He was shaking his head with a scowl, but he didn't look at her. He couldn't tell her what to say. He looked down at his papers, pretending to be studying something else. Chloe didn't answer. Thorne hadn't asked her a question.

~

Chloe was eager to hear Ruby's testimony. Ruby had been subpoenaed because she didn't want to testify. Chloe knew that Ruby's testimony would support Chloe's and Mim's case. She had never accused their father of anything, even though she had practically begged Social Services to take her out of the home. It had been a long time ago, but Chloe could remember lying in bed listening to Ruby and their parents fighting. Screaming matches that would lead to the neighbors calling the police. Ruby was older than Chloe, and they had shared a room during those early years. Chloe had been five, Ronnie three, and the twins still newborns. But in spite of all the fighting, Ruby had never accused either parent of any wrongdoing. She just wanted out. She even returned for a night now and then, or for a brief visit during the day. If she had come back voluntarily, then it had to be obvious to anyone that she wasn't being abused.

Ruby struggled on her crutches to the witness chair that Chloe had vacated. She didn't want to be there, and she did all she could do to get out of it, but the judge addressed her firmly and insisted that she had to give testimony, even if it was just to say that she didn't know anything about the case.

Voychuk took Ruby through the expected questions. Ruby's answers were not scripted like Chloe's and Mim's. She had never rehearsed with them. And because of her stroke, her speech was slow and stuttering, almost painful to listen to. She confirmed she'd never been molested. Then Thorne asked questions that highlighted the parallels between her history, Ronnie's, and June's, but he didn't confront her or bully her. Chloe supposed that if he did, he would look like the bad guy, with Ruby being so obviously disabled.

Ruby's brief testimony made Chloe uneasy. Ruby's eyes kept going to Mim, looking puzzled. Ruby said she didn't remember what had happened so long ago. But if Chloe could remember the fights when she'd only been five, then why couldn't Ruby remember?

CHAPTER
Four

I 'm so glad that's all over," Chloe told her mother, as they finally left the courthouse. "Aren't you?"

"I'll be happy when the prosecutor calls to tell me that they are putting Justin in prison for the rest of his life," Mim said, her voice hard.

Chloe nodded. She wouldn't be glad to hear that Justin was going to prison, but she would be happy if Mim were happy. She was confident that the jury would see through all the lies that had been told and do the right thing. That's how it always worked on TV.

They were sleeping at the home of one of Mim's friends from way back when she was a kid, going to high school. They had worn out their welcome at many other similar homes. Mim was sleeping on the couch, groaning and snoring all night with how the couch hurt her. Chloe slept on the floor. No mattress, not even an air mattress. Just a couple of blankets on the grimy rug beside the couch where Mim tossed and turned. Chloe put the two blankets together and doubled them over like a sleeping bag so that she had two layers under her and two layers over her. But it didn't cushion her from the hard floor. It didn't keep her warm enough. And somehow Chloe was always on the bare rug in the morning with the blankets in a tangle around her elbows and knees.

But Voychuk had the friend's phone number so that he could reach them when the jury came back. And it wasn't long. The next day, they were on their way back to the courthouse in Mim's battered station wagon. Chloe hoped that, like the house, the car could be replaced once the insurance money came in.

"They'll convict him, right?" Chloe asked, filling the silence. "They know that he did it. He admitted it. So they'll convict him, won't they? He'll go to prison for twenty years."

Mim scowled at her. "If the verdict was that sure, there wouldn't be any need for a trial," she said. "It's the jury that decides, and they were crying during June's testimony." She had a pronounced frown. Chloe had looked at the jury while Justin and June had testified. Mim was right; they have been very sympathetic. But June's tears didn't excuse what Justin had done, did they? Just because somebody cried about it, that didn't make it all right.

"They'll convict him," Chloe assured her.

"They'll say it was justifiable," Mim said heavily. "They think that all this nonsense is true, and they will say that it was justifiable. That it was okay for Justin to shoot his own father if he thought June was being hurt."

"No!"

Mim slapped her heavy hand down on Chloe's thigh, bare under the hem of her shorts. Chloe gasped and put her hand over the red mark.

"Don't you talk back to me!"

"I'm sorry." Chloe peeked at the skin, burning and throbbing. It was just her leg, not her face. It shouldn't hurt that much. She rubbed it and stared out the window, not bothering Mim anymore with talk of the trial.

They arrived at the courthouse. Chloe got out of the car and pulled the hem of her shorts down to cover the angry red mark. It didn't quite cover, but she didn't think it was very noticeable. No one was going to be looking at her legs. They would all be looking at the judge and the jury. And Justin. No one would be looking at Chloe. When she sat down at the courthouse and her shorts rode up, Chloe covered the bruise up with her hand and paid close attention to the court procedure, not wanting to draw anyone's attention to herself.

She didn't comprehend what was going on. The words 'hung jury' and 'mistrial' echoed in her head, and she looked over at Voychuk, trying to understand it. His expression was closed. The usual friendly smile and air of amusement were gone, and he was doing his best to show nothing.

"What does that mean?" Chloe asked.

Mim raised her hand, and Chloe flinched away. Voychuk's eyes riveted on Mim's threatening hand, and Mim lowered it again. On the other side of the courtroom, June and Justin hugged, and June started dancing around excitedly.

"Are you stupid?" Mim demanded. "You know what it means. A mistrial. He's not going to prison. He doesn't get any punishment. He can just commit murder and walk away scot-free."

Chloe looked at Voychuk for confirmation. She didn't say anything else that her mother might take as stupid. They would really just let Justin off after what he had done? After he had confessed?

"Unless we choose to retry it," Voychuk said. "We could try again."

"But you won't, will you?" Mim snarled. "You know better than that. The jury all think that these were poor, abused children and that what Justin did was right. You're not going to convince another jury to send him away."

"Unless we can find something compelling," Voychuk said, "we won't try him again. It's a waste of time and money. You can see how it would go."

The money from the insurance finally came in. Mim and Chloe both looked at the digits on the payout check with reverence.

"We can get a new house with that, right?" Chloe said excitedly. She'd never seen such a large check before.

Mim studied it carefully. "Enough for a down payment on a little place," she said cautiously. "Trade in the car. And we can start fresh." She swiped at the corner of her eye. "Just you and me."

Chloe gave her a little squeeze around the shoulders.

"It will be good, Mom. It will be nice."

Mim shook her head.

"Can we look today? I've seen some for sale signs around here."

"You want to live in this neighborhood? It's a dump."

"Oh." Chloe thought about it. "Where, then? Near our old house?"

"I'll call a Realtor. Figure out what we can afford... find a better neighborhood..."

"Can we start looking today?"

"Not today." Mim touched Chloe's hair and wrapped a lock around her finger. "Maybe we can have a celebration dinner today. You can clean yourself up?"

Chloe felt her face flush pink in embarrassment. Sleeping on people's couches and floors, she hadn't been very diligent about showering or brushing her hair. She didn't want to be in the way of the homeowners. Monopolize their time and hot water.

"It will only take me a few minutes to shower and do my hair."

"Take your time and do it right. We'll do dinner when we have both had a chance to pretty ourselves up."

"Okay!" Chloe bounced on her heels. "Where are we going to go?"

"Somewhere nice. I'll think about it."

Chloe nodded, excited. She had never gone to a nice restaurant for dinner. She and Mim had been making do at the cheapest, greasiest places. It was the first time that they could celebrate together, and it made her feel warm right down to her toes.

Being the second of four girls, Chloe had never had her own bedroom. She loved the little house that Mim had picked out, and she loved her new bedroom. She put down her bag of clothes and hugged herself, walking around the room. Her own room. A room of her own. For the first time ever, she had her own place. Her own space. A place she could go that was away from everybody and everything else, that belonged to just her.

"I love my room, Mom!"

For once, Mim was not crabby and wasn't scowling at Chloe's exclamation when she came to the doorway and looked in. She glanced around the little room and nodded.

"You can pick out a paint color, and we'll put a fresh coat up on those walls," she said.

Pink. Chloe was going to pick pink. And she was going to get a bed with a pretty white frame that made her feel like a princess. Maybe even with a canopy. A bedroom of her very own.

"I love our house!"

Mim smiled slightly. "It's a nice little house," she allowed.

It was perfect for just the two of them. A doll house, the real estate agent had called it. Just two bedrooms upstairs and an unfinished basement only half the size of the rest of the house downstairs. It wouldn't do for a large family. It wouldn't have worked for them if the other children had still been at home. But for just Chloe and Mim, it was fine. After couch-surfing for so long, it was paradise. They wouldn't be underfoot at friends' and strangers' houses anymore. No more sleeping on the floor—except for the first night. Showers whenever Chloe wanted them, as long as she didn't use up all the hot water. It was only a few blocks from the new school. Chloe wouldn't have to get a ride or take the bus. After all the disruption since the shooting, Chloe was looking forward to getting back to school. She craved the normality of a daily routine. Seeing her friends every day. Even sitting in a neat, tidy classroom and learning something new each day, and sitting down at the end of the day in her own bedroom with her schoolbooks to do her homework. She had missed a lot of school, but Mim shrugged it off. Chloe would be able to catch up easily. She'd always been able to manage at school before.

Chloe left her bag in the bedroom and walked excitedly through the rest of the house. They would be able to cook their own dinners. No more fast food. Chloe's clothes were too tight with the amount of weight she had put on since they had lost the house. Eating greasy junk hadn't done either of them any good. Chloe hoped that Mim would be in a better mood when she started eating healthier food. And now that she would have her own space.

"You're making me crazy with all of your back and forth," Mim growled. "Why don't you go to your room and just stay there for a while?"

Go to your room. Even that wasn't a punishment anymore. Chloe was happy to go to her room. She went back and whirled around like a ballerina so that she could see her whole room at once. She whirled around and around and around until she was too dizzy to stand.

"When are we going shopping?" Chloe called out. "We need

bedding for tonight, and to get some furniture. And pots and pans. And towels."

There was a pause while her mother considered this. Even without any furniture, they still needed somewhere to sleep. A bag of clothes each wasn't going to help when they needed blankets. And towels and toilet paper. There were just some things they couldn't do without.

"We'd better make a list. We'll need some things tonight," Mim agreed.

They couldn't even make a list, with no pen and paper between them. Mim rifled through her purse, and eventually pulled out her checkbook. There was a pen and the check register.

"You write it down." Mim thrust them at Chloe. She wasn't illiterate, but Chloe knew that reading and writing were difficult for her mother. Tasks Mim would avoid whenever possible. "Make two lists. Things we have to have tonight. And what we need soon."

"Okay!" Chloe was happy to be the keeper of the lists. She used one page of the check register, putting two headings at the top, neatly underlined and enclosed in pretty flower brackets. They crunched through the lists, both making suggestions, but Chloe not writing anything down without Mim's approval.

"That's a lot," Chloe said, looking at the cramped-together words when they started to run out of ideas.

"But it's not all for today," Mim reminded her. "We'll get what we need today. The rest will wait."

The air mattress was much heavier than Chloe had imagined. It hadn't been on the list, but Mim wanted something to keep her bones off of the cold, hard floor. Chloe wasn't sure of the purchase. Why get something that they would only use once? In a day or two, they would have beds of their own with proper mattresses, and they would have no use for the air mattress.

But Mim was in charge, and she said they needed the air mattress or she wouldn't get a wink of sleep. Chloe knew what it would be like if her mother didn't get enough sleep. It was best to keep her happy. So Chloe loaded the heavy, bulky box into the shopping cart and they moved onto the next item.

"We might need two carts," Chloe observed.

"We can fit everything we need for one night into one."

They walked down the housewares aisle.

"We need coat hangers." Chloe looked over the racks and selected a package of white plastic hangers.

"The plastic ones break. Get wire ones." Mim pointed them out.

Chloe swallowed. She had a strong aversion to wire coat hangers.

"The wire ones are so expensive," she countered. "And these white ones are pretty! The wire ones could get rusty if you have to hang something up to dry."

Mim considered these arguments, then flipped a hand at the plastic ones and continued to walk down the aisle. Chloe breathed a sigh of relief and added them to the shopping cart.

While Mim had agreed to Chloe sharing the air mattress with her until they could get proper beds, Chloe ended up on the floor by morning. Every time Mim had moved, Chloe had been jounced around and had to hold on for dear life. And even though Mim was able to sleep on a couch when necessary, her body somehow took up the whole double wide mattress and had left only a sliver of space, if any, for Chloe. Within a couple of hours, Chloe moved to the floor, exhausted by all the bouncing around. The floor was still, at least.

Mim snored away like a buzz saw, and in a couple more hours Chloe took refuge in her own bedroom, wrapped up in a cocoon of blankets. Sleeping the first night in her own room.

As usual, by morning she was sleeping directly on the bare floor, with the blankets all tangled up around her arms and legs. Chloe got up, unable to sleep any longer. The floor was cold and uncomfortable, and Chloe was too excited about going back to school to settle her brain back to sleep.

She got up and went to the kitchen, where the new coffee maker sat gleaming on the counter. They had both agreed that coffee was a must for breakfast. Chloe didn't care whether she had cold cereal or something hot like scrambled eggs. She had to have her coffee. And Mim agreed. Chloe put a filter in the hopper and carefully measured out the coffee grounds. It was a good thing the coffee can had a tear-off foil seal, because they had not thought to get a can opener.

With her first cup of coffee, Chloe sat against the wall in the living room and watched the sun come up and the neighborhood begin to awaken. When she started to see little kids walking to school, she went in to waken Mim.

"Mommy... what time do we have to be at the school?" she asked tentatively, loathe to wake Mim, but not wanting to be late for the first day of classes. "Mom...?"

"Shh. Let me sleep," Mim growled.

"What time do we have to be at the school? It's almost eight."

Mim snorted and rolled over. "What?"

"It's almost eight. What time do we have to be there?"

"Twenty past."

"Twenty past eight? Then we have to go now. There's coffee, Mom. You have to get up now."

Mim groaned and made no sign of getting up. "I didn't sleep a wink last night. You go. They know you're coming today. They have your paperwork. Just go to the office."

"Mom!"

Mim pulled the blankets over her head and refused to respond to Chloe's repeated pleas.

"If you say one more word, I'm going to beat the tar out of you," Mim growled, reaching her limit.

Chloe stepped back from her.

She was scared to go to school by herself, but she knew it was no idle threat. And if Mim beat her badly, she wouldn't be able to go to school. Maybe for a few days, even a week. She backed off, retreating to the kitchen and pouring herself another mug of coffee. Her hand was shaking as she lifted it to her lips.

She knew where the school was, and there was nothing for her to do but walk over by herself, and like Mim had suggested, present herself at the office.

CHAPTER
Five

The secretary didn't seem to know what to do with a student who showed up on her own explaining that she was to start there that day. The principal and vice-principal were busy with other pressing issues, and she ended up calling one of the guidance counselors for help.

He was a tall man, his skin very white, and he was completely bald. He didn't look old enough to be bald; maybe he was one of those people who shaved his head when it started to thin or recede. He had on a tight t-shirt that showed off a muscled chest. He looked more like a gym coach than a guidance counselor. He smiled in Chloe's direction and went over to the little-labeled shelves where papers were sorted. He looked through a couple of slots and pulled out a thin sheaf of papers.

"Would you be Chloe Simpson?" he asked.

Chloe nodded, relieved. "Yes. That's me."

He really looked at her for the first time, meeting her eyes and giving her a careful examination. He smiled warmly. "Where's your mother, Chloe?"

"She wasn't feeling well this morning. But I still wanted to start today, so she said I could come over by myself."

"Well, I'm sorry to hear she's under the weather. Why don't you come into my office, and we'll sort through all the logistics?"

Chloe nodded. She followed him into a cramped little office space, and he shut the door, muting the busy noises of the outer office. He motioned her to the chair in front of his desk, crowded close to a fake palm, and he sat down on the other side.

"I'm Mr. Gnatsky," he introduced himself. There was a brass nameplate on the front of his desk, and Chloe studied it, trying to memorize the odd name.

"So, I have your records from your last school. It looks like... you've had a prolonged absence."

Chloe nodded nervously. "We got kicked out of our house, and we've been moving around, all over the place. I wasn't in anyplace long enough to register somewhere new, so..."

"You were still registered at George. You should have gotten a ride or taken a bus there."

"Yeah, I guess. It's just... there was other stuff going on." She raised her eyes to look at Gnatsky, who was looking skeptical. "My dad was killed," she said. "He was murdered, and we had to testify at the trial and all. It took up lots of our time. I couldn't... I couldn't go to school while all that was going on. And Mom was afraid that I'd be bullied. It was in the papers..."

She saw comprehension enter his expression and knew that he had now connected her to the notorious Simpson trial. He knew who she was and that her brother had killed her father. No one could be expected to go to school with all of that going on.

"I see. Well, you will need to do some work to get caught back up with your class, or you will end up needing to repeat the grade. You've missed a lot of time. I'm not sure it's reasonable to expect you to catch up. But we'll keep you where you are and see what happens. Maybe with some hard work you'll be able to figure it out."

"Okay."

He stared at her. Chloe wondered if it was his baldness that made his eyes seem so prominent. So intense.

"You may need some special tutoring. I'll talk to your mother about looking into that."

Chloe nodded.

"Okay. Let's get you orientated with your schedule and a map of the school. I know it's awkward starting somewhere new so late in the year, but you seem like the type who will adapt quickly."

"I've gone to lots of different schools. I'm not scared." Even though she was. A little. It was always scary starting at a new school, with no friends and no idea where all her classes were. And no siblings at the school this time.

Gnatsky gave her another pleasant smile. He pulled out a computer printout with her schedule on it and turned it around so that it was right-side-up for her. He walked her through her schedule and showed her where everything was on a floor plan of the school.

"I'll walk you to your first class and help you get a sense of how everything is laid out," he promised.

When he walked her to her first-period math class, he put his hand on the small of Chloe's back. She thrilled a little at the warmth of his touch.

It was a couple of days before Mr. Gnatsky managed to pin Mim down to come in and meet with him about Chloe. Chloe thought that he would just meet with her mother privately, but he wanted Chloe there as well. So after school one day, she went down to Gnatsky's office and sat and waited for Mim to arrive. Another chair had been set up in the tight space. Chloe inched her chair over into the tree to give her mother a little more space. She and Mr. Gnatsky talked casually while they waited for Mim. He looked at Chloe's homework stacked on her knees.

"Don't you have a backpack or book bag?"

"No, not yet. I'll get one soon." Chloe gave a little shrug. "We haven't been able to get everything we need yet."

"You need a way to cart your books back and forth. Don't want you leaving books you need for your homework in your locker because they're too hard to carry in your arms."

"I won't. I'm strong."

"And what about your lunch?"

Chloe shifted in her seat. "I don't usually bring lunch," she confessed.

"You buy it in the cafeteria?"

Chloe bit her lip and shrugged. Mr. Gnatsky took in her answer, his lips pursed thoughtfully.

"Are you not eating lunch, Chloe?"

"I'm not usually hungry."

"You need to nourish your brain if you want to do well in school. What about breakfast?"

"I usually have coffee. That gets my brain started. My stomach doesn't like anything much first thing in the morning."

"I need my coffee too," he admitted with a smile. "But we need to make sure that you're getting the nutrition that you need. You can't skip breakfast and lunch, even if you *are* trying to lose weight." His eyes flicked over her figure. "Do you need a voucher for the school lunch program?"

It was a double-whammy that left Chloe sputtering. First, a dig about her weight, which Chloe didn't like to admit might be a problem, and then the suggestion that they were too poor to be able to afford proper meals. After her period of homelessness, Chloe was proud of the fact that they had money. They could afford a house and clothes and food. They didn't need any charity.

"No!" Chloe insisted. "I just... don't get hungry during the day."

"You need to start bringing a lunch. Even if you only eat a little. Our bodies are not designed to run all day without food. Skipping meals slows down your metabolism and causes... other issues."

Another slam about her weight. Chloe sucked in her belly. She wrapped her arms around her schoolbooks, holding them against her chest like a shield. Like he couldn't see how fat she was with the books there.

Chloe heard Mim's voice in the outer office, inquiring as to where to find them. A few seconds later, she was shown into the room. She looked at Chloe with a frown and sat down. Chloe's heart was immediately hammering against her ribs. Did Mim think that she had been called in because Chloe had done something wrong? Mim had been called in to school before to talk about problems with the other children, but never about Chloe. Chloe worked hard and behaved herself. She never got in trouble at school.

Mim let out an exasperated sigh.

"Mrs. Simpson, I'm Mr. Gnatsky," the counselor introduced himself, reaching across the desk to shake Mim's hand. Mim hesitated, then connected with him. "Gunter," Mr. Gnatsky added, smiling at Mim and holding onto her hand for an extra few seconds.

Mim started to blush. "Mim," she offered with a girlish giggle.

"Mim?"

She nodded. Mr. Gnatsky let go of Mim's hand. "What a charming name. I don't think I've ever heard it before."

"I've heard of Gunter before," Mim teased.

It was all Chloe could do to keep her mouth closed and not blurt anything out. Her mother and the school counselor flirting with each other? How gross was that? And Mr. Gnatsky knew that Chloe's father had just recently been murdered. What did Mim think she was doing, giggling at him?

Mr. Gnatsky settled back into his seat again. "I can't tell you what a pleasure it has been working with Chloe these last few days. If Chloe's hardworking attitude is any kind of reflection on your parenting, you have done well."

After all the news articles and slurs that they had put up with since the shooting about what awful parents Chloe's mom and dad were to abuse their children or to raise a child that would shoot his own father, Mim couldn't help but like Mr. Gnatsky. The compliment was appreciated, whether it was sincere or not. And in spite of the fact that Chloe knew Mr. Gnatsky was just trying to flirt with Mim, she felt warm and happy at the compliment about her attitude and behavior. He had only known Chloe for a few days, but Mr. Gnatsky recognized that she was a good student and a good person. He had taken notice.

"Chloe is a good girl," Mim allowed. "We've worked hard to raise our kids right, and she's turned out okay."

Chloe touched Mim affectionately on the arm. Mim didn't give compliments often. Mim looked at her but didn't pull away. Chloe set aside, for the time being, the sting over the affronts about her weight and poverty. Mr. Gnatsky hadn't meant to hurt her. Chloe chose to bask instead in the warmth of their compliments.

"So why am I here?" Mim prompted Mr. Gnatsky, getting back to business.

"Chloe is working hard to catch up, but I'm not sure that she can do it on her own. She has missed an awful lot of school, and she may end up having to repeat the grade." He spread several papers in front of him on the desk. "Before leaving George, Chloe's marks were... lackluster. Maybe the result of moving from school to school, so she didn't get the benefit of a full course of study. Maybe the result of her considerable number of tardies." He looked up from the papers, raising an eyebrow at Chloe.

"I didn't skip," Chloe insisted. "I had to get the twins off to school, and if they were slow, it made me late."

"That won't be a problem anymore," Mim promised. "It's just me and Chloe now, and she can get herself here on time."

"So far she's done well. But I will be watching for any continuing problems."

Chloe shook her head. "I'll do better here. I promise."

"In any case," Mr. Gnatsky sighed, "that rocky beginning, compounded by missing an extended portion of this school year, has left Chloe in a very disadvantaged position."

He looked at her, and with the word disadvantaged, Chloe thought he was going to segue into a discussion about her not eating properly and needing charity. But he didn't. He went on without mentioning it.

"I wonder, Mrs. Simpson—"

"Mim."

He smiled at her. "I wonder, Mim, if you and I could get together, in another setting, to discuss possible solutions to Chloe's problems."

Mim's brows drew down.

"In another setting?" she repeated stupidly.

"Maybe... dinner...?" he suggested.

Mim was blushing again. Even more deeply now. She didn't argue that the suggestion was inappropriate. Instead, she looked at Chloe.

"I'm sure Chloe could make some macaroni and do her homework while you're gone," Mr. Gnatsky suggested. "She's old enough to be on her own for a few hours."

"Oh, yes. She's very responsible. She babysat the younger kids."

"Well, then... tonight? Could I pick you up?"

Chloe sat there in dumb disbelief as they made arrangements for their date.

It was the first time Chloe had been alone in the new house, and she wasn't sure how she felt about it. It wasn't scary, but it was weird.

Even at the old house, she had rarely been alone. She needed to be there when the twins were home, to make sure they didn't get into too much trouble. And she helped to prepare meals and keep house. The rest of the time, one or both of her parents were there. Then she wasn't in charge, but she wasn't alone, either.

She moved around the house, bouncing from one room to another, looking at everything in a new light. They only had a few pieces of furniture, a few pots and dishes, and the necessary toiletries. Mim had a bed, queen size, and Chloe now had the air mattress. The pink paint for the walls and the princess bed were still a fantasy. Chloe wasn't sure whether they would ever materialize.

Mim was looking for work now, knowing that the insurance money wouldn't last for long. She had worked before, odd domestic jobs, Chloe wasn't sure what. Mim seemed to float from one job to another and one employer to the other without bothering to tell anyone. Her hours changed and everyone was just supposed to know what it was all about.

Chloe watched the clock. They went out to dinner at seven, so Chloe assumed Mim would be home around nine. The bogus 'meeting' about Chloe's education couldn't really be stretched out longer than that. But at nine there was no sign of Mim. Chloe turned on the TV to distract herself, and she pretended that she wasn't really watching the minutes tick past. It was ten, and then eleven, and Mim still hadn't returned.

Chloe started to worry. Just what did they know about Gunter Gnatsky? He could be a serial killer. How would they know? People like that hid in the open, acting like everyone else and never giving away their real personalities. He could have taken Mim off to some lonely road, murdered her, and buried her body. It would take time, of course. But maybe she was never coming home. Since Chloe knew that Mim had gone with him, Gunter have to get rid of Chloe too.

Chloe gave a little shiver at the thought. She turned her attention back to the TV, but once she had thought it, she couldn't get it out. What if something had happened to Mim? What would Chloe do then?

Just after midnight, Chloe heard the door. She tensed and looked around the room for some kind of weapon. They didn't even have a baseball bat. What if it was Gnatsky, coming after Chloe now?

But it was Mim. She floated into the room, her face aglow. Her hair was mussed and makeup smeared. She seemed to have had the time of her life.

"What are you still doing up?" she asked Chloe. But it was just a question; there was no threat behind it.

"Just waiting for you. Making sure you got in okay."

"You don't have to do that. You should have gone to sleep. Teenagers need to get plenty of sleep."

Chloe shifted uneasily. The only time that Mim concerned herself with Chloe's sleep was when she gave her a sleeping pill, announcing that Chloe hadn't been getting enough sleep lately, or claiming she had been up in the night. Occasionally, Chloe *had* been up in the night, but she knew she wasn't supposed to, and she wouldn't get up unless she absolutely had to go to the bathroom or throw up.

Or when the police dragged her out of bed in the middle of the night.

"I'll go to bed now, Mommy. I was just waiting to make sure that you were okay."

Chloe immediately turned off the TV and headed for the bathroom to brush her teeth. She always brushed her teeth before bed and never complained about having to do it. She actually liked that part of the routine. She liked the fresh minty feeling when she climbed into bed.

"Did you have a nice time?" she asked her mother, even though it was obvious from Mim's aspect that she had enjoyed herself greatly.

"Yes. Gunter is a very nice man. Very concerned about his students. You are lucky to have him as your counselor."

Chloe nodded. "He seemed nice." She agreed.

Mostly.

"He is going to come to the house on Saturday to do some private tutoring with you."

"He's coming here?" Chloe repeated, freezing in the act of pulling the toothpaste out of the bathroom drawer. "Why is he coming here?"

"To help you with your work. To teach you privately and help you get caught up."

"Why would he do that?"

"Because he cares so much about his students," Mim repeated. "You're very lucky to have him. I don't know of many teachers or counselors who would do something like that. But he really wants to help you."

Chloe put toothpaste on her toothbrush and brushed her teeth slowly, thinking about that. She had never had a teacher come to her house before. She had never heard of a teacher doing such a thing. Chloe wondered if he was coming over just because of Mim. It was just another way for him to see her.

～

Chloe could tell that Mim was anxious about Mr. Gnatsky coming over to tutor Chloe. She would have cleaned the house from top to bottom if it had been dirty and there was anything to clean. But there was so little there really wasn't anything for her to do after she had dusted, vacuumed, and cleaned the bathroom. So Mim bounced from room to room, fussing over the lack of furniture and decoration.

"He knows we just got the house," Chloe pointed out. "It's okay."

"We'll have to get you a bed," Mim muttered. "I don't want him thinking that I'm neglecting you or not providing for your needs. A dresser for your things."

What things? Chloe wanted to ask. But she didn't. She knew when to keep her mouth shut. She got her school books out and arranged them neatly on the table. She got out the juice mix and made some lemonade, which she put in the fridge to chill until they wanted it. She made sure that her pens worked, and her pencils were sharp, even though they were brand new and she knew very well that they were.

Finally, the doorbell rang, Mr. Gnatsky was at the door. Mim answered it and brought him into the kitchen where Chloe was waiting. He nodded and gave her a smile.

"Hello, Chloe. All set?"

Chloe nodded.

"What's your biggest problem area? What are you having the most trouble with?"

"Math. I don't understand what we're doing."

"Makes sense," Mr. Gnatsky observed. "You need to build on what was taught earlier in the year. Which you've missed. Let's look at what you're working on."

He sat down with her and patiently worked through the problems. For a while, Mim stood around, expecting his attention, but it turned out that he really *was* there to tutor Chloe. He paid no attention to Mim. Chloe was happy to have his help and worked diligently on all her homework.

Mr. Gnatsky patted her on the back.

"You're doing really well, Chloe. I know this is hard work. And you're not going to learn it all in a day. We'll need to spend more time together."

"Okay. Thank you for doing this."

"I want you to succeed. I want to give you a chance."

Chloe nodded. She sighed and sat back in her chair, rubbing the back of her head and neck.

"Can we take a break?"

"I think we're probably about done today. I know you've still got more schoolwork to do, but there's only so much you can be expected to do in one session. You need to get away from this and unwind for a while before you go back to it again."

"Do you want some lemonade?"

"Sure. That sounds good." He smiled at her. "I'm pretty dry from all the talking."

Chloe could have kicked herself. She should have offered it earlier. At the beginning, instead of waiting until the end. She poured a couple of glasses.

"Mom? Do you want lemonade?"

Mim came into the kitchen. "Are you done? You've been at it for hours."

"We're done for now," Mr. Gnatsky agreed. "Chloe can work on her other subjects later, after a break. You're okay on the other subjects?"

"Better," Chloe said. "Math is the hardest."

"Yes, because it builds so much on what has been taught before."

"Do you want to do something...?" Mim suggested. "Go out for a bit?"

Mr. Gnatsky considered, then nodded. "Sure. What would you like to do? Go out for a walk?"

Mim wrinkled her nose. "A walk? I'm on my feet all day; I don't want to go for a walk."

"Oh. Of course. Maybe a drive? There's a nice spot I know that looks out over the lake..."

This seemed to be more to Mim's liking. "Yes... that sounds nice."

Chloe rolled her eyes.

CHAPTER
Six

A t first, they had fallen into a routine where Mr. Gnatsky would come by once or twice a week to help Chloe with her schoolwork, especially the math. He and Mim would go out together afterward. Sometimes he would call on Mim days when he wasn't tutoring Chloe, and would lavish Mim with the attention she craved. Chloe liked the way that Mim sparkled after her dates with Mr. Gnatsky. She was kind to Chloe and stayed in a good mood for hours.

Chloe had gone to bed before Mim got home. She had sat up for a while, but Chloe started to get drowsy, and she no longer had the fear that something would happen to Mim while she was out. She and Mr. Gnatsky would have a nice time, and she would come home happy, and all would be well. Mr. Gnatsky had reprimanded Chloe a few times for yawning during tutoring, telling her that she needed to get more sleep, and Mim echoed the words when he was gone. So instead of staying up, Chloe put herself to bed and fell asleep before Mim got home.

She woke up before her alarm in the morning, which was unusual. But that was probably the result of actually getting enough sleep, so her body was ready to wake up. As she pulled on her clothes and brushed her hair, Chloe thought she could smell coffee. But that didn't make sense because Chloe was the one who always put the pot of coffee on in the morning before Mim was mobile.

The light was on in the kitchen. At first, Chloe panicked that she had left it on all night, wasting electricity and making the bills skyrocket. But she remembered turning off all the lights, so her next thought was that Mim had left it on when she got home. It was out of character, but anyone could make a mistake. So she was shocked when she walked into the kitchen and found Mr. Gnatsky there, pouring himself a cup of coffee.

At Chloe's gasp, Mr. Gnatsky turned around. He smiled at Chloe. "Morning, Chloe," he greeted, and he gave Chloe a fatherly kiss on the forehead.

Chloe gaped. "What—? You spent the night?"

"We were pretty late getting in, so it made more sense for me to just sleep over. I'm sure you don't have any objection."

"Um… no…" Chloe had no idea what to say to him. Even if she did have an objection, she would never dare voice it.

"Coffee's ready. Does Mim usually have a cup in the morning?"

"Yeah. Just one."

"I'll take one in to her. You make sure you have something to boost your blood sugar. A piece of toast. Fruit."

Chloe nodded wordlessly. He filled a mug for her mother and went back to the bedroom.

Chloe stood at her locker, trying to sort out the books she needed for her morning classes. Despite her coffee and breakfast, her brain still wasn't working properly. She couldn't stop thinking about Mr. Gnatsky and her mother.

Even as she was thinking about him, Mr. Gnatsky strode down the hall toward her.

"Morning, Chloe," he greeted and gave her a wink.

Chloe fumbled for words. "Uh… hi… Mr. Gnastky."

He continued on his way as if everything was perfectly normal.

There was a giggle from beside Chloe, and she closed her locker door slightly to look at Leesa, at the locker beside her.

"Chloe's got a crush on Mr. Gnatsky," Leesa said with another giggle.

"I do not!" Chloe protested.

"You better watch out for that perv," advised Callie, another locker down.

"I don't even like him," Chloe insisted, though she could feel her face flaming red as she remembered his kiss of that morning, and the various other affectionate touches when they talked or studied together.

She grabbed a random assortment of books, slammed her locker closed, and hurried in the direction of her first class.

Mr. Gnatsky's nights over became more and more common, until he was there more often than he was at his own home. More and more of his possessions made their way into the house. Even a few pieces of his furniture.

One day, Chloe walked into her bedroom to find Gnatsky standing in the middle of it, his hands in his pockets, gazing at the air mattress on the floor.

"Umm… what's up?" Chloe asked.

Mr. Gnatsky smiled at her and ran a hand over his bald head.

"Just thinking," he offered, without saying what it was that he had been thinking of. He moved toward her door. "Need to talk to your mother. You got math homework tonight?"

"Yeah. But I think I can do it okay."

"Good. Do it before supper, so I can help you if you run into any problems."

Chloe had been planning to take a break before attacking her homework, but she couldn't argue with him. He wasn't her parent, but he was a concerned teacher and was offering Chloe his own time and efforts to help her.

"Okay," she agreed. She spread her books out on the floor as he walked back out.

Chloe could hear him in the next room, talking to Mim.

"She needs a bed and a proper desk and a place where she can study properly. If you want her to do well in school and not have Social Services on your case, you need to think about these things."

Mim muttered some reply. Gnatsky's voice got louder, his anger more pronounced.

"You don't care what she eats or wears. You don't care about her sleep or her marks at school. She walks around the school and neighborhood looking as unkempt as a beggar or a hooker. You think you're being a good mother to her?"

"I know how to look after my own kids, thank you!" Mim snapped.

"Oh, you do? Is that why they are all in care of the state, other than Chloe? You treat her like trash, Mim. If I don't take a stronger hand, I can see what's going to happen to her."

"Yeah? What are you going to do about it?"

"I'm going to take care of it myself." Gnatsky's voice had dropped the angry tone and was closer to his usual calm demeanor. "I will get her a bed and a desk and fix up her room. I'll talk to her about her appearance. I'll work with her, but you have to do your part. You're her mother."

Chloe couldn't believe what she was hearing. The barbed comments about her looks hurt, but were counterbalanced by his offer to help and provide for her needs. He would get her a bed and a desk? And how would he fix up her room? Chloe couldn't help but be excited. Gnatsky had so far done everything that he said he would. Despite his relationship with Mim, he hadn't abandoned Chloe's education, but was there to help her and tutor her even more often than he had initially offered. She had thought that he would be distracted by Mim and lose interest in Chloe, but if anything, he was more interested than ever in looking after her.

Mim's voice had dropped down to where Chloe couldn't hear her properly. They murmured to each other for a while, and Chloe tried to focus on her schoolwork, suspecting they were headed toward a romantic interlude. But shortly, Mr. Gnatsky was in Chloe's doorway, looking down at her, sitting cross-legged, hunched over her books.

"How's it coming?"

"Almost done the math," Chloe assured him.

"Good. You've come a long way in a very short time. I'm impressed with how hard you have been working."

She felt goosebumps, followed by a warm flush, and looked away from him, pretending to be looking at her work.

"Mr. Gnatsky..."

He put his hand on the doorframe. "You can call me Gunter at home, Chloe."

Chloe cleared her throat. On one hand, it was awkward changing how she addressed him, but on the other, calling him Mr. Gnatsky when they were talking casually around home had felt very stilted. "Gunter..."

She got a little knot in her stomach calling him by his first name. A little flutter, uncomfortable and pleased at the same time.

"Yes, Chloe?" he replied in an over-serious tone that made Chloe grin.

"Thank you... for all the stuff you're doing to help me."

He glanced in the direction of Mim's bedroom. "You heard?"

Chloe nodded. "Some of it."

He came into the room and sat down on the floor across from her. Most adults couldn't sit so easily on the floor, but Gunter was supple, in good shape, and he didn't groan getting down or complain about his back or his tailbone. He sat directly in front of her, and he grasped her hands in his.

"Chloe. I'm going to be candid here because there's really no other way to approach this. I know it hurts, but someone needs to talk to you."

Chloe swallowed and nodded.

"You're fat. And you dress like a little slut."

Chloe recoiled, drawing back like she had been slapped. She tried to pull out of his hands, but his grip tightened, and he wouldn't let her go.

"Do you hear the way the other kids talk about you? Do you see the way people look at you when you go by? I don't know what Mim is thinking, letting you dress the way you do. It's disgusting. You need to have some respect for yourself. Showing off your body in skimpy, tawdry clothing doesn't show any respect for yourself of anyone else."

Chloe became suddenly aware of the spaghetti-strap halter-top she was wearing, which admittedly bared her belly if she lifted her arms up. And the shorts that, sitting on the floor as she was, probably showed off a plumber's crack. With a complexion as fair as her hair, Chloe's fat thighs looked like porpoises stuffed into the shorts, which rode up almost to her crotch with the strain being put on them. Her face burned, and she wanted to cover her face with her hands or pull up her shorts in the back. Or both. But Gunter wouldn't let go of her hands.

"It's not your fault. It's the way you were raised. But it's time someone explained it to you."

Chloe nodded. She stared down, her eyes filling with tears. She realized that her top was stained. Another strike against her. How could she think that he liked her and cared about her? He was embarrassed by her. By having to see her at school, parading around like a hooker. That's what he had called her.

"Do you want to grow up to be like your mother? A fat, slovenly cow that can't satisfy a man?"

If Chloe had thought that she couldn't be shocked by anything else he could say, she was wrong. He was insulting Mim when he was dating her? Pretty much living with her?

"But... you're..." Chloe sniffled, sucking back tears and snot. She tried to get the words out, but she was crying too hard, trying to keep from sobbing aloud.

Gunter's voice dropped to a near-whisper. "I am seeing your mother for one reason only, and trust me that it is not her looks. She is repulsive. I can barely stand to touch her. The only reason I am with her is to help you, Chloe. Do you think she would stand for me doing anything for you if I was a stranger? Just the school counselor?"

Chloe shook her head. She had seen how teachers, counselors, and social workers had been treated by Mim over the years with suspicion, scorn, and distrust. Mim would never allow a school counselor into their home. No matter how much he claimed he wanted to help.

"I don't understand," she murmured.

"You don't need to. There are some things that children just don't understand. All you need to do is to listen to what I tell you. I want to help you, Chloe. Not just with your schoolwork. With all the rest, too. I can help you to lose the excess weight and to find clothes that are appropriate. And I'll make sure that you have a proper bed and a place to study."

"Okay."

Chloe pulled her hands back again and this time, he let them go. Chloe wiped the tears from her face, trying to settle her breathing into a calm, relaxed pattern. Gunter took her face between two hands and stared into her eyes. It was so intense; Chloe had to look away.

He turned her face slightly and gave her a kiss on the cheek. "It will be okay, Chloe. Don't cry."

CHAPTER
Seven

C hloe awoke to the noises of hammering and power tools. For a while, she tried to go back to sleep, but she couldn't understand what all the racket was about, and her body wouldn't let her settle back down to sleep again. She wandered out of her bedroom, rubbing her eyes. There was coffee in the kitchen, so she helped herself to a mug, while listening and looking around. The noise seemed to be coming from downstairs, so she wandered down the stairs, rubbing her sticky eyes and squinting around to see what was going on.

"What are you doing?" she asked Gunter, who was putting up framework in the basement.

He put down the drill he was using and lifted up his protective goggles.

"I'm building your bedroom," he said with a smile.

"My bedroom? My bedroom is upstairs," Chloe pointed in the direction from which she had just come.

"Your new bedroom is downstairs. You see, this will be your bedroom here," he gestured to the space he was standing in. He walked through the framework into a smaller space. "And this will be your bathroom." He grinned, waiting for her admiration.

Chloe blinked. "My bathroom?"

"Your very own," he confirmed. "You won't have to come upstairs to use that one. And you won't have to fight for it in the morning.

You just get out of bed," he pointed, "and step into your very own shower."

Chloe preferred baths. But she didn't suppose he was putting a tub in a basement bathroom.

"Why are you building a bedroom down here?" she asked. "When I already have one upstairs? I don't understand."

"You need your space and independence. If you are down here, then we don't need to worry about waking you up when we get in late, or about... er... privacy issues. And you don't have to worry about being in the way. You'll have a space all your own, quiet to study, your own bathroom..."

He raised his pale eyebrows expectantly. Chloe took another sip of her coffee. She couldn't fathom why he would take on such an unnecessary project when she had a perfectly good bedroom of her own upstairs. It was the first time she'd ever had her own room, and that had seemed a great luxury. Now he was telling her she needed a whole floor all her own?

"Wow," Chloe said. "That's really... really nice of you, Gunter." She looked around at all the work that he had already done. He was obviously handy. Something that Mim had always complained that Chloe's father was not. He had griped about having to heat up his own dinner or mow the lawn. He had never done anything to fix up the house. "Are you sure we can afford this...?"

"Just some sheetrock and screws. A bit of mud and paint when it's done. You need a bed and a desk whether you're upstairs or down. And the bathroom fixtures... I can source them cheaply. There are salvage places that sell perfectly good fixtures for next to nothing. If you know a contractor in the middle of a renovation, sometimes you can even get them for free, just to take them away."

Chloe felt overwhelmed at the thought of a brand new room built just for her, and her very own bathroom. She didn't like the idea of being relegated to the basement, but she knew that any sane teen would jump at the offer of more independence and a place of her very own.

"Can I..."

Gunter waited for her to finish, then grew impatient. "Can I what? What do you want, Chloe?"

"Can I..." she swallowed and took a deep breath. "Can I have pink walls?"

"Of course! You can have whatever you want. You just tell me and I'll get it for you."

Chloe went back upstairs to her old bedroom. She sat on her air mattress on the floor and drank her coffee, thinking about it.

The mattress needed to be pumped up again.

The new bedroom and bathroom evolved over the next few weeks. There was also a storage space lined with shelves, even though they had nothing to store. All that they had, they were using. There was nothing extra. Nothing seasonal to be put away. No pantry goods waiting for them to run out of something.

Chloe looked at the new bedroom every day. Gunter didn't work on it every day. He was busy with work, with tutoring Chloe, and with going out with Mim. But Chloe went down and looked at it every day anyway, to see what might have changed. Gauging how long it was going to take to complete, and imagining what it was going to look like when it was done.

When the mudding was dry, Chloe put on a dust mask and helped with the sanding. The drywall dust caked her clothing and got all over everything in the house, even though they brushed off before they went up the stairs. They sanded everything satin smooth. Gunter had a day off and rolled on primer while Chloe was shopping for clothes, with explicit directions from Gunter on the pieces of clothing that he wanted her to get. He described styles, fabrics, colors, and the appropriate lengths and cuts for each thing. Shopping took a long time, and when she was done, Chloe went downstairs and admired the primered walls.

"It's very bright," she observed.

"Too bright," Gunter agreed. "It will be softer when we put the pink paint on. And my work lights are too bright for this little room," he gestured at the lights that he had set up to ensure that they got the paint on perfectly flat and didn't miss any spots. "We want enough light to work and do the tasks that you want, but without it glaring or being overwhelming."

"Yeah," Chloe agreed, glad that her oasis wasn't going to be as bright as a hospital operating room. "Is it ready to paint soon?"

"I'm done in today, and you probably are too after a day of shopping. I'm ready for a beer and to relax in front of the TV. We can start painting tomorrow after you're done your homework."

Chloe smiled. She could help with the painting, and then her room would almost be ready to move into. She tried not to get too excited about it, sure that it wouldn't live up to her princess fantasies. But it would be hers. Built and furnished just for her. Not just leftovers that no one else wanted.

Turning around, Chloe noticed Leesa's quick look away. She'd obviously been looking at Chloe, and didn't want to be caught at it. Chloe tugged at her shirt, but everything was in place and laying as it should. She didn't have to worry that Leesa was staring at her because Chloe had unintentionally exposed some part of her body or her clothes were stained or ill-fitting. Not only had Chloe followed Gunter's clothes-purchasing instructions to the letter, but Gunter was checking her outfit every day before she went to school to make sure that it was appropriate and flattering.

But she still could have spilled something on it at lunch, or brushed up against wet paint or a smudge of drywall dust they had missed cleaning up before stepping out the door, so Chloe checked just to be sure.

She made a shrug at Leesa. "What?"

Leesa's eyes widened. "What?" she echoed, "I didn't say anything."

"You're staring at me."

"No, I'm not. Why would I be staring at you?"

"I don't know." Chloe shook her head and closed her locker door.

"You look nice," Leesa said suddenly, as she turned away.

Chloe watched her walk away down the hall and wondered if she had imagined it. *You look nice?* Was Leesa actually complimenting her? Or was it some kind of set-up and she was just trying to get Chloe off her guard? Chloe moved on to her next class frowning, trying to figure it out.

"When can I see my room?" Chloe pestered, so impatient to see her new room completed that she felt like she couldn't stand it any longer. "It's my room; I should be able to see it!"

"You'll see it soon," Gunter promised. "I just have a few more final touches to put on it."

"I don't know what you're so excited about," Mim complained. "It's just a room. In the basement, like a dungeon."

Gunter gave her a sharp look. "It's not a dungeon," he snapped. "I've gone to a lot of work to make it nice."

Chloe hadn't been able to see the bedroom for several days. While he had promised that she could help with the painting, Gunter had quickly become impatient with Chloe's inability to paint without drips running down the wall and spattering all over her clothes. No matter how careful she was in applying it, she just couldn't seem to get it to go on evenly and not leave trails running down the wall. He'd kicked her out and hadn't let her back into the room since. There was a lock on the bedroom door, and even when he left the house, Gunter locked it so that Chloe couldn't get in and peek.

"When?" Chloe repeated.

"Tomorrow. Maybe. If everything is done." Gunter hedged, stopping just short of promising her that it would be the next day.

"I can't wait to see it!"

When Chloe got home from school the next day, she went to her room to put down her book bag before getting a snack, so that no one could complain about having to trip over it. And for a moment, there was a stab of pain in her chest when she saw that the room was empty. Completely bare. For a moment, she felt like she had been erased. They had thrown all her things away and left her without even a place to sleep. But within a few seconds, she realized the logical reason there was nothing in her bedroom. Because it wasn't her bedroom anymore. If the mattress was deflated and put away, it was because she would be sleeping in her new bed in her new bedroom.

There were no clothes in the closet because they had all been moved to her bedroom downstairs.

Chloe didn't put her book bag down in the empty room. She ran through the living room and kitchen and down the stairs. The door to her new bedroom stood open, and Chloe belted through it like a kid on Christmas morning.

Gunter straightened up from plugging a desk lamp in and looked at her, smiling.

Chloe looked around, taking in the room. Her new room. The walls were a soft, warm pink. The bed was a metal bedstead with powder white paint that was either brand new or just recently refinished. There was a white dresser of drawers, and a natural color wood student's desk. It wasn't a princess's room, but it was close enough. Everything she needed was there. Her clothes were hung in the closet. She had a bed of her own to sleep in. And her own bathroom.

Chloe ducked into the tiny bathroom to have a look around. Everything was put away. All the fixtures were sparkling clean. There was a strip of lights around a bright new mirror. She went back into the bedroom.

"Wow," she said. "Everything is so beautiful. Thank you, Gunter!"

She threw her arms around him impulsively. She knew it had taken a lot of work, and it had all been for her. Because he cared about her health and happiness. Gunter's arms tightened around her. He gave her a kiss on the cheek. Chloe released her hold and tried to step back, but he continued to hold her. Chloe squirmed and didn't think that he was going to let her go. But then he released her, and Chloe was left wondering if she had imagined him holding onto her for that extra second or two.

Gunter licked his lips and looked around the room with a satisfied expression. "I am glad you like it."

"I really do. And I know it took a lot of work. Thank you so much."

Chloe sat down on her new bed. It was soft, but firm. The springs bounced when she moved around but didn't squeak. Chloe put her book bag down beside her on the bed.

"Don't do your work there," Gunter warned. "You have a study desk to do all your work at. No more hunching over with bad posture. Back straight, shoulders back."

"I wasn't going to. I was just putting it down."

"Put it down over there," Gunter insisted, pointing at the desk. Chloe walked across the room and put it down where he indicated. He nodded.

"We should celebrate!" Chloe suggested. "Why don't we get a pizza?"

Gunter raised his eyebrows and looked at her. Chloe lowered her eyes, knowing what he was going to say before he said it. They had talked before about how she needed to change her eating habits if she was going to lose weight. Eating a proper breakfast and lunch. A modest supper with lots of veggies and no fat or salt. No junk food at any time. Pizza definitely wasn't on the menu.

"We talked about your food choices, Chloe. I'm sure we can think of another way to celebrate that doesn't include empty calories and foods that are going to make you feel depressed and bad about yourself."

Chloe nodded. "Yeah. I'm sorry. I wasn't thinking. Maybe we could go for a walk together. All of us. Get some exercise."

"You know Mim won't go walking."

"Right... well, you and me, then."

"I'd love to go for a walk with you, Chloe, and I think that's a great way to celebrate that will help your body instead of hurting it. But I don't think it would be appropriate for me to go out for a walk with you. People might misinterpret. Think that I was behaving inappropriately. I'm your counsellor, people might think I was taking advantage of you."

"For going walking together? Dads take their kids out for walks all the time."

"I'm not your dad, though."

"You're like a stepdad."

"I'm not married to your mom. And you and I know that we're not even really together. It's just a sham. It's too risky, Chloe. I think you'll have to take that walk by yourself."

"Great," Chloe sighed. "I'll celebrate by eating dry salad and walking by myself. Woo-hoo."

Gunter cracked a smile. "Getting in shape isn't always a lot of fun. But you've been doing very well. You just keep it up."

Chloe nodded, looking down at herself. She hadn't weighed

herself to see how much weight she had lost. Mim wouldn't have a scale in the house, and Gunter agreed, saying that Chloe would be setting herself up for an eating disorder. But she knew that her clothes were looser, and she thought that when she looked in the mirror, she looked a little slimmer, her body just a little bit firmer.

"I've really noticed the changes in you," Gunter said encouragingly. "I'm sure that you have too. It won't take you long to drop the excess weight."

"It does make me feel better," Chloe admitted.

"Of course it does. You're nourishing your body. Getting the proper sleep and exercise. Everything will work better. More energy, more alert and focused, a glowing complexion..."

She met his eyes and looked away again, flushing.

CHAPTER
Eight

H ey, chloe. Did you write down the homework Higgins assigned?"

Chloe turned around and saw Slader, one of the boys in her math class, hovering behind her as she packed her school bag.

"Just the next exercise," she said.

He didn't move on. "Which one was that?"

Chloe looked at him. How could he not know where they were in the text? They had homework every night. He must have done the previous assignments and would know where they were. But he just stood there, looking at her, his eyes soft and liquid, like a sad puppy dog's. Chloe smiled, her heart giving a few extra beats. She dragged her math text back out of the bag and opened it up.

He looked over her shoulder, his breath warm on her ear he was standing so close.

"Right here," Chloe pointed. "One-oh-three. Just..." she just about lost her train of thought. She could feel his body heat, even though he wasn't touching her. "The first half. We'll cover the next exercise in class tomorrow."

"Great, thank you," he whispered. He gave her a sort of a pat on the shoulder and moved away. "Thanks a lot, Chloe."

Chloe blew out her breath and giggled. She caught surprised glances from a few of the other girls close by, but no one said anything to her. She wished, not for the first time, that she had a best friend that she could confide in about the encounter. Or any friend at all. But in spite of being a veteran mover, she just couldn't seem to put the energy into making friends this time. She was still too anxious about everyone knowing about the shooting and all the stupid allegations that had been made. No one had said anything to her about it, but she couldn't help wondering how many people knew the stories and were speculating about Chloe and her father. It just made her sick to think about it.

"What did you eat for lunch today?" Gunter asked, as Chloe set the table and he prepared dinner.

"Just a sandwich and an apple," Chloe reported. "And water."

"That's it?" Gunter didn't turn around from the vegetables that he was chopping to look at her. Chloe shook her head, but then she remembered. She bit the skin around her thumbnail.

"I... they had that fundraiser, and I bought a muffin," she admitted.

"Well, that was nice of you to support the fundraiser. I suppose that means that you ate the muffin."

"Yes."

"The whole thing?"

They weren't exactly small muffins. Chloe had relished every bite and licked every last bit of melted chocolate chip off of her fingers.

"Uh... yeah. The whole thing."

"Do you know how many calories are in a muffin like that? About six hundred!" He looked at the food he was preparing. "That's your whole meal allowance. For one snack. I guess that means you're not having supper."

Chloe gaped at him. "What?"

"You're already through your allotted calories today. You're done. May as well put your plate back away."

"No way!" Chloe objected. "It was just one time. For a fundraiser. I'm not going to skip supper!"

He whirled around, his face grim. Chloe stepped back, her heart in her throat.

"You stupid, fat sow!" Gunter grated. "Are you talking back to me?"

Chloe took another step back, tears springing to her eyes.

"No. No, I'm sorry. Of course you're right. I won't eat supper. I won't have anything the rest of the night. I was being weak, a glutton. I should never have had that muffin."

"People have weak moments," Gunter said, his voice still tight with anger. "But you will *not* talk back to me like that. You will show me the respect I deserve, or I will slit your throat!"

Chloe gasped in shock.

"No, sir!" she agreed. "I won't do that again. Ever!"

With a shaking hand, she picked her plate up from the table and put it back into the cupboard. Then she fled to her room.

For a long time, Chloe just lay curled up on her bed, sobbing, hugging the pillow to her like a teddy bear. She could hear her mother's heavy footsteps overhead, the chairs scraping as Gunter and Mim sat down to dinner. Eventually, she wiped her tears away, blew her nose in the bathroom, and sat down at her study desk with her schoolbooks. She was in no mood to do homework, but when Gunter came down to check on her, she didn't want him to find her crying in bed. If she wanted to redeem herself from having talked back to him, she had better be caught doing what she was supposed to be doing, rather than crying about being corrected. It wasn't like he'd whipped her. She'd talked back, and he'd admonished her. That was all.

She found it hard to focus on her work. Her mind kept going back to his words and the fire in his eyes when she should be concentrating on her math problems. Her stomach growled and ached to be filled. Despite how many times she had complained about the sparse dinners of salads and vegetables, Chloe longed for one. She wouldn't ever complain again. At least they filled her belly.

There was a quiet tread on the stairs. Chloe looked down in panic at her notebook. She'd only done half of her math. She should have been a lot further along. But there was nothing she could do about it now. She couldn't scribble random answers to make it look like she was further along than she was. He would know that it was wrong, and she had to show all her work anyway. At least what she had done was neat and tidy, and she was reasonably confident that it was right.

Gunter entered her room without a word and stood looking over her shoulder at her work.

"Good," he approved. "It's coming along."

Chloe breathed out a slow sigh of relief and nodded. Gunter went over to her bed and sat down.

"How was your day at school? Any problems in your classes?"

"No. I got paired with Theo in social. He's not going to do any work. That means I'm going to have to do the whole project myself."

"You're probably right about that. But at least Mr. Terry is showing confidence in you. He wouldn't put together two people that won't do any work. He knows that you can do it."

Chloe ventured a glance at Gunter. There was no hint of his earlier anger in his face. She saw only the regular features and piercing eyes she was familiar with. She tried an appreciative smile. "Yeah, I guess."

"I saw you talking in the hallway with Slader today."

Chloe swallowed, and her face got hot as she remembered how Slader had hung over her, his body nearly touching hers. And how she had not objected or moved away, enjoying his closeness. Gunter's tone was disapproving. He didn't like it if he thought the boys were giving her too much attention.

"He was just asking about the math homework." Chloe gestured at her textbook. "I just told him what the assignment was."

"Oh, he was doing a lot more than asking what the assignment was," Gunter assured her. "Math homework was the furthest thing from his mind."

Chloe looked down. "That's all that happened."

"And you didn't have fantasies about it being more?"

Chloe covered her burning face with both hands. "I didn't try to," she protested.

Gunter laughed. "I don't know how any red-blooded girl could have avoided it. You're only human." Chloe ventured a look at him. "That boy was practically on top of you. You didn't do anything wrong."

"I didn't do anything," Chloe repeated.

"No." He chuckled again. "You see what a difference it makes when you start taking care of yourself? You don't need to wear slutty clothes to get attention. You take care of your hygiene, and your weight and people do notice. I notice you getting a lot more looks from the boys. And not because they're disgusted by what a mess you are. Because they appreciate the hard work you are putting into looking nice."

"Yeah. I guess."

"You be careful. Girls who are loose with the boys get themselves into trouble. You don't want to end up with a baby, or an STD, or rumors spread all over the school about you."

"No. I'm not going to do anything."

"They can look but not touch. I expect to hear from you if any of them think they can take liberties. They can keep their hands to themselves. And so can you."

Chloe wiped her hot face. "Nobody's going to do anything."

"They will if you let them. You make sure they know where the boundaries are."

"Yeah. Okay."

"Anything else I should know about? Anyone else we need to keep an eye on?"

"No. Nobody's done anything."

His gaze washed over Chloe's body.

"Make sure they don't. You are starting to look like a very pretty girl. People are noticing."

Chloe shifted uncomfortably in the folding metal chair. With less padding, her tailbone ached when she sat for long periods of time. She was incredibly bored sitting through the end-of-term awards ceremony. They had been through all the sports and extracurricular awards. Then awards for each of the various subjects. Honors list. Award after award, she was yawning and struggling to stay awake. Next came the most-improved awards. Chloe shifted and smothered another yawn.

"That's you!" Everett nudged Chloe.

Chloe straightened and looked at him. "What?"

"They called your name. You got most-improved. You have to go up."

Chloe looked around her. She hadn't heard her name called, and she wasn't going to go up without being sure that it was her name that had been called. How embarrassing would it be if Everett was just trying to prank her and she went up to receive an award in front of the whole school when she hadn't been given one?

Other people down the row of chairs were looking at her, waiting for her to get up.

"They called you," Everett insisted.

Leesa was looking back at Chloe, motioning for her to go up. Chloe rose uncertainly to her feet.

"Chloe?" the principal said, squinting over the audience. "Chloe Simpson?"

Chloe walked up to the front of the gym her heart beating hard. She had to walk down the gauntlet of teachers and administrators, shaking hands with each one, until she reached the principal. Gunter was part of the line. He gave Chloe a two-handed shake, holding her hand warmly between his and gripping it an extra second longer.

"Good job, Chloe," he murmured.

"Thanks."

He released her, and Chloe continued down the line, shaking each person's hand and accepting their whispered congratulations. The principal gave Chloe a big smile and handed her the certificate.

"You deserve it," he told her. "You've made amazing progress in a very short time."

"Thank you."

There was applause from the student body, which died away as the principal read off the next list of names. Chloe returned to her seat. Everett turned his head to look at the certificate, and Chloe turned it toward him.

"Nice," he complimented. "Good for you."

Chloe heard her mother arrive home from work and went upstairs to see her.

"Mom, I got an award," Chloe announced, flapping the certificate at her.

Mim kicked her heavy shoes off, her forehead wrinkling. "Hello, Mom, how was your day?" she suggested, an edge to her voice.

Chloe froze, no longer waving the certificate around.

"Hi, Mommy," she said in a small voice. "Did you have a good day?"

"While you were sitting around, I was on my feet all day, breaking my back to feed you."

"I'm sorry. Do you want me to get you a drink? Or... do you want a bath, to soak your feet?"

"Get me a drink," Mim agreed. She fell heavily into the couch, feeling for the remote without looking down.

Chloe went into the kitchen. She put down her certificate and made a fresh pitcher of lemonade, letting the water run for long enough to get cold. There was no ice in the freezer. She refilled the empty ice cube tray so there would be some the next time. She poured Mim a glass and took it and the certificate back into the living room to Mim. Chloe sat down on the couch next to her mother. Mim took a long drink of lemonade and looked toward the paper in Chloe's hand.

"What is this, then? Show me what you got."

Chloe held it out so that she and Mim could both see it. Mim's eyebrows rose.

"Good for you," she approved. "You've been working really hard on your schoolwork." She took another sip of the lemonade. "You and Gunter."

Chloe darted her eyes sideways at Mim, not sure if she heard jealousy there.

"He's helped me a lot," she agreed.

"He's a good man." Mim looked like she would say something else. Chloe tried to think what it would be. A warning to stay away from Mim's man? Complaints about their lack of intimacy? A suggestion it was time to go work on her homework? But Mim didn't air her grievance, whatever it was. She rubbed her stomach like she was having cramps.

"Do you need an aspirin?" Chloe suggested.

"No. Is Gunter home?" Mim's head turned toward the kitchen.

"No, not yet. He might have gone to his house. He didn't say if he was coming. Did he tell you...?"

"He gave up his place. The rest of his stuff is in the spare bedroom. He said he'd help with the bills, instead of paying rent on a place he wasn't spending any time at."

"Oh." Chloe thought about this. Mim didn't seem as happy with this arrangement as Chloe thought she would. "Then I guess he's not at his house. Do you want me to start on supper?"

"No. I think I'll go soak in the tub. He might have something planned for supper."

Chloe didn't know where Gunter had gone after school. They waited until they were both hungry and grouchy and it was obvious that Gunter was not coming home for supper. Chloe rifled the fridge and cooked up some scrambled eggs for them. She added lots of vegetables for good nutrition, but she used the whole eggs instead of just the whites, and added cheese, salt, and plenty of ketchup on top as a way of thumbing her nose at Gunter for leaving them to fend for themselves, not even saying that he was going to be late getting in. She felt guilty about it and later had an upset stomach, but it tasted so good, and they finished every last bit between them. Chloe was sure to wash up the dishes and put everything away to hide the evidence of her rebellion.

When she went to bed, he still wasn't home. She was dozing off when she heard him come in. Mim had gone to bed early, and Chloe didn't hear her awaken at Gunter's arrival. Chloe dozed, listening to Gunter moving quietly around the house above her. Then he was on the stairs, and Chloe turned over and propped herself on her elbow as he came into her doorway.

"You asleep?" Gunter whispered.

"No. I'm still awake," Chloe murmured back.

He slipped in through the door and sat on the edge of the bed beside her.

"You were surprised by the award?" Gunter asked. Chloe could hear the smile in his voice.

"Yeah. I really was. You never said anything!"

"Of course not, it was a surprise. I'm proud of you. You've shown vast improvement since you arrived at the school. You're almost making honors, after missing months of instruction."

"It's only because you helped me," Chloe pointed out. "I couldn't have done it without you tutoring me."

He reached over and gave her a one-armed hug.

"We make a good team," he conceded.

Chloe snuggled against his chest, feeling warm and protected. He put his other arm around her and held her firmly, squirming closer to stretch out on the bed beside her. She traced a circle on his chest with her finger and closed her eyes. He kissed her on the top of the head and was still.

CHAPTER
Nine

C hloe got home from school early, the last class of the day being cancelled because the school's football team was in the finals and they wanted everyone to go support the team. Chloe had no interest and snuck out before she could be herded out to the field with everyone else.

Mim's car was outside the house, which surprised Chloe. Her mother was usually still working when Chloe got home from school. But maybe she had a day off or had switched jobs or schedules.

"Mom?" she called as she walked in through the door. "I'm home, they let us out early."

There was a groan from the direction of the master bedroom. Chloe was immediately anxious. Had something happened? Was Mim hurt? Chloe's mind went instantly to the shooting of her father, so sudden and unpredictable, and she was sure that someone had attacked her mother too.

"Mom? Are you okay?"

She peeked in the bedroom door. Mim was in bed, but nothing seemed to be sinister or out of place. Mim groaned again, a loud groan of pain. Chloe crept closer.

"Mommy? You sick? Do you need a bucket? Tea?"

She tiptoed up to the bed. Mim grabbed for her hand. Chloe held Mim's hand in hers, trying to comfort her.

"Is it the flu? You could have called me at the school; I would've come home."

Mim breathed heavily. She let go of Chloe's hand and pushed both hands down on her stomach.

"You have to take it," she told Chloe feverishly. "You have to hide it, so he doesn't see. He'll know!"

"Take... what? What are you talking about?" Chloe touched Mim's forehead tentatively to see if she was hot. Mim was sweating but didn't feel like she had a fever. Chloe stroked a lock of hair back from Mim's face.

"Baby," Mim breathed. "Have to hide it from Gunter."

Chloe still couldn't understand what she meant.

"Hide what from Gunter?"

Mim didn't answer, groaning and pushing down on her stomach. Chloe stared at Mim's big belly and started to comprehend. She fought against the idea. "There's no baby, Mom. What do you mean?"

"Don't be stupid."

"You're not... you're not having a baby."

Mim slapped Chloe, but missed her face and hit her shoulder. "Help me. Don't be such an idiot!"

"But I thought you and Gunter didn't... couldn't... he said..."

"No. He couldn't. So he would know the baby isn't his. He can't see it. You have to take it. Deal with it."

Chloe stood there, paralyzed. Mim couldn't expect her to do such a thing. She couldn't expect Chloe to somehow hide a newborn from her stepfather. And do what? Raise it in secret? Abandon it on someone's doorstep? Chloe couldn't wrap her mind around it.

Mim was groaning again, rocking back and forth and pushing down with her arms. Chloe pulled back the sheets, terrified at what she would find. Mim lay on a plastic sheet and layers of towels. Her nightgown was hiked up over her hips. Chloe turned away, feeling nauseated.

"Don't you bloody well faint!" Mim hissed.

Chloe steadied herself on the side table. "I won't," she promised, but still couldn't look at her mother. Mim labored alone, Chloe could do no more than stand there speechless.

A thin cry broke the uncomfortable silence between them. Chloe couldn't look at Mim.

"Here," a towel-wrapped bundle was thrust into Chloe's arms.

"Mom, I can't—"

"Shut up. Take it away. Don't let Gunter see. He can't see! Tell me you understand."

"Yes, Mom." Tears were dripping down Chloe's cheeks.

Mim was sitting up, gathering together the stained towels and wrapping them in the plastic sheet. She got out of bed, pulling her nightgown down and gathering it all together in a bundle.

"Should you be up?" Chloe asked. "I should do that—"

"You do what I told you. Hurry. He could be home anytime."

Chloe left the room and went downstairs to her own bedroom, dazed, with no idea of what to do. It wasn't until she was in her own room that she dropped her gaze to the bundle in her arms. A red, mucousy face topped with a black fuzz of hair. Chloe wiped at it with the towel. She put it down on her bed and unwrapped the towel, looking at the rest of the baby's body. Its limbs seemed thinner than they should be. It was a boy. She couldn't think of what to do next, and ended up just wrapping it up again. What should she do?

Her paralysis remained until she heard Gunter arrive home. Then she was forced to take action. Gunter might start on dinner, or he might check on Chloe right away. She should be sitting at her desk working on her schoolwork. Chloe darted into the bathroom and lay the bundle in the bottom of the shower stall, pulling the curtain around to hide it from sight. Then went back to her bedroom, closing the bathroom door.

If the baby was to start crying again, the game would be up. Chloe had a small stereo that Gunter had bought for her. She turned it on and tuned to a radio station as quickly as she could. She turned up the sound carefully. If she didn't turn it loud enough, it wouldn't hide any noise the baby made. If she turned it too loud, Gunter would turn it down himself, and again it might be too low to mask the sounds of the baby.

Praying she had it set at the right volume, Chloe left the stereo and sat down at her desk, pulling out he school books as quickly as she could. Normally she did math first, to get it out of the way. Then Gunter could help her if she ran into trouble and he would still have the evening free to do other things. But she hadn't started on her math, and it would take too long to get anything down. Instead she pulled out her English Language Arts. There was a novel to read and comprehension questions to answer, followed by a short essay. Chloe opened the novel and pretended that she had been reading it. She put the date on her notebook page and copied down the first couple of questions. She had most of the first answer down when Gunter got to the bottom of the stairs. Chloe looked up.

"Hey."

"Hi, Chloe. I didn't see you at the game. Did you stay?"

"Uh... no. I had a bunch of reading to do." She held the novel up. "So I wanted to get home and try to get it done while it was still quiet."

He studied her for a minute, then nodded. "Your mom is sick in bed, so it's just you and me for dinner. How did school go?"

Chloe focused on remembering her day. Everything that had happened before arriving home had fled from her memory.

"Um... yeah. Pretty normal day. Nothing much happened."

"What did you eat for lunch?"

"Soup, and carrot sticks, and an apple."

"Good," he approved. "Plenty of calories left for supper. You want to come up and help me make it?"

"Uh... I've got quite a bit of homework. Do you need me?"

"No, you go ahead. I'll call you when it's ready." He didn't leave immediately, watching her. "That Stoneman boy still hanging around you?"

"No. I don't think I saw him at all today. I guess maybe he's given up."

"You talk to any boys today?"

Chloe concentrated, thinking about it. She could just tell Gunter 'no' because that was what he wanted to hear. But she was scrupulously honest with him, always giving the details, even if she knew he wouldn't like the answers.

"Um... I'm not sure... I have that joint project in social. Had to talk to Theo. And Mr. Terry. He's a boy."

"I'm not interested in Mr. Terry. Unless he's showing improper interest in you..."

Chloe wasn't even sure what was appropriate and what was inappropriate anymore.

"No, he just talks to me about my work," she said uncertainly.

Gunter nodded. "Anyone else?"

"I don't think so."

"Are you telling me the truth? Look at me, Chloe."

She raised her eyes to his intense gaze and tried to keep eyes gaze steady and not be distracted by thoughts of the newborn hidden in the bathroom. Gunter stared into her eyes for a few seconds, then nodded.

"I'll call you for supper," he told her, and went back upstairs.

Chloe breathed a sigh of relief. She took a few seconds away from her homework to check on the baby. Then she sat back down to ensure that she would have a good amount of work done when Gunter checked it after supper.

Chloe was nervous all throughout supper. Any minute the baby could start crying, and baby's cries could be loud. Or Mim might come into the room and say something that would give her condition away. Or, Chloe knew, women who'd just had babies could bleed to death.

She was afraid that Gunter would be able to read Chloe's face and know what had happened. So many times it seemed like he could see right into her soul and pluck out her insecurities. She kept waiting for him to do it now. To look at her and just know that she had hidden the baby.

Chloe didn't know what to do next. She puzzled through it while she ate the chicken breast and salad that Gunter had prepared. In spite of how little she had eaten, her stomach felt full and sick before she even started. What was she going to do with the baby? How could she feed or care for it by herself without Gunter finding out? Could she get it out of the house without Gunter's knowledge? What if Mim changed her mind and charged Chloe with kidnapping? Chloe couldn't think of a single optimistic result. No matter what she did, it was going to end badly.

"Are you not feeling well?" Gunter asked, watching Chloe poke at her dinner.

"My stomach feels kind of bad," Chloe admitted.

"You're sure you didn't have anything else to eat, other than what you told me?"

Chloe shook her head. "No. I was good. Maybe... I've got the flu like Mom."

He stared at her, frowning. Chloe felt a flush beginning at her neck. He was going to figure it out.

"Can I leave this? And take my milk downstairs? Maybe if I just sip it while I'm working, I can get something down..."

Gunter grimaced. He didn't like her to have food downstairs in her room. His eyes flicked over in the direction of Mim's room and he made up his mind.

"Okay. But don't force it if you're not feeling well. You don't want to just be bringing it back up again. Call me if you get a fever or start to feel worse. I'm going to sit with your mom for a little while."

Chloe breathed a sigh of relief. "Yeah. Okay. Thanks. And thank you for supper... sorry I couldn't eat it."

He shrugged and picked up both of their plates, his empty and Chloe's still mostly full. Chloe picked up her cup of milk and headed downstairs to her room.

She shut and locked her door, something that she had never done before. As a precaution, she put on her jammies. She could say that she just locked the door to change if Gunter happened to come downstairs and was upset about it. Then she went into the bathroom. The baby hadn't moved. Babies didn't crawl or roll around when they were only a day old. It was making noises that Chloe thought were preliminary to crying. She looked at the glass in her hand. How was she going to get the milk into him without a bottle? She couldn't just pour it in. He would choke.

She dipped her finger into the milk and touched it to his lips. He opened his mouth to suck on her finger. His suck seemed strong, but she couldn't feed him one drop at a time. She dipped her finger again and watched him suck. He was getting restless and more fussy instead of less. Chloe grabbed the washcloth that was hanging next to the sink and dipped it into the milk, and then put it into the baby's mouth. He made faces and didn't want to take it, crying and pulling back, but inserting her finger and then sneaking the washcloth in beside it, the baby sucked the milk out of the cloth. Chloe kept re-saturating it until he fell asleep. There was still half a glass left, and Chloe put it on the edge of the sink for his next feeding.

Just as she set it down, Chloe heard the doorknob rattle as Gunter tried to open the door. He swore and called out to her.

"Chloe? Why is this door locked? Open it now!"

"I'm coming." Chloe shut the bathroom door and hurried to unlock the bedroom door. As she opened it, she saw that Gunter had his keychain out and had already found her bedroom key. He was quick. A locked door was not going to do anything more than delay him a few seconds.

Gunter's eyes went over her, noting the pajamas and then going to the clothes she had left on the floor. "Hang up your clothes. Never leave them on the floor."

"Sorry. I was just getting changed and my stomach felt worse, so I went to the bathroom…"

Chloe picked up the shirt. He bent down to pick up the pants and took the shirt out of her hands.

"You'd better lay down," he advised.

Chloe watched him move toward the closet with the clothes. "You don't have to do that for me. I can still do it."

"Lay down."

Chloe climbed obediently into bed. He hung up the clothes and shut off the overhead light, leaving the lamp on her bedside table on. Gunter sat down on the bed and stroke her hair gently, giving every indication that he planned to stay with her. But he couldn't stay with her any longer than the baby would sleep and Chloe wasn't sure how long that would be. She remembered how colicky and fussy June and Justin had been as babies. Mim could never get more than a twenty-minute break without one of them crying. Chloe remembered rocking them for what seemed like hours on end, trying to give her mother a break.

"I think I'm going to go straight to sleep," Chloe told Gunter, trying to discourage him from settling in.

"I'll sit with you a while. You can go to sleep."

"I'm really restless, I need to move around."

"Go ahead."

"I don't want to give you this flu…"

"Why do I get the feeling that you don't want me around?" Gunter asked, raising an eyebrow. While his tone was amused, Chloe could tell he was upset by the rejection. She hastened to soothe him.

"It's just that I'm not feeling good," she said. "I like it when you stay with me. But right now... I just feel so gross... You won't want to be in here while I'm all... gassy and icky... I might throw up. I hate it when people see me throw up. Or hear me."

He chuckled. "Fine, Chloe. I'll leave you alone. Will you be able to call if you need me?"

Chloe nodded. "I can still yell."

He tousled her hair and turned off her lamp before leaving.

The baby slept most of the way through the first night. Or at least, if he woke up, Chloe didn't hear him until it was almost morning. She managed another washcloth feeding. He still didn't finish the whole glass of milk. She was glad that she still had a little more to give him in the morning when she got up, without taking the chance of raiding the fridge and waking Gunter up. She stared at the fine lashes that lay on his cheeks as he slept. He should have a name. Even if she found someone else to take care of him, she could still give him a name to start life with. She gazed at him and tried to think of an appropriate name. She liked June and Justin, so she tried to think of a J name for the baby. Eventually, she settled on Joshua. Joshua Simpson, her newest brother. Her only brother, since she couldn't think of Justin as her brother anymore.

In the morning, she did her best to fake sick when Gunter came down to check on her. She had held a hot cloth to her face so that it was pink and moist. She acted tired and sluggish when he talked to her, but didn't do anything to suggest that it was serious enough for him to be concerned or take her to the doctor.

"My stomach is doing better," she said. "But I'm so sleepy and achy... I just need to sleep for a while. Maybe I'll be well enough for school this afternoon..."

"No, you stay home this afternoon. No need to drag yourself out before you're over it. Don't need to infect the rest of the school, either." He felt her forehead and her cheek. "You're warm. Just rest today. Tomorrow you'll probably be back to your old self."

"Yeah," Chloe agreed in a tired voice. "Tomorrow I'll be fine."

He gave her shoulder a quick squeeze and went back upstairs.

Chloe listened carefully for him to leave the house, and when he finally did, she waited five more minutes and then went upstairs.

"Mom?" She went into Mim's bedroom and saw that she was still in bed. Chloe sat on the edge of the bed. "Are you okay?"

"Yes, I'm fine. Just need a day or two to recover."

Chloe nodded. "What am I supposed to do about the baby? We need bottles, milk, diapers... we can't keep him hidden for very long. How can you just not tell Gunter?"

"We can't tell him," Mim insisted. "You need to get rid of it, Chloe. It was a boy?" She looked wistful for a moment. "After so many girls."

"And Justin."

"No. Don't ever talk to me about him."

"I named him Joshua. Unless you want to name him something else."

"You have to get rid of him. Gunter can't know about him. He'll leave me. That can't happen."

"Then... what do I do? Give him to someone? Leave him at the hospital?"

"No! He can't leave this house. They would do tests, figure out where he came from. He can never leave this house."

Chloe's stomach clenched into a tight, hard, ball. "What? What do you mean? How can I...?"

"Get rid of him," Mim repeated in a harsh voice. "Don't go all soft on me, miss! This is a matter of survival. We *need* Gunter. Just get rid of the wretched thing." Her beady eyes stared fiercely into Chloe's. "Baby's aren't difficult. They're fragile. It only takes a few seconds..."

Chloe ran from the room.

She ran down the stairs and into her room and locked the door. As if the monstrous woman who was her mother might chase her down there and dispose of the baby herself. Chloe's eyes were wet with tears.

She looked in on Joshua. The last feeding had not put him back to sleep. He moved his head when Chloe entered the room. Like a baby bird peeping for his mama. Chloe picked him up and cuddled him close. How could anyone consider a baby disposable? He was a person. A living thing. Human. Just like her. With proper care, he would grow up to be a big strong man.

You couldn't just squash the life out of him like a bug.

He was tiny. But he nuzzled against her, rooting for milk. She wished she could nurse him like a real mother. His little nose was so small; she was careful not to press it against her. Mim was right; it would take little effort to cover up his nostrils and let him suffocate.

But she couldn't do it. Chloe had never willfully disobeyed her mother. But this time, she had to. She couldn't do anything to hurt the tiny infant. She wouldn't do it just for her mother's convenience.

But she wasn't sure what the alternatives were. If she didn't obey, what was she to do? How could she protect the baby's best interests and her mother's at the same time?

Chloe went upstairs and got another glass of milk. She would have to deduct the baby's calories from her own. Gunter was sure to notice if she was suddenly drinking more milk. Chloe couldn't tell him the truth, so the only option was to claim that she was the one drinking it and forego those calories. She could do that for Joshua.

She decided she'd better change him before feeding him, so she wouldn't have to wake him up to change him after he drifted back off to sleep. She unwound the wet towel, rinsed it in the sink, squeezed it out, and put it on the edge of the hamper to dry before going into the laundry. It wasn't soiled very badly. She could maybe hand wash and reuse it once or twice before putting it into the laundry so that no one would notice her using extra towels. She would have to find a better solution once he was bigger and moving around, but it would do for the present.

It wasn't until the next morning that Chloe realized she had another problem. She could not feed Joshua during the day if she were at school. And she couldn't ask anyone else to do it. She couldn't take the baby to school. A live baby in her locker or backpack might attract attention. So she would have to get home during the day to feed him.

Lunch she could manage. If she went to school late and went home before last period, maybe that would be often enough. Three hours apart didn't seem too bad for feedings. As long as she fed him plenty.

It would be a lot easier if she had a bottle. But she couldn't risk being seen buying one or getting caught shoplifting one. And if she had one, Gunter might see it.

Gunter insisted on driving Chloe to school with him rather than letting her walk after being sick. So the baby was going to have to wait longer than three hours until she could manage a lunch feeding. But he'd been waiting that long at night, so hopefully it would be okay.

Chloe was distracted all through her morning classes. She was sure her teachers were wondering why she was being such an idiot when they asked her questions. Hopefully, they would just chalk it up to her still being a little bit under the weather.

As soon as her last morning class was over, Chloe was out of the school like a shot and ran all the way home, ignoring her burning lungs and leg muscles.

Joshua was crying, but she was relieved to find that she couldn't hear him until she got down the stairs. At least Mim and Gunter would not hear him upstairs. He was a very quiet baby. She unwrapped the towel to change him. It wasn't very wet, but she put a new one on him anyway. He fussed throughout the feeding, never settling down properly, but she got as much milk into his tummy as she could. His eyes seemed darker and more deep-set than they had previously. His skin was papery and dry. She wondered if he was coming down with something.

Chloe settled Joshua into a nest of towels once more, washed out the previous towel, and headed back to school. It was too late for her to buy any lunch, but Joshua had had to wait for his meal, so it seemed only right that she should have to suffer as well. Her stomach growled all the way through her afternoon classes, serving as a reminder that she needed to get back home as quickly as possible.

She slipped out of the school during the class change before final period and hiked home. She was too tired and weak to run again. But it hadn't been as long as it had been in the morning, and Joshua had still been okay then.

When she got home, she was relieved to find that he was still sleeping. She woke him gently to feed him and make up for being so long in the morning. He was drowsy and didn't seem very hungry. Chloe decided that he needed sleep more than food and left him to rest.

∾

"Did you skip final period?" Gunter asked Chloe when she went up to help him prepare supper. He didn't turn around to look at her.

Chloe stood there for a moment, the question hanging in the air.

"Yes," she admitted eventually. "I got through the rest of the day, but I was pretty useless... I just couldn't manage one more class."

He paused in chopping vegetables and looked over his shoulder at her. It was a brief look, and then he went back to chopping.

"Might have been too early for you to go back to school today. You walked home?"

"Yes. The fresh air helped a bit. But I'm wiped out now."

"You'll need to go to bed early again tonight. You can get caught up on homework once you are feeling better. If you try to do everything before you're well, you're just going to make yourself sicker. What have you eaten?"

"Just milk. And a piece of toast at breakfast."

"Can you manage some supper, do you think? Some steamed rice with vegetables would be pretty gentle."

Chloe's stomach growled, but not loudly enough that he heard it. "That sounds good. I think so." Her stomach felt like it was going to consume itself if she didn't get something into it pretty soon. She would need to be sure to eat slowly. He would wonder what was going on if she gobbled it down like she was starving. Which she was.

The smells of the food cooking were a tantalizing torture. Chloe set the table and poured herself a tall glass of milk. It felt like an eternity before the food was on the table.

"Is Mom having anything tonight?" Chloe asked.

"I'll take some in on a tray after we're done. She's a little hungrier today. It will take time for her to recover her strength. Both of you."

Chloe took a tiny bite of rice. She chewed for a long time and then went for a piece of carrot. She ate as slowly as she could manage. After the first few bites, her stomach settled down, and she could feel the boost in her blood sugar, calming her anxiety and helping her to breathe again. Gunter kept a close eye on her while she ate, so she was careful to continue to eat slowly, and to leave just enough on her plate to convince him that she wasn't quite up to par yet. She wanted those last few bites. But she was no longer starving. She could do without them.

"You'd better get off to bed," Gunter advised. "And I don't think I heard your shower this morning. If you don't have one tonight, be sure to have one in the morning. You don't want to stink, and with being sick, you can get smelly pretty quickly. Your hair needs to be washed."

"Okay."

With the baby in the shower stall, Chloe hadn't even thought about her hygiene. But he wasn't going to crawl away; she could just leave him on the floor while she showered and then put him back in once she dried out the stall. She wondered if she should be washing Joshua too. He didn't smell that she had noticed.

After being excused, Chloe changed into her jammies and took her glass of milk into the bathroom to feed Joshua.

He was making a cute snoring noise, his breath raspy. Chloe decided to wait a while to see if he would wake up on his own. She looked over her school books. Gunter had said she didn't need to get all her homework done, but she didn't want to get too far behind. She could get a few things done to make it easier.

After shooing Chloe off to bed and tucking her in, Gunter gave her a kiss on the forehead and one on the cheek and admonished her to go to sleep.

"No staying up reading more tonight," he instructed, with a glance at her English books. "You need your sleep. You can catch up tomorrow."

Chloe nodded drowsily and waited for him to leave. Once she could hear him upstairs talking to Mim, she went into the bathroom to feed Joshua.

He was quiet, no longer snoring.

When she touched him, he didn't stir.

Chloe shook and poked him gently, then harder. There was still no response. Her heart beating rapidly, Chloe leaned close to him.

"No, no, no," she whispered.

Putting her ear directly over his mouth, she could not hear or feel any breathing. She pulled the towel away from his chest and pressed her ear to his body, listening for the sound of his heartbeat. Still, she could detect nothing. Chloe squeezed his arms. Ran her sharp fingernail down the sole of his foot. There was no response. Chloe cuddled him to her, sobbing.

"No, no, no!"

Babies are fragile. That's what Mim had said. *It doesn't take much…* Had he smothered on the towels? Was the milk not nourishing enough for him? Had the four hours between his morning and noon feeding been too long?

She didn't know what she could have done to save him

Chloe cried long into the night. She slept a sparse few hours, Joshua's tiny body cuddled in her arms in her own bed. When she woke up before dawn, she realized she needed to face the problem of what to do with his body. Burying it seemed out of the question. Gunter was bound to notice any digging in the back yard. She couldn't put him in a garbage bag to be taken out with the trash. That would be heartless.

That didn't leave many options. Chloe looked around her room, the tiny bathroom, and the store room. The store room seemed the only possibility. There were a few plastic bins there. A few things that had been put away for when the weather got cooler again. A few of Gunter's things. The box with the unused air mattress in it.

Gunter's bins were out of the question. Who knew when he might dig around in one of them? But the quilt box or the mattress box seemed like good possibilities.

In the wee hours of the morning, Chloe watched herself, face set and tearless, as she wrapped Joshua's body up in a big bath towel and tuck it away into one of the boxes.

CHAPTER
Ten

C hloe went through the day in a daze. She saw herself moving from one class to the next like a sleepwalker, not talking to anyone or taking in a word of what was being taught. Even in social studies, where she was supposed to be doing a group project with Theo, she sat at her desk with her face buried in her folded arms and didn't say anything to him. Theo shrugged his shoulders and drew patterns all over his arms with a black pen.

When school was finally over, she made an effort to organize the books she would need and headed for home. Her thoughts were far away, unaware of her surroundings until she heard her name repeated several times. She finally looked around to see the source of the voice.

"You think you're better than anybody else? Walking around with your nose up in the air?" he accused.

"No." Chloe rubbed her eyes, trying to focus on the boy and to remember his name. "I didn't hear you."

He looked her over. "Come here." He grabbed her arm. Chloe jerked back, but he didn't let go. "I just wanted to show you something, don't act like that!"

Chloe looked at him searchingly. He wanted to show her something? What was this all about?

"What?" she stalled. She glanced around for help, but the street was quiet. Most of the students lived in the opposite direction.

He gave her a smile that looked predatory. "I just want to show you something," he wheedled.

"I don't… I don't know what you're talking about. Let go of me."

He jerked her closer to him. Chloe resisted.

"Just leave me alone. Let me go."

The boy didn't. His grip on her arm was tight. No longer pretending that he just wanted to show her something. No longer hiding behind the mask of a smile. He swore at her. "Get over here. You do what you're told."

Chloe always did what she was told. But he wasn't her parent or her teacher. Or her counselor. She didn't have to listen to him. And she had an inkling of what would happen if she did.

He dragged her off of the sidewalk, and struggling, through the break in a hedge back behind an ancient, crumbling church. Chloe let out a scream and fought him off.

He threw her down on the ground, and with the weight of her books and the impetus of the push, she couldn't keep her feet and went down with a crash. Then his weight was on her, pinning her down, clawing at her clothing. Chloe screamed again, trying to kick him or to free her arms. He was swearing, punching her, covering her mouth to stop her from screaming, but then letting it go to hit her or tear at her. He called her names and punched her in the mouth. Chloe tasted blood. The weight of him on her body made it hard to get enough air to breathe, let alone to scream anymore. She tried desperately to fight him off, but it was a losing battle. He was going to have his way.

Then the boy went flying off her. She heard his head clonk on the ground or on one of the pathway paving stones. For a minute, Chloe couldn't comprehend what had happened.

Gunter was bending over her. "Chloe! Chloe, are you okay?" He was an inch from her face, his tone urgent.

Chloe blinked her eyes, trying to sort out all of the input from her senses. "Gunter?"

"Shh, it's okay. Are you all right, Chloe?"

Chloe put her hands beside her to push herself up. She turned her head and looked for her attacker. He was groaning, twisting his body around, trying to get to his feet. Gunter paid no attention to the boy.

"He… he grabbed me. He was trying to…"

"He's not going to hurt you. I'm here. I'll protect you. Are you hurt?"

"No... I don't think so."

There was saliva running down her chin. Gunter wiped it with his thumb and Chloe saw that it was blood, not spit. She explored the inside of her mouth with her tongue. It had been cut on her teeth when the boy had hit her.

"It's okay," she said. "Just a little blood. It's not bad."

"Can you get up?"

Gunter grasped her arms with strong hands and helped to pull her to her feet. Chloe felt a little steadier once on her feet. She was still wearing her backpack. She readjusted it on her shoulders and took a deep breath. Out the corner of her eye, Chloe saw the boy stumbling away, ducking out through another hole in the hedge. She raised a warning hand to point him out to Gunter.

"I know him," Gunter said. "I'll call the police once we get you taken care of." His eyes traveled over her torn shirt. Her pants were intact. "He didn't... he didn't have a chance to..."

Chloe shook her head. "No. How did you know? I thought he was going to... I couldn't fight him off..."

"I was looking for you, to give you a ride home from school. I heard you scream."

Chloe nodded. She tried to take a step to walk to his car and leave the abandoned churchyard behind. But her knees buckled, weak as water. Gunter wrapped an arm around her and supported her, helping her back out to the street, where she saw his car pulled over haphazardly at an angle to the curb. He helped her in, then went around his side and got in. They drove back to the house without any conversation. Chloe was cold and starting to shake.

"It's okay," Gunter soothed. He took her into the kitchen and lowered her into a chair. She watched blankly as he looked through the cupboards, and pulled out a bottle of wine that he must have purchased for a romantic meal between him and Mim. Chloe shook her head when he prepared to open it.

"I can't have wine."

Gunter turned his head and looked at her. "Just a little bit to counteract the shock," he said. "It will fortify you. Steady your nerves."

"I can't. I'm allergic."

His brows drew down. "You're allergic…?"

"To wine."

"How do you know that?"

"Because I had a reaction." Chloe thought this rather obvious.

"When did you drink wine?"

"I… don't remember. It was a long time ago."

He seemed even more puzzled by this answer. Chloe shrugged it off.

"I think… I'd like to go lay down. Would that be okay? I'm so cold…"

"Yes, of course." He didn't need to escort her all the way from the kitchen to her bedroom. Chloe could have managed that on her own. But he did anyway. Chloe collapsed onto the bed. He took her backpack and put it by her desk. And removed her shoes and put them neatly beside the door. He shut and locked the bedroom door. Chloe stirred, trying to figure out why he had done that.

Gunter started to unbutton the torn shirt. Chloe clutched it to her.

"No!"

"We'll get you into something else clean and whole. Let's get these muddy clothes off of you."

Chloe still resisted. "No. I can do it myself."

"Are you talking back to me?" All of the gentle solicitation was gone from his tone. This was the Gunter she feared. The one who called her filthy, degrading names and berated her for mistakes or perceived disobedience.

Chloe froze. She didn't dare move or protest again. She was a good girl. An obedient girl. She did what she was told. She was always the perfect daughter, the one that her parents could rely on. Gunter had stepped into that role as well as others. Absolute obedience was the imperative.

Gunter's hands went back to her shirt, unbuttoning it and removing it. Chloe shivered, and her bared skin broke out into goosebumps.

"You see?" Gunter was looking at her scratched and scraped body. "You look so much better having lost the extra weight. You don't look like a fat cow anymore. You're pretty. Desirable."

"Would you get me a shirt?" Chloe whispered. "I just want to go to sleep now."

But Gunter shook his head. "We need to get the rest of these clothes off," he said. "You'll feel much better when you're into something fresh and clean."

She didn't dare protest.

But she couldn't be there to experience it. She floated away as he stripped off the contaminated clothing.

Then lay down with her to help to warm her shivering, shuddering body.

Then kissed away her tears.

Chloe woke gradually, groggy and confused. Her whole body ached. But she knew there was something more than just scrapes and bruises from the boy's attack. She had that same feeling as she had had over the years when she took the sleeping pills her mother gave her. Waking up in the morning with that heavy pelvic pain, tenderness, and spots of blood on her underwear, even though it wasn't her period. She hadn't had a sleeping pill this time, but still had the same weird feeling of unreality. A feeling that she was separate from the rest of the world and not really experiencing the same things as her body was.

She didn't want to feel the pain and the rawness of her body. She didn't want to remember what had happened the previous day. So much trauma in such a short period of time. She just wanted to completely rewrite the last few days and pretend that none of it had ever happened.

Chloe burrowed down further under her covers and tried to find sleep again. She would tell Gunter that she was still too sick to go to school. She could miss one more day. She had caught up to her peers after weeks and months of absence; she could certainly recover from a few days.

He did come down to get her to get ready for school, but when he found her still in bed, he changed his mind and spent some time with her before heading off to the school himself, a satisfied smile on his face.

Chloe tried locking the door, but there was no point. He had the key on his key ring and it provided no barrier to him. The only person the lock would keep out was Mim, and there was no need to keep her away. She never came down to Chloe's bedroom, even the nights that Gunter didn't go back upstairs.

～

Gunter poured them each a cup of coffee and set them out on the table just as Chloe entered the kitchen from the stairs. Mim sat heavily on one of the sturdy kitchen chairs, fat thighs lapping over the sides of the seat, and let out a noisy sigh to let the world know that she was not ready for the day to start.

"Morning, Chloe," Gunter greeted.

Chloe sat down and took a sip of her coffee. "Oh, that's so good," she approved. "My brain needs a kick start this morning."

Gunter placed a plate with two slices of dry toast in front of her and sat down himself. "I like that outfit," he told her. "It really suits you."

Chloe flushed with pleasure at his compliment. She liked the way that the blouse and pants fitted her shape and had admired the effect in her mirror, but that wasn't the same as hearing it from someone else. Someone that she trusted to always tell her the truth, good or bad.

"She's skin and bones," Mim complained. "Just look at her arms. They're sticks. She's not getting enough to eat."

Gunter looked at Mim with an expression of distaste. "Chloe is a healthy weight. If you have concerns about it, maybe you should look at some weight tables yourself."

Mim looked away from him and took another sip of her coffee. Chloe wondered, not for the first time, about the strange relationship between the two. Mim seemed desperate to hold onto Gunter, despite his insults and their lack of intimacy. Was it just the money? Appearances? Having someone around who was handy and would voluntarily make meals?

She already knew what it was that Gunter got out of the relationship.

CHAPTER
Eleven

The first sign that something was wrong didn't come from Gunter or Mim, but from one of the girls at school.

Chloe didn't really have any friends. Her school life was monitored and controlled by Gunter, so that didn't give Chloe much opportunity for social contact. Her meals, study time, and other routines were dictated for her, and though she had gotten to know the others students by name, she didn't really know any of them personally.

"Chloe."

At a tap on her shoulder, Chloe turned around and saw Leesa, who had been just a couple of lockers down from her the previous school year. Chloe cocked her head.

"Yes?"

"I just wanted to say... you know he never sticks long with one girl, right?"

Chloe stared. "Who? What are you talking about?"

"Mr. Gnatsky. He's been sniffing around Caitlyn Summers lately. Just thought you should know."

Chloe stared at Leesa, horrified. A jumble of thoughts tumbled through her head. Leesa, and others at school, knew about Gunter and his interest in Chloe. She didn't know if they knew that Gunter lived with her or not. Not only that, but Gunter was known as someone who had inappropriate relationships with students. Multiple students, not just Chloe. How could the other students be aware of it and not the administration? Surely someone had reported if they had suspicions about Gunter's behavior? They wouldn't just let a staff member continue to have contact with students if it was known. Would they?

And the worst of the facts that Leesa had just relayed. That Gunter had bored of Chloe and was moving on to someone else.

Chloe didn't say anything to Mim or to Gunter. She went home as usual, got out her schoolbooks as usual, and did all of her chores and anything else she was expected to do. Gunter didn't call her up to help with dinner preparations, but Chloe went anyway, volunteering her services.

"Set the table," Gunter said absently, flicking a hand in the direction of the table.

"Okay." Chloe looked over the pots on the stove. "What are we having? Chicken and rice?"

"Yes. And salad. Just plates, nothing special."

Chloe pulled things out of the cupboards and slowly put them in the settings. She waited for Gunter to ask her about her day. Making sure that she had not overeaten. That there had not been problems with any of the boys at school. If she needed any help with her schoolwork. Chloe had not needed much help with schoolwork lately. She was caught up to the rest of her classes and only occasionally ran into problems. Usually with math.

But Gunter was quiet, thinking his own thoughts and not sharing them with her. Was he thinking about Caitlyn Summers? Preparing a brand new strategy of seduction? Chloe stood there in silence after she was finished the table, watching him.

"There's lemon water in the fridge," Gunter said without turning around. "You know what to do. Don't just stand there like a moron."

"Sorry." Chloe went to the fridge and fetched the water. She added salt and pepper shakers to the table. "Should I get Mom? Is it ready?"

"Yes, it will be on the table by the time she gets herself out here."

Chloe found Mim in front of the TV in the living room and invited her for dinner. Mim sighed at having to leave in the middle of her show, but was hungry enough not to delay until the end. She waddled into the kitchen and sat down.

Gunter brought the serving dishes to the table and dished up his own and Chloe's. He sat down and chewed a forkful of chicken and rice.

"I'm moving out," he said.

Chloe and Mim both stared at him. Mim's fork clattered to the floor. Gunter wiped his mouth with his napkin and retrieved it for her, setting it down beside her plate instead of putting it into her hand.

"What did you say?" Mim demanded.

"I'm moving out. This weekend."

"But... what are you talking about? Moving out? What happened?"

"Nothing happened. I'm done here. I'm moving on." He took another bite and shook his head at Mim. "It shouldn't come as any great shock. You know how fat and ugly you are. You've figured out by now that I have no desire for you."

Mim took the insult with barely a flinch. "But... what has changed? I thought we had worked things out. So that you were..." her eyes drifted to Chloe, "...satisfied."

Gunter snorted. "What a horrible mother you are. Even an animal has better maternal instincts than you do."

While Mim flapped her jaw at this, trying to figure out how to respond, Gunter turned and spoke to Chloe.

"I'm sorry for you. Having to stay here with her and no one else to look out for you. But I've taught you what to do. How to study and take care of your body and dress properly. You're going to have to take care of yourself and do those things on your own now. I'm sure it won't be long until your mother brings another man home." He got out his keys and took Chloe's bedroom key off of the ring, handing it across to her. "There's a lock on the door for a reason. Keep it locked."

It had never stopped him.

Chloe picked up the key, staring at him. "Are you really leaving? Just like that?"

"I'm sorry. Yes. I'm done here."

~

Chloe felt like a sleepwalker over the next few days, not quite believing that Gunter was really going to move out. Not believing that he didn't care for her anymore. She was sure that he would change his mind, or she would wake up and find out that it had just been a nightmare. How was she going to manage without him?

He had a friend with a truck come and help him to carry out all his things. The spare bedroom was cleared out. He took his bins from the store room. The pots and pans and kitchen appliances that were his. Chloe half-expected him to come down to her bedroom and demand back the clothes that he had bought for her or that had been bought at his direction. But he didn't. It was his friend who went down to the storeroom to fetch Gunter's boxes, clearly marked with his initials. Gunter didn't even venture downstairs.

After Gunter had taken whatever was his from the master bedroom, Mim had retreated and shut the door so she didn't have to watch him taking everything else. Chloe went upstairs and watched Gunter walk slowly through the house, looking for anything else that he may have missed. Gunter looked at her, standing there by herself with her arms folded. His friend was still taking out the last few boxes, so Gunter's voice was low.

"I'll still see you at the school," he commented.

"But it won't be the same."

He gave Chloe a brief hug. She clung to him. "Please don't go. Stay here. I don't care if there's someone else. Just don't leave me here all by myself. Please."

Gunter stroked her hair for a moment.

"You're a sweet girl, Chloe. You're a lot smarter, and you've got a lot more going for you than you think. If you'll be strong and stand up for yourself, you can go far. Don't let... people... push you around. You're young, but there are kids your age already living on their own, on the streets, independent. Don't forget that. You're stronger than you think."

"Like my sister, Ruby."

"Like your sister, Ruby," he agreed. Of course he had heard all about Ruby over the months that he had lived there. "Now I have to tell you goodbye." He kissed her once on the forehead. "I'll see you at school. Take care of yourself."

And with that, he pushed her away and walked out of the house.

～

The front door closed and Chloe listened to the truck pulling away from the house a couple of minutes later. That was it. Gunter was gone.

Mim had apparently also heard the final exit and knew what it meant. Chloe heard the bedroom door open. Her mother thumped heavily down the hall and walked into the living room to face Chloe. Her eyes were rimmed with red and her eyes and nose moist.

"This is your fault," she accused.

Chloe just stood there. She couldn't disagree. If she was the reason Gunter had come and had stayed, then Chloe was also the reason he had left. If he had been distracted by another girl, then it was because Chloe hadn't been able to hold his interest. Maybe she hadn't lost enough weight, or hadn't dressed well enough, or hadn't pleased him in other ways. He had frequently had reason to berate her. There had been too many of those things and he had decided he'd had enough.

Mim had a yellow extension cord in her hand, looped through her palm several times. Chloe heard it whistle through the air. It hit her with a loud smack that burned and smarted. She didn't run away. She didn't retreat to her bedroom and lock the door. She stood there and took it as Mim screamed and whipped and worked herself into a frenzy.

Chloe watched from the ceiling, feeling nothing, as the blond girl was beaten to the floor.

CHAPTER
Twelve

C hloe had missed several days of school. But she had recovered enough to go back, and there was no joy in rattling around the house on her own when Mim went to work. So Chloe put on her clothes and her makeup, grabbed her book bag, and headed back to school.

She was late getting there and didn't stop at the office for a tardy slip like she was supposed to. The teachers didn't really want more to do and never read the tardy slips anyway. It was just extra work for everyone. Chloe walked in and sat at her desk without a word, even though it was halfway through the second-period class.

The seat was hard and cold, and it hurt her bruises in unexpected ways, the jolts of pain catching her off-guard whenever she shifted her position. Chloe tried to focus on the lesson, but her thoughts kept wandering far from the course of study.

"Chloe?"

Chloe looked at the teacher, who had apparently just asked her a question. Trying to draw her attention back to the class. Chloe rubbed her forehead.

"I'm sorry. I wasn't listening, Mr. Harris."

"I was asking you about the role of Germany—"

"I don't know. I'll have to re-read it tonight."

He opened his mouth, looking for a way to get her re-engaged with the lesson, then changed his mind. She had apologized and been respectful; there was no reason for him to embarrass her in front of the class. She was obviously far from being able to deal with it.

"See me after the lesson, please."

"Yes, sir."

He went on with the lesson. Chloe put her head down on her desk and closed her eyes. She listened to the rhythm of his voice, but his actual words washed right over her. Germany. The war. She would read the text when she was home to get caught back up. Or maybe she wouldn't. There wasn't anyone left at home who cared about whether she got good marks or not. If she wanted to, she could just coast through and not try to stay on top of the courses of study. What difference did marks make?

When he was finished his lecture and had given the day's assignment to the class to begin work on, Mr. Harris turned his attention back to Chloe.

"Chloe, would you come up and talk to me, please?" he requested, sitting at his desk.

Chloe roused herself. She sat up and wondered whether she should take all her books up with her, or just go up with nothing to speak to him. She decided to leave everything at her desk and walked to the teacher's desk.

"Are you not feeling well today?" Harris asked in a low voice.

Chloe shook her head. "No."

"You're pale. Should you be at home in bed?"

"I already missed the rest of the week," Chloe pointed out. "I gotta be here…"

He frowned, studying her. Chloe drew back slightly, uncomfortable with his scrutiny. Mr. Harris pulled a pink slip out of his drawer and wrote something on it. He folded it over and stapled it closed.

"I want you to talk to your counselor," he advised, handing it to her. "You may as well go now; you won't be missing anything."

Chloe took the slip reluctantly. "I'm just not feeling well," she protested. "I don't need to see anyone."

"I gave you a slip. You need to go to the office."

She stood there looking for an argument. Then she went back to her desk, gathered her books, and left the room.

At the office, she approached the secretary, fluttering the pink slip at her. "I'm supposed to see a counselor."

"Your name?"

"Chloe Simpson."

The secretary looked at her for a moment, then back at her computer as she typed Chloe's name in.

"Your counselor is Mr. Gnatsky. He's free to see you."

"Uh... could I see another counselor instead?"

"Mr. Gnatsky is your counselor."

"But... could I change? Could I change to one of the other counselors instead?"

"Not without a reason. Do you have a valid reason for switching?"

"I... no, I just... how about a female counselor? What if I want to discuss... feminine issues?"

"You'll have to be more specific. All our counselors are trained to deal with anything to do with pregnancy, STDs, or other issues regarding sexuality."

The conversation was not going the way Chloe had hoped. Now, not only did she still have to meet with Gunter, but the secretary was going to be speculating on what nice juicy topics Chloe needed to be counseled on.

"Never mind. I'll see Gunter," Chloe said quickly.

She headed for his office. She didn't know what she was concerned about. Their relationship now ended, Gunter would be nothing but professional in any discussions he had with Chloe.

She knocked on the open door. Gunter looked up and gave her a polite smile.

"Chloe. Come in. What can I do for you?"

Chloe handed him the pink slip. She watched him get out his staple remover and carefully take the staple out instead of ripping the folded note open. It had been stapled so that Chloe wouldn't read it, but she had simply pulled the two sides apart as far as the staple would allow and peered into the tube that the note had formed. It was unenlightening. Harris's scribble said simply 'evaluate situation.'

Chloe looked at the chair that Gunter motioned her into. It was softer than the classroom chairs, but it still wasn't going to be comfortable for her to sit down. She stayed on her feet and folded her arms.

"I don't need to talk to anyone," she informed him.

"I know you're upset about me leaving," he said reasonably. "I know that you've missed school all week. You want to talk about it?"

"No."

He stared at her, those intense eyes reading her soul.

"Do you have a black eye?"

"No."

Of course she did, but it was covered with a thick layer of make-up. If Gunter couldn't tell for sure, she'd done her job well.

"You have a cut on your cheek. And at the corner of your mouth."

"Zits," Chloe insisted. "I scratched them. Made a bit of a mess."

"If I called the police and they examined you, what kind of injuries would they find?"

Chloe set her jaw. "No one has got any right to examine me. There's no cause."

"If I report suspicion of child abuse, they have cause."

"If you report suspicion of child abuse," Chloe countered, "I'll report you."

Gunter didn't flinch, but she knew she had him. He couldn't afford to have the police looking at him. Since it was widely known among the student body, he had obviously been pursuing students for some time, An inquiry would find something, even if it was just gossip. And if Chloe wanted to push it, she could give them details. Details that would prove her allegations.

"Chloe. If Mim is hurting you, all it would take is one report from me and I could have you out of that house. They could find you a foster home. Somewhere you would be safe."

Chloe shook her head. "I'm not going to a foster home. I'm staying with my mom. You stay out of it."

Gunter tapped his pen on his desk. "Are you sure?"

Chloe nodded. "If I wanted to leave, I could make the phone call. I don't need anything from you."

"Do you want me to talk to her?" he persisted.

"Are you *kidding*?" A call from Gunter to Mim would just send her back over the edge, and Chloe could expect a beating that was worse than the last. "Stay away from her! I mean it."

"Okay." He sighed. "I'm here if you want help. I haven't aban-doned you."

~

Chloe felt rudderless. Ever since Gunter had moved in with them, he had been in control of her life. She ate when and what he said. She wore what he told her to. Studied when and what he told her to, for long hours on end. She washed and slept when he told her to. Now that he was suddenly gone, she didn't know what to do. For a few days, she tried to follow the schedule he had dictated, but without him there to enforce it, it quickly fell apart. She had no desire to study or do her homework. Mim didn't want the types of meals that Gunter had made, and Chloe fell back into making the high calorie, highly processed comfort food that Mim craved. Press a few buttons on the microwave, and it was done. She stopped showering and washing her hair and rarely had the energy to do the laundry.

After school one day, Chloe saw Gunter coming down the hallway toward her, walking beside Caitlyn Summers, talking seriously with her. Without time to think, Chloe grabbed the hand of the nearest boy, a football player called Hobbs, and spun him around to face her. Hobbs looked confused.

"Uh... what...?"

Chloe smiled up at him. "Hey. Aren't you in my math class?"

"Uh... sure."

When Gunter walked by, Chloe made sure that he saw her holding Hobbs' hand and openly flirting with him. Gunter had always been jealous of any of the boys even speaking to her. Maybe if he thought there was some competition now, he'd be more interested in her again. Guys were like that, more attracted to a girl when there was competition.

"Are you very good at math?" Chloe asked Hobbs. "I could really use a tutor."

She was sure that she could have tutored him, but how else was she supposed to get him to meet with her to pursue the relationship further?

"Well, I dunno..."

"My mom won't let me *date*," Chloe said, planting the idea, "but she'll let me get tutoring. You know. To bring my math scores up."

"Uh, yeah. Maybe I could help with that."

She pressed up close to him, making sure that he couldn't mistake her purpose. "You're not, uh *tutoring* anyone else, are you?"

He was looking at her with a dazed expression.

"Uh... no..."

"How about the library, during lunch tomorrow?"

"Sure."

CHAPTER
Thirteen

C hloe awoke during the night to all kinds of noise filtering down from the upstairs. Mim had been out when Chloe went to bed. She hadn't said where she was going or when she would be back, and Chloe just went to bed as if that was perfectly normal. And lately, it had been.

But Mim had not brought all her dates home. From the crashing around and the baritone voice upstairs, she had this time. Chloe had no inclination to go upstairs and meet the new man. He would probably be gone the next day and never heard from again. And from the sounds of things, they were both drunk, clumsy, and angry. Chloe considered getting up to lock her door but didn't think that either of them would venture down the stairs in the condition they were in. Chloe pulled the pillow over her head in an attempt to block out the noise and tried to go back to sleep.

~

In the morning, things were quiet. Chloe considered waking her mother up. What if she was late for work? Would she lose her job? Did she even have a job to lose? Was it a day off? Chloe made herself a pot of coffee and waited for it to perk. While she was waiting, there were noises from the bedroom, and a man went down the hall to the bathroom to relieve himself. Chloe hoped he wasn't too hung over to hit the bullseye. She had no desire to clean up after him.

On his trek back toward the bedroom, he glanced into the kitchen and looked surprised to see her standing there. He walked into the doorway and studied her, brows down.

He looked younger than Mim. Five o'clock shadow that might be a day or two old. Short hair that was charmingly mussed and probably looked fabulous when he took the time to pretty himself up. He was wearing only a pair of blue boxers, obviously not having expected there to be anyone else around. He looked around the rest of the kitchen, and then back at Chloe.

"Who are you?"

"Chloe. Mim's daughter."

"She has a daughter? News to me."

Chloe shrugged. "Yeah. She does."

"Huh."

"And you?"

"Walter. Bose." He rubbed his eyes. "Really? She has a daughter?"

Chloe laughed. "She has four daughters. But I'm the only one living here."

"Yeah? So what's so special about you?"

Chloe took the coffee off of the burner and poured herself a mug. She wasn't quite sure how to answer that. So she sipped the hot coffee instead. He shrugged and went back to the bedroom.

Chloe had known that it was Gunter's day to supervise the library at lunch, so she made sure that she wore one of the shirts that he labeled slutty and that he would see her making out with her new tutor. They weren't exactly hidden away in the back.

Hobbs was an eager participant in her plan, though he had no idea of her motives. He obviously appreciated her dressing for him but was frustrated by the roadblocks he encountered. He had made several suggestions of places that they could go for some privacy so that he could investigate further, but Chloe was where she wanted to be. Right under Gunter's nose, where he had to see them every time he made his rounds. He had broken them up several times, and even suggested that they needed to go somewhere else. But Chloe declined, explaining that they were studying and needed to be there to get any work done.

"It doesn't look to me like you're getting any work done," Gunter pointed out. "Why don't you pack your bags and move on? Other people here *are* trying to study, and you're very... distracting."

"We're allowed to be here," Chloe maintained.

"Not if you're going to be disruptive."

"We're being quiet."

Gunter growled and moved on.

"What's that guy's problem?" Hobbs asked with a nervous laugh. "Repressed much?"

Chloe laughed and continued with the study session.

Walter was not gone the next day, but seemed to have become a permanent fixture. Chloe couldn't understand what Mim saw in him. Had she just looked for someone who was the complete opposite of Gunter? Walter was sloppy, undisciplined, and drunk at least half the time. She assumed that Mim must be getting something out of the relationship, or she wouldn't have put up with his abusive behavior.

Chloe was making dinner according to Mim's orders. Mac and cheese with fish sticks. It was a bizarre combination, but who was Chloe to question it? She did what she was told, and if Mim was craving KD and battered fish, then that was what Chloe would make.

Mim and Walter had been watching TV in the living room, but after some argument over nothing and a bit of shoving, Walter made and appearance in the kitchen to find out what was going on with dinner.

"What the hell is that smell?" he demanded, nose wrinkling. He leaned into the fridge to take out another six pack.

"It's fish."

"Smells like rotten garbage! Why would you cook something so disgusting?"

"That's what Mom wanted," Chloe snapped back. "You heard her ask for it."

Before Chloe even finished turning around, he was on top of her.

Spitting invectives, he grabbed Chloe by her long, blond hair and threw her to the floor.

"You don't talk to me like that!" he snarled. He hadn't put down the six-pack, and Chloe counted herself lucky that he hit her with his free fist rather than the one holding the beer, or he would have broken bones for sure. She rolled over and tried to avoid him, but he dropped the cans of beer, grabbed her by the arm, and held her still while he pummeled her.

Chloe was gone.

Just like that, she was out of her body, watching the incident as an observer. Far enough away that she didn't have to feel the blows, taste the blood, or hear the crunch of her bones beneath his fists.

It was always best not to fight back and not to resist. In time, he wore himself out, picked up his beer, and returned to the living room to argue some more with Mim. Chloe gathered her strength and got back to her feet. Holding a tissue to her nose to keep from bleeding into the pasta, she finished cooking supper and retreated to her bedroom.

CHAPTER

Fourteen

The days turned into weeks and then months. Chloe gradually came to the conclusion that it didn't matter how many boys she paraded past Gunter, he no longer had even a passing interest in being with her. She worried that she had pushed him further away with her efforts, but she had to remind herself that he had left her before she started fooling around with the other boys. He had already been gone then. There was nothing she could have done about it. She watched Caitlyn Summers change day by day, noting the gradual adoption of different clothes and a new hairstyle, softening of her makeup, and other subtle changes. She knew that behind the scenes, Gunter was molding another girl into his ideal. By then, Chloe had thrown out most of the clothes that he had bought for her.

Chloe listened to footsteps coming down the stairs as she worked half-heartedly on her homework. It had been nice when she had been able to understand everything and get good marks on her assignments. She felt like she had lost IQ points when Gunter left, taking all her motivation and discipline with him.

Mim was out of breath as she came in through Chloe's door. A momentous occasion. Chloe could probably count on one hand the number of times that Mim had come into her room.

"What's up?" Chloe asked.

Mim breathed heavily, looking around. It wasn't neat and tidy like it had been when Gunter lived there. There were dirty clothes on the floor, dirty dishes on several surfaces, and the bed was unmade. Mim frowned at a hole in the wall.

"What happened there?" she demanded.

"Walter."

Mim shook her head. "What was he doing down here?"

"Looking for someone to punch, I guess." Chloe shrugged. "Where is he now?"

"Passed out."

Mim still hadn't said what she had come downstairs for. Chloe studied her. She had gained weight. At least to Chloe's eye. It was hard to tell, because Mim's weight fluctuated wildly from month to month as she tried out new diets and then gave up on them, eating to more than make up for the weight that she had lost in the preceding days or weeks. Mim hugged her lower abdomen and caught Chloe's inquiring gaze.

"It's nothing," Mim said. "A cramp."

"Oh?" Chloe considered. "The kind of cramp you get before a baby comes?"

Mim gave her a sharp look, and Chloe knew she'd gone too far. She tensed and looked for something to say to reverse the damage.

"I'm sorry Mommy, I didn't mean..."

Mim held her stomach she sat abruptly on the bed. She rolled over onto her side. "It's too early," she moaned. "Much too early."

So Chloe *had* called it correctly. She left her desk and sat on the bed beside Mim.

"Can I help? Should I call an ambulance? What should I do?"

"No need to go to the hospital for a miscarriage," Mim objected. "I've been there before. Parked in a hallway for everyone to see because there were no beds. Laboring alone, doctors and nurses coming and going, acting like you're just passing a kidney stone or something." She gripped herself, grimacing. A tear squeezed from her eye. "I'm not doing that again."

Chloe rubbed Mim's back to soothe her, but Mim jerked away under her touch. "Oh!"

"What's wrong?" Chloe grasped the edge of Mim's shirt. "Are you hurt?"

The bruises answered her question. Mottled blue and black marks over Mim's flank and spine. "Ouch. When did he do this?"

Mim groaned and didn't answer, writing to find a more comfortable position on the bed. Chloe stroked Mim's hair away from her forehead, where she could see that there were no bruises.

"Is the baby coming because he hit you?"

Mim grasped Chloe's hand and squeezed. "Help me to the bathroom," she ordered. "I need the toilet."

"Okay. Let me help you. I'll come around this side..." Chloe did her best to get Mim up and find a way to support her to the bathroom. "Are you sure I shouldn't get an ambulance?" she asked again.

"Go out. Leave me alone."

Chloe obeyed, pulling the door shut most of the way behind her, but leaving it cracked slightly so that she could hear if Mim called her back.

She tried to ignore the grunting and moaning and to go back to her schoolwork, but there was no way that she could get anything else done. She stared at the questions without any comprehension as to what subject she was even looking at.

"Chloe."

Chloe returned to the bathroom and peeked in the door. Mim shuffled toward the bedroom, head down. She thrust a wet mass toward Chloe.

"Get rid of this. It's too big to flush."

The warm, wet bundle was in Chloe's hands before she could comprehend what was happening. She stared down at the wet, bloody, grayish blob in her hands. She gradually came to realize what it was. Chloe wiped fluid away from the tiny baby's nose and mouth, feeling nauseated. There was movement. A gasping breath, a twist of the head. Chloe's senses were overwhelmed. She followed her mother into the bedroom, where Mim again lay on the bed.

"Mom... it's alive..."

"No. It's too early to survive, Chloe. Much too early. Throw it out."

"I can't! It's breathing! It's not garbage!"

Mim groaned and held her stomach. She closed her eyes and was soon asleep.

Chloe sat on the edge of the bed. She should do something. She knew logically that it didn't matter what she did. The outcome would be the same. Whether she tried to get help, against Mim's orders, or tried to save the baby herself, or just abandoned it to its fate, the results would be the same. It wasn't going to live. It was no bigger than Chloe's hand. Such a tiny thing could never survive. By the time she did anything, it would breathe its last.

Chloe went back to the bathroom and took down a pink, fluffy washcloth. She wrapped it around the purple, alien-looking baby, and then went back to her bed and squeezed in beside Mim. She watched her tiny sister, knowing that each breath was likely to be her last.

And by the time Mim awoke again, it was. The baby lay still and quiet, cradled in Chloe's hands. Mim gave it barely a glance.

"I told you."

"I know."

Mim lay with one hand on her pelvis, frowning. Chloe didn't say anything for a while.

"What?" she asked finally. "Are you okay? Do you need a doctor?"

Mim shook her head. She turned her head toward Chloe. "I can still feel the baby kick," she said.

"But the baby died."

Mim nodded. Then after a few minutes, she shook her head. "No," she said. "I can still feel it." She took one of Chloe's hands and held it over her. "Tell me you don't feel that."

Chloe waited, feeling nothing. Then there was a flutter. She remembered that feeling from when Mim was pregnant with June and Justin. That miraculous feeling when Mim pressed Chloe's fingers against her belly and Chloe realized that there was, in fact, something inside of her.

"Twins again," Chloe said. "Like June and Justin?"

Mim looked at her. "But I couldn't lose one and keep the other, could I?"

Chloe looked at the baby held in one hand and Mim's belly under the other hand. "I don't know. How do you feel?"

"The cramps have stopped. I don't think... I think it has stopped."

"Then maybe it will be okay..."

In class, Chloe's head was down as she struggled with the math problem, trying her hardest to work it through without checking the answer at the back of the book or asking for help. It was so much harder now that there was no one to help her.

"Chloe."

There was a hand on her shoulder and Chloe flinched away so violently that she nearly fell out of her chair. There were a few giggles from the other students.

"I'm sorry," Mrs. Straus said, real apology in her tone. "I didn't mean to startle you." She laid a pink piece of paper down on the desk. "You're wanted at the office."

Chloe looked at the slip. Her name and the word *counselor*.

Gunter? It couldn't be that he wanted her back after all the time that had passed. Could it? Chloe closed her math books and picked everything up. At the office, she presented her slip to the secretary.

"I'm here to see Mr. Gnatsky," he explained.

The woman shook her head.

"Miss Fry," she said. "You have Miss Fry this year."

"They changed it?" Chloe was confused.

"We like to keep students with the same counselor through all their time here, but sometimes there are changes. You'll like Miss Fry."

Chloe looked at the cluster of offices. "Which one?"

"On the far left."

The door stood open. Chloe had been summoned, and Miss Fry was waiting for her. Chloe walked slowly toward it, no longer anticipating the meeting. Her stomach was a tight knot. She tried to swallow the lump in her throat, not sure why she suddenly felt like crying. There had been that one instant of hope, and now she felt crushed, like the rejection was fresh, and Gunter had just announced that he was leaving.

She hovered in the doorway. Miss Fry, a young-looking woman with silky blond hair whom Chloe had seen around the school before, looked up at her.

"Chloe. Come on in. Have a seat."

Chloe obeyed. She rubbed at a tear that escaped her eye, and gave herself a harsh lecture, just like Gunter would have. *It's time to stop being a crybaby and grow a spine, Chloe. No one gets anywhere in life by crying. Quit being such a needy little baby and shape up!* By the time she looked up at Miss Fry, all threatening tears were gone, and her eyes were dry.

Miss Fry smiled, with teeth, like it was a photo shoot. Chloe wondered if she had been a model before she had started her career as a school counselor. Who would give up that job for one of drudgery, working with troubled, oppositional youth all day?

"I don't know why you wanted me," Chloe said. "I haven't done anything." She breathed out slowly. She hadn't, as far as she knew, done anything to attract the attention of the administration. She had stopped trying to use they boys to try to get back at Gunter or to make him jealous so that he would come back to her. Though she still made the occasional study date, they were no longer out in the open, and were purely for physical comfort, endeavoring to fill the emptiness inside her.

Miss Fry got up from her desk, and Chloe watched her walk around the little office to shut the door. Then she returned to her seat. She pulled two or three tissues from the box on her desk and handed them to Chloe. Chloe looked down at them in her hand, stupefied. Miss Fry was expecting her to cry? If Chloe hadn't already determined not to cry, that action would have fortified her. She wasn't some weakling who was going to break down because the school counselor got after her.

"Chloe," Miss Fry folded her hands together on top of the thick file on the desk in front of her. "We're really very concerned about you."

Chloe remained stone-faced, waiting for an explanation.

"You were one of our most improved students last year. You were doing very well academically; you looked well and happy, and we were all so impressed with your transformation."

Chloe just waited. Miss Fry didn't need to point out how her marks had plummeted. And while Chloe had not gained back all the weight she had lost, she had gone back to wearing the clothes Gunter had decried as slutty. Walter liked them just fine, and he was the one Chloe had to appease now. The boys at school liked them just fine too. Gunter was the one who had a problem, not Chloe. She wrapped a hank of hair around her finger. It was tangled, and Chloe picked the knots out of it, waiting for Miss Fry to go on. When was the last time Chloe had washed her hair? When was the last time she'd even bothered to shower? Most of the time now, she slept in too late to shower in the morning, already late for school, and she didn't like to go to bed with wet hair in the cold of the basement.

"You can talk to me, Chloe," Miss Fry said earnestly.

She hadn't even asked Chloe any questions yet. Exactly what did she expect Chloe to say?

"Your teachers have noticed bruises."

They'd have to be blind not to, even with the makeup. Chloe shrugged. "I'm fair. I bruise easily. I'm clumsy."

"I don't think that's true. Who's hurting you, Chloe? Is it your mother?"

"No. She'd never do anything to hurt me," Chloe snapped. "No one is hurting me. It's just stupid accidents."

Miss Fry gazed at her, waiting for her to break down and admit it. But Chloe refused. She stared at the tip of Miss Fry's nose, waiting for her to back off. Miss Fry looked down at her hands or her papers.

"Your marks are way down. What's going on there?"

"It's just harder than it was."

"You're not handing in most of your homework assignments. Do you have a place to study and do homework at home?"

"Yes."

"Why are you not doing it?"

Chloe shrugged. "It's just too hard."

"Then you're going to need to talk to your teachers about getting extra help. You can get resource room help, afterschool help from your teachers, sessions with me, peer tutoring... There are a lot of options. We'll do everything we can to help you get back on track."

"Okay," Chloe agreed. Of course, she wouldn't, but arguing wouldn't get Miss Fry off her back. "Is that all, then?"

"Are you drinking, Chloe? Is there a problem with substance abuse or addiction?"

"No. I'm allergic to alcohol. Couldn't get drunk if I wanted to."

A small crease appeared between Miss Fry's eyes. She sighed. "I want to help you, Chloe."

"I've had enough of people trying to help me. It just makes things worse. So leave me alone."

Miss Fry unfolded her hands and started to write something in the file. "I have some very serious concerns," she said. "I had hoped that you would open up to me, and we wouldn't have to get anyone else involved."

Chloe couldn't help it. Her mind went immediately to Gunter. "Who?"

"I'm going to be putting in a call to Social Services. They can look into things at home, offer you a safe haven. Whatever else is needed."

It was like having a bucket of ice dashed over her. Chloe scowled. "You don't need to call them," she growled. "I already have a social worker. He knows everything is fine. You don't need to make another call."

"I'm required by law to make the call where I suspect abuse."

"I'm not abused."

"I can't make that judgment. All I can do is make the call."

Chloe stood up. "Thanks a lot," she snarled, and stormed out of the office.

Chloe couldn't go back to class. She wouldn't be able to concentrate on her work. She wouldn't be able to stop thinking about the teachers talking about her and the other kids all looking at her, whispering behind their hands. She considered not going home at all. What would happen if she just kept walking and never returned? No social worker to deal with. No Mim to be angry over the report being made. No Walter with his raging benders. She could find her way somewhere else. On the street. In a shelter. Ruby had done it, why not Chloe?

But Chloe's temperament was the opposite of Ruby's. Where Ruby was rebellious and wanted to break away, Chloe clung to her mother and her home, determined to be the perfect daughter and make it work by sheer force of will.

Chloe could never abandon Mim. She supposed that when she was an adult, she would have to leave and support herself, but that day was still far in the future.

So after walking aimlessly for a number of hours, not wanting to get in trouble for being home too early if Mim happened to be home from work, Chloe finally went home. In the end, she estimated the time wrong and arrived home late. Chloe stopped and stared at the house. There were police cars, lights flashing, all along the street in front of the house. Mim wouldn't have called the police because Chloe was late getting home. And if she did, they wouldn't show up in force. Not for a teenager being an hour or two late getting home from school.

Worried, Chloe approached the house. No one stopped her from going in. Chloe stepped in the door and looked around at the uniformed policemen and men in suits bustling around the house, talking, barking orders, looking busy. For a moment, she was thrown back to that night, waking to find the house overrun by officers. It was nightmarish.

"What's going on?"

One of the men who was not wearing a uniform turned around and approached her. "You must be Chloe."

"Yeah."

"Please just stand somewhere out of the way while we conduct our search."

"What search? What are you looking for?"

"This is the residence of a Mr. Walter Bose. He has been arrested for drug trafficking. We are executing a search warrant for further evidence."

Chloe relaxed and breathed out, relieved that it wasn't anything to do with her or the meeting with Miss Fry.

"Oh. Okay. Can I got to my room?"

"Which is yours?"

"Downstairs."

The man in charge motioned to one of the uniformed cops.

"Jensen. Take Miss Simpson down to her room. Stay with her. Take a look around."

"Not in my room!" Chloe protested, outraged.

"The warrant covers the entire house. It wouldn't be the first time that a dealer hid drugs in his kid's room."

"He's not my dad. And he doesn't live downstairs. He lives upstairs."

The boss nodded at Jensen, who was patiently waiting. "Go with her," he repeated.

Chloe flounced off down the stairs, with Jensen immediately behind her. Even when Walter wasn't there, he was causing her problems. Once down in her room, Chloe wasn't sure what to do. After hesitating for a moment, she went over to her desk and pulled out her books. She was just a kid doing her homework. Not suspicious and not a threat to anyone. Jensen looked around the untidy room.

"So... how long has Bose been living here?" he asked.

"A few months." Chloe didn't try to recall any specifics. "But not down here. He doesn't come down here."

"I understand. But I've got a job to do. You heard my orders."

Chloe watched him check through the drawers, not taking any clothes out, just moving them around. She looked down at her books and pretended to be working, though of course she couldn't do anything with him right there, going through all of her things. She wasn't concerned about him finding anything incriminating. Walter wouldn't have left anything down there to indicate his presence. Jensen ducked into the bathroom for a moment, but there was nowhere to hide anything in there. He left the bedroom and Chloe listened for his feet on the stairs. But he didn't go up the stairs. It took her about five seconds to realize why not, and she dashed out of the bedroom. He was in the little shelved storage room.

"That's not his stuff," Chloe insisted, as Jensen looked over the bins and boxes on the shelves. "That stuff's mine and my mom's. Can't you just get out of my stuff?"

"Sorry, no." His voice was flat, unemotional.

"This is our stuff!"

All of the boxes and bins were neatly marked with the contents in Gunter's fussy printing. Jensen could see that none of it was Walter's. But that didn't dissuade him. He opened each box and bin in turn, putting his hand in to shift the contents and then closing them back up. Chloe was frantic.

"That's not Walter's stuff. You're not allowed to touch it."

He looked at her for a moment and then continued with his search. Chloe's knees went weak, and she sat on one of the stairs, unable to look away.

But Jensen wasn't performing a thorough search. He didn't unwrap each bundle or look closely at every item. He had a general look at the contents and went onto the next bin.

Chloe breathed out, relieved. Jensen finished with the last box on the shelf, then turned around and walked past her on the stairs.

"I'm sorry," he said. "Just doing my job."

Chloe wondered if she should go upstairs to see how Mim was taking the search. There were too many people up there already, and it was quiet downstairs. So she stayed where she was.

As things started to quiet down, a man in the suit came down the stairs. Not the same one as had been giving orders upstairs. He looked surprised to find Chloe on the stairs.

"They already searched down here," Chloe growled.

"I'm not police," he said, and he displayed the ID on the lanyard around his neck. Social Services.

"I'm not talking to you," Chloe said immediately.

"Let's go into your room. This is it?" he indicated the doorway.

Chloe sat there for a minute longer, being stubborn. But social workers were experts on stubborn, and this one was not going to leave until he had talked to her.

At least it was not Mr. Clive. He had been too eager to take Chloe away and would have jumped at any opportunity. Such as the suggestion that Chloe might be in a bad environment due to her mother's boyfriend being a drug dealer. Walter was such an idiot. Stupid to start dealing drugs. Even stupider to get caught.

Chloe walked into her room and sat down on the bed. The social worker had been standing at her desk looking down at her homework. He turned around and faced her.

"Mr. Johann," he introduced himself. He gave her a grim, tight-lipped smile. Mandatory. Not the least bit reassuring. He sat down on the edge of the bed as if he was her friend or confidante. Chloe backed away slightly, shaking her head.

"Off my bed," she ordered. She pointed to the chair at her study desk.

Johann got back up, his face reddening. He wheeled the chair over and sat down. She had him off balance. He was obviously new at this. Any experienced social worker knew never even to touch a girl's bed. She could feel threatened. She could make accusations. Johann's inexperience made his dangerous. Someone like Mr. Clive knew the way the system worked. He wouldn't take Chloe out of the home without a reasonable expectation that they could keep her out. There was no point in removing her if she was simply returned a couple of days, weeks, or months later, with no changes having taken place. But a new, idealistic social worker might take her out without any real proof that anything was wrong, disrupting her life for months to come and making things worse than ever for Chloe when she returned.

Johann tried to get comfortable in the study chair. Or to look like he was comfortable, at least. But it wasn't adjusted for his height or for leaning casually back, so that didn't work. He was forced to sit rigidly, his knees too high. But he made the best of it.

"It's pretty unusual to have two independent calls on one child in a single day," he said.

"What?"

"You already know that your guidance counselor called in a report. And we also got one from the police," he raised a finger to point at the footsteps overhead, "to check on you."

Chloe scratched at the blanket on her bed. The bedclothes hadn't been changed for a long time. The blanket was pilling and had bits stuck in it. Dirt, hair, bits of meals, even though she wasn't supposed to bring food downstairs. She wasn't sure what had spilled on it and dried into a crusty yellow.

"You want to tell me what your counselor was concerned about?" Johann prodded.

"I expect she told you."

"Why don't you tell me, in your own words?"

"My grades are bad. The work got too hard."

"Uh-huh?"

Chloe shrugged.

"You know it's more than just grades, though the precipitous drop is disturbing."

"They're overreacting. I have different teachers this year. They mark differently."

"I see." He wrote this down in his notepad to follow up on. Chloe watched him. "Your counselor was also concerned about your behavior. And about unexplained bruises or injuries."

"I bruise easily," Chloe said. "You know, like those babies with brittle bones. Everyone thinks they're being abused, but it is completely explainable."

"Do you have a disorder that makes you bruise more easily?"

"No... but I'm very fair," Chloe indicated her blond hair. "My skin shows every little thing..."

"You still have to have been hit in the first place. Nobody gets a black eye from running into a door."

Chloe looked away. "They're exaggerating. Does it look like there's anything wrong with me?"

Johann studied her. The lighting was not good in the basement, one of the lights in the fixture had burnt out, and Chloe hadn't bothered to replace it. The study lamp threw strange shadows around the room. Chloe didn't stay still. She got up and went over to her bookshelf, pretending that she was looking over her book collection.

"How about these charges against Walter Bose?" Johann asked.

Chloe looked back at him, surprised at the change of subject. "What would I know about that?"

"I don't know. What would you know about it?"

"I don't have anything to do with Walter. He's mom's boyfriend. I don't know anything about him or what he does. I didn't even know he was dealing drugs."

"No?"

Chloe shook her head firmly. "I didn't even know he used drugs. If he does. He drinks like a fish, but if he was taking anything else, I don't know anything about it."

"What about your mom?"

"What?"

"Does she do drugs?"

"No."

"You didn't know that Walter did. Maybe you should think about it."

"No, she doesn't," Chloe insisted.

"What about drinking?"

"A little. Not like him. Just a little wine now and then, you know. A glass at supper or before bed."

"She never gets intoxicated?"

"No."

"Why would she put up with it in Bose?"

Chloe rolled her eyes. "I don't know. I wouldn't if I had a choice."

"Why not?"

Chloe decided she'd better shut up. Anything more she said would only give Johann reason to remove her. So she just clamped her mouth shut and stretched out on her bed, hands behind her head, and stared up at the ceiling.

"Chloe...?"

Chloe stubbornly kept her mouth shut.

"Chloe, I need you to cooperate with me. I know you're uncomfortable, but these are important questions. I need to judge whether you should remain in this house or not. Right now... I think it's a bad idea. The school has suggested that you're being physically abused, you've got a drug dealer living in the home, and..." His eyes traveled over the detritus on Chloe's floor, the stains on the blanket, and the holes in the wall and door. "I'm concerned about the conditions you're living in."

"Teenagers are messy!" Chloe protested. "It's not like there are rats or rotting garbage. It's just clothes and junk. Go look in the kitchen cupboards. There's food. No drugs, just Walter's beer. I got everything I need. My own room and bed, even my own bathroom. They arrested Walter, so he's not going to be here and you don't need to worry about anything."

"Is Walter hitting you?"

"Nobody's hitting me. But if they were, it would be him, not my mom. So now I'm safe. That's all your concerns, right?"

"What about your schoolwork?"

"Miss Fry said they'd get me tutors and extra help. It's not like marks are such a big deal. I'm not going to university."

"No? Why not?"

"I couldn't ever afford it, even if I wanted to. I don't need any education to flip burgers or vacuum offices. I don't need school, so why should I be wasting all my time and effort on it?"

"If your marks were good enough, you could get a scholarship to go to university."

"They're *never* gonna be that good. I'll probably drop out once I'm sixteen."

Johann made notes in his notepad, a frown creasing his forehead. His eyes went around the room once more. He got up and wandered around, prodding the piles of clothes on the floor, checking the bathroom and the garbage. He looked at the hole that Walter had punched through the door.

"What happened here?"

"I was mad. I punched it. I know, pretty immature."

"It's a bit high, considering your height. And from the outside."

"So?"

"I think it was someone else. Someone who wanted access to this room. Maybe Walter?"

"That's stupid. Why would he come down here?"

Johann didn't come up with an answer.

"Walter's not here anymore," Chloe reminded him again. "They're putting him away for dealing drugs. How long is that? He's not gonna be back here next week."

He sighed. "I'm going to need to talk to your mother. And to the officers about Mr. Bose."

"Be my guest."

Mr. Johann eventually decided that there wasn't enough hard proof that Chloe was being abused or was in any danger in the home environment, and left her there. So it was back to being Mim and Chloe again. Chloe was glad that Walter was gone. She was wary of her mother for the first few days after Walter's removal, ready for a beating, but Mim seemed more ambivalent about Walter being gone. She couldn't really blame Chloe for what had happened. She hadn't had anything to do with the drug charges against Walter. And maybe Mim was tired of being hit too.

Things were much more peaceful with Walter out of the way. Chloe liked it when it was just the two of them.

But that wasn't to last either. Chloe had been watching Mim get heavier, though she got heavier all over instead of having that cute basketball belly that women always had on TV. Chloe couldn't tell looking at her that she was pregnant. But Mim had said nothing more about the surviving twin, and Chloe assumed that if Mim miscarried, she would have told Chloe.

Still, Chloe was surprised to be woken up in the middle of the night when the time came. Mim shook her roughly and slapped her around the head and face. Chloe held up her hands to protect herself and tried to get oriented. Whenever she was woken up in the night, her mind always went first to that night, when she was woken up by the police. The initial confusion always took her back to that place.

"What? What, I'm awake!"

Mim stopped hitting her.

"Are you okay?" Chloe asked, rubbing her eyes. "Is it time? For the baby?"

Mim pressed a squirming bundle into Chloe's arms.

"Oh!" Chloe blinked and tried to see the baby better in the dark. "Okay... we should take him to the hospital. And you too, if you need a doctor."

"No. Nobody needs a doctor," Mim said.

"The baby might. We should get him checked out."

"You take care of him," Mim said. "We don't need a doctor."

"Me? I can't... I won't know what to do." Chloe thought back to those few short days with Joshua. She had made mistakes, and Joshua had died. It had been devastating. She couldn't let that happen again.

"Just take care of him. I don't want to."

"I need things. Bottles and formula and diapers. Why won't you take him to the hospital? You don't have to hide him from anyone this time."

"No. No one can know. You want Walter claiming him? Insisting on visitation or joint custody?"

"He wouldn't do that."

"Don't be so sure. A man like that will do anything."

"Can you turn on the lamp?"

Mim wasn't familiar with the room, and it took her a few minutes to locate the lamp and the switch on it. The bright glow lit the room immediately. Chloe was able to see the baby for the first time. He was wrapped in a worn blue towel, most of the wet stuff wiped away. Though he was very small, it was nothing like when Chloe had held his twin. He looked like a baby instead of an alien or medical mistake.

"Is he breathing okay?" she asked, leaning closer to listen to the new baby's chest. "Premature babies can't breathe very well sometimes."

"It doesn't matter," Mim said. "He'll just die like the others."

"No! You go get me bottles and formula this time! He's strong. He can survive if you give him a chance!"

Mim slapped her across the face. Chloe held the baby close to her chest.

"Please, Mommy!"

"You don't talk to me like that. You don't order me around!"

"I'm sorry. But please, please help me. I don't want him to die. Please get bottles."

Mim didn't hit her again, but walked out without another word. Chloe sat and rocked the baby, tears starting down her cheeks. She wasn't going to let this happen again. She couldn't let it happen. In the morning, if Mim refused to get bottles, Chloe would get them herself. She didn't care if she didn't have any money and had to steal them. She wasn't going to be talked out of it. This baby would live.

The night was long. Chloe was afraid to go to sleep in case the baby should stop breathing in the night. She agonized over whether he would be able to go all night without a bottle. But he slept most of the time and in the morning still had good color. He didn't have the deep-set eyes that Joshua had before he died.

Chloe dressed, doing her best to look older than she did. She didn't have any baby clothes. And no proper baby blanket. She couldn't walk into a store with a baby wrapped in a towel. The police or social services would be there before she left the store. Chloe searched for a solution, and in the end, ripped apart a flannel nightgown and tucked it around the baby. With the edges tucked in, it looked enough like a baby blanket to pass muster. No one would know, even close up, that it was a nightgown. She folded other pieces of the nightgown to serve as a diaper until she could get some of those too.

She didn't know how she was going to walk into the store with a baby, and walk out with all the goods that she needed, without being detained. There were a lot of surveillance cameras in the store and a lot of people who looked at Chloe or watched her covertly. She had to be patient. But eventually, she was able to sneak the baby and a few clothes and diapers into the bathroom, where she dressed him properly. Then she wound the makeshift blanket around him again to hide the change of clothes. She had worn a baggy jacket to the store, and she hid a bottle and a can of formula the best she could in the large pockets. She wouldn't be greedy. She needed a lot more than she took, but she would have to pick it up a little at a time. At different stores so that no one would grow too suspicious of her.

Chloe was elated when she got home. She could do it. She could save the baby and raise him to be strong. She didn't have to lose this one like Joshua.

She didn't even try to go to school. Not this time. This time, she would stay home and put all of her efforts into saving the baby. And if they sent a truant officer or social worker to the house to find out why she had stopped going to school, then maybe they would find the baby and take him away, and he would have a better chance at survival. So she didn't even care about getting caught. She couldn't call Social Services. She would never do that. But if they happened to get called, let them come.

She was afraid to give the baby a name, but after a day of whispering 'baby' to him, she knew she had to think of something better. Eventually, she settled on Phillip. She didn't know anyone named Phillip, so the name wasn't tainted. It wasn't close to the names of any of her other brothers or sisters. It was just his.

Mim had little energy. Normally a sedentary woman, other than when she had to be out working, she seemed barely able to even get out of bed. Chloe urged her to go see the doctor, but she refused. Each day she recovered a little more, ate a little better. Chloe could see she was on the mend and left her alone.

Then it happened. Phillip had seemed fussy and irritable for a couple of days. He was warmer to the touch and started turning away from the bottle when Chloe tried to feed him.

"You have to eat," Chloe encouraged him, knowing that it wouldn't help a bit. "Come on, Phillip. You have to eat if you're going to grow up to be big and strong. Come on, take the bottle... take it, sweetie..."

In time, Chloe despaired of getting him to eat and took him upstairs. She hadn't let Mim see Phillip since he was born, afraid that she would do him harm, but now she was desperate.

"Mommy, Phillip is sick. He needs a doctor."

"Phillip?" Mim looked sharply at the baby in Chloe's arms. "Oh. I'm surprised he's still alive."

"We need to call an ambulance. Or take him to the hospital. Please, Mommy. Please, don't let him die too."

Mim shook her head. "He's going to die. You may as well give up."

"No." Chloe headed for the front door. "I'm going to take him out. I'm going to get him help."

She should have left him somewhere that first time she took him out, when Mim had been in bed and hadn't had the energy to care what Chloe was doing with him. Surely someone would have found him and taken care of him if she had left him in the store washroom. Or she could have found a way to get to the hospital instead of the store and left him there.

But she had left it too long, allowing Mim to get stronger again. And Mim wasn't going to let Chloe take the baby to anyone else. She smashed a wine bottle into the back of Chloe's head. Chloe stumbled to her knees with the force of it. But she held Phillip close, protecting him, and didn't drop him. Another blow fell at the crown of Chloe's head.

"Mommy, please, no! Let me take him. Please!"

"You will not take that baby out of this house!"

"Let me call a doctor! An ambulance!"

"You will not!"

The blows continued to fall, some glancing off and some so heavy that Chloe felt nauseated and feared that she would black out. She held the baby to her protectively. Somehow she had to shield him from the blows. She couldn't black out and let Mim hurt him.

But it was impossible. Chloe heard her own heart-wrenching cries as she watched herself being beaten and watched Mim yank the baby out of her arms. There was nothing she could do for the young blond girl who wept and screamed for the baby that would never snuggle in her arms again.

CHAPTER
Fifteen

Chloe attended school only haphazardly after that point. She went to school because there was nowhere else for her to go, but she was blind and deaf to everything around her. The days passed by. She could feel nothing, because when she did feel, the devastation was overwhelming. She couldn't think about what was happening to her or about what had happened.

She didn't take her schoolbooks home; she just dumped them in her locker at the end of the day. Miss Fry tried a few times to have her come in for some kind of counseling, but Chloe refused. When they told her to go to the office, she just went home. What could they do about it?

Eventually, Mim brought home another boyfriend. Sal Durrant. Each man that she had hooked up with had been progressively worse, and Chloe didn't know if it was possible for anyone to be worse than Sal. Gunter and Walter together had not been as bad as Sal.

One of the first things that he did was to reverse the lock on her bedroom door, so that instead of the door forming a barrier to the outside, it became Chloe's prison. He could then have access to her whenever he pleased, and she had nowhere to go. No truant officer came, or if he did, they somehow dealt with him, because Chloe did not see another face for a long, long time. In the beginning, he chained her as well as locking the door. He didn't need to chain her for Chloe to stay. She never tried to escape. And so after the first few weeks, he didn't bother. Unless he particularly wanted her chained during the abuse.

Though she knew his name, she thought of him only as Blue Jeans. That was what he invariably wore. She saw nothing above his waist. Never his face. She had no need to look into his eyes to see the evil darkness he was filled with.

She saw the blue jeans. She saw the silver belt buckle grow bigger and bigger as he approached her, filling her vision. Then Chloe was out of herself, floating up to the ceiling. And then further and further away, her body getting smaller and smaller until she couldn't see it anymore, and couldn't see or feel anything he did to her.

Blue Jeans brought her a teddy bear once. Chloe didn't try to understand him, but this new behavior was so bizarre that she sat and thought about it for hours, trying to comprehend his action. He showed her the teddy bear, let her touch it to feel the soft, fluffy fur, and then he put it on the study desk across from the bed.

"You are not allowed to touch it," he told Chloe. "You are never, ever, to touch or move it. It stays right there, like that, and if I ever think you have touched so much as a hair..."

He didn't need to threaten her. Chloe was always obedient. And the threat was empty since it didn't matter if she obeyed him or not, she knew he would torture her in the most evil ways he could invent.

She never touched the teddy bear again. And she never looked at it. It sat on the desk watching her, as if it had become Blue Jeans itself keeping an eye on her, making sure that she was obedient.

The footsteps that Chloe heard coming down the stairs to the basement did not belong to Blue Jeans. She recognized her mother's heavy tread.

The door opened. Chloe had not seen her mother for a long time. Weeks, or maybe even months. Mim had almost ceased to exist altogether. She looked at Chloe, her dark eyes angry about something.

"I want you to come make dinner," Mim told her. "You never do any chores around here anymore. You're always just down here, lolling around in bed. You think you're some kind of princess we should be feeding sweets to and bowing to all day long. You heard me. You come upstairs and make dinner."

Chloe put her feet over the edge of the bed and stood up. She was shaky on her feet. Far from eating sweets, she couldn't remember the last time she had eaten.

"Get some clothes on," Mim snapped.

Chloe looked down at the tatters that hung from her body. She looked at the floor for something that was in better shape. But everything was in similar condition, stained and torn. She shuffled over to her dresser to see if there was anything in the drawers she could wear. She found a housecoat that she had never worn and pulled it on over her tatters, tying it around the waist.

"Go on, then. Upstairs," Mim ordered.

If she'd had a whip, she would have cracked it. Chloe was glad that she didn't have a whip. The light upstairs hurt Chloe's eyes, making tears stream down her cheeks. Mim misinterpreted the tears and berated her. Chloe didn't even hear her words. She moved mechanically, pulling out dishes and looking in the fridge and cupboards for Mim's favorite foods.

Mim slapped her a couple of times, but Chloe was way beyond being hurt by a few slaps. Eventually, Mim left her alone and went to the living room to watch TV while Chloe got supper together. Chloe didn't ask where Blue Jeans was. He wasn't in the house, but Chloe could still feel his presence. She made no attempt to leave the house or call for help.

Chloe was the perfect daughter. She was always obedient. She had no intention of leaving her mother.

CHAPTER

Sixteen

Bill Maynard clicked on the next video uploaded by user SD1392. His stomach was already churning. All the videos he watched were disgusting and heartbreaking, and every time his heart went out to the victim. This girl was a teenager. Stick thin. Blond. He watched for her to turn toward the camera so that he could get a better clip of her face, but she seemed to be avoiding it. He turned his attention to the man. Small and wiry. No identifiable tattoos caught by the camera. Bill turned the sound down and looked for anything in the frame that would help them to pin down where their victim was. The uploads were recent and appeared to extend back in time over a period of months. Tech was working on the usual details like IP addresses and location coordinates in the video. Hopefully, the perp wasn't too tech savvy, and they could get a good fix on him.

After the next video, he would take a break. Turn off the horror show, get a drink of water, take a walk around the block. Maybe stop and watch the kids in the park. Happy faces, an antidote to the torture and abuse that he had to watch over and over again.

~

Following up on leads, Bill waited in the school office, watching all the kids who walked by in the hallway outside or who came through the office area. He couldn't stop himself from looking at their eyes to try to determine which might be victims. Visible bruises? Neglected air? That look of pain or blankness in their eyes. Even when he was around normal kids, he couldn't help looking for the signs.

He watched a brunette teen come into the office and approach the secretary with her pass.

"Um, I'm supposed to see…"

The secretary nodded toward Bill, and the girl turned and looked at him.

"Oh. Hi. Are you…?"

Bill stood up and offered his hand. "I'm Bill Maynard. You're Leesa?"

"Yeah."

"They put us in here," Bill motioned to a small conference room that they had allocated to him.

Leesa preceded him into the room. Bill let her choose a seat and then selected a chair that was perpendicular to her. Not directly across from her where he might seem confrontational. They were friends, there to help each other. Not quite side-by-side, but as close as he could manage without making her feel uncomfortable. He left the door open.

Bill started with small talk. The weather. How her school year was going. How the school football team was doing. She started to cast questioning looks at him, ready to move to the business of the meeting. Bill took a breath and placed first the initial inquiry poster on the table in front of him, the one that she had seen. Then a series of other shots of the girl. A few different angles, different lighting. Nothing that was graphic or hinted at the contents of the video they were taken from. But no one could have doubted where they came from.

Leesa picked photos up and looked at them. She didn't ask about where they had come from or what had happened to the girl. Businesslike, looking only at the lines of the face.

"I don't know," she said finally. "She looks sort of like a girl I used to go to school with. But she's different. I'm just not sure."

"If you can give me her name and any information that you have, I will look into it. We won't use your name. If it isn't the right girl, no harm done. But we can't find her without help from the public.

There's just not enough information in the pictures to track her down."

Leesa's eyes strayed to the poster again. She had been sure enough to call the hotline. That took a lot of guts. She hadn't just taken it to a parent or teacher or her peers, asking if they thought it looked like the girl they had once known. Maybe she had started with that. But by calling the hotline, she indicated a level of certainty, even if she was waffling now.

"I can't imagine," Leesa said. "She looks so awful. Chloe didn't always take care of herself, but she didn't look like this."

Bill wrote it down. "What's Chloe's last name?"

"Um, Simpson, I think. Something like that. You'll have to check with the junior high. She didn't come here."

"Okay. That would be at Lincoln? PS 2?"

"Yeah."

"How long ago was this?" He evaluated her. "About... two years?"

"Yeah. We were in the same grade for a couple of years. Then she moved away or something. She stopped coming. I don't know where she is now."

Bill was disappointed. Would the school know where they had moved to? They would have had to send records somewhere. To her new school. But he doubted the victim was going to school any longer. She couldn't go to school in the condition she was in without the warning bells going off.

"How well did you know Chloe?"

"Not at all," Leesa said quickly. "She had a locker near mine. We were in phys ed together, I think. That was all. I just knew her name."

"What kind of home did she come from?"

Leesa's eyes slid away from him. Some secret there. Something wrong that she wasn't ready to tell him yet.

"She lived with her mom. Dad wasn't around."

"So just the two of them."

"Um... yeah, I guess..."

"Who else?" he pressed deeper. "A brother or sister?"

"No."

"Border? Friend of the family?"

"No... like... I think..."

Bill waited. *Who else?*

"There was this guy at Lincoln..."

"Chloe had a boyfriend?"

"He was one of the school counselors. There were rumors about him. I don't know how they got started. Or if they were even true. But he was definitely creepy..."

"What was his name?"

"I don't remember. It was a weird name. I haven't thought about him for a long time."

"And you think that this school counselor might have... been involved with Chloe?"

"There were rumors that he was dating Chloe's mom. Living with them."

"Ah." Bill nodded. He scribbled down a few notes. "That *would* be kind of weird, wouldn't it?"

She nodded in agreement. "It really was. I can't believe now that none of us ever said anything. You know, to the principal or something. We all figured that the adults knew what was going on too. I mean... *we* all knew."

"That he was living with Chloe's mom."

"That he... chased girls. Students. I don't know how far it went... but it was... weird."

"He was having relationships with junior high girls?"

Even if he wasn't the perp in the video, Bill would have to pursue the guy. Make sure that if he was having relationships with young girls that they put a stop to it.

"I don't know... Yeah. Of some kind."

"And you don't remember his name?"

"I can't right now. But he was one of the school counselors."

"What did he look like?"

"Bald. Shaved his head, I think. Thirties or forties. Old. Really intense eyes."

Bill jotted this all down. "Great. I'll look into that."

Leesa looked at the pictures of the girl. "He wasn't still with her, though. He'd moved on to another girl."

"And what happened to Chloe after that? Is that when she stopped coming to school?"

"No, she still came the year after that. But by the time I started high school... I don't remember what happened to her. I don't think I knew. I just figured... she moved away."

Bill nodded.

"She was quite a bit heavier than that," Leesa said. "Like, in the beginning, she was... fat. I know you shouldn't say that. Lots of people are overweight. But she was, you know, pudgy. She slimmed down after that. But this..."

Bill looked at the sharp, angular lines of the victim's face. She wasn't overweight anymore. She was either anorexic or starving.

"We'll find her," he promised Leesa. "We'll make sure she gets better."

Leesa nodded. "I'm really sorry I never said anything about that counselor," she said. "I don't understand how we all knew what was going on, or thought we did, and never said anything."

Bill nodded. "Kids tell stories," he said. "Embellish them. Make the lonely old widow out to be a witch or a monster. We enjoy telling exciting stories. But we know that they aren't entirely true. Maybe you thought that it was a story. An exaggeration. The guy who takes a peep down a girl's shirt when she bends over becomes a raging pedophile. Everybody repeats the stories, but no one really believes them."

"Yeah, I guess. Something like that."

"We'll look into it. If this guy is doing something wrong, we'll put a stop to it. Put him away."

～

The woman at the office at PS 2 typed the name into the computer.

"Chloe Simpson... no, we don't have a Chloe Simpson."

"It would have been a couple of years ago. She's not a current student. I want to know where she went. Her new address."

"The record would be closed. It might be purged after two years. We're not allowed to keep private information on students." Her eyes flicked up to him. She didn't like the idea of sharing a student's address. It had been drilled into all the school administrators. Never share a student's information with anyone. Not even someone who claimed to be a family member.

"I have the warrant," he pointed out. "Privacy Act doesn't apply. If you have the information, you need to give it to me."

"I'm just saying I don't know whether we have it."

"Two years isn't that long ago. I'm sure you must keep information that long."

"Some of it. Not sensitive stuff."

She nevertheless tapped keys, searching for archived records.

"The file has been closed," she advised. "Sent to storage."

"I would like the file to be retrieved. And in the meantime, you must have an address attached to that computer record."

"Sure, but you said she wasn't there anymore."

"If I could get it, please…"

She read it out to him reluctantly.

"What school did she transfer to?"

"I don't see here where we sent records to any other school."

Bill waited while she examined the electronic record.

"Ah, They gave notice that they were homeschooling."

Bill shook his head. That was one way to escape the extra layer of monitoring that school attendance enabled. And it meant that they might have moved anywhere and not re-registered in the new school district.

"Thanks, that's great," he said. "By the way, who was her guidance counselor?"

"That would have been… Miss Fry."

"I thought it was a man. Maybe the year before?"

"We try to keep them with the same counselor all three years they are here. Unless there's a particular reason to change."

"Did you have a counselor here, he was bald? Not an old man." Despite Leesa's assertion that thirties or forties were old.

The secretary nodded, smiling. "That would be Mr. Gnatsky. He's still with us."

"Oh, he is? And did he live with Chloe?"

She frowned and shook her head. "Why would he live with a student he wasn't related to? That doesn't make any sense."

"I thought he did at some point."

"No. I keep the staff addresses updated on the computer and he hasn't moved in the past few years."

"Great. What is his address?"

She chewed on her lip, studying Bill. He did his best to look as if it was a routine inquiry.

"Why would you need that? You can just go talk to him."

"I need it for my report. Just routine."

She looked in the direction of the warrant he had laid on the counter. "That said anything about Chloe Simpson, not our staff members."

Bill squared the warrant on the counter in front of him and read it. "It says, 'all information relevant to the investigation of allegations of abuse against Chloe Simpson.'"

"Uh-huh."

"This is relevant to the investigation. I need Mr. Gnatsky's address from your records."

She took her time and gave it to him.

Before going to talk to Mr. Gnatsky, Bill made a phone call to have the desk perform what searches they could on Chloe Simpson's former address and her mother's name. Then he showed himself into Mr. Gunter Gnatsky's office.

He would have recognized Gnatsky by Leesa's description. Bald head, late thirties or early forties, intense eyes. He gave Bill a cautious smile.

"Officer? How can I help you?"

Bill stepped in and placed himself into the visitor's chair in front of Gnatsky's desk. He leaned forward, staring Gnatsky in the eye.

"I'm here about Chloe Simpson."

Gnatsky did well, his face giving no indication that the question caused him any concern.

"Chloe... It's been a few years. I'm not sure I can help you with anything. What's the problem?"

"Among other things, we're trying to track her down. Your name came up in the investigation."

"I was her guidance counselor the first year," Gnatsky agreed. "Is she... missing? I heard they started homeschooling."

"She dropped out of sight at that point. I'm looking for her current address."

"Really. I wasn't aware that they had moved."

"They're still at the same address?"

Gnatsky scratched the back of his skull. "I've seen her mother in the neighborhood occasionally. I think so."

The searches that the desk was performing would confirm it within a few minutes. Bill nodded. It would make the investigation much simpler if they had a current address.

"You had a relationship with the mother."

Gnatsky raised his eyebrows. He considered the question carefully before saying anything. "There's no rule against having a relationship with the parent of a student."

"It's not exactly advisable if you're the student's guidance counselor. Wouldn't you say that's a conflict of interest?"

"Not at all. In fact, it aligns all interests. You want the child to succeed in every facet. Not just school, but home and family. And you get a lot more insight if you see the child outside of school as well."

"It seems to me that the role of a guidance counselor is to be a refuge the child can go to when there are problems at home. She can't very well do that if the counselor is part of the problem."

Gnatsky shook his head. "There was never a problem between me and Chloe."

"We'll be looking into that."

Gnatsky swallowed, but didn't blanch in the face of the warning. A tough nut. He was going to be a slippery one.

"Is that everything, then, officer?"

Bill nodded. "For now," he said, and gave Gnatsky a pleasant smile.

CHAPTER
Seventeen

As soon as the desk confirmed that Mim Simpson was still the registered owner of the last address the school had for Chloe and that her driver's license was also registered to that address, Bill headed over. They had also confirmed that there were prior Social Services reports on Chloe, including one filed by the school counselor. Not Mr. Gnatsky, but his successor on Chloe's file. While the task force assembled a team to organize a rescue, Bill started knocking on neighbors' doors.

"The people next door," Bill said, jerking a thumb over his shoulder. "They have a daughter?"

"No, no kids over there," said the woman who had come to the door in her housecoat. She moved to shut the door.

"A teenager," Bill persisted, putting his toe in the door to prevent her from closing it. "A blond girl. How long have you lived here?"

"I've been here for ten years!"

"And they never had a girl next door? Chloe? Does that ring a bell?"

The woman frowned and ran her fingers through her already-messy red curls. "Chloe? A blond?"

"Yes."

"Well… I think there used to be. But it's been a long time since I saw her. Maybe she moved out. Living with an auntie or a boyfriend."

"Did she have a boyfriend?"

"How would I know that? They're not going to talk to the next door neighbor about it!"

"You never saw her bringing a boy home?"

"No, but I'm not nosy, I wouldn't notice."

"How about Mrs. Simpson? Does she have a boyfriend? Is there a man living there?"

"Oh, yes. She always has a man around. Some of them not too nice. Drinking, swearing, calling names…"

"Can you describe the current boyfriend?" Bill didn't have a picture. The man had never faced the camera. But he knew the general shape and size of him.

"Slim, wiry. Dark hair. I don't really know. I don't pay attention."

"Do they fight? You ever have to call the police on them?"

"Wouldn't you know that?"

"We're pulling up the records. It takes time."

"They're not too bad," the woman said grudgingly. "No loud parties or smoking weed outside my windows."

"No yelling? Screaming?"

She shrugged. "Maybe an argument from time to time. Nothing unusual."

If Bill were to judge from the videos he had viewed so far, there wouldn't have been a lot of screaming. Nothing that neighbors could have been expected to notice.

"Okay, ma'am. Thank you for your help."

"What's going on over there? What did they do?"

"I'd like you to stay in your house for the next few hours. There is going to be a lot going on, and we'd like all the neighbors to stay out of the way, safe in their own homes."

Her eyes glittered, alive with interest. As soon as she shut the door, she was going to go call all her friends to speculate on what was going on. As long as she stayed in her house, Bill didn't care who she called.

There were last-minute instructions. Logistics to be ironed out. Everyone carefully coordinated. Bill straightened his coat, making sure it was clear of his sidearm. He touched his vest just to make sure he had remembered to put it on. Mistakes could be costly. Whoever the man living with Mim Simpson was, he hadn't registered his vehicle at that address. They didn't have a name on him, which meant they didn't know what his history was or if he was likely to be carrying a weapon.

The other cars rolled in, and Bill led the door approach. He rang the doorbell and rapped on the door, standing to the side. They could hear voices within. Arguing about who was going to get the door. Bill rang again, hurrying them along, trying to keep them off-balance. Even though he could hear footsteps, he knocked on the door again.

It was wrenched open, and the man glared at Bill, furious at the interruption and rude manners. Before he had a chance to process the crowd of uniformed figures on his doorstep and react, Bill grabbed him, twisted his arm up behind his back, and pushed him into Carson's waiting arms.

"Go, go, go!" he shouted, pushing the door open the rest of the way with a slam against the inside wall and leading the charge into the house.

Mim Simpson, a dark-haired, overweight woman was sitting on the couch in front of the TV, a plate of chicken fingers and fries balanced on her knees.

"Put your hands behind your head!" Bill shouted at her. "Do it now! Do it now!"

She tried to catch the plate of fries and figure out what to do with them, then dropped them as she obeyed him, putting her hands on her head. Her eyes were alarmed. She was confused and panicked, not understanding what was going on. She couldn't even find her voice to complain to him and demand to know what was going on.

"Where's your daughter?" Bill demanded, getting right up in her face. "Where's Chloe? Keep your hands on your head!"

"In her room."

Police were already fanning out throughout the house.

"Where's her room?"

"Downstairs."

Bill headed toward the kitchen, where he knew he would find the stairs. At the same time, there was a voice in his earpiece.

"Maynard, down here. Basement."

"On my way."

He didn't run down the stairs. The lighting was dark and the steps felt soft under his feet. Rotting through. There was no hurry. No altercation or take-down in progress. Just three members of the task force standing around a closed door.

There was a hole in the door. Bill could see light through it. Not bright, but the room appeared to be occupied. Bill nodded to the others and reached for the door handle. He expected to find it locked. It was a flimsy, hollow-core door and he'd be able to break through it if necessary. But it wasn't locked. The knob turned easily in his hand, and he swung it open with a slight creak.

At first, the room seemed empty. But then he saw the slight movement from the bed and realized the girl was hiding under the covers, her body so slight that he hadn't even seen her shape under the blanket.

"Hi, there," Bill said softly, dropping to his knees beside the bed. "Are you Chloe?"

She stared out at him, her eyes so deep-set and shadowed that he couldn't see them. Her face looked like a skull in the dimness.

"Chloe, I'm here to help you. I'm with the police. I'm here to stop him from hurting you."

Her thin body shuddered. Still, she said nothing and made no move to crawl out of the bed to greet her rescuers.

"He's not going to hurt you anymore. You can come out, now. We'll take care of you."

There was an uproar upstairs, Mim screaming for her boyfriend. Bill assumed that they had gotten around to putting the cuffs on her, and she had finally begun to realize the trouble that they were in.

Chloe's face pushed out from the blankets. "Mom!" she said in alarm.

"Your mom's okay." Bill touched the blanket, seeing if she would let him pull it back further. "No one is hurting her."

Chloe clutched at the blanket to keep it over herself. "No." She pulled it more tightly around her. She struggled to sit up, pulling the blanket around her like a robe. She looked around the room, her head twisting this way and that. Bill looked, trying to anticipate whatever it was she was looking for.

Chloe's eyes fastened on a bathrobe on the floor, and she made a little nod toward it. Bill moved around the bed and picked it up. He handed it to her. He turned his head away for a few seconds to let her slip it on. When he looked back, she was tying the belt around her tiny waist. The robe swam on her. She folded her arms protectively as if she was afraid it was going to fall off or he would be able to see through it. Bill touched his transmitter.

"We're going to need an ambulance," he said quietly.

Chloe looked at him. "I'm okay," she said. "I don't need anything."

He didn't argue with her and point out what awful condition she was in. "It's routine. Someone needs to look you over for the report."

She looked at him for a moment. Neither of them sure what step to take next. Chloe's eyes went up to the ceiling.

"Is my mom okay?"

"Your mom is fine. No one is going to do anything to hurt her."

"*He* hurts her," Chloe confided. "Someone should look at her too."

"He?" Bill repeated.

Chloe flapped a hand toward the upstairs. "Him. Blue Jeans. Sometimes she's black and blue. I don't know why she lets him stay."

"She might have tried to get rid of him. It can be pretty difficult, sometimes, especially if she doesn't want to involve the police."

Chloe nodded.

"Does Blue Jeans have a name?" Bill asked.

She considered for a moment, looking blank. Then it came to her.

"Sal. I don't remember his last name."

"We're going to take Sal away so that he can never hurt you again. I know you must be scared, but it's going to be okay. We're going to make sure that you're taken care of."

"Can I see my mom?"

Bill held his hand out to help her up. He held it low, and not too close to her, so that she wouldn't see it as an aggressive gesture. Chloe took it and slid out from under the covers. Bill held her steady as she stood. She looked like she would blow away in a strong wind. But Chloe seemed to be okay with her legs under her, so Bill let go of her hand and she led the way upstairs.

He knew that the other officers wouldn't let her interfere with Mim, but he needed to get her out of the house, and it was best if she did it under her own power, rather than having to be dragged. Bill expected Chloe to have problems with the steep basement steps. She gave the other cops gathered around her bedroom door a fleeting glance, then went up the stairs without a pause. Bill marveled at her strength. She didn't even stop at the top for a breath, but continued into the living room, where they had handcuffed Mim, face-down on the floor, and she was refusing to get back onto her feet. She was a big woman, and getting a dead weight up and out of the house was tricky.

"Mommy!" Chloe pattered into the living room in her bare feet. "Mom, are you okay?"

Chloe knelt down beside her mother to look at her face and talk to her, fussing over the big woman as if she had been brutalized. Bill blinked his eyes, trying to keep tears from forming. The contrast of Chloe's stick-thin arms against Mim's fat, fleshy ones was horrifying. In the sunlit room, he could see Chloe's deathly pallor for the first time. She obviously had not gotten out of her prison very often over the past couple of years. The bathrobe she had on was thin and worn, and it was obvious that she had barely a stitch on underneath.

"Your mom is okay, Chloe," Bill told her.

Chloe stroked Mim's hair. "I'll help you up, Mommy. You want me to?"

Bill opened his mouth to object, but Mim nodded. She would be much easier for them to maneuver once on her feet. Chloe put one of her tiny arms under Mim's shoulder and strained to lift her. Bill and the other officers could do nothing but watch; Mim wouldn't let any of them help. Puffing and straining, Chloe managed to get Mim back on her feet. Mim looked at her daughter for a long moment.

"You need to go get some clothes on. What do you think you're doing, walking around the house like that?"

Chloe ducked her head and nodded. Mim looked at Bill.

"You should get her some of the chicken on the stove. The girl's nothing but skin and bones."

Bill nodded. "I might just do that," he agreed.

Chloe touched her mother's face. "Mom has a black eye," she pointed out to Bill. "You see, it's not her fault. He hurts her too."

Mim glared at Chloe. "You keep your mouth shut, brat," she snarled.

Chloe was immediately cowed, lowering her head and pressing her lips shut. Bill was shocked at the control Mim exercised over her.

"Come on, let's get you something to eat," he suggested, touching Chloe's elbow to steer her into the kitchen.

Chloe was reluctant to leave her mother again, but her lips parted, obviously feeling the pull of something to eat. How long had they been starving her? He gave her a stronger tug and Chloe moved with him, into the kitchen where the remainder of the chicken fingers that Mim and Sal had heated up were in a pan on top of the stove.

He looked through the cupboards to find a plate and put two chicken fingers on the plate for her. "Here, sit down. Eat slowly, or you're going to get sick, okay?"

Chloe didn't argue. She took the plate from him and sat down to eat, nibbling at the chicken fingers and chewing carefully.

"Could I... could I have a drink too?" she suggested.

"Of course!" Bill looked in the fridge, but there was nothing but beer. He ran the tap until it was cold and filled a glass halfway for her. "Be careful," he warned again.

Chloe nodded.

The ambulance had arrived as Chloe finished off the chicken fingers, so Bill left her with the paramedics and went back downstairs to see what the rest of the team had found. Cotter had taken charge of the scene, and he walked Bill through what there was to see.

"Teddy bear is a nanny cam," he said, nodding to the stuffed toy sitting on the dresser. "It has remote access, so there's no need to swap tapes. There's a red light on, which the techs tell me means it has footage that still needs to be downloaded."

"Which is good, because that means we have some unedited video," Bill said. Sal had only uploaded edited video clips, which started with his back to the camera, never coming into the frame with his face visible. The unedited footage would help the court convict him.

"Yep." Cotter looked around, not sure what else to say. The windowless room was sparsely furnished. There wasn't much else to point out.

Bill went to the dresser and pulled out drawers, looking for something he could give Chloe to wear. But it was obvious why she was dressed in rags. She didn't have anything else. Most of her remaining clothes were scattered on the floor, stained and torn.

He checked the closet but found it in similar condition. While it looked like the closet had once been neat and well-furnished, with matching hangers all across the rod, it was now nearly empty. There were some boxes up on the shelf, neatly labeled with school subjects.

"Bathroom through that one," Cotter pointed to the other door. He grimaced a warning look at Bill.

With dread tight in his belly, Bill walked through the door into the tiny bathroom. There wasn't much to see. No girlish shampoos or make-up. There were painkillers in the medicine cabinet, some of them narcotics. There was a laundry basket filled with tattered, blood-stained towels, smelling rank. Under the sink, tucked into one of the front corners where it wouldn't be seen at a casual glance, was a container of birth-control pills with Mim's name on the prescription.

CHAPTER

Eighteen

Chloe had repeatedly said she didn't want to go to the hospital, but they needed to document her condition, so she was forced to go against her wishes. Bill was given a packet of photos, x-rays, and examination notes to take back to the task force with him. He took a quick flip through them. There were pictures of black and blue bruises. The x-rays showed numerous healed breaks, especially to her ribs and orbital bones. The internal exam confirmed what they already knew from the videos.

She didn't want to stay. She kept saying that she wanted to go home, and couldn't accept that she no longer had a home to go to.

"I want to stay with my mom," Chloe insisted. "Mom will look after me."

"Your mom has not been able to look after you. Your mother has, at the very least, stood by while you were being abused and neglected. She is in custody. You can't go back to her."

"You arrested her?" Chloe demanded, even though she had seen her mother in handcuffs. "You can't arrest her. She didn't do anything. She takes care of me."

"You can't go back to her. We need to keep you safe."

Chloe wiped at her eyes but didn't produce tears. Bill suspected that she was too dehydrated to cry tears.

"Where am I going to go, then? I don't have any other family."

"We'll find you somewhere safe," he assured her.

They had found her some clothes to wear, though they hung off of her and she had to walk with a hand on her waistband to keep her pants from falling down. The clothes seemed to give her a little confidence. She stood up taller and was less tentative. He couldn't help but wonder what she had been like before. Despite what she had been through, Chloe wasn't a cowering, shrinking violet.

Bill sat her down in a conference room. Not one of the cold, clinical ones that they used for suspects, but one of the cozier ones designed for families of victims or for the victims themselves. A couch and upholstered chairs. A little toy chest. And of course, audio and video recording.

Chloe sat down and looked around. "This is nice."

"Thanks. Make yourself comfortable."

She shifted a little and shrugged.

"So... I know this is difficult, Chloe, but I'd like to talk to you about what has happened over the past couple of years."

She looked at him and said nothing.

Bill started off with a simple, factual question. "Sal—Blue Jeans, as you called him—did he move in two years ago?"

Chloe wrinkled her forehead. "Two years? No. Just... I don't know how long it has been. A few months, maybe."

"So what happened before that? When you stopped going to school."

"I didn't stop. I missed sometimes when I was... sick... but I still went the rest of the time."

Bill studied her expression. There were no indicators that she was trying to mislead him. She seemed confused. The timeline was muddled for her; that was all. He tried to clear it up.

"The school was notified that you were not going back. You were going to be homeschooled."

"Okay."

"That was two years ago."

"No. I was still going to school two years ago. They must have the dates wrong."

But Bill had received the thick paper copy of Chloe's file the school had retrieved from storage, and he had already verified all the dates.

"It was two years ago, Chloe. That's when the school closed your file, and you dropped out of sight."

Chloe looked around the room in disorientation. There was no calendar to clear up the confusion. But there was a stack of magazines on a side table, reading material for when people had to wait. Chloe grabbed a handful and started to look through them. Her eyes went frantically over the dates on the fronts.

"No. That doesn't make sense." She looked at her own hands as if she expected to be able to tell by their appearance the length of time that had passed. She rubbed her eyes. "No!"

"I'm sorry."

"Two years?" She swore.

"You just lost track of time, being shut in the basement. No window. No way to keep track of the days."

"But it couldn't have been that long. I would have known."

Bill took her thin hand between both of his to calm her. She didn't jerk away. "You couldn't see the sun go up and down. You probably didn't eat every day. There was no way for you to know how much time passed."

"But... how could they... how could they do that?"

Bill shook his head. "I can't explain it. I don't understand how anyone could be so... heartless. But there is evil in this world. I've seen it."

She pulled away from him and put her hands over her face. Her stomach heaved with silent sobs. There were still no tears.

"Chloe."

"No. Don't talk to me right now."

Bill closed his mouth and sat back. It was heartbreaking to watch her. He felt helpless, yearning to do something that would comfort her. After all she had been through, she had just lost two years of her life. Like her innocence, she could never get them back. In her mind, she was still fifteen, but she was seventeen, nearly an adult. Finding her appropriate care was not going to be easy. But that part was not his job.

"Do you want me to go?" he asked. "Do you want some time alone?"

Chloe shook her head. "No. I don't want to be alone again." Her voice cracked but was not broken by sobs.

"Okay. I'm here," Bill assured her. He just sat with her.

That much, he could do.

～

It had been a long day. Bill wasn't sure how many hours it had been since he had slept. He had taken a brief nap in the afternoon while Chloe had been at the hospital, but it hadn't been long and hadn't chased away the sleep-deprived headache. Tylenol and caffeine had kept him on his feet. Despite his tiredness, he couldn't go home and rest while his brain whirled with details of the case and unanswered questions.

Social Services had found Chloe a bed for the night, in a shelter for abused women. On paper, it sounded appropriate, but looking at the waifish child in front of him, Bill wasn't convinced that it was the best solution for her. She wasn't an adult.

It wasn't a permanent solution. They would keep looking for an appropriate care solution while she recovered. Hopefully, something that would work even past her eighteenth birthday. Seventeen was such a difficult age to deal with. Too old for traditional foster care. Too young to qualify for an adult program. Too often kids her age just fell through the gaping wide cracks of the system.

Tech had uploaded the latest video from the teddy bear cam. Bill pulled it up and watched it dispassionately, looking for information that be could used to build the case against Sal and Mim. The recording was started and stopped remotely from upstairs in the spare bedroom, Bill had been told. So the unclipped video showed Sal's entrance into the room. The angles were still bad, not affording a full view of Sal's face. But enough, Bill thought, to make him identifiable.

He turned the sound down and watched it again. The end of the video was gut wrenching. After Sal had fallen asleep on the bed, Chloe cuddled up against his body, starving for the warmth of human contact, even if it was with her abuser. It made Bill sick. Made him want to go to the prison and beat Sal Durrant senseless. Every day. For at least two years.

Bill went back to the beginning of the video to watch it again. There was a moment near the beginning when Sal's head cocked to the side, and his face turned toward the door as if someone had walked up. Had Mim come down the stairs? Was there someone else nearby? Bill studied Chloe, watching her carefully for her reaction. Did she also hear someone approach? Did she feel threatened by it?

But Chloe's reaction was the opposite to what Bill would have expected. Rather than looking worried or frightened by whatever Sal heard, Chloe reached out to Sal, pulling him closer to her, distracting his attention from whatever he had heard. Bill blinked, trying to process it. Why? What had Sal heard?

He played the rest of the video, watching for either of them to look toward the door again. Neither of them had. Had Sal really heard something, or only thought that he did? Had Mim been there for some reason? If they could prove that she had seen what was going on with her own eyes and failed to act, she would be going away for a long time.

When he had watched it the first two times, Bill had only watched the video up to the point at which Sal left the room. He had to go upstairs to stop the recording, which meant there were a few minutes of video of Chloe alone in the room after his departure. A few seconds after he was out the door, Chloe whipped back the blankets and got out of bed. Then she too was out the door. Bill watched, frowning. He knew that the door had been left unlocked when they arrived to free Chloe. But he had assumed that the rest of the time it was locked, that it was merely an oversight. He assumed that Chloe didn't know it had been left unlocked, or she would have escaped. A few seconds after Chloe left the room, the video cut out.

Bill sat back, considering. He looked for an explanation that made sense. They were only fractions of a second on the video. Something that no one else would probably even notice, mesmerized by the horror the bulk of the video showed. But Bill was trained to search out every last detail. To analyze every possible clue the video yielded up.

He went back to the beginning of the video, turning the sound up higher this time to see if he could hear the footsteps or whatever noise had attracted Sal's attention.

"Tell me what you hear," Bill ordered, playing just the audio of the portion of the recording that he had isolated.

Mercer sat attentively. It was jus a second. Maybe a second and a half. Mercer shook his head.

"I don't know. A voice. Maybe someone crying. Or a cat."

Bill nodded. "Doesn't make much sense, does it? There wasn't a cat at the Simpson house."

"Well, no, but there were people. It could just as easily be someone calling from another room. Or someone crying. The girl herself."

"Look at the video."

Bill played back a few seconds of the video. Mercer frowned.

"Okay, so it's not the girl. It's something outside the room. Must be the mother. She called from upstairs. It's very faint."

Bill raised an eyebrow. "Did it sound like the mother? She doesn't exactly have a quiet voice."

"No. But she might not have been calling. Just talking to herself, or on the phone. She could have been watching the TV. It might be a noise from the TV."

"That would be directly overhead. Sal wouldn't look toward the door."

Mercer shrugged. "Is that all you've got? Do you have any explanations?"

"One more thing."

Bill selected a point at the end of the video. Mercer watched Chloe jump out of bed and hurry out the door.

"So she knew the door wasn't locked?" Mercer said with surprise. "I assumed it was like the old story about training an elephant. You tie it with a rope as a baby, and it is conditioned to believe that it cannot escape the rope, so it doesn't try when it's bigger and stronger and actually could. She had been locked up for so long that she never tried the door and just assumed she was locked in."

"Apparently not," Bill said. "She was still just as much a prisoner in that house, but she knew the bedroom door wasn't locked."

"So why is that important?"

Bill played the last few seconds back again. "Where is she going?"

"Upstairs, apparently. Maybe she figured she was safe to go get something to eat, now that Sal was all mellowed out."

Bill shook his head. He played it again, waiting for Mercer to notice.

"Where is she going?" he repeated

There was a flash of understanding from Mercer. "She turned the wrong way. Not toward the stairs."

"Toward the storeroom," Bill said. "Why? What's in the storeroom?"

They both looked at each other, sorting through the possibilities. Food? A way to escape? Something too valuable to her to be left in her room, which Sal treated as his territory?

"Whatever made that noise," Mercer said finally. "But… what was it?"

Normally, they would not have gone back at night. They would have gone home to sleep. Rest up and get the whole team out there in the morning to help out. More eyes, better light, minds alert. There were plenty of reasons to wait until morning.

But they were too worried about what might be awaiting at the house that had been missed amidst the chaos earlier in the day, when Sal and Mim were arrested and Chloe was rescued.

Perhaps it was just a cat that would need to be fed and cared for and turned in to the Humane Society. Perhaps it was something else.

They turned on the stairway light and went down the stairs to the basement. There was a light with a pull cord in the storeroom. Not the brightest bulb, but there were also no outside windows, so it wasn't going to be any brighter in the morning. Bill and Mercer had both brought along flashlights and turned them on as they looked the room over, touching nothing.

There was no sign of a cat. No sign that one had ever been present. Bill shone his flashlight along the ground, looking for any disturbance in the light layer of dust coating the floor. There were some faintly scuffed spots. Mercer played his flashlight over the fronts of the bins on the shelves. If Chloe had gone into the storeroom, then why? Was she looking for something? Planning an escape? Going after something that she had hidden?

"These ones have been moved, I think," Mercer suggested.

Bill nodded. The dust on the shelf had been disturbed, as if the bins had been moved around. He reached around behind each bin but didn't find anything hidden behind.

"I guess we open them up and see what we can find," he offered.

He pulled on a pair of gloves to avoid getting fingerprints on the bins and lifted a couple down from the shelf. Bill opened the first bin with a pop. He wrinkled his nose at the foul smell and started breathing through his mouth. With one more glance at Mercer, he tugged loose the towel-wrapped bundle jammed into the top of the bin and unwound the towel.

And with that, everything changed. Bill swore, staring down at the decomposing corpse of a newborn.

Within a couple of hours, the storeroom had been filled with bright work lights, and each bin was being removed and carefully inventoried. By morning, they had four bodies of varying sizes and states of decomposition. Three were old, partially mummified. Only the first, the one that Bill had found, was relatively fresh, just beginning to decompose. The coroner who examined it on the scene offered a preliminary guess that the baby had been dead for three days. A bottle and a can of powdered formula a couple of years old had been found in another box. They had been recently used, moisture still clinging to the inside of the bottle.

"So the video was taken just a day or two before the baby died," Bill said.

"Assuming the date stamps are correct," Mercer pointed out.

Bill shook his head, at a loss for words. "I'll want Chloe at the station as soon as possible," he sighed.

Mercer nodded. "I had them put a detail on the shelter while you were calling for reinforcements. He confirmed Chloe was still there, sleeping soundly. I think the shelter usually has them up at six, so after she has had some breakfast, Marvin will get her over to the station." Mercer rubbed his own temples, looking Bill over. "You might want to go home for a shower and a nap before that. Chloe will wait."

~

Mim had displayed shock when confronted about the dead babies in the basement. She swore up and down that she had never had any children while living in the house and had no idea that Chloe had.

"You hear about that sometimes," she said, shaking her head. "Teenage girls having babies when no one even knew they were pregnant. They wear a baggy sweater and keep it hidden, somehow. I don't know how; I was always as big as a whale with my pregnancies!"

Bill, looking at her, figured it was far more likely that Mim could hide a pregnancy than Chloe could, all skin and bones.

Chloe's reaction to the discovery of the babies was not shock, but fear. "I never did anything to hurt them," she insisted. "It's just... none of them survived."

"Were they your babies?" Bill pressed.

She looked at him, her eyes narrow, frown lines around her mouth. She didn't answer right away, apparently thinking it through.

"Yes," she agreed finally. "They were mine."

"Nobody knew about the pregnancies? How did you hide them?"

"I just... I don't know. You couldn't really tell."

"I think you're lying to me, Chloe. You had birth control pills in your bathroom."

"They don't always work," Chloe pointed out. "People still get pregnant on the pill. Sometimes."

"Four times?"

She slouched in her chair. Not one of the comfy rooms this time. One of the cold, hard-backed chairs. Even though he knew Chloe had to be treated as a suspect and questioned in one of the appointed interrogation rooms, Bill felt bad about it. Chloe shifted constantly for a more comfortable position. She had no fat to cushion her and Bill suspected the chair was painful for her to sit in.

"Yes."

While the coroner had not yet confirmed the approximate dates of death for all of the infants, he had given Bill a timeline that stretched as far back as four years. When Chloe was only thirteen and was still going to school. It seemed unlikely that she'd been able to hide a pregnancy while going to school, but Leesa *had* said that Chloe had been overweight and then had slimmed down. Which led to another topic that Bill hadn't yet addressed with Chloe. But maybe it was time.

"Was one of the babies Gunter Gnatsky's?" he asked.

This time, Chloe's face did register shock. She sprang right out of her chair. Her mouth formed the word 'no,' but no sound came out. She shook her head.

"But you were in a relationship with Mr. Gnatsky," Bill said confidently as if it were already proven fact.

"No!" The sound came bursting out. "You don't know. You're wrong!"

"I don't think so. Sit back down, please."

Chloe kicked at the chair. "I can't sit in this stupid chair. It hurts my butt. I want to go home. I don't want to answer any more questions."

"I can understand that. But we can't just let you go. Not when you may have murdered your own children."

"Murdered?" Chloe repeated, horror in her voice. "I loved those babies! I wouldn't do anything to hurt them! I didn't murder anyone!"

"You kept them a secret from everyone. Including Sal. But you were afraid that someone was going to find out about them. They would cry too much and attract attention. You wouldn't be able to keep them a secret any longer. So... you put your hand over their mouths... just for a minute... to keep them quiet..."

"No!" Chloe kicked again, the leg of the table this time. But it was bolted to the floor and didn't budge. "You don't know what you're talking about. I never did anything to hurt them. I tried to save them! Mom—" she cut herself off abruptly.

"Mom what?"

"Nothing. Mom didn't know. It was a secret. But I never hurt them!"

Bill called up the doctor at the hospital who had examined Chloe and outlined the situation to him. The doctor clicked his tongue.

"A newborn? In the past week or two? There's no way that a girl that undernourished had a baby recently. And with those hips... she certainly hasn't had four pregnancies!"

This just confirmed what Bill's instincts had already told him. Though Chloe and Mim had separately come up with the same story of the babies being Chloe's, there was no way that it was true. They had either discussed the story ahead of time, or Chloe was so used to being the mother's scapegoat that she automatically took it upon herself. They would order DNA testing of the remains, and that would confirm who the mother was, and if they could get Gnatsky's DNA, whether his genes were in the mix.

He had already arranged to stop by the coroner's office, so he went by with an update on the situation and to see what they had been able to determine so far.

"Horrible situation," Hodge said, shaking his head. "You didn't use to hear about these cases, but there have been at least two in the past year where six or more infants were discovered. Maybe it's just because people don't have a field or woods to bury them anymore. So it's closets and garages. Maybe it has always happened..."

"I don't know," Bill shook his head. "Seems like a new thing to me. So, could you determine cause of death in any of the babies?"

"Of course, the most recent death was the easiest," Hodge said, picking up one of the four slim file folders in front of him. "We don't have to guess; everything is still intact. This baby had a severe bacterial infection. Intestinal tract. Hard to say whether fever or dehydration took him. It was probably pretty quick."

"Could anything have been done?"

"If they got him to the hospital in time and antibiotics were administered... possibly. If he became dehydrated overnight, he might have been dead by the time they woke up in the morning."

"What was the infection caused by? Was he born with it?"

"Intestinal tract; not likely. Probably picked it up from mom or a bottle that wasn't sterilized or had been left out too long."

Bill remembered the bottle they had discovered in the boxes. "What if they only had one bottle?"

"Then it was probably never cleaned properly between feedings. Could be harboring all kinds of bacteria."

"Could you test it?"

"I could swab it. Would that help your case?"

"Maybe. Okay, one down. Bacterial infection. Possible neglect. How about the other three?"

"Moving back in time to the baby who died before that. Judging by the skeletal structure, he was small. Maybe premature, but not by more than a few weeks. For this one, in spite of being desiccated, it was also not difficult to determine cause of death." He opened the next file and snapped an x-ray up onto the light box. Bill immediately recognized the shape of the baby's skull. He followed the lines that Hodge traced with his capped pen. "These are fractures. Massive head trauma."

Bill's stomach gave a twist. Neglect or a contaminated bottle was one thing. At least a bottle proved that they had tried to take care of the baby. But a fractured skull was clearly abuse, taking them over the line into willful murder.

"Damn. Any idea as to the age of the baby? How long it would have taken death to occur?"

"Still a newborn. With this degree of trauma... I would expect death to have been instantaneous."

"Right then. Two down, two to go. Next?"

"The one before that was very tiny. Did you see it?"

Bill nodded. He had seen all of them. Pulled most of them out of the bins himself.

"Micro-preemie or a miscarriage," Hodge said. "Way too early to have any good chance at survival. Even born at the hospital with a good NICU, a lot of doctors wouldn't attempt to keep it alive."

"So that one can't be counted with the others. And the oldest body?"

The doctor shook his head. "It's been too long. No trauma to the body. No deformities. I can try rehydrating some of the tissues, but we probably wouldn't be able to find anything out. SIDS. Smothering. Maybe infection, like the last one. Dehydration. There's not enough evidence to pinpoint."

"One definite homicide and one possible neglect. Whatever charges they want to lay for indignity to a dead body. It will shore up the abuse charges concerning Chloe. Every little bit helps."

Hodge had heard enough about Chloe's case to look sad. "That poor girl. How does anyone live a normal life after going through something like that? No matter how long the parents go away for, it's not long enough."

Bill sighed. "Yeah. They're trying to pin the deaths of the babies on her. But I'm not going to let that happen."

CHAPTER
Nineteen

Chloe had been returned to the good room. The one with the comfortable chairs that looked like someone's living room. She supposed that meant that she was no longer being treated as a suspect in the deaths of the babies. Whenever her mind went back to them, she pushed the memories away. She didn't want to think about that. She wanted all the bad memories to go away, to be like they had never happened. She closed her eyes, forcing herself away. It had never happened. It had happened to someone else.

Instead of Bill, the investigator who had spent the most time with her since he'd coaxed her out from under the covers in her bed, a man with a suit came in to talk to her. Chloe shifted uncomfortably. She didn't want to talk to anyone else. While this man smiled at her, she could tell that he didn't mean it. He wasn't warm and friendly like Bill. He had an insincere manner that she didn't trust.

"Chloe. I'm very glad to meet you. And sorry to hear about all that you have had to go through."

He offered his hand to shake but Chloe didn't take it. She sat back in the seat, keeping her body as far away from him as possible. He sat down, resting his file folder and notebook on his knees.

"My name is Mr. Temple. I am the prosecutor in the cases against Sal Durrant and your mother."

A lawyer. That explained the slimy feeling. Chloe said nothing.

"I'd like to spend some time with you, going over what happened over the past couple of years and what your testimony will be."

"I already talked to the cops," Chloe said. "That's all I'm going to say."

"I don't expect you to tell me anything different. But I have to hear it from your own mouth."

"I'm not talking to you."

"Let's start with the easy stuff. Sal is your mother's boyfriend?"

Chloe stared at the ceiling. "I wouldn't know."

"You wouldn't know."

"You'd have to ask her. I didn't hang out with them. I don't know anything about their relationship. Maybe he was just a border."

"I think you know the specifics of their relationship pretty well."

"Nope."

"Did he pay rent?"

"I wouldn't know. I don't pay the bills."

"Did he sleep in the same room as your mother?"

Chloe gave another shrug. "I wouldn't know, would I? I was downstairs."

"Chloe. I need you to cooperate. Would it be easier for you if I just let you tell me your story? I can do that. I'll just be quiet and not ask difficult questions, and you can explain to me what went on."

"Nothing went on. Don't know what you mean."

"You were being abused. There are videos, Chloe. We know exactly what happened."

Chloe looked at Temple in shock, feeling the blood drain from her face. "What?" she demanded.

Temple looked taken aback. "You didn't know about the videos?" He flushed. "I assumed you had been told."

"Videos of what?" Chloe scoffed, her mouth as dry as sand. "No one ever took videos. Blue—Sal didn't have a camera."

"The teddy bear on your dresser was a video camera. One of the eyes was the lens."

Chloe felt sick. She had never had a clue. She felt naked in front of Temple. Like he had stripped her. She folded her arms across herself protectively, hunching over.

"He recorded me all the time?" Chloe demanded. Her mind went unwillingly to the latest baby. Bill had acted like he didn't know anything about Chloe taking care of the baby, or its death. Had that all been an act? "All day long?"

"No. Only... when he was with you."

Chloe held her stomach. "I'm gonna be sick." The pain seized her in the gut and in the chest simultaneously. She could barely breathe. Temple grabbed the wastepaper bin and thrust it at her, then went hurriedly to the door to flag down a policeman to escort her to the restroom. Chloe didn't even get to her feet before the pain and nausea overwhelmed her, and she retched over the garbage can. Temple turned away from her, looking ill himself. Chloe's face was sweating like she had a fever.

The vomiting couldn't last long, though her stomach still hurt. She had only been able to eat tiny amounts at a time. She asked to be taken to the bathroom to clean up and rinse out her mouth.

When she finished and was reaching to open the bathroom door, she stopped, listening to the voices on the other side. She heard a familiar voice. Bill's voice, furious.

"What the hell were you thinking?" Bill demanded. "Why would you tell her that? She doesn't need to know what that pervert did! You think she needs to know that he uploaded them to the internet? That anyone who wanted to pay twenty bucks a download has copies? There's no way for us to ever get them all back and keep them from being reposted on another site. They're out there. Forever. She doesn't need to hear that!"

Chloe leaned against the wall and closed her eyes. Temple hadn't spilled that part, but she supposed she would have found out sooner or later anyway. She spent a few minutes trying to regain her composure. With a few breaths, she managed to separate herself. She didn't need to experience this pain. She could remove herself from it, just like she had so many times before.

She watched herself from a distance as she lifted up her head and walk out of the restroom to where Temple and Bill were talking.

"I'm not going to testify," she told them crisply. "You have everything you need. I just want to go home."

~

The trouble was, there was no more 'home' to go to. Chloe continued to stay at the women's shelter until Social Services came up with what they figured was a good solution. It was a group home. Other teenagers and young adults like Chloe. Most of them in one kind of trouble or another. Released from prison. On probation or parole. Runaways. Drug addicts. You couldn't tell by looking at them what they had done to get there. And everybody would just assume that Chloe was in the same boat. Maybe a homeless crack addict, if they judged by her wasted body.

"Time to get up! Hey! Come on, wake up!"

Chloe eventually groaned and shifted, forced to consciousness by the continued shaking and badgering.

"What? What is it?"

"It's time to get up," the woman enunciated impatiently. "Man, you'd sleep through an earthquake, wouldn't you? Up and at 'em. Move it."

Chloe stretched her body out. She'd slept in a tightly-coiled, protective ball, and her muscles and joints ached. "Why?"

"You can't sleep all day. There's chores to do. You gotta look for a job. We don't sleep once the sun is up around here."

Chloe scratched her head. Dry hair broke off under her nails. She smoothed her hair with her fingertips, trying to pat the thin hair that remained down into place. They had insisted that it needed to be cut off, it was so tangled and matted. But Chloe had spent hours with a brush and comb, trying to work out all the knots so that she could keep her hair. Mim hated short hair. Chloe didn't want anyone to cut it off.

Joelle was the name of the woman who had woken Chloe up. She was a dark-haired, petite woman, her hair in a pixie cut, with lots of earrings. She was one of the 'mothers' at the group home, ordering the residents around and generally treating them like stupid children.

"I'm up," Chloe confirmed. She rubbed her eyes. It was hard getting used to waking up each morning. She had spent so much of her captivity sleeping, forcing consciousness away. Her body was having trouble adjusting to a normal schedule.

"You'd better stay up," Joelle warned. She left Chloe sitting on her bed yawning, and went on to wake up the next malingerer.

Chloe squinted at the window. It was nice to see the sun again. She hadn't realized how much a person could miss something so basic. Sunlight. Food. Clothing. Emerging from the dark period of her confinement, they were almost painful to experience again. But at the same time, it seemed like her body was far away, and she couldn't fully feel them. Like she was in a bubble, a thick barrier between her and the rest of the world.

The thought of food started her stomach rumbling. Chloe untangled herself from her blankets and went to the bathroom, then headed downstairs to the kitchen.

"Morning, sleepyhead!" John greeted in a booming voice.

Chloe flinched back from the Samoan's loud voice and impressive bulk. "Hi."

"You're supposed to dress before breakfast."

Chloe looked down at her nightgown. "Oh. Yeah. Can I have breakfast before I shower? Just this once?"

"Just because you're my favorite," John conceded. "Get dished up and take it to the table."

Chloe looked sideways at him, trying to study him without appearing to look. Despite his declaration that she was his favorite, he didn't appear to be looking at her body or expecting any special favors. Chloe grabbed a plate, scooped one serving spoon of scrambled eggs onto her plate, added one piece of toast, and went to the table.

She glanced at the others at the table. Marilla, a dark-skinned woman, her face disfigured by scars that covered more than half of it. Burns, Chloe thought. And Jackson, a baby-faced redhead who was working his way through at least four times as much scrambled eggs as Chloe had taken, in spite of his slim build.

"No wonder you're so skinny," he commented. "You don't eat anything."

Chloe studied him before sitting down, decided he wasn't a threat, and took her seat.

"This is a lot for me," she said.

He frowned at her. Marilla was staring. Her head was bowed like she was totally intent on her meal, but her eyes were fixed on Chloe. "How come you don't eat more?"

Chloe hadn't shared her story with anyone there. She didn't know how much the supervisors knew about how she had ended up there. But the other residents didn't have any way to know unless Chloe chose to tell them.

"Just not used to eating much," she said, not explaining the reason.

Chloe started to eat, carefully chewing each bite and giving her stomach lots of warning to prepare for more food. She spent a lot of time cramped or bloated. The doctor had said she'd get used to it. Her stomach would adjust to having food regularly. But he hadn't said how long it would take.

"What are you doing today?" John demanded, waddling over and placing a glass of orange juice beside Chloe's plate. She'd forgotten to get something to drink. "You got plans to look for work?"

"I don't know... how would I do that?"

It was hard to think of herself as seventeen. Nearly an adult. She didn't have to go to school anymore. But she had suddenly been dropped into an adult's world, expected to get a job to help support herself, to learn how to be independent and look after her own needs. She no longer had a mother to look after her or the school keeping track of her welfare. She was alone.

"How would you do that?" John chuckled. "You can go down to the job bank and look through listings. You can burn some shoe leather going door to door to local businesses seeing if they need anyone. Look in the newspaper advertisements. There are lots of things you can do."

Chloe chewed on the corner of her toast. "Where is the job bank?"

That sounded like a good option. The word bank made it sound prosperous, like they had plenty of jobs to go around for everyone. Maybe even for someone like Chloe, who had no skills to speak of.

John gave her the address and some basic directions to get there. Chloe wasn't familiar with the neighborhood they had dumped her in, and was going to have to spend some time walking around, getting to know the landmarks. John's description was gibberish to her.

"Job training is what you need," Jackson advised, after taking a huge gulp of milk to wash down an even bigger mouthful of food.

179

Chloe wondered how he could even taste the food eating it so fast. Not that she could really taste her own. Her taste buds, like the rest of her senses, seemed like they had been turned off, or at least muffled. "You can't expect to get a job when you don't know how to do anything."

That was logical. Chloe had no idea what she could apply for with no experience and no training. "Where can I get that?"

"Exactly!" Jackson said emphatically.

Chloe frowned at him for not answering the question. Marilla looked at Chloe and rolled her eyes. Chloe looked down at her food and took another tiny bite of eggs.

"Do you have a job?" she asked Marilla.

"None of us have jobs," Marilla said. "How are you supposed to get a job when you've got no experience? Or when they find out you're just out of prison? Exactly where are we supposed to find a job that would support us?"

"None of you have jobs?" Chloe repeated, stunned.

"Lenny does," John argued. "He's got a job at the bottle depot."

"Yeah, but he's handicapped," Marilla pointed out. "That's different." At Chloe's baffled look, she explained further. "He's mentally challenged. So the government finds him a job that doesn't require any skills and subsidizes his salary. How can we compete against someone an employer only has to pay less than minimum wage? Why would they hire you or me to put bottles in crates when they can have Lenny at half the price?"

Chloe shook her head. "That doesn't seem fair."

"You think it's easy for someone like Lenny to get a job?" John challenged. "He didn't get that job by sitting around here whining."

Chloe shifted away from John an inch, not liking how close behind her shoulder he was standing.

Chloe had taken a long time getting showered and dressed. Much longer than it should have taken, when she only had one outfit to wear, and no makeup or accessories. She felt like a child learning how to dress herself for the first time. Her fingers were awkward and didn't move the way they should. The clothes felt scratchy and constricting. Nothing looked right, ballooning over her skinny, flat figure.

Marilla came to her rescue as Chloe stood in front of the mirror, looking at the stranger on the other side of the glass. "Hey, are you okay?"

Chloe smoothed the lines of her clothes, shaking her head. She had never cared much about fashion or spent a lot of time on how she looked, other than when Gunter was guiding her and showing her how to dress properly. But she felt sick looking at the body in the reflection. That wasn't her.

"What can I do?" Marilla asked. "You need makeup?"

"Yeah."

"Come on. I've got plenty." Marilla caught Chloe's arm and tugged her into her bedroom. 'Plenty' consisted of foundation, a palette of blushes, and a jumble of tubes of lipsticks, most of them store testers. But it was more than Chloe had. The foundation was too dark for Chloe's fair skin. Marilla fussed over her, making suggestions and doing what she could to soften the sharp angles and prominent cheekbones of Chloe's face.

Marilla turned her attention from Chloe's face. "Those are your only clothes?"

Chloe nodded.

"They didn't exactly bother to get you anything that fit, did they?"

"I don't know if anything will," Chloe said, patting the ill-fitting clothes sadly. "I just don't have a body anymore."

"Well, what you don't have, you can fake."

Chloe's figure had developed earlier than most of her peers', so she had never been one to worry about stuffing her bra or wearing a training bra when she had nothing to support. "It wouldn't look normal," Chloe said, shaking her head. "You'd be able to tell."

"Think so?" Marilla laughed.

Chloe looked at her doubtfully. Marilla went to her dresser and took out two oddly-shaped chunks of pink foam. Marilla handed them to Chloe. Chloe looked down at two prosthetic breasts. It took all her control not to throw them back like hot potatoes.

"Why do you have these?" she asked blankly.

"Those are my back-ups." Marilla made a casual gesture toward her chest. "I lost my breasts the same time as this happened." She touched her scar-ravaged face.

Chloe looked at Marilla's bust line, then up at her face.

"What happened?"

"I'll tell you someday. Maybe. You want to try them? Just slip them into your bra. You can see what direction they go."

Chloe looked down at the fake flesh, then at herself in the mirror. She glanced at Marilla one more time and then turned away from her slightly to reach down her shirt and try to settle the prosthetics into place. She was surprised when she looked back at the mirror. They didn't feel perfectly comfortable, but they looked good. It was such a small change, together with the little bit of makeup, but it boosted her self-confidence immensely. She smiled at Marilla.

"Thank you! I never would have thought…"

Marilla nodded. "Makes you feel a lot different, doesn't it? Makes you feel like a woman."

"Yeah."

Marilla next found a scarf she tied artistically around Chloe's waist to hide the bulges and folds in the jeans that had to be cinched tightly around her tiny waist.

"There. And you can wear my coat if you're going out somewhere. The lines will look good on you. It'll make you look taller."

Marilla offered her the coat. Chloe was taken off-guard by an over-whelming urge to cry. She rolled her eyes upward to the ceiling and took a deep breath, trying to settle the emotions. Marilla's helpful-ness and understanding touched her heart. She had guarded her feel-ings so carefully that it took her by surprise.

"Don't you cry," Marilla ordered. "Off you go."

"Thank you…"

"Don't thank me. Just get out of here. Don't make a nuisance of yourself."

Grateful for the excuse to flee, Chloe quickly made her exit.

When she got outside, she walked very fast. The group home was downtown, so there weren't a lot of houses in the surrounding area. Instead, Chloe was immediately surrounded by a variety of small businesses, condos, and coffee shops. Chloe breathed in the brisk, cool air and just struck off in a random direction.

Though John had described where the job bank was, Chloe didn't know any of the landmarks he had mentioned, so her walk was just reconnaissance. Get familiar with the area. Learn where everything was. Make it her own. She had a good sense of direction that had never failed her before. She had lived in a lot of different neighborhoods before her father was killed, and she was always the first to get comfortable finding her way around, acting as a human directory for the rest of the family when they were looking for a bank or a grocery store, or a twenty-four hour pharmacy when one of the younger kids was sick. That was a skill Chloe had, though she wasn't sure it could translate into anything marketable. It was a practical talent, but not of much real value.

She felt good to start out with. Out on her own for the first time in months. In years. Free, independent, not required to obey or serve anybody but herself. The fresh air felt good. She was full of energy. She was embarking on a new adventure.

But it wasn't to last. Chloe's energy flagged after just a couple of blocks, and she was forced to slow down and look for somewhere to sit and rest. She didn't want to admit that maybe her body wasn't ready for a new adventure, and pushed on.

She kept getting jostled by the crowd. People were rushing past her in both directions, some of them talking or yelling at each other. She tried to leave space around her so that she wouldn't get pushed or elbowed, but people just got more impatient with her as she slowed down and tried to find a space where she wouldn't be trampled. There were too many people. Way too many after having lived the past two years completely isolated from the noisy, bustling, chaotic outside world. Chloe was having a hard time breathing. She felt dizzy and nauseated. She knew she should go back to the group home, but she was suddenly disoriented, not even sure which way she had been walking down the street, never mind what route she had taken to get where she was.

"No," Chloe murmured to herself. "Just calm down. You're okay. It's time to go home."

She spun in a circle, looking for something familiar. The condos towered over her. The smells from the little restaurants and food trucks was making her sick. Someone shoved past Chloe, making her topple over.

Chloe landed awkwardly on elbows and knees and tried to steady herself and get her head on straight. But it was whirling dizzily, and she barely knew which way was up. A couple of people kicked her or tripped over her. Someone muttered about drunks, and a knee in her back shoved her out of the main walkway.

"Hey! Hey, look out!" a man's voice ordered, rising above the noise of the street. "Watch where you're going!"

Hands landed on Chloe, and she prepared herself to be thrown again.

But they weren't cruel this time. The hands steadied her and stopped people from running into her. Chloe tried to catch her breath.

"Are you okay?" his kind voice asked.

"Yeah, thanks," Chloe muttered. "I'm fine."

When she raised her head up further, she felt nauseated, like she had a concussion. The sounds and movement of the crowds were too much to handle.

"Take your time," he soothed. "I saw you get pushed down. I can't believe no one even stopped to say sorry."

Chloe put her hands over her eyes, trying to block everything out.

"Just breathe." His voice was calming. Chloe tried to obey and just get oxygen into her brain. There was enough air. The crowds had just panicked her. She was perfectly okay.

"Yeah," she gulped. "Yeah, I'm okay."

"Can you get up? I'll help you."

Chloe uncurled and sat up cautiously, her knees under her. She blinked at the man who had stopped to help her. Young. He didn't look past his twenties. Dark hair and a thin growth of whiskers that couldn't decide whether to be five o'clock shadow or a goatee. Dark eyes that twinkled with humor and exuded concern for her at the same time.

"Up?" he suggested.

Chloe gave him her hand and got stiffly to her feet. Her knees held, and the dizziness was receding. People still looked at her as they went by, but they didn't collide with her. Not with the man standing right there looking out for her.

"You're bleeding," he said.

Chloe touched her nose, but it was dry. She looked at her hands and elbows and saw that they were grazed from her fall. Her knees probably were too, but she couldn't see them through her pants. They weren't as bad because they were covered.

"It's nothing," Chloe brushed crumbs of gravel out of the abrasion. "Just skinned."

"Always stings so much," he said sympathetically.

Chloe thought about it but really didn't feel any pain. "Thanks for helping me."

"Are you going to be okay? Where are you headed?"

She thought that she probably shouldn't tell him. The stranger could have evil intentions. Stalk her back to the group home. But she didn't think that she was in any danger. She looked around her, trying to orient herself. Which way had she come? Where was the group home?

"I'm... where am I? I got turned around."

"Main," he said unhelpfully. "Where were you headed?"

"I don't know. I was just... taking a look around."

"You don't have anywhere to go?"

"I do. I'm... in a place..." Her face burned. "A group home. Not because I did something wrong. I wasn't in prison."

He nodded slowly. "Okay..."

Chloe tried to collect her thoughts. "I think... I came that way?" Chloe pointed. "No... that doesn't look right..."

"Where is your group home? I can at least point you in the right direction."

"I don't actually know. I think if I just stand here for a few minutes... It'll come back to me. I just panicked."

He stood with her. Chloe shifted. "You should go. You have to be somewhere."

"No, I can stay with you for a bit."

"I'm okay now. I'll just stand here a few minutes. You go on."

He frowned at this. But he chose not to argue with her about it, and reluctantly went on. Chloe watched him make his way down the street until he finally turned a corner and was gone. She took a deep breath and looked around.

Pay attention. Look. You know which way you came. Just look and you can figure it out.

But her brain was not cooperating. She continued to look at the world around her as if she had fallen out of an alien aircraft. It all seemed completely foreign.

Chloe was paralyzed. She'd always been able to find her way around before. Just start moving her feet and she would find her way back to the group home. But she couldn't even take that first small step. What if she went the wrong way? What if the crowd started to jostle her again? She was fine standing off to the side, but once she started walking again, she'd be in the crowd.

So she was still there when the man, apparently finished whatever errands he was off on, walked down the street again, going the opposite direction. He looked at her and didn't approach her at first. He stopped and looked in some shop windows and then glanced over at her. Looked in the shops again, and looked back at her. Eventually, he gave up the subtleties and sidled up to her.

"Are you okay?"

"Yes."

"Are you still lost?"

Chloe swallowed. "I'm not lost... I just don't know... where to go from here."

He must have thought her mentally challenged like Lenny. A girl who is old enough to know better than to get lost says she lives in a group home, but doesn't know where she lives. Had to be something wrong with her.

"You don't know what street your house is on?"

"No." Chloe glanced up and down the street. "They all look the same. There was a big elm tree in the front yard."

But this description didn't enlighten him.

"What else was close by?"

"There were condos and stores... I don't really know."

"Does it have a name? The group home? Sometimes they have a creative name...?"

"No. I don't know if it does. I haven't been there very long."

He pondered on this for a few minutes. "Do you have anyone you can call? One of the supervisors at the group home, or a friend or family member?"

Chloe shook her head.

"A social worker? Police officer? Someone must know where you belong."

"Social worker..." Chloe echoed. It had been her new social worker who had taken her there. But she didn't want to call Social Services and have them think that she wasn't capable of living on her own. She didn't want to be locked up because they didn't think she could take care of herself. What about a police officer? Bill would help her out, and he wouldn't tell the social worker that she was a flake. At least, she didn't think he would. "There was a cop. Bill..."

"Bill?" her good Samaritan echoed.

"Yeah. Umm... Bill..." Chloe struggled to remember his last name. He had told her at least once. She had seen it repeatedly on his name bar when he wore his uniform. "I can't remember his last name. And I don't know his number."

The man sighed. "Let's go sit down. You look dead on your feet." He gestured toward a bus bench down the block. Chloe walked with him and sat down on the bench, sighing with relief to get off of her feet. He sat down beside her.

"So, somebody must know where your home is. There must be some way to find out."

"What's your name?" Chloe asked.

He looked surprised.

"Oh! Sorry. Jozef."

"Jozef. I'm Chloe."

"It's nice to meet you. I'm sorry I didn't introduce myself. I was just thinking of your problem."

Chloe nodded. "I know. Thank you for helping me before." She looked around at the bustling street. "It's really busy out here."

"It is," he agreed. "I love the feeling, all bustling with life. But if you're not used to it, I can understand how it would be over-whelming."

"Yeah. I'll get used to it... someday."

"I know you will." He smiled at her. A friendly, sincere smile. Not the kind she'd been getting from all the social workers and lawyers and everyone else who knew they were supposed to smile at her but really didn't care a bit about her.

"If we called the police," Chloe said, "do you think they could help me find the cop who was helping me? And he could help me find the group home again? Or would that cause a bunch of trouble?"

She didn't want to cause any trouble. In the past, Mim had always told her what to say or not to say. Chloe had experience in some areas, like dealing with social workers, but she had no idea what would happen if she called the police station to ask about Bill.

"I don't think it would get you in any trouble," Jozef said. "If you're sincerely asking for their help, and you think this officer could help you, then why would they be upset about it? I think they're pretty understanding."

Chloe bit her lip. "Bill would help me... if I found him. I just don't know... if I can find him."

"Well, let's give it a try."

"Okay. I need to find a phone."

Jozef smiled and pulled a phone out of his pocket. "Done."

"Do you know the number? I don't think we should call nine-one-one."

"I don't know. Being lost or missing probably qualifies as an emergency."

"I don't want to make a big deal. I'm not in danger. Just..." She sighed. "Disoriented."

"Okay. I'll get directory assistance. They'll track it down."

"Good." Chloe nodded, relieved. She didn't think she could handle any more police sirens. Her nerves were already frayed. She tried to relax and not let Jozef see how she was shaking. If he could help her to find Bill, Chloe could get home and climb into her bed. It was probably too early, and they wouldn't let her go to bed yet, but if she told them she was sick, she thought they would.

Jozef chatted pleasantly with the directory assistance woman and in a couple of minutes was connected with a police switchboard. He handed the phone to Chloe. "Okay, tell them about Bill and they'll track him down for you."

Chloe took the phone from him and held it to her ear.

"Uh... hello?"

"How may I direct your call?"

"I need to reach a policeman who helped me out. But I don't know his last name. His first name was Bill."

"We have a number of Bills," the switchboard operator said. "Do you know what department he was in?"

"No…"

"What was it that he helped you with? Can you tell me the nature of the crime?"

Chloe cast a look at Jozef and didn't want to say anything in front of him. She turned away from him slightly, lowering her voice still more.

"I… I can't say," she said.

"If you can't tell me anything about what he was working on, I can't track him down for you, honey."

Chloe looked at Jozef again, cupping her hand around the mouthpiece of the phone to try to keep him from hearing her conversation. Jozef suddenly got the idea and stood up, walking away from her.

"I'll just be down here," he pointed further down the block. "When you're done."

Chloe nodded and watched him walk out of earshot. She still whispered into the phone, not wanting to be overheard by anyone walking by.

"He was on a special task force. To help… to help kids…"

"The Child Exploitation Unit?" the woman suggested. Then her voice suddenly changed. "Are you in danger? You should call the emergency line if you are in immediate danger."

"No. I just… need to talk to him."

"I'll put you through."

Chloe listened to the phone ring through. There was no immediate answer. It went on and on. Chloe prepared to hang up, knowing that it was going to go through to his machine. Then just as she put her finger over the 'end call' button, there was a click.

"Maynard."

"Uh…"

"Bill Maynard here. Can I help you?"

Chloe sighed, relieved. "It's Chloe. Simpson."

"Chloe! Are you okay? Is everything all right?"

"I just wondered… I'm sort of… stuck."

"Stuck. Stuck how?"

"I… I kind of got lost. And I can't remember where the group home is."

There was silence, and then a low chuckle. Chloe was relieved. He wasn't going to yell at her or impose some kind of consequence for wasting his time and valuable police resources. She let her breath out, suddenly realizing that she had been holding it. When she drew it back in, she couldn't stop him from hearing her sob of relief.

"Chloe? Chloe, I'm sorry. I'm not laughing at you. I'll help you."

"I know."

"You have to admit; it does sound a little funny."

Chloe sobbed again. "Yeah." She looked up and caught Jozef's eye, motioning for him to come back.

"Do you want me to have someone pick you up?" Bill suggested.

"No. If you can just tell me the address, I can find it."

"Okay. Do you have a pen and paper?"

Chloe mimed writing to Jozef. He patted his pockets and found a pen. Chloe scribbled on her palm to make sure it worked.

"Okay. Go ahead."

Bill gave her the address slowly and Chloe wrote it on her palm.

"Okay, I got it."

"You'll be able to find it?"

"Yeah."

"Do you have my direct line? In case you need me for anything?"

"No. Do you want to give it to me?"

"You bet." Bill again recited the number slowly, giving Chloe lots of time to get it down.

"Thank you... I don't know what I would have done if I couldn't get a hold of you."

"Happy to help, Chloe. You're going to be okay now?"

"Yeah."

They said their goodbyes and hung up. Chloe handed the phone back to Jozef.

"Thanks. You're really nice."

He smiled in return. "I take it you got everything you needed?"

"Yes. I've got the address now so that I can find my way back."

"Do you want me to walk with you, at least part way?" Jozef eyed the busy sidewalks. "I'd like to be sure you're okay."

Chloe looked down at the address on her hand and was forced to admit that she really had no idea which direction to start out in. She assumed that once she started to get close, she would recognize the streets and be able to get the rest of the way herself. But she wasn't even sure what street she was currently on, and still had no sense of what direction the group home was. She displayed her hand to Jozef.

"Do you know where that is?"

"Sure. I can help you find your way back."

"Okay."

The first thing he did was to get her onto a parallel street that was much less busy. Chloe tried to relax her tense muscles.

"That's better."

"Yeah, I thought so. You're a little agoraphobic, huh?"

Chloe stared at the sidewalk as they walked, not wanting to look at his face.

"I don't know what that is."

"Fear of crowds. Or open spaces. I think it applies to both."

"I don't know... I never used to be. But... a lot has changed."

"We don't have too far to go. Just a few blocks."

Chloe nodded sheepishly. "My sense of direction used to be a lot better. I never got lost. I don't know what happened to me."

"You just panicked. It could happen to anyone, getting knocked down like that."

"People can be jerks."

"You're right about that."

He was good at small talk and the walk back to the group home went by quickly, without any awkward silences. Chloe hadn't meant to let him walk her all the way home, but suddenly they were there, in front of the house. Chloe didn't even recognize it until she saw the elm tree out front.

"Oh... this is it."

"Good. I'm glad to know you're home safe. I enjoyed talking with you. Do you want my phone number? We could talk anytime."

"Don't you work?"

"Well, yes. But I could still talk to you."

"No..." Chloe was uncomfortable with the idea of a relationship so soon. "I better let you do your job. Thanks for helping me out. When I fell and when I got... stuck."

"Any excuse to rescue a damsel in distress," he said with a smile.

Chloe returned the smile with less sincerity and hurried into the house.

~

"Chloe, you're back!"

Chloe turned around to see who had spoken, a little pleased that someone had been worried about her. Someone had noticed her absence and was relieved to see her back home unharmed.

But the woman who had spoken, Adele, was not smiling or looking pleased to see her.

"Yeah, I'm back," Chloe agreed.

"You need to keep us informed about your schedule. Where you are going and what you are doing. Who you are going to be with. Is that understood?"

Chloe dropped her eyes. "Okay. I didn't know."

"I think you can figure out that you need to be responsible and keep us informed. You're not a child anymore, Chloe."

Chloe hadn't been required to report her movements when she was a child. She took care of her responsibilities and her mother never asked for an accounting of the rest of her time.

"Okay," she agreed.

"You are here because you are in need of supervision. You're not ready to be on your own yet."

"I know."

"So where were you?" Adele stepped closer to Chloe, staring directly into her eyes. Chloe stepped back, startled by the aggressive attitude. "What do you have to hide?" Adele challenged.

"Nothing!" Chloe stepped back again, trying to preserve her personal space. Adele pursued her, backing her into the wall. She grasped Chloe's chin and stared into her eyes. Then Adele finally released her and stepped back.

"If you take drugs, I will know," Adele warned.

"I didn't. I don't take drugs."

"Not while you're here, you don't. No addicts here."

"I'm not."

Adele's eyes flicked over her, and she smirked knowingly at Chloe's thin body. "Sure."

Chloe turned away from her. "I'm not feeling good. I'm going to bed."

"Withdrawals?"

"No. I'm just…" Chloe didn't want to have to explain why she was so thin and weak, what it was that she was recovering from. Social Services had promised not to give the group home details, to preserve Chloe's privacy. She sighed and shook her head. "Just a bug, I guess."

She could feel Adele's eyes on her all the way up the stairs. It was a relief to turn the corner and be out of sight.

Chloe went straight to her bed and didn't even bother to change out of her clothes. She was too exhausted. She just crawled in under the covers of the warm, soft bed, and closed her eyes.

CHAPTER
Twenty

C hloe slept like the dead, but she awoke some time later with a jolt when someone else's weight depressed her mattress. She knew that sensation and was immediately alert. Her eyes flew open, and she saw Mr. Dietz, one of the other supervisors, sitting on the edge of her bed.

"Just checking in on you," he said in an even tone. "Adele said that you weren't feeling well."

Chloe tried not to flinch when he put his hand out and touched her forehead. He then took her by the wrist and felt her pulse. Chloe knew that her heart was racing hard, even though she was trying to slow down her breathing and calm her body. Even though her brain knew that she was safe from the supervisor, her body had been conditioned and knew that pain was inevitable once he was that close to her. She was helpless to stop him.

"Pulse is pretty fast, there," Mr. Dietz commented. He released Chloe's pulse, but still held her arm lightly supported in his hand. He stared down at her wrist. "I can see all your bones," he observed, surprise in his voice. He stared into her eyes. Did they all have to do that? Didn't they realize how invasive it was? Chloe lowered her lids as if sleepy, blocking him out.

"Just the flu or something," she told him.

"Do you need anything?"

"No. Just want to sleep."

He patted her thigh. "Well, you just give a shout if you change your mind."

Chloe went rigid at his touch. Mr. Dietz looked at her for a moment, his expression a blank mask. Then he removed his hand and left the room to let her go back to sleep.

It was evening, and the first day that Chloe hadn't felt like going to bed at five o'clock. Maybe that meant her body was starting to heal. She wandered around the group home, looking for something to do. The fallback activity for most of the residents was watching TV, but Chloe didn't feel like her brain needed to be any more numb than it already was. Marilla was sketching in a notepad propped against her knee. Lenny was working on a small puzzle on the cleared kitchen table. There were packs of playing cards, but Chloe didn't feel like solitaire.

In the living room, stuffed partway behind the couch, she found a guitar case. Chloe pulled it carefully out and opened the case. All the strings of the guitar were intact. She looked around.

"Does this belong to someone? Is it okay if I look at it...?"

Mr. Dietz looked at it, his lips pursed. "I haven't seen that for a while! It belonged to Samuel. He... he's not here anymore. Go ahead, if you know how to play."

"He won't be back looking for it?"

He shook his head. "No. He won't be back."

Chloe sat down on the couch and held the guitar in her lap. She picked the strings one at a time, but they didn't sound right. She played with the tuning pegs, playing each string one at a time and trying to get them to match the sound in her head. After a few minutes, she strummed it, and felt a thrill at the chord that came out.

"Sounds good," Mr. Dietz said. "I didn't know you played."

"I don't," Chloe admitted. "But I'd like to learn."

"Well, that sounded pretty good."

Chloe shrugged. "But that's just one chord. And it probably still isn't tuned right."

"It sounded right to me."

She picked each of the strings again, running up and down the scale one or two strings at a time.

Marilla walked into the living room and watched Chloe play. Chloe grinned at her. Marilla clapped politely. "Very nice. They should give you a job at the symphony."

Chloe shook her head and strummed quietly.

"I don't really know how to play," she admitted.

"Well, I guess not. Most people don't know how the first time they pick one up."

Chloe sighed and moved to put the guitar away again.

"You could watch videos on the internet," Marilla suggested. "There's lots of basic teaching videos like that. You could at least learn the chords and a few songs."

"Really?" Chloe considered this. "I've never seen anything like that."

"Sure. We could see if they'll let us borrow the computer here for a few minutes. And the library has put some in for the public to use. We can go there tomorrow."

Chloe picked the guitar up again. "Cool," she said, holding it against her. "Videos would be a good way to learn."

Marilla was as good as her word and took Chloe with her to the public library the next day to show her how to find guitar lesson videos on the computer. Chloe was excited. She leaned in while Marilla tried a few different search strings and pulled up a few sites that hosted guitar tutorials.

Then a wave of cold passed over her as she remembered Bill's words. About how Blue Jeans had uploaded videos of Chloe, and now they were out there, and no one could ever ensure that they were all erased. She watched the hands of the video tutorial that Marilla played, but she didn't see the guitar player's hands. She saw herself. There must be dozens of videos. And maybe hundreds of perverts who had downloaded them to watch her and stare at her body.

"Chloe?" Marilla shook her. "Chloe, are you okay? What's wrong?"

Chloe realized that her cheeks were wet, and rubbed away tears.

The first tears that she had cried since being taken away from her home. Chloe sniffled.

"No, I'm fine. I was just thinking of something."

"Do you want... to watch another one? Or is this too much for you?"

Chloe blinked and scrubbed at her eyes. "Can you play that one again? I didn't really see it."

"Are you sure?" Marilla's hand hovered over the mouse, reluctant to play it again.

"It wasn't the lesson, it was something else," Chloe assured her. "I'm okay. I'll pay attention this time."

Marilla nodded and clicked the play button once more. Chloe forced herself to listen to the tutorial, watching the finger positions carefully, rather than thinking of any other videos that might be in existence.

When they were done, Chloe picked up her guitar case, eager to try out what she had learned.

"Let's go outside so I can try," she suggested.

"Sure," Marilla agreed. "You think you got all that?" Marilla shook her head. "That was an awful lot of information."

"I have to try it out before I forget anything."

They didn't go back to the group home, but found a bench under a tree on the library grounds and sat down. Chloe took her guitar out and tuned the strings again. It was easier this time. She strummed it a few times and then tried out the chords that the videos had shown. The strings hurt her fingers, unused to playing and with no padding of flesh or callous to protect them. Marilla sat watching her.

"I'd swear you've been doing it for years," she said. "How did you remember all the string combinations?"

"There were only three of them in the first lesson," Chloe pointed out. "That's not so much to remember." She ran through the three chords in a quick progression. Then she tried one of the simple songs that the tutorial had taught. She did it more by ear than by memory, pressing down the strings and then looking for the notes or trying to remember where they were from the last time she had played them. In a few minutes, she ran through Three Blind Mice from start to finish, with only a couple of fumbles.

Someone walking by tossed a coin into Chloe's guitar case. Startled, Chloe looked at Marilla. Marilla laughed.

"This just gets better all the time. And you thought you had no marketable skills."

"Yeah, as soon as I find a place where the rent is only twenty-five cents, I'll be golden." Chloe strummed a loud chord for emphasis. Marilla laughed again.

Chloe continued to practice, eventually getting two songs down pat. As she played and laughed with Marilla, more people tossed coins into the open guitar case. Marilla picked a few of them up.

"Put these in your pocket. If people think you are getting too much money, they won't give any more."

"But I don't need it," Chloe pointed out. "I didn't ask for money. People just did it because they wanted to."

"You're not going to turn down a good thing! You're getting money, so keep playing. Don't tell me that there's nothing you want to buy. Clothes, makeup, I don't know what else you want. Money is money, girl. You don't throw away the opportunity."

"I guess," Chloe agreed. She pocketed the money as Marilla had instructed and continued to practice.

Playing guitar was something that occupied Chloe's time and that she got a little bit of pleasure out of. And as Marilla said, money was money. And Chloe needed money to buy the little things that Social Services and the group home did not provide. They gave her a bed, a roof over her head, food, and the bare minimum in clothing, but that was it. Residents were expected to find jobs and become independent, though Chloe wasn't sure how. In just a few days, she had already seen a couple of residents 'bounced' out of the house for breaking the rules, sent back to prison or out on the street. She was terrified they would decide she had done something to break the rules and bounce her too. Chloe always followed the rules, always did her best to be good, but the rules at the group home overwhelmed her, there were so many. She was sure that she would make a mistake and end up bounced as well.

But no one seemed to object to her new routine of going to the library to watch some more guitar tutorials, and then sitting for a few hours playing for change. Chloe didn't say that she was playing guitar instead of looking for work, but she thought the supervisors probably understood that without her saying so.

"You're looking better."

Chloe was jolted out of her thoughts and looked around for the source of the voice. It was Jozef again, the man who had helped her when she got lost. He stood nearby with his hands in his pockets, listening to Chloe play.

"Oh—hi. Jozef."

"Hi, Chloe." He gave her a warm smile. "You're feeling a lot better today, huh?"

She nodded and started playing again, realizing that she had stopped. "Yeah. I'm doing good."

"You mind if I keep you company for a little while?"

Chloe looked at the empty seat next to her on the bench. "It's not my bench. You can sit where you want."

He sat down next to her. "Thanks."

She nodded.

"You play very well. You didn't have a guitar with you the other day."

"I'm just learning. I didn't have it yet that day."

"You're just learning?" Jozef raised his black eyebrows. "You sound like you've been playing for years. Are you putting me on?"

"No." Chloe laughed. "I just started a few days ago. I never played before that."

"You're like a musical genius. That's amazing."

Chloe waved it off. "It's just fooling around," she said. But she was pleased with the compliment. When she was little, she had wanted to learn to play the piano, but Mim had told her that she had no talent, and Mim wasn't going to waste her money on lessons for something Chloe would only want to give up after a month.

Learning guitar was better. You couldn't carry a piano around and play it on the street.

She glanced up from her guitar at Jozef and looked away again. He was a nice guy. He had helped her out. But she wasn't sure if he was actually interested in her. He had stopped to talk with her when he saw her playing, and he didn't look like he was going to be leaving anytime soon. Maybe he was.

For a while, they talked a little while Chloe played through the songs that she had learned and practiced the finger placements for the new chords that she had learned. But a couple of people could only talk about the weather and how busy the streets were for so long. A couple of times, Jozef had floated more personal questions, but Chloe resisted. She didn't want to share anything about her personal life. He didn't need to know about Mim and Blue Jeans and the police and the babies. Chloe was trying to forget about all of that.

"I could really go for a coffee right about now," Jozef said. "How about you? Can I treat you to a coffee? Maybe a muffin?"

Chloe chewed on her lip, thinking about it.

"Chocolate chip muffin..." Jozef wheedled.

Chloe's stomach liked the sound of that, giving a little pulse of hunger that spread through her body, crystallizing her desire for food. And not just any food, but a chocolate chip muffin. Chloe's mouth watered.

"Umm... maybe. Where?"

"There's a little coffee shop just about a block over. With the red and white awning? You've seen it."

Chloe thought that she had. She was still wary of getting too far away from the home, worried that she was going to get turned around again and not know her way back. But the coffee shop was only a block away. And Jozef knew which direction she needed to go if she had problems getting home again.

"Yeah... okay." Chloe picked the loose change out of her guitar case and added it to her pocket. "I can pay, though. I owe you a favor for helping me out."

"No, not at all. That didn't cost me anything, and it wasn't even a long walk. I suggested coffee, so I'm buying."

Chloe considered this but decided she didn't feel too bad about him paying. "If you really want," she said finally.

Jozef smiled with approval. "Good." He watched Chloe put her guitar away. "Can I carry that for you?"

Chloe was reluctant to hand it over, even though she knew he was a good guy. He wasn't going to run off with it, steal the one possession that she owned. But she couldn't bring herself to hand it over.

"I... um... I want to carry it myself."

"Okay." His smile assured her that was all right; he wasn't angry with her. They walked together to the coffee shop. It wasn't too crowded, so they were able to find a table where Chloe could put her guitar down without tripping anyone up.

"Chocolate chip?" Jozef asked. "Or did you want another kind? They have an awesome cranberry orange. Lots of different flavors. Whatever looks good to you."

"Chocolate chip," Chloe said. That was what she had been anticipating ever since he had said it. If she were to change to another flavor now, her body would not be happy about it.

"Perfect. What kind of coffee?"

Chloe looked up at the densely-written menu board. They had all the fancy kinds of coffee a person couldn't make at home. And different kinds of spices, creamers, and flavorings to add to each one. She could be there all day just trying to read through all the different choices.

"Um... You know, I just like regular coffee. Black. Nothing else. I'm already having a dessert. Don't need sugar in the coffee too."

She remembered how Gunter had rolled his eyes at the fancy designer coffees. *Six hundred calories for a hot drink? What kind of moron drinks all their calories like that?*

"You're sure. Just black?"

Chloe hesitated. Did Jozef *want* her to have one of the higher-calorie drinks? Did he think she was too skinny, so he was suggesting a coffee that would help her put on more weight? Chloe tried to read his expression so that she could give the right answer. He didn't seem angry or stern. Just inquiring. Coming to a fancy coffee shop and then just ordering a plain cup of joe did seem a little odd. But she had come for the chocolate chip muffin.

"Yeah. If that's okay with you," Chloe said tentatively.

"Of course. I don't care what you drink," Jozef said, with a 'whatever' gesture.

Chloe smiled back and nodded, but inside her stomach had started twisting. Maybe he didn't care anything for her. Maybe he was just bored and thought that buying a weird, nearly-homeless girl a meal was a nice thing to do. He didn't care what she ate because he didn't care about her.

When he returned to the table and distributed their coffee and treats, Chloe tried to analyze him. He wasn't angry, and he wasn't bored and distracted. Not that she could tell from his pleasant expression. They both settled in, taking small bites of their food—Jozef had ordered one of the cranberry orange muffins he had extolled—and waiting for their coffee to cool enough to drink. Maybe she should have ordered the cranberry orange muffin that he had suggested. He hadn't acted like it mattered, but maybe it did. Maybe that was the way that he expected her to show him that she returned his feelings for her. And by not ordering it, she had hurt him.

"Would you like a taste?" Jozef asked, seeing Chloe's eyes on his muffin. He broke a piece off and held it out to her.

Chloe took it and chewed slowly. She wasn't a big fan of cranberry. She liked her berries sweet, if she was going to have any. The tart berries always left a funny taste in her mouth, and it wasn't erased by the acidic tones of the orange cake.

"It's good," she lied. "Really nice."

"Delicious, right? Do you want to go halves? You can have half of my muffin if you want to trade."

"No," Chloe said hastily. "It's so sour after the chocolate chips..." She looked down at the muffin. "Did you want a taste? Here."

She quickly broke off a piece and handed it across to Jozef. He tried to protest, but took it when she put it into his hand.

"I always feel a little bit guilty when I eat those," Jozef said. "Like I'm sneaking dessert before dinner. When they are warm right out of the oven..." he rolled his eyes in ecstasy. "They are just unbelievable."

Was he telling Chloe that she should feel guilty for eating it? Chloe was so confused by his easy-going manner. Gunter and the other boyfriends had always been clear what they wanted. There was no guessing. They just said it straight out.

Joelle gave Chloe's arm a sharp pinch to wake her up. Chloe pulled away and curled up into a ball to protect herself.

"Ouch!" she protested. "That hurt!"

It was sure to leave a bruise on Chloe's fragile, fair skin. She had suffered much worse abuse and injury in the past, but she was outraged over being woken up that way.

"You've been here long enough to know what time to wake up. I shouldn't have to be in here every morning shaking you awake!"

"That wasn't shaking; that was pinching!"

"And I'll do worse if you don't shape up," Joelle said nastily. "Seven o'clock is plenty late to sleep in, especially when you go to bed so early. Get yourself up tomorrow, or I won't be nearly so nice."

Joelle went on to wake up any others who needed to be rousted out of their beds. Chloe sat up, rubbing her bruised arm. Ivy, the girl that she roomed with, had apparently woken up before the seven o'clock reveille and was getting dressed. She shut the door behind Joelle, shaking her head.

"Man, who crapped in her cornflakes?"

Chloe giggled. "Guess she got out on the wrong side the bed," she offered.

"Maybe her boyfriend dumped her," Ivy said, pulling on a pair of pants.

Chloe frowned. She knew how that felt. If Joelle had been dumped by her boyfriend, then she deserved sympathy, not to be made fun of by the residents.

"What?" Ivy demanded.

"That's mean."

"What are you, two? She was being *mean* to you."

"I know, but... we don't know why she's acting like that. Maybe something bad did happen to her."

"Yeah. She has to wake up with that face every morning. That's enough to make anyone cranky."

Chloe went over to the dresser to get clothes out of her drawer. Ivy made a snorting noise and left the room, not shutting the door behind her. Chloe shut the door firmly and changed out of her nightgown.

When she went down the hall to the bathroom, she found a short lineup outside. With a groan, she fell in behind Masoud to wait.

"Wicked Witch of the West roll you out of bed too?" he asked with a grin.

Chloe shrugged. "Yeah, whatever. I don't know what she's in such a bad mood about this morning." She looked at her arm where Joelle had pinched her. It was a dull red.

"She do that to you?" Masoud inquired.

"Yeah. It's nothing. Just a little tender."

He called Joelle a name under his breath. At least, Chloe thought that he was referring to Joelle, and not to Chloe. "You want me to kiss it better?" Masoud asked in a teasing voice.

Chloe looked up at him, surprised. Before she could prepare herself, Masoud bent down and kissed her on the lips. Chloe recoiled, banging into the wall.

"Whoa," he said, "take it easy!" He wrapped his arms around her and pulled her close to kiss her again. Chloe struck out wildly, but her blows had no effect on him.

"Leave her alone!" Chloe recognized Lara's voice, and Lara apparently struck him, because Chloe felt the blow through Masoud's body, and he loosened his grip and backed off.

"What's your problem?" he demanded, turning on Lara. "Mind your own business!"

"Leave Chloe alone, Masoud!" She shoved him again.

Masoud raised his hands, looking offended. "I don't hear *her* complaining. We're just having a little fun."

"Keep your hands to yourself."

"I don't hear her complaining," Masoud repeated.

Lara turned toward Chloe. "Tell him!"

Chloe's mouth was dry. A lump burned in her throat and she couldn't get a sound out. She pushed past both of them. Abandoning the wait for the bathroom, she went down the stairs to where the supervisors were.

Instead of John serving breakfast, it was Darnell, a supervisor who had just started a couple of days before. Chloe was sure it was John's day, so she was taken aback to see the skinny, braided black man instead of the fat Samoan.

"Good morning," Darnell greeted. "What's the big hurry? You're going to fall down the stairs."

Chloe let out her breath. She still couldn't seem to find words. Lara hurried down the stairs behind Chloe, swearing under her breath.

"You know what that Masoud is doing?" she demanded of Darnell.

"He grabs Chloe and kisses her. Just holds her still and lays it on her. You gotta bounce him! You bounce him, or I'm calling the cops."

"Settle down, Laura." Darnell scooped another batch of scrambled eggs into the serving dish. "Why don't you let Chloe tell me what happened?"

"It's Lara," she snapped. "Never call me Laura!"

He blinked at her. "I'm sorry. I didn't mean to offend you. Names can be tricky. Lara."

Lara nodded and turned to face Chloe expectantly. "Well? Tell him! Bounce Masoud right out of here!"

Chloe said nothing. She went to the table and sat down and poured herself an orange juice. She drank it, rinsing the foul taste of the boy out of her mouth and trying to calm herself down enough that she could speak. She was so outraged and angry and flustered that she couldn't find her voice. She took a few deep breaths and pulled herself out of the situation. Masoud could do what he liked. It didn't hurt Chloe. Chloe had been hurt too many times for a little thing like that to bother her. When she pulled herself away from feeling anything, her body relaxed and she was able to take a deep breath without feeling like she was drowning.

"It was nothing," she said. "I can handle it myself."

"What?" Lara screeched. "You gotta tell Darnell. And he'll get rid of Masoud. You don't have to put up with that."

And who would replace Masoud? Within another day or two, another boy would be transferred in. Likely fresh out of prison. Maybe he'd toe the line for a few days and maybe he wouldn't. Chloe knew from experience; each one could be worse than the last. It was best for her to keep quiet and keep her head down.

"Okay, leave it be," Darnell told Lara. "Give Chloe a little time and space, and if she changes her mind and wants to talk to me about it, she can." He met Chloe's eyes and made sure that she understood this. "Until she's ready to make a report, you need to just let it go."

Lara swore, first at Darnell and then at Chloe. "Great job! You know what you're doing to the rest of us when you won't report it? Who's next, huh? Who's gonna be next? And what if nobody's there to stop him? What then, huh?"

Lara stomped off up the stairs. Chloe stared down at the table, aware that Darnell and the rest of those who were eating were looking at her. Darnell threw some more buttered toast onto the stack and turned off the burners on the stove.

"Come with me for a minute, Chloe," he said.

Chloe took another drink of her orange juice and followed him. She didn't feel any anxiety about it. All her emotions were already turned off. He led her to one of the main floor bedrooms that now served as an administrative office and retreat for the supervisors.

"You're okay?" Darnell asked.

Chloe nodded.

"You know that you have the right to report if anyone is bullying you or behaving inappropriately."

"Yeah. I said I'm fine. I don't want to report anyone."

"Okay." He shrugged. "You're not required to. I'm not going to push you."

Chloe nodded again. He motioned for her to step out of the office ahead of him. Chloe turned sideways to squeeze by him, as he was standing in the doorway. As she slid by in front of him, he reached out and smacked her on the rump.

Chloe was too numb to care. She didn't even look back at him.

CHAPTER
Twenty-One

Chloe's stomach was too upset to eat anything for breakfast. And she was used to going long periods of time without food, so it didn't bother her to skip one meal. Sometimes it was more work to eat than it was to go without. It was one less thing to worry about. She gathered together her few possessions and stuffed them into a backpack from the closet. She didn't know whose the backpack was, but it wasn't in use and a lot of stuff just got left at the group home when previous residents were bounced or moved on somewhere else. With the backpack and her guitar, she left the group home. Good riddance. She would be better off on her own than having to deal with all of the rules and personalities at the group home.

She had slowly been learning her way around the neighborhood, and she was aware of others who were homeless, living on the street or in emergency shelters. She didn't need to contend with the group home and its dangers and endless rules. She was earning enough with her guitar playing to buy something to eat. She didn't need much. And she'd keep going to the library and learning more songs on her guitar. She could try setting up in some new places, where there was more foot traffic, so it wasn't always the same people seeing her, who would get tired of giving her money after a few times. The bus and train stations were good places to get lots of people on their daily commutes or shopping trips.

Ruby had been living on her own for years, hanging out with gangs or sleeping with friends. If Ruby could do it, Chloe could too.

~

"Mommy, I want to listen!"

Chloe didn't stop playing, but followed the mother and child with her eyes. The mother was similar to Chloe in many ways. A girl in her late teens or early twenties. Blond, slim, around Chloe's height. She wore dirty blue jeans, and a worn hoodie pulled up over her head. The little girl was maybe four or five, her hair and eyes dark. She wore a little pink jacket that was a size too big for her. Better than too small, Chloe supposed.

The mother looked exhausted, but at the little girl's insistence and pulls on her hand, she stopped to listen to Chloe's guitar playing. When Chloe finished the song that she was on, she switched to another she had been working on. The theme song from the newest Disney release. The little girl's eyes lit up, and she tugged on her mother's arm.

"Listen, Mommy! She's playing *my* song!"

The woman smiled faintly. When Chloe was done the song, she stopped and put her hand over the strings to stop them from vibrating.

"Hi," she said to the little girl.

"Hi! You play really good! That's my favorite song!"

"I thought you might like that one."

"I do!"

The mother stood there looking Chloe over. "I don't have money for you," she said, a bit of a challenge in her voice.

"That's okay," Chloe said with a headshake. "You need it more." She took two dollars out of the guitar case and held it out to them.

The little girl moved forward to grab it, and the woman jerked her back. "No, Babe. We don't take money from people like that."

Babe looked up at her, face crumpling like she was going to cry. "People like what?" she whined. "People give us money."

"Not homeless people," the mother snapped. She rolled her eyes at Chloe and shook her head. "Sorry. She just doesn't understand."

"I meant it, though. You can have it. Buy a muffin or something for supper."

"We'll go to the soup kitchen for supper. That's where we're headed right now. Are you going?"

Chloe glanced up at the sky, estimating the time. "It's too early for supper."

"If you want to get something and get to a shelter in time for a bed, you've got to head over pretty early. Before the working stiffs start getting off. Later there's a bottleneck."

"Is it open this early?"

"No. We'll get in line. Be first in and first out."

Chloe thought about this. "I'm okay," she said eventually. "I don't need a shelter. The weather's warm enough."

"You want to start going when it is still warm so that you can get one of the permanent beds once it gets cold. It's the regulars, the people they know, who will get into the special winter programs."

Chloe considered it for a few minutes, then nodded. "You don't mind a tag-along?"

"No. Feel free."

"Okay. Thanks."

Chloe put away her money and laid the guitar in its case.

"Is your name really Babe?" she asked the little girl, as she stood up.

"Yes."

"I'm Chloe."

"I've never known anyone named Chloe," Babe said seriously.

"Well, I've never known anyone named Babe."

The mother touched Babe on the back to move her along. "I'm Jenny," she said.

"Nice to meet you."

They walked in silence for a few minutes. "I don't think I've seen you around before," Jenny said. "Are you new around here?"

"Pretty new, yeah."

"Yeah, well... welcome," Jenny said with a little laugh.

Chloe took a slow look around at their surroundings. The busy sidewalks and dusty storefronts might not be homey, but they were home. "I've been worse places."

Jenny gave a little nod. "Me too, I guess. Better to be out here, trying to make it on your own, then somewhere you're getting hurt."

"Uh-huh."

Chloe went to the soup kitchen with Jenny and Babe, but when it came time to go to the shelter, she grew anxious.

"I think... I'll just sleep out, tonight."

"Remember what I said? You won't be able to get into any of the winter programs," Jenny told her.

"Maybe tomorrow. I just... tonight I want to be out in the open air, where I can breathe."

"It's not that bad," Jenny said. "It's warm, and it's safe. Out on the street, anyone coming along can hurt you. You can't protect yourself from some dude with a baseball bat or a gang of teenagers."

Chloe thought about the shelter that she had been at in between being taken away from her home and put into the group home. The babies crying, the coughing and yelling, other disruptions in the night with people wanting to leave or to get in after closing.

The babies crying.

She shook her head, touching her temple as it throbbed.

"I know. I just... can't tonight. Maybe tomorrow."

"Won't you wait with us?" Babe asked, her lower lip sticking out in a pout. "I thought you were going to stay in the line with us. We have to wait for a long time!"

"I know, Babe... maybe I can wait in line with you for a little while, but I'm not going to go in to sleep."

"Okay." Babe accepted this cheerfully. "Will you play me some more songs on your guitar?"

"Sure."

Most of the others who were lined up were already sitting on the pavement, knowing that they were going to be there for a couple of hours. So it was not strange for Chloe to sit down to take out her guitar.

People watched her as she played, but she didn't care. She played the songs that she figured Babe would like and ran through the rest of her limited repertoire. A few of the homeless people sitting and waiting smiled at her or gave her a thumbs-up.

"I thought I recognized that guitar."

Chloe looked up at a passerby who had stopped and spoken. It was Jozef. He smiled at her.

"I'd know your playing anywhere, Chloe."

"That's just because you've heard all my songs," Chloe dismissed. But she smiled at his words.

"So..." His eyes went to the main entrance of the shelter and then back at her. "Everything okay?"

"Fine. Just visiting with some friends," Chloe nodded to Jenny and Babe. Babe gave Jozef a little wave, and he smiled broadly.

"Well, hi, there," he greeted.

Babe smiled back at him, but Jenny put her arm around Babe, pulling her closer and scowling.

"You don't talk to strangers," she growled.

Jozef's face fell. "Oh, I'm sorry. I didn't mean..."

"You should know a little girl can't be talking to strange men."

"Yeah. Sorry. I wasn't thinking about that."

"If I let every sicko off the street talk to her, I would've lost her a long time ago. You don't talk to little girls."

Jozef stood there awkwardly. He looked back at Chloe. She rolled her eyes at him.

"Sorry," she apologized for Jenny's attack.

"Do you want to go somewhere, have a coffee?" he suggested. "I mean, I understand if you're busy here. I'm interrupting..."

"Yeah." Chloe shrugged. "Maybe next time. I'm gonna stay here and visit for a while."

"Okay. Um... I guess I'll see you around. Are you still at the... at the same place?" he was cautious of what he said in front of the others.

"No. Not anymore."

"Where are you staying? Here?" He gestured to the emergency shelter.

"No. I'm not sure where yet. I guess... we'll run into each other again."

"Sure." He smiled. "I'll be listening for your guitar."

Chloe nodded. She strummed the guitar, then started playing a song, looking down at it. He walked away down the street.

"That your boyfriend?" asked another woman waiting in the line.

Chloe looked at her. Black. She had a young, unlined face, but could have been anywhere between sixteen and forty. She looked tired and worn. A drug user? Chloe pushed the thought immediately away. How often had she been judged lately as a junkie just because of her gaunt appearance? The woman was tired from working all day. Anyone could be tired.

"No," Chloe said. "Just… a friend, I guess. Helped me out one day."

"He's cute. Seems like a nice guy. You should hook up with him, get yourself off the street."

Chloe was shocked. "I hardly know him!"

"Yeah, well you said he helped you out, didn't you? Just tell him you need a place to sleep for the night. He'll invite you to his place, and you just make yourself at home. You'll be his girlfriend in no time. He doesn't already have a girl, does he?"

"No… I don't know. I don't really know anything about him. I just know his face, to say hi to."

"Get yourself in there. You gotta take the opportunity. Before someone else does."

Chloe looked down at her guitar, picking the strings in random scales and riffs.

"I couldn't do that."

"Sure you could. You deserve it, don't you? A warm bed? A roof over your head that's not a place like this? Permanent? Or for as long as he'll keep you."

"I guess. But I don't know him that well."

"Well, get proactive, girl. That's the only way to survive."

Chloe looked over at Jenny to see what she thought of this suggestion. Jenny was cuddling Babe close, giving her a sip from a water bottle. Jenny's eyes were dark and angry.

"Not exactly an option when you've got a kid, like me," she said. "Guys don't want someone else's baby under their feet. Sometimes not even their own baby."

Babe looked up at her mother, her eyes sad, mouth pointing down. Jenny kissed her roughly on the top of the head. "You're my Babe and I'm not giving you up for any man," she assured the little girl. "We can make it on our own, can't we?"

Babe nodded and snuggled down. "Just you and me," she whispered.

"That's right. Just you and me. We don't need no one else."

"You wouldn't be here if you didn't need no one else," the black woman challenged. "You'd be living in your own pad and feeding your own kid. You need help just like the rest of us. I'm just talking about a different kind of help."

Jenny shook her head. "Not for me," she asserted.

Chloe didn't look at either one of them. She was pretty sure that Jozef had no thoughts of taking her under his roof and providing for her. He hardly even knew her. A guy didn't just pick up a homeless girl off the street and let her into his house. Jozef seemed like a nice enough guy, but he wasn't that interested in her. She didn't mean anything to him. He was just a nice guy who had stopped to help her once.

"I'm Abony," the black woman introduced herself abruptly.

Chloe glanced in her direction.

"Ebony?" she repeated.

"No, Abony. With an A."

"Oh. Okay. I'm Chloe."

"Nice to meet you, Chloe. You're not going to stay here tonight?"

"Uh... no."

"You should. You're crazy to be thinking of sleeping rough." She looked at Chloe's backpack. "You don't even have a sleeping bag or blanket. Where are you going to sleep that the cops aren't gonna roust you? Thought of that?"

"I got a few places in mind," Chloe said cautiously.

Abony shook her head in derision. "You're gonna end up in the pokey first night," she predicted. "That, or beat up."

Chloe looked away from Abony and back at her guitar. She was growing more and more uncomfortable sitting there in the line. Not just her tailbone, which was killing her sitting on the cold, hard concrete, but she didn't particularly want to stay around people who thought she was being stupid. They didn't know anything about Chloe. They didn't know how tough she was or if she could handle a night on the streets. Or living on the street permanently. Chloe hadn't thought about how long it might be. She would like to work her way up to having her own little apartment, but she wasn't going to be able to afford anything playing her guitar on the sidewalk.

She stopped mid-song and put her hand over the strings. "I gotta go."

Jenny looked at her, surprised at the abruptness. "Are you okay?"

"Yeah. I just gotta get out of here. I'll... I guess I'll see you around, right?"

"You gonna go to the soup kitchen for breakfast? It's not much, but you can get something warm in your belly."

"Breakfast is the most important meal of the day," Babe said seriously.

Chloe shook her head. "Probably not. I don't eat much."

"That's obvious," Jenny said, looking at Chloe's body. "You got anorexia or something?"

"No, I was..." Chloe busied herself with putting her guitar away. She didn't want to talk about what had happened to her. She wanted to put that as far away from her as possible. She remembered what Marilla had said to her before. "Maybe I'll tell you about it sometime."

Jenny shifted Babe in her lap, looking for a more comfortable position. "Whatever."

Chloe got creakily to her feet. "See you later," she told them, as a group. "Bye, Babe,"

Babe smiled at her. "Bye-bye." She waved.

Despite Abony's prediction, Chloe did not get rousted by the cops the first night. Nor did she get beaten up by a random passerby. But she didn't get much sleep either. Abony was right about the sleeping bag. Chloe needed one if she was going to make it through the night comfortably. Or in some semblance of comfort. Chloe stayed on the move most of the night. Stopping and sleeping under a tree or in a sheltered back alley for a few minutes, and then waking and moving on again. When the sun started to come up, she walked along the street, quiet for once, and watched the sky get brighter. Before long, they would be waking the sleepers at the group home. And for once, Chloe was already awake. No one would be pinching her, or worse. Not anymore. She was in charge of herself now.

Chloe counted her money out of sight of anyone on the street and considered whether to get herself something for breakfast. She didn't much feel like eating, and could save her money for another time, so she didn't bother.

She selected a park bench that was passed by the morning commuters getting off the bus and train, and started to play. She kept the music quiet, not wanting to irritate anyone who hadn't had their morning coffee yet.

A police car rolled up and stopped in front of her. Chloe stopped playing as the officer got out and walked up to her.

"You got a license?" he demanded.

Chloe looked at him, uncertain. "A driver's license?" she asked.

"Don't play games with me! You got a busking license?"

"Busking...?"

He kicked at her guitar case. "Busking. Performing in public. Panhandling. You got a license?"

"Um... no. I didn't know... where would I get one?"

"City Hall, where do you think?"

"Okay. I guess... I'll go and get one."

He sneered at her. "Yeah, you will, huh? You don't have one, so you're getting a ticket." He pulled out his small clipboard of forms and pulled a new triplicate over the cardboard divider to the front. "You got the money to pay a ticket?"

"No... I have a little. How much is the ticket?"

"Hundred bucks. You don't pay it; you're going to jail until you can."

"How can I get the money if I'm in jail?"

He smiled, showing his teeth. "That's not my problem."

"But..."

He continued to smile. He looked more like a predator baring his teeth than someone who was friendly or amused. "Name?"

"What if... what if I give you the money I have? It's not a hundred, but..." she trailed off.

He didn't say no, which gave her a little hope. "How much have you got?"

"I have... thirty-three."

"Are you trying to bribe an officer of the law not to give you a ticket?"

"No! I'm just... um... negotiating... It doesn't help you if I get thrown in jail and can't pay anything. I just thought..." She smiled weakly, trying to charm him, but knowing that she wouldn't succeed.

"Thirty-three isn't much."

"It's all I have."

"How are you going to pay for your busking license?"

Chloe's stomach clenched. "I'll... get more money."

"By busking? Without a license?"

She shrugged hopelessly. He held out his hand, and Chloe just looked at it.

"Your money."

Chloe realized that he was going to let her pay up front and dug into her pockets. She transferred all the bills that she had into his hand. When she started to scoop out the coins, he shook his head.

"Keep the change; I'm not going to walk around weighed down with all that coin."

"Oh, okay. Thank you."

"Next time, I'll expect you to have more. And a license."

Chloe stared at him. He wanted to be paid off *and* for her to have a license? He was going to shake her down even if she got a busking license?

He smiled at her again and got back into his car. Chloe watched him drive away, her brain whirling. She let her fingers play the guitar without her brain engaging, trying to understand what had just happened. She was going to have to revise her ideas of finances if she was going to have to pay off a cop every day. What if it was more than one cop? More than one a day? She wouldn't be able to give them all her money. Not if she was going to survive.

Chloe's entrance into the little shop was heralded by tinkling bells that made the woman at the till look up to see her new customer. Her welcoming smile changed to a scowl.

"Customers only," she snapped. "No bathroom here and no coming in 'just to warm up.' You want to be in here; you buy something."

Chloe's face flushed. She had received similar responses at other establishments all day long, but it still embarrassed her. She didn't know how they could classify her as homeless the instant she walked into the store. She wasn't dirty or unkempt. She had a backpack, but lots of shoppers had backpacks. Did the guitar in her hand give her away?

"I'm... looking for a job," she explained. "I wondered if you had any openings."

The woman looked her over more carefully, considering her reply.

"You have a social security number?"

"Uh... no."

"You got a permanent address?"

"No."

"Then how do you expect me to pay you? I have government forms to be filled in, remittances to be made."

"Can't you just..."

"What? Pay you under the table? That's not the way things work here."

"I don't know... how do I get a number?"

"You'll have to figure that out yourself. But they're not going to give you one without a permanent address."

Chloe apologized and walked back out of the store. It seemed like there were roadblocks everywhere she went. If they wanted homeless people to work, they should make it easy for them. If they didn't want people on the streets, how were they to get jobs?

"Mommy! The guitar lady!"

Chloe turned toward the little voice and smiled at Babe and Jenny. Babe smiled excitedly and ran toward Chloe, already begging for her favorite song, hauling on Jenny's hand to make her move faster.

Jenny smiled, her eyes far away. "Hi, Chloe."

"Hi. How's it going?"

Jenny's eyes focused in on Chloe for a moment; then she looked away again. "Well, not so good. But I should be used to that, right?"

"What's wrong?"

"They're trying to take Babe away from me. Say I can't provide a safe environment for her. Well, how am I supposed to provide a safe environment when no one will give me a place to stay?   All the programs are filled up, overflowing. Moms with kids are supposed to get priority, but I can't get in anywhere. They give me a week to find a place to live. How do they expect me to find a place in a week? They think I haven't been looking for the last three months?"

Chloe nodded. "I'm sorry."

"Nothing you can do about it." Her eyes went down to Babe, then back to Chloe again. "At least you're not using up resources. It's not like you got a room and I didn't."

"Yeah... but I feel bad. They should be able to find you something. I wish I could help."

"You know the biggest problem? All the places that won't take addicts. How am I supposed to get clean if no one will take me? Addicts' kids don't matter? We didn't choose this life!"

Chloe nodded uncertainly. "I... didn't know you were..."

"Who isn't? They want to take away all the programs if you're not clean. Drug testing for food stamps. Employment services. Housing. They think an addict is just going to trash the room. I don't know, have a big party or something." Jenny snorted. "Get clean with no supports, and then you can have the services. Once you don't need them anymore."

Chloe looked down at Babe and realized she was crying. She bent down to the child's level. "Oh, Babe. Don't cry. Your mom will figure something out."

Jenny gave Babe a tight hug and kissed her on the head. "Don't be a baby," she said sternly. "Don't let no one see you cry. You be strong, no matter what happens."

Babe struggled to stop the flow of tears. "I don't want them to take me away from you, Mommy!"

"No. I know. I don't want them to either. But you need a place to live. Somewhere you have a bed every night, and food every meal, three times a day. I just can't give that to you."

"I don't care about that!" Babe wailed.

Chloe flashed back to the days after her father was killed. Sleeping on couches and floors, with nowhere to call her own. Losing all her possessions. But she wouldn't have wanted a house and a bed and toys instead of her mother. She would have willingly given all that up to stay with Mim. Chloe's heart ached for the little girl.

"Oh, sweetie..."

"Don't baby her," Jenny ordered. "She's gonna have to be tough. Do me proud. I don't want anyone thinking I raised a crybaby."

Babe sniffled. "I'm not a crybaby."

"Then quit crying. Life sucks sometimes. Deal with it."

They were all quiet, considering the problem.

"How will they take her away?" Chloe said. "If they don't know where to find you..."

"I don't have any skills like you do," Jenny said. "I don't have cash to buy food and stay under the radar. If I want my little girl to eat, I have to take her to the kitchens. Even if I don't meet with my social worker, she knows I have to go back there. She'll be there with the cops, waiting."

"Oh. Yeah."

Jenny ruffled Babe's fine blond hair. "At least if they put her in a foster home, I've got a better chance at finding a guy who will help me out. Maybe you can give me your boyfriend. We're both blond. Small. He won't even know the difference."

Chloe managed a laugh that was really more of an embarrassed cough. "I told you, he's not my boyfriend. Just... a guy who says hi now and then."

"If you won't take him, don't be surprised if I do."

Chloe patted at her burning cheeks like she was cold. "Do what you like. He's not my boyfriend."

Jenny yanked on Babe, pulling her on down the street, away from Chloe.

CHAPTER
Twenty-Two

The nights were getting colder and colder. Chloe's bones ached all the time. Coffee houses wouldn't turn her away as long as she was a paying customer, so she frequently used them to warm up. But that ate into her finances, the less grungy coffee shops charging exorbitant amounts, even for just a regular cup of joe. Chloe had noticed that the hair on her body had started to grow in thicker, and thought of an animal putting on its winter coat. But her thin layer of fur didn't seem to warm her at all as the weather got colder.

She had gloves with the fingers snipped off so that she could still play her guitar, but she could only play for short periods of time before having to bundle up or go inside to warm herself again.

Chloe decided she had had enough, and it was time to go retrieve her sleeping bag and curl up for the night. While it didn't keep her as warm as she would like, it would be warmer than sitting around without it. Chloe had squirreled it away in an alley, stashed with care in the thin space between a dumpster and a building, where no casual observer would find it. She made her way across the intervening blocks and into the alley, and looked uneasily around.

Everything was wrong. The dumpster had been moved and emptied. Chloe knew the collection schedule, and the dumpster hadn't been due to be cleared. She looked behind it, but it was too far away from the wall to secrete anything, and her sleeping bag was nowhere to be seen on the ground. If the truck lifted and emptied the dumpster, the sleeping bag would just fall down. It wouldn't end up inside the garbage truck. Chloe circled the dumpster. Looked underneath it. Growing more frantic, she moved up and down the alley, looking behind any obstacle where the sleeping bag might have been hidden.

"No... no, no, no..."

She searched the entire alley three times. She even walked out of the alley to check the store fronts and street signs to make sure that she hadn't somehow ended up in the wrong one.

Without a sleeping bag, she would freeze overnight. There was no doubt about it. And she didn't have time to get a new sleeping bag. Too much of her money had gone to coffee she didn't need and cops padding their pension plans, she couldn't afford to buy another one. Even a couple of blankets were beyond her resources.

One of the doors into the alley opened, and the restaurant cook, who she thought was also the owner, glared out at her with bloodshot eyes.

"Get out of here!" he shouted. "No loitering or I'll call the cops! I've had enough bums digging in my dumpster and pissing in my doorway. Get lost!"

Chloe turned and ran. He yelled and swore after her, warning her not to come back. And she wouldn't. She would never go into that alley again.

She walked down the street, letting the crowds jostle her along. She didn't care now if they touched her. If they shoved her. She was used to it. She had no more personal space.

Chloe found herself in front of the women's emergency shelter. But it was late, and she could see that they had already closed their doors for the night. A few women hung around looking as desolate as Chloe felt. All the shelters were filled to overflowing. There just wasn't room for everyone.

"Hey, Chloe!"

Chloe focused in on the young black woman closest to her. "Oh... Abony. Hi."

Abony nodded and sidled up to her. "Down and out?" she asked. "What happened to being self-sufficient? I thought you didn't need anyone's help?"

Chloe rolled her eyes upward, blinking, and managed to stay in control. "Lost my sleeping bag," she said in as casual a voice as she could manage. "So I guess I'm not sleeping tonight. I'll walk to keep warm and get another one tomorrow, once I can scrape up enough cash."

"Come with me. I've got a better solution."

Chloe hesitated. "What? There's no other shelters that will still have space."

"No, but shelters aren't the only ones with beds."

What did she mean? Chloe ran through the possibilities. A hotel? Abony knew that she didn't have enough money. Hospital? A minor injury or faked illness could sometimes be turned into a bed for the night. Maybe a couple of meals too. Was that what Abony had in mind?

In the end, she went with Abony without demanding answers to her questions. Abony wasn't long on words, but Chloe trusted that she knew what she was talking about. They passed homeless sleeping on the sidewalks and cold-looking prostitutes working the street. Abony slowed and looked around carefully, looking anxious about being seen. There were a few other young girls and boys in the otherwise empty courtyard. Chloe strained to see what building they were beside. It was an old high school, rundown, now being used for government offices and some small businesses that rented the space.

"There's nowhere to sleep here," Chloe said, irritated. Did Abony think they could break into the building and sleep on some reception area couch? She couldn't fathom what the plan was.

"Not yet," Abony said, looking amused. "But there will be. Just hang on and wait."

The other young people there didn't have much to say. A few nodded or greeted Abony. None of them knew Chloe, and they didn't say anything to her. A car pulled up, and a few of the youth went over to talk to the driver.

"Are they hookers?" Chloe demanded. "I'm not doing that!"

"Not hookers," Abony said. They both watched as a boy got into the car and the car drove away. "It's only prostitution if you're getting money," Abony explained. "It's just survival. Getting a warm bed for the night."

"What?"

"Don't get all squeamish," Abony said. "You could have asked that boyfriend of yours, but you didn't. So, meet someone new. It's just one night. Though there's always repeats. And sometimes a guy will decide he wants a relationship. Then you've hit the jackpot."

"I'm not doing this," Chloe insisted.

"Why not?"

Chloe tried to come up with a logical reason to refuse. It wasn't like she was untouched. It wasn't illegal. Was it so wrong just to want to survive? To have a warm bed for one night, a soft bed where she could rest her aching bones for once? She hadn't had any human contact for a long time, and the thought of a warm body next to hers was not unpleasant. She knew that her mother would say that it was wrong for her to do, but Mim wasn't there. And Chloe was coming to understand that Mim herself had not always chosen the most virtuous path. And she'd frequently put Chloe in harm's way.

"Why not?" Abony persisted.

Chloe couldn't come up with a reason.

Abony assured Chloe that the only people who knew about the pickup area were those who were deemed to be safe. 'Friendlies' who provided a safe haven for a night and wouldn't ever hurt the person they took in. Chloe doubted there could ever be a foolproof screening system. But she'd been through enough abuse that she just pushed it out of her mind. What was one more? Especially if it meant a bed and hot food without having to resort to a shelter or group home. Abony said some of them gave gifts if they liked her. Clothes, drugs, or even some cash. She made it sound so good. Chloe had no use for drugs, but anything else a guy wanted to give to her was fine.

Another car drove up. Abony and Chloe were the closest and walked up to it together. In spite of her decision not to be worried about the consequences, Chloe's gut tightened and she half-decided to back out.

"Come on," Abony hissed, grabbing her by the arm. "Don't mess with me."

Chloe went with Abony obediently. They bent down to talk to the driver. Chloe experienced a little jolt of shock when she saw it was a woman. White, classy hair and jewelry, and a nice, newest-model car.

"You want?" Abony murmured to Chloe.

"Uh—no. That's just... weird."

Abony smiled at the woman. Nice broad smile, lots of teeth. "Hiya. Looking for some company?"

The woman smiled politely. "Yes... but not you." Her eyes went briefly to Chloe, then flicked away.

Abony nodded understandingly. "Boy or girl?" she inquired.

"Boy."

Abony straightened up and waved at one of the boys. "Jeremy. Here." She tapped the top of the car. "Think you might know this one."

Jeremy, a skinny white boy who was not dressed for the frigid weather sauntered over. He cheered when he saw the occupant of the car. "I'd move in with this one!" he agreed. "If she'd only offer."

He opened the door and slid in, and in a couple of seconds, the car pulled away.

"Women come here too?" Chloe said to Abony.

"Probably eighty percent men," Abony said with a shrug. "But women get lonely too."

The shiny black car had barely pulled out when a red sports car pulled in. A Mustang, old model, not in top condition, screeched up to where Abony and Chloe were standing. Chloe hung back and as before it was Abony who made the first contact.

"Hey," she greeted, giving a flirty little wiggle. "What's up?"

Chloe was close enough to see the male driver wave Abony away. "White girl," he insisted. "That one." He pointed directly at Chloe.

Abony backed up to let Chloe in. "Okay? See you tomorrow, maybe. Meet me by the shelter again, 'cause we'll be moving the meet somewhere else tomorrow."

Chloe hesitated. "Do I just..."

"Just go have some fun. Stay warm tonight." She winked. "Nice and warm."

Chloe slowly opened the car door and slid into the seat. The man driving was dark blond, with close-cropped hair. Really broad across the chest; a linebacker or body builder, maybe. He didn't seem too tall, but with his legs folded under the dash, Chloe couldn't tell for sure what his full height would be.

"Hi, there," he greeted. He gave her a couple of glances as he pulled out and headed back to the main streets. "Don't think we've met before."

"No. It's... uh... I haven't done this before. But it's cold..."

"Not at my place, it's not. How does a hot shower sound to you?"

Chloe sighed, settling back into her seat. "Sounds heavenly," she admitted.

"Yeah. Maybe some wine and some lasagna, you'll be forgetting all about the cold."

"No wine," Chloe said immediately. "I'm allergic."

"That's a new one by me. Okay, then. Hot beverage of your choice. How's that sound?"

Chloe smiled tentatively. "Really nice," she said.

Maybe it wasn't such a bad idea after all. Chloe was looking forward to getting the frost out of her bones.

He had been so polite and gentlemanly all evening that Chloe was surprised when they slipped into bed, and he started swearing and calling her names. She had almost forgotten who she was with, thinking of him as a friend instead of a man with an agenda.

Chloe remembered the first time that Gunter had switched off his usual politeness and started calling her such filthy, degrading names that her jaw dropped to the floor in astonishment. No one had ever talked to her that way before. But she had quickly grown accustomed to men talking to her like that. It became so common that she hardly even noticed.

She had thought that John—he swore that was his real name, and he wasn't just putting her on—was different. She had let herself slip into a fantasy, imagining that he was Prince Charming. So attentive to her needs, offering her every amenity that she might want. Hot water, food, music, low lights... until they got to the crux. Then he was suddenly every man she'd ever been with, all over again. Chloe changed the channel in her brain, withdrawing from him, going to a place where she could see and hear what was going on without having to feel anything.

When he was done, she would have her soft, warm bed.

Until morning.

Then, like Cinderella leaving the ball, it would all be over.

She was at the library the next time she saw Jozef again. Chloe was watching videos on the public computer, as usual, to learn some new techniques and songs. Her fingers were hard and tough now. No more blisters from playing all day. No more cuts from sliding them up the string too quickly. She was familiar enough with the sound of her guitar now to immediately feel the songs and techniques in her body as she watched the videos. She had only to complete the circuit by picking up her guitar and trying them out. There was a lot of competition for the computers, so she had to be there soon after the library opened, and do her research before people started to hang over her, waiting for her to finish.

"That looks hard."

Chloe had seen Jozef coming, so she didn't startle. He never seemed to say hi, he just jumped right in on a conversation as soon as he was close enough to speak to her.

"It's not bad," Chloe said, miming the fingering as if she was holding her guitar in her lap. He stared at her hands.

"It looks even harder when you do it. How can you move them that quickly?"

"Just practice."

"You're really good."

He always said that. Chloe yawned and rubbed her eyes before remembering the bruise around the right eye, puffy and tender. She flinched at her own touch and pulled away.

Jozef's eyes lingered on her face, but he didn't ask her how she had gotten hurt. It was such a slight bruise; maybe he didn't even notice.

"How's it been going?" he asked. "I've been watching for you, but I haven't seen you around."

"Yeah. I haven't been playing a lot lately," Chloe admitted. "It's cold out. And I've been trying to get a job."

"Oh!" His eyes lit up. "What are you looking for? Maybe I can help."

"Well... anything. I want to be able to get a little apartment. A place of my own."

"You had a place, at the group home. Where are you now? Why didn't you stay?"

Chloe gave a shrug. "Here and there," she said, careful not to answer his question or to dwell on the fact that she hadn't given him any information. "I don't have any experience, so... I don't know what you do or what kind of openings you might know about..."

"I'm a professor, actually. At the college." Chloe looked at him blankly. "I teach."

"You're a teacher?"

"Yes."

"Well, I can't do that. There isn't going to be anywhere at a college where someone like me with no experience, can work."

Jozef tilted his head up stubbornly. "Don't discount it right away! There are a lot of places on campus where kids who are just starting out can work. They're used to hiring kids right out of high school."

Chloe raised her brows. "Really?" She didn't dare hope that he actually could find her a job. She'd been running into dead ends everywhere that she asked. No one wanted a street kid with no papers and no experience. They all thought that she would rob them. Or be unreliable. Or do some other horrible thing that Chloe had never thought of, like throwing up on a customer. Chloe had never done that.

"Really," Jozef assured her. "I'll ask around and see what I can find. Where can I get a hold of you if I do? You don't have a phone number, I guess."

"No... I'm here most mornings when it opens. If it's warm enough in the afternoon, I like to play near the train station. When people start heading home from work."

"Where are you spending the night? At a shelter?"

"Sometimes."

Chloe had yet to spend a night at a shelter. Most nights now she spent the night with John or one of the others. Clients, Abony called them, even though Abony and Chloe didn't charge any money, just trading on a bed and a meal. And on a night when she didn't get picked up or didn't feel safe, Chloe spent the night walking to keep from getting frostbite. The morning after, she frequently fell asleep in the warm library, until someone would complain and she'd get kicked out.

Jozef didn't ask where she stayed the nights that she wasn't at a shelter. Maybe he already had a pretty good idea.

"You're looking good," he remarked. "I think you've put on a little weight."

"A little." Chloe swept her hair back from her face. It was getting fuller too, starting to grow back in, not so dry and brittle as it had been when Bill had taken her away from her home. She wondered if Jozef was one of those guys who liked fat women. How much weight would he expect her to put on if he wanted to be with her? She didn't want to be fat like she had been before Gunter. She needed to add a little flesh so that she was stronger and her energy would last longer. And a little bit of fat to help keep her warm and pad her behind so she could sit comfortably, but she didn't want to be as big as she used to be.

"I'd like to help you," Jozef said. "Would you let me know what else I can do?"

Chloe shrugged. "A job is the biggest thing right now... I've really been trying, but everyone thinks I'm an addict, and I'm going to mess up." She considered, scratching her ear. "I can't do anything for you, though... I don't like to just take charity."

"It's not charity," Jozef laughed. "I'm not giving you anything, just putting in a good word for you. Helping to network. It's not like I'm writing you a check and expecting something back in return. Just being a friend."

Chloe nodded, but was uneasy. When someone did something for her, especially a guy, it was because he wanted something in return. And so far, Jozef hadn't told her what he wanted. It made her anxious not to know what he expected on his end of the deal.

∾

Abony had told Chloe that if one of her clients decided that he wanted a relationship with her, that was the jackpot. That was the best possible outcome of trading services for a bed. For a chance at survival. She'd had repeat encounters with a number of the men, and eventually some women too. But John, the man with the Mustang, was her most regular. She had assumed that he wasn't interested in anything long-term, since he'd never had her over for more than a night at a time, with no commitments as to when he would pick her up again. So it came at her out of the blue.

"You could stay." He said it as Chloe sipped her coffee in the morning and prepared herself mentally to head back out in the cold again. John was nice and would usually drop her off somewhere close to the library. Not like some men who thought it was clever to drop her miles away from anywhere, forcing her to walk back to the neighborhood. Chloe made sure that those types got blacklisted. Kept out of their little circle of friendlies.

Chloe just about choked on her coffee. She put her mug down carefully.

"What?"

"Why don't you just stay here? For a while. You know, while it's cold out. Why waste your time on the stroll, when you could just stay here with me, where it's warm and comfy."

"Really? I wouldn't be in your way?" Chloe checked. "I mean... you're sure?"

"I wouldn't have said it if I wasn't sure."

"I'd... I'd be okay with that." Chloe was cautious about sounding too excited. While it was cold, he had said. That could mean anywhere from a few weeks to a few months, but didn't mean forever. He wasn't committing to a long-term relationship. It would be a short-term arrangement of convenience to both of them. But it meant no more nights spent walking the streets to stay warm. Or hoping that the next guy she exchanged services with wouldn't abandon her outside the city limits. Or break any bones. Or strangle her and leave her in a shallow grave. John wasn't bad. She could put up with any negatives in exchange for the stability he would offer. She had put up with much worse before.

John smiled at her, pleased. "You can leave any of your stuff in the closet," he said, "so you don't have to take it all with you. When you go out."

"Thanks. That's really nice of you."

Chloe was playing her guitar and saw Jozef coming.

"I might have gotten a lead on a job for you," Jozef advised.

Chloe stopped playing and held her hand over her strings. "Really? A real job?"

"A real job." He brushed off the bench and sat down beside her, leaning in close. "There's a coffee shop on campus that's looking for a couple of baristas. Students aren't always reliable workers, and they have a lot of turnover. I put in a good word for you, and they said if you're interested, come in and talk to them."

"What does a barista do?" Chloe asked. "I'm not sure I could do that."

"All you have to do is make coffee and take orders. I'm sure you could do that."

Chloe thought about it and nodded. If it was like the coffee shop that Jozef had taken her to, it might be hard to keep track of all the different flavors and add-ins, but she could learn them. It wasn't like she had to use any advanced math. The register would even tell her what change to give; she didn't have to do it in her head. Chloe already knew how to make coffee. That wouldn't be hard.

"Um… okay, I could try that. If they would really hire me."

"I explained the best that I could. They'll help you with the paper-work, figuring out what you need to do. The boss said he'd be happy to help you get your life turned around. He said the job would mean more to you than to a student, so you'd probably be more reliable."

"Yeah. I'd be good. I wouldn't just quit on him."

"Good! Do you want me to show you where it is? Take you over there?"

"Sure. Right now?"

Jozef nodded. Chloe packed away her guitar and stood up. She jiggled around a bit to loosen up her stiff joints and pulled on mittens without any finger holes. Jozef walked along beside her. He didn't take her arm or put his hand behind her back or around her waist when they walked. He didn't touch her at all. She chided herself for expecting him too. He wasn't interested in her; he was just helping her out with a job. Just like the people who chucked change into her guitar case weren't interested in a relationship. They were just being nice and helping her out.

They had to ride the train, which Chloe hadn't done before. She watched Jozef closely so she wouldn't do something stupid. She paid her own fare. She tried to appear casual and unimpressed on the train, not to look around her with wide eyes like she'd never done it before. She was just like the rest of the blank-eyed commuters.

Jozef was good at small-talk and kept Chloe engaged in conversation without digging into questions about herself. He talked about some of his classes and students, telling her funny stories. A few times Chloe found him looking at her expectantly and realized that she had disengaged and was staring blankly out the window without any idea what he had been saying. It had been a long time since she had been required to actually participate in a longer conversation. It was hard to keep her focus on it.

Eventually, they made it to the campus. Chloe tried not to stare at the students. So many young people. A ton more than she had ever gone to school with. So many people around her age, walking around chatting, carefree. She studied them covertly as they went by her. No one seemed to be poor, or hungry, or scared or worried about anything. They just chatted about their classes or their social lives, laughing as they scurried along from one building to another. Chloe tensed, her heart starting to race.

Chloe realized that Jozef had stopped talking to her. She turned her gaze back to him, raising her eyebrows. What had he been talking about?

"Are you okay?" he asked.

Chloe nodded quickly. "Yes, I'm fine."

"Is it the crowds? I never even thought..."

"I'm better than I was," Chloe hurried to reassure him. "I'm not going to freak out. It's just a little... weird. All these students, all in one place, and no one... like me."

He cocked his head. "What do you mean, like you? I thought you actually had a lot in common with them."

Chloe shook her head vigorously. "With me? No. They all..."

Chloe tried to put the feeling into words. How alien she felt. How she lived in a whole different world than they did. She felt unreal, like a ghost walking through the midst of them unseen. "They're... they are all smart, have money and homes... they haven't... lived the kind of life I have..."

"Those are just outside things." Jozef scratched his chin, frowning at Chloe. "Superficial. On the inside, they're just like you. Young, hopeful, looking for a start..."

She could see that he didn't understand. Chloe's experiences were not superficial. They weren't just something that had happened to her, like tripping over a crack in the sidewalk. They ran all the way down to her bones. They had changed her and shaped who she was. They separated her from everyone else in the world. Everyone who hadn't gone through the same things.

She felt like she was floating along up above herself and Jozef. She watched herself smile and nod and engage with Jozef, wearing a mask of normality.

Inside, she was just waiting for him to show his real feelings toward her.

"I'm looking for someone who will be a hard worker," Adrian said to Chloe. "It doesn't matter if you have any experience or not. What matters is that you are willing to work hard, put in your hours, and learn. I'll teach you everything you need to know. But I expect something back."

Chloe nodded her understanding. She glanced over at Jozef, feeling self-conscious with him standing there listening to them.

"Jozef said I should give you a chance, so I'm trusting his judgment. You're not going to let the two of us down, are you?"

"No. I can work hard." Chloe looked around at the various machines, taps, and toppings. "I don't know how all of these work, but I can make a pot of coffee."

"You'll pick up on the other machines easily enough. They're all just push-button. Put in the grounds, make your selection, and push a button to start brewing. You just need to be able to take an order and then fill it."

Chloe nodded. "I can do that."

"Let's get you started, then. Aprons are on the wall. Put your stuff in the staff room. You need to tie back your hair."

He gestured to the hooks hung with red aprons like Adrian and the other staff were wearing. Chloe looked at Jozef.

"Thanks... I guess I'll see you later."

Jozef gave her an encouraging smile. "You'll do great. Don't worry. I have faith in you."

"Okay. Thanks."

In a few minutes, Jozef was gone, Chloe was suited up, and Adrian was walking her through the preparation area showing her where everything was, one hand on the back of her shoulder.

CHAPTER
Twenty-Three

C hloe looked at the clock beside the bed and started to get up. John grunted something and grabbed at her.

"Come 'ere."

"I have to get ready. I need to get to work."

He swore and pulled her in. "Forget work. You've got work to do here."

"I'll get fired!" Chloe protested.

"Too bad."

After, he refused to drop her off at the train like he did some mornings, so Chloe ran, and was exhausted and dripping with sweat when she got on the train. In spite of running, she was still late getting to the coffee shop. Adrian scowled at her.

"You're late. Again."

"I know. I'm sorry. I had an emergency, and then the train…"

"You need to get here earlier. I don't know whether you need to get up earlier or what, but you need to figure it out. I need you here for the rush."

The rush was on, and there was no more time for discussion, but Adrian continued to put the coffee pots down with a loud clatter and made no effort to avoid running into Chloe as they both moved around the preparation area. She had to watch out for him, jumping out of the way whenever he charged in her direction, frequently fumbling with pots and cups, spilling, and losing her place. Several times he stepped on her foot or shouldered her out of the way.

Chloe rubbed a bead of sweat from her hairline with the back of her hand and realized that a lock of hair had escaped from her ponytail. If she stopped to retie her hair, she would have to wash up again, and she would be that much further behind.

"What's the hold-up?" a customer complained, still waiting for his fancy java.

"Chloe!" Adrian barked.

"I'm sorry. I'm sorry, it's coming." Chloe hurried up to the counter and set the cup down. The man looked at her and looked at the cup.

"Mochaccino!" he growled.

Chloe looked at the cup. A latte.

"Oh… who had the latte?" She scanned the waiting customers, but no one claimed it. Her face hot, Chloe left it on the counter and went to get a mochaccino.

At Adrian's glare, she ducked her head. "I'm sorry. I know I'm behind. I'm trying."

"Slow down. You try to go too fast, and you just mess stuff up. Do one order at a time and get it right the first time."

Chloe nodded. She knew he was right. But he was also the one cracking the whip and telling her to go faster. She couldn't go faster and slower at the same time. "Okay. Sorry."

He motioned for her to get on with it, and Chloe got the mochaccino, handing it to the customer with her face burning hot. He didn't tip her.

Luckily, it wasn't during a rush when Jozef stopped by for a coffee, expecting to be able to chat with Chloe.

"How's it going?" he asked with an expectant smile.

Chloe glanced in Adrian's direction. He wasn't listening, but would probably overhear if Chloe said anything negative.

"I'm still learning," she said. "It's not as easy at it looks."

Jozef looked up at the menu board and shook his head. "It looks pretty complicated, actually," he said. "There's a lot to remember. And I know what it looks like in here when it gets busy."

Chloe rolled her eyes. "It's crazy," she agreed.

"I'm sure you're doing great. Don't get discouraged. Any job takes time to get settled in."

Chloe nodded. "What can I get you?"

"Cappuccino?" Jozef suggested.

Chloe nodded. She moved to get it ready for him. While she was waiting for the machine to finish, Adrian jostled her elbow.

"Didn't you take that girl's order?" he asked.

Chloe looked at the young student that he indicated, standing there jiggling impatiently, eyes rolling up to the ceiling. Chloe hesitated, trying to recall.

"I... I don't think so."

"You'd better go ask her."

Chloe sidled up to the girl. "Um... 'scuse me... did you already order?"

"Yeah, like an hour ago!"

"I... uh... guess I forgot. What did you want?"

The girl recited her order, a complicated half-and-half with various shots and toppings.

"Okay, one second." Chloe pulled out an order pad, which she rarely used, and started marking off the various items.

"No, vanilla," the girl corrected impatiently.

"Uh..." Chloe stared down at the order slip, looking for the checkboxes.

"Give it here," the girl snatched the order pad away from her and filled it out herself. "There. Think you can manage that?"

Chloe swallowed the lump in her throat and went to fill the order. She could hear the girl making comments and giggling behind her. It didn't take a genius to figure out that she was badmouthing Chloe. She handed the half-and-half to the girl, and turned away, closing her eyes for a moment to try to regain her composure. When she opened them again, Jozef was watching her with an expectant smile.

He had ordered something. Chloe had no idea what. It had flown right out of her mind.

"Mocha?" she guessed.

"Cappuccino."

"Oh. Yeah. Hang on."

She went back to the cappuccino maker, where the cup had been filled and was still sitting there waiting for her. She turned back to Jozef and slid it across to him.

Adrian closed in on Chloe while Jozef took a sip of his cappuccino.

"You should explain to your girlfriend," he growled at Jozef, "about being on time for work. And not forgetting when she's on shift. I'm giving her a lotta leeway on your account, but my patience isn't going to last much longer. Explain to her."

"She isn't my girlfriend," Jozef said quickly, his face getting red. He glanced aside at Chloe. "I'll see if I can help out."

Adrian nodded and moved away from them.

"What's up?" Jozef asked quietly. "You know you have to get in on time if you want to keep your job. I don't want to be in Adrian's bad books."

Chloe looked away from him. "It's not that easy."

"What can I do? Do you want a wake-up call? You've got change for the train, right?"

"It's not that... it's just... other stuff I gotta do..."

"More important than keeping your job?"

Since the job didn't give Chloe enough money to pay for a roof over her head, her arrangement with John had to take precedent.

"Well... yeah..."

Jozef was taken aback by this. He had been sure that Chloe would realize that the job was more important than anything else. But he didn't understand how it was. How she couldn't live on poverty wages.

"You want to talk about it? Maybe we can work something out."

"No. Sometimes... I just forget... but usually, I got other things I gotta do before work. To survive."

"Like...?"

Chloe shook her head. Jozef sipped at his coffee, a wrinkle between his brows. "And there's nothing I could do to help? You know I would do it."

She couldn't expect him to step into John's place, not when he didn't have any interest in her. Jozef was a nice guy, but he wasn't going to do that.

John had fallen asleep. Chloe, looking around the apartment, decided that she should do a little tidying up. John had never required her to do any cooking or cleaning for him, but she liked things to be orderly. And wanted to express her gratitude for him putting a roof over her head. The weather was miserable. There had been reports in the news lately about homeless people perishing overnight. Chloe just shook her head, thankful that it wasn't her. At least she had a warm place to sleep every night.

She tossed discarded clothing into the laundry hamper, takeout boxes in the garbage can, and put a few mugs and dishes in the sink, careful to lay them down with barely a clink so that she wouldn't wake him up.

Standing in front of the sink, Chloe stared out the window at the night sky. It was a clear night, the moon shining brightly with no clouds in front of it. Stars twinkled where the streetlights were not shining too brightly.

She breathed and stared at the moon. For two years, she had not seen the moon or the stars. She had been so isolated from the rest of the world that she had completely lost track of time, losing years of her life. Even Bill couldn't grasp how devastating it had been to be resurrected like Rip Van Winkle, discovering that the whole world had moved on without her.

Hands closed over Chloe's shoulders, and she gave a yell, throwing them off and whipping around to face her attacker. He towered over her, face angry, yelling at her. Chloe held up her hands in front of her face to ward him off, showing submission, begging him not to hurt her. Her knees collapsed, and she fell to the floor, still pleading.

"Chloe! Chloe! What the hell is wrong with you? Stop it! Calm down!"

The world spun around her, not just in a circle, but like a kaleidoscope, everything fragmented and scattered. She couldn't make out the face. Couldn't understand what he was saying or why he was shaking her arm.

"Chloe! Stop it now!"

A hard slap convinced Chloe to be quiet and stop jabbering, pressing her eyes closed and just sobbing to herself. Everything whirled out of control.

"Chloe." Softer now.

Chloe breathed, recognizing her own name out of all the wild sensory input.

"I'm here," she said.

"What's the matter with you? Are you high? Are you tripping out?"

Chloe tried to push through the panic and confusion. "Jozef?"

"Who's Jozef?"

Not Jozef, then. He couldn't always be with her when she had a meltdown. That had only been one time. Just a chance meeting.

Chloe realized that she was prostrate on the floor, like someone in prayer, knees down, face to the ground, crying into the grimy carpet. She opened her eyes and tried to process the visual input.

The man beside her, bent over, his face showing complete confusion. The small apartment. The kitchen she had been standing in before her brain imploded.

"John?"

"Yeah. Who else would it be?"

"What happened?"

"You tell me!" His voice was angry and plaintive at the same time. "I wake up in an empty bed. Got up to see where you were. You're standing in the kitchen in some kind of trance. You don't hear anything I say to you. And then when I touch you..." He shook his head, baffled. "You totally freak out. What *was* that?"

Chloe rubbed her arms. She was cold. Her skin was rough with goosebumps. She wanted him to hold her close and give her some of his heat.

"I just... you startled me."

"Startled you? I was calling your name. Standing two feet away from you and you acted like you were deaf or unconscious on your feet. Are you on drugs? You don't take any meds."

"No. It wasn't anything like that. I was just thinking. I didn't hear you coming. You just scared me."

He shook his head. "Someone doesn't behave like that because you just startle them. That's full-on crazy!"

Chloe didn't know what else to say.

"Are you going to get up or just stay there on the floor?"

She was as weak as a kitten. A drowned kitten. Just sitting up was exhausting and made her dizzy. "Can you help me? To the bed?"

Chloe reached toward him, reaching for his arm to support her. He bent over and lifted her up bodily, carrying her in his arms to the bed. He set her down in the nest of messy blankets.

"You'd better stay in bed and quit wandering," he ordered.

He left the bedroom. Though Chloe couldn't see him, she could see the lights going out one at a time and the rest of the apartment going dark. Then he came back in through the bedroom door. The bedside lamp was on, and moonlight shone through the window. John got into bed and jerked the blankets around, pulling them up around himself and then over Chloe.

"Come here."

They were both in the warm nest now, but Chloe was shivering. She had frost in her bones. She withdrew from it all, watching herself lying in the bed. Since she didn't slide over to John, he wiggled closer to her and put his arms around her, pulling her in close, so she was pasted against his body.

"You're as cold as ice."

He pulled the blankets closer around them so that their body heat would warm the space faster. He nestled her face against his neck, and she could count his pulse, evenly beating the seconds away. He rubbed her skin, trying to warm her up.

"You must have had a nightmare," he decided. "Maybe you were sleepwalking. You just stay with me and forget all about it."

Chloe was too far away to feel the cold anymore, or even his touch. She concentrated on the beating of his heart that filled the room, drifting away.

Chloe had been having a good day. She had arrived at work in good time and hadn't made many mistakes. She moved around the preparation area and the seating area smoothly, as if she knew what she was doing. It was all finally coming together for her. Jozef had promised that if she worked hard and were patient, it would eventually work out, and he had been right. She was finally feeling calm and capable, getting drinks on automatic pilot, her muscle memory taking her from one job to another without her brain having to engage so much.

She grabbed the fresh pot of French roast from the machine and moved into the seating area, looking for people who needed refills. She moved from one table to another, offering the fresh coffee at each one.

Somebody ran into her from behind, and Chloe steadied herself, focused on the hot pot of coffee and not spilling or dropping it. The man who had run into her started swearing and calling her names.

Chloe turned around to apologize to him. He had run into her, but it was probably her fault for moving too slowly or being erratic.

She saw the bald head and the prominent eyes; a t-shirt stretched across his broad chest. She heard the invectives he was spewing at her.

Gunter.

Chloe went numb all over, stunned. She wasn't aware of her hand dropping, tipping the nearly-full pot of scalding coffee. All down the lower part of his shirt and the front of his pants. He bellowed in pain and struck out, sending Chloe flying across the room, to land with a crash on empty chairs and eventually the floor.

There was chaos around her. Babbling voices, his screams and curses, hands jerking Chloe back to her feet, and Adrian's face in front of her eyes, red-faced, yelling.

Tears started down Chloe's face. She tried to staunch them. Gunter would mock her for crying over nothing. Crying over spilled coffee. But *he* was crying over spilled coffee. Bellowing about it. Pulling his clothes away from his body to keep the coffee from burning him any further.

Adrian pushed Chloe into a chair with the order that she stay put. She knew that she should go back to the preparation area. People needed their orders filled. But his glare kept her in her chair, obeying his order.

They brought Gunter ice packs. Someone said something about calling an ambulance. He was bellowing about police and suing the coffee house, and he continued to call Chloe names. She'd heard them all before. It was nothing but background noise to her now.

Chloe floated up away from herself, trying to get perspective. She looked over herself and the coffee shop and the spilled coffee on the floor and everyone rushing around trying to help Gunter.

Only it wasn't Gunter.

It wasn't until then that Chloe realized that she had been wrong. All the pieces were there. Bald head, intense eyes, t-shirt stretched over his pecs. But it wasn't Gunter. He was younger than Gunter. There was a tattoo on the bare skin over his left ear. He wore jeans like the rest of the students, not Gunter's customary khakis. There had been a school backpack slung over one shoulder, though now it lay on the floor forgotten as they tried to administer first aid for the burns.

Chloe had just dumped scalding coffee down a customer's pants. A stranger. Granted, he had run into her, and it had been an accident, but it was still her fault. She should be the one helping him, assisting with the administration of first aid.

Chloe got up and took a couple of steps closer to render her assistance. The stranger started a fresh list of imprecations aimed at her.

Adrian got in front of Chloe. "I told you to stay there," he pointed back at the chair, "so that's what you do. You stay there until I tell you that you can get up."

Chloe meekly returned to the chair.

There were sirens outside, and an ambulance pulled up. Chloe tried to blink away the images that flashed in front of her eyes. The night of her father's shooting all over again. The ambulance arriving too late to do anything for him. The police cars everywhere. Flashing lights in her eyes, sirens splitting her head.

Chloe covered her eyes, trying to erase the flashbacks.

Words and phrases seeped into her consciousness. *Blisters. Second-degree burns.* The man who wasn't Gunter swearing and cursing a storm of words, insisting that the police be called, that Chloe be charged with assault. Chloe didn't try to protest that it had been an accident. She didn't say anything to defend herself. She just sat in the chair where Adrian had told her to sit and waited for it all to unfold.

Police cars pulled up. The cops came into the coffee shop and looked around, their movements calm and leisurely. There was no emergency. The man who had been burned had been loaded into a gurney and taken outside behind the ambulance, and the cops went over and talked to him, their voices calm while he continued to rage and whine.

They talked to bystanders. They talked to Adrian, and eventually, they talked to Chloe.

"You want to tell us what happened here?" one asked. His name was Watkins. He was tall with dark hair and a voice that was quiet and calm. He didn't yell at her like the cops that had gotten her out of bed the night of the shooting. He didn't order her around and push her harder when she didn't respond immediately. He was more like Bill, taking his time, waiting to get to the bottom of the story if she would just tell her side of it.

But like with Mim and Blue Jeans, Chloe could only tell him that she was at fault.

"I did it. Spilled coffee on that man. I didn't mean to."

"Accidents happen. You want to tell us how?"

"I didn't mean to," Chloe repeated. She looked over to the coffee counter. She really should be taking orders. Adrian wouldn't like her slacking off. But he had told her to sit in that chair, and he hadn't yet told her that she could get back up.

"No. How did it happen, then?"

"I just... I thought he was someone else."

Watkins frowned and looked over at the other officer, Symes.

"You thought he was someone else. Someone that you *did* want to hurt?"

"No! No, I wouldn't hurt anyone. Not on purpose. I never meant to hurt anyone. He just startled me. He ran into me, and I turned around, and I thought he was someone else. It... scared me. I just... I don't know what happened. One minute I was holding the pot of coffee, and the next..."

"Niagara Falls," suggested Watkins.

Chloe supposed she should laugh. It was a joke. Meant to bring some levity to the situation and to help her relax. But it didn't help. Chloe knew that she was in big trouble. The man was charging her with assault. He was going to get her put in jail. Just like Justin. Only Justin hadn't stayed in jail, Chloe remembered belatedly. They had acquitted him. The jury had hung. Mistrial. He had still had to go to jail until the case had been tried, though. And Chloe would have to go to jail too and sit in a cell, once more a prisoner, until they decided whether she had intended to scald the man who looked like Gunter.

Chloe covered her eyes, overwhelmed. Watkins pulled her hands gently away from her eyes.

"Everybody's overreacting just a little," he told her. "It doesn't sound like anything was done maliciously. He can try suing the coffee shop if he wants, but I don't think he'll get anywhere. If he does, the shop's insurance will pay for it. Accidents happen."

"I did it, though. I hurt him. Dumped boiling hot coffee all down him! Is he... is he going to be okay?"

"He'll live," Symes said crisply. "He's doing a lot of yelling, but it's not like he was doused in gasoline and lit on fire like he'd have you believe. He got scalded. I'm sure it hurts like hell. But he's not crippled for life. He may have some scars. But maybe not even that, if they do grafts."

Chloe covered up her face again. Skin grafts. That was serious. That was expensive. Painful. She'd heard about it on TV.

"No, none of that," Watkins admonished. He pulled over one of the coffee house chairs and sat down facing Chloe. "Let's get an initial report filled out, okay? I'll need your name and address."

Chloe gave him her name, but she hesitated over her address. She didn't really live with John. That was only temporary. Until the weather warmed again. It was his home, and she didn't have any claim over it. Even though he'd told her that she could, she didn't leave any of her things there. She brought her guitar and her backpack in to work every day. She took them to the library and everywhere she went. She didn't leave them in John's closet like it was her own home.

"I don't actually... I don't have an address," she explained awkwardly.

"No address? Where are you living? You have to be living somewhere."

"No... just... wherever I can. I got this job so I can try to get enough money to get my own place. But it doesn't pay enough."

"Are you staying with a friend? At a shelter? YMCA?"

"No."

Watkins studied her for a few moments, his eyes probing. Then he finally nodded and made some kind of notation on the form to indicate that she didn't have a fixed address.

"How long have you been employed here?"

"Just... I don't know. A few weeks. Couple months."

"And before that, where were you working?"

"Nowhere. I just... played my guitar a little. For change."

"And nothing like this has ever happened before?"

"No," Chloe assured him, shaking her head vehemently. "Nothing like this ever happened. I never hurt anyone before. Sometimes I spill. But I never..." She shook her head, unable to get the words she was feeling all out at the same time. "Never hurt anyone."

"Have you ever been charged with assault?"

"No."

"Have you ever been charged with anything?"

Chloe shook her head. "No. I don't... I don't think so."

"You don't think so. Well, wouldn't you be the one who would know?"

Chloe was trying to be honest. Just like she had tried scrupulously to tell the truth when Gunter would ask her questions. It was better to expose every little flaw and take the consequences for them than to be in fear that he would find out that she had lied to him.

"I was questioned before," Chloe said. "But I don't think I was ever charged with anything. And sometimes the cops—the police—say they're going to give me a ticket or arrest me for something, but then they don't. So that doesn't count, right?"

"They say they're going to give you a ticket or arrest you for what?"

Chloe shrugged. "Busking without a license. Loitering. Trespassing." She looked down. "Being homeless."

"No... that doesn't count," Watkins agreed. He looked at Symes. "Who's been threatening you like that?"

Chloe kept her eyes down. "I don't remember their names," she evaded. "Different cops different times."

"So they tell you they're going to ticket you or charge you unless you move on."

"No... unless I... pay. Or... *something*..." Sometimes it wasn't money they were after.

"That is illegal," Watkins said. "An officer can't take money from a citizen for anything, certainly not to get out of an arrest."

He didn't believe her. Chloe stared at his feet.

"Any cop who does that should be reported," he said. "You get his name and his badge number and report him."

Chloe shook her head. She wasn't going to get out of line and do anything that was going to bring the cops down on her harder.

"Who would believe me? Why would anyone believe me over a cop?"

He took out a business card and held it out to her. "I would."

She shook her head and refused to take it. Watkins sat there with it out for a long time, then finally withdrew it and put it away again, sighing.

"And what else have you been questioned about?"

Chloe thought about being in that cold, hard chair, with Bill interrogating her about the babies. She closed her eyes and for a minute felt the pain in her chest over their loss. Then she locked it up and didn't feel it anymore.

"I dunno… some stuff to do with my mom and her boyfriend. He got arrested."

Mentally, she apologized to her mother for saying anything about her. She knew better than to talk about the family. Even to save her own skin. But it would never get back to Mim. It wouldn't hurt her.

"What was he arrested for?"

"I'm not sure what all the charges were…" This was true. She didn't know what they had decided to charge him with. She might have a pretty good idea, but it had never been confirmed.

Watkins studied her, then decided that he wasn't concerned with this.

"We're going to need to run your background. Make sure there are no outstanding warrants."

Chloe nodded. He leaned forward with his elbows on his knees, looking down for a while.

"Have you had any drug issues, Chloe?"

"No! Everyone thinks I'm on drugs because I'm skinny, but I'm not!"

"I had to ask. Anything that might be relevant to this incident. I need to make a full report. So you've never experimented with drugs? No addictions?"

"No."

"What about alcohol?"

"I'm allergic."

"Really? Well, that puts a crimp in the partying, doesn't it?" His eyes were sharp.

"I don't party."

"Why don't you tell me, in your words, what happened today?"

Chloe closed her eyes, frustrated. She'd already explained what had happened. She hated the way that the cops always asked the same thing over and over again. Like if they asked her a hundred times, maybe they could catch her in some inconsistency on the hundredth. And she couldn't refuse to answer, or they would get suspicious that she was trying to hide something.

"I was just refilling coffee cups. He ran into me from behind and started swearing at me. I turned around, and I thought it was... a guy I used to know. It startled me so much... I was just so shocked that I dumped the coffee pot."

"You were scared?"

"I was startled. I thought it was someone I used to know."

"And this someone that you used to know..."

"Gunter," Chloe supplied in almost a whisper.

"This Gunter. Is he someone you would have wanted to see? Or not?"

She could see where this was going. "I didn't do it on purpose. I wasn't trying to hurt anyone."

"Just answer the question. Someone you would have wanted to see, or not?"

Chloe thought about this. *Would she want to see him?* She longed to be back with him, the way that she had once been. But how would it be to see him again and know that she couldn't be with him? She knew what it had been like going to school and still seeing him in the hallways, knowing that he was no longer interested in her.

"I'd like to see him," she said slowly, "but I wouldn't want him to be mad at me. Swearing like that guy was."

Watkins nodded and wrote something down. "Go on, then. What happened next?"

Chloe looked at him blankly. "That's it. I dumped the coffee on him."

"And then? What happened next?"

She frowned, feeling the wrinkles crease her forehead. What had happened next? There hadn't been anything else. Just chaos.

"I don't know... he hit me. They gave him ice packs. He was still yelling. The ambulance. The police car."

"He hit you?"

Chloe tried to tease this memory out from the rest. "I guess. I mean... I just poured hot coffee down his pants."

"Are you injured? Do you want to prefer charges against *him* for assault?"

Chloe blinked at him. "No."

"What you did was an accident. What he did was on purpose. And he's the one you say ran into you in the first place. Maybe you should charge him."

Chloe shook her head. "I dumped hot coffee on him. Of course he hit me."

"Are you hurt?" Watkins measured the area from the pool of coffee on the floor to the chairs that Chloe had landed on when the man hit her. "That must have been quite a hit. Has anyone treated you?"

"No... I'm fine... just bruised."

Watkins got to his feet. "I think I'd better let him know that he may be charged with assault as well. It seems like the only balanced approach. Maybe he'll change his mind about charging you. His behavior has been very aggressive. We'll probably want to drug test him."

Chloe watched him go back outside to talk to the man on the stretcher.

Eventually, the police left. Watkins again tried to press a business card on her, but Chloe refused it. She wasn't going to be calling him. If she needed to talk to the police, she'd call Bill. She knew him and she already had his number.

Chloe tensed to get up from the chair that she had been confined to. Then she remembered that Adrian had told her she couldn't leave it until he said so. She looked around for him.

Adrian walked over. He didn't look so angry anymore. Just determined. He held something out to her. Chloe looked down at the check in his hand, not comprehending.

"This is what you are owed," Adrian said. "I've paid you out for the rest of the week, in lieu of notice."

She took the paycheck from him, still not able to understand what he was saying. He could obviously see the confusion in her eyes.

"You're terminated," he said flatly. "Fired. Out of here. Get your stuff and don't come back."

"Fired? But…"

"But what? I've had some bad workers, but you take the cake. I don't want to see you again. You try coming back here and I'll take out a restraining order."

"I didn't mean to—"

"I know that. You're just a complete flake and you're dangerous walking around here with scalding hot liquids. No more. There isn't insurance enough in the world to keep someone like you on staff."

Chloe swallowed hard. She folded the check and put it into her pocket. Adrian waited while she removed her apron and he took it out of her hand. He didn't even trust her to go hang it up. She went into the staff room to collect her guitar and backpack. Then without another word between her and Adrian, she walked out.

Chloe tried to play guitar, but she was so numb she couldn't seem to find the right strings. After fumbling around for a while, she decided to go back to John's. Maybe she could just sleep until he got home. Shut the whole world out, and just sleep.

When she got home, though, John was there already. He looked at her and checked his watch. "You're home early," he observed. "Everything okay?"

"I got fired," Chloe said dully.

"Oh." He gave a little laugh. "Well, never mind that. I never liked you working anyway. I'm taking care of you, aren't I? What do you need a job for?"

Chloe didn't have the energy to discuss it. She just shrugged and put her things down.

"You look beat," John said. "Why don't you lay down for a while?"

That was all that Chloe wanted to do, but she knew by the look in his eye and the fact that he followed her into the bedroom that she wasn't going to get any time to herself for a while.

Later, as she dressed, Chloe felt a tug on her shirt. She looked around to see that John had a hold of the shirt and was preventing her from putting it back on. She stopped, not sure what he wanted.

"You're hurt," he said. His eyes narrowed. "Who's been beating up on you?"

He knew that he hadn't been the one to hit her in the back. Chloe got up and went into the bathroom, to look at her back in the mirror. There were dark black and blue bruises where she had landed on the chairs at the coffee shop.

John had followed her and stood in the door of the bathroom, which was too small to admit two people comfortably. "Doesn't it hurt?" he demanded. "You never even flinched."

Chloe considered. She was numb. She supposed that the bruises would hurt if she let them. But she didn't want to feel anything. It was easier to shut the pain off than it was to feel it.

"It's fine," she said.

She pulled her shirt on, and this time, he let her. "Maybe I should take you to the hospital," he suggested. "You might have broken ribs. Or a vertebrae."

"No. I'm fine. Nothing broken," Chloe assured him. Though if she was to feel the pain, he was probably right. Her bones were fragile from malnutrition. The crash into the chairs had undoubtedly been violent enough to break a rib. But ribs would heal on their own. She didn't need a hospital for that. She never had before. "I just... want to sleep."

CHAPTER
Twenty~Four

J ozef sought Chloe out at the library in the early morning. Chloe stared at the computer, not wanting to look at him. She knew that she had disappointed him by royally fouling up the job that he had lined up for her. All the work that he had done to prepare the way for her was flushed down the toilet, and he probably couldn't ever go back to the coffee shop again.

"Chloe, I'm so sorry about the job," Jozef said, leaning in close to her when she wouldn't look at him. "I heard all about what happened and... I'm just so sorry it didn't work out."

She glanced sideways at him, not turning her face away from the computer. "It's my fault, not yours."

"I'm the one who got you into the job. I set you up for failure. I never meant you to get hurt. I just wanted to help."

"You didn't do anything wrong. It was all my fault."

"No. No, it's not your fault, it was an accident. I can't believe that Adrian would fire you over an accident."

Chloe rubbed at her eyes, burning from staring so hard at the computer screen. "They had to call an ambulance. And the cops. The guy is going to sue Adrian."

"Still..." Jozef trailed off.

"I wasn't any good at it," Chloe pointed out. "I was always messing up. I'm not a good employee."

He put his hand over hers, resting on the mouse. Chloe froze.

"Don't say that about yourself. This wasn't the right job for you. That doesn't mean you're not a good employee. It just means we have to find something that's a better fit for you."

Chloe shook her head. "Nothing like *that*. And I don't have any schooling, so I'm not gonna get anything in an office. Not much I'm good for."

"Don't say that," he protested again. "Chloe, you're a wonderful person. We just need to find something that fits. Maybe somewhere that needs an entertainer, someone playing guitar while people are eating."

She was irritated by him saying she was a wonderful person. He didn't know anything about what kind of a person she was. He barely knew a thing about her. He didn't know where she had come from or what she had done. She could be a serial killer; he wouldn't know the difference.

It took her some time to tear her brain away from these thoughts and think about what he had said. Playing background music on her guitar? She was such a beginner; the thought seemed ridiculous. But when she got good enough, she would love to do something like that. It probably wouldn't pay well. Maybe not even as much as the coffee shop. But it would be something that she enjoyed, instead of being useless at it.

"Don't worry about me," she told Jozef. "You don't need to do anything for me."

He sat there beside her, not saying anything. His hand was still on hers, and Chloe shook it off to point the mouse at the next tutorial video.

"I like you, Chloe," Jozef said, his voice so low that she could hardly hear it. "I want to be able to help you. Don't keep pushing me away."

How could Jozef care about her? He didn't care what Chloe ate or what she wore. He didn't understand or care that she was living with another man. Had never asked her if she was seeing someone else. She had embarrassed Jozef in front of Adrian, a friend who had trusted his judgment and who would probably never speak to him again. And instead of Jozef screaming at her and telling her how she had screwed up, he just said it didn't matter.

A few cups of coffee together or chance meetings on the sidewalk didn't make them a couple, or even friends. If he wanted to pursue a relationship, he would expect something from Chloe. It would be a reciprocal arrangement. Not just throwing a job at her in the same way that people threw pennies into her guitar case. He didn't see her as a person. She was just a cause. A good deed to be performed.

"Chloe?"

"I like you too," Chloe conceded. "But I don't need anything from you."

Chloe went back to the routines that she had followed before the barista job. Going to the library to learn more guitar. Playing on the street for as long as she could keep warm. Going home to John at night, keeping him happy so that he would keep a roof over her head. It was the best she could hope for. There were few demands. Nobody shaking her awake or yelling at her for their coffee. There weren't people in her personal space all day long. She dealt with the cops when she had to and also tried to avoid the toughs who thought they owned the street and everybody on it. At least they didn't spend much time causing trouble when it was so cold out.

When it started to get warmer out, she worried. How long would it be before John decided that Chloe no longer needed the shelter of his bed full time? It would be warm enough to sleep rough without freezing, and she would go back to living on the street, with no access to a warm bed, shower, and meals every day.

They had just finished a meal of microwaved frozen burritos from the convenience store on the corner when it happened. Chloe didn't like the burritos. They reminded her too much of the meals that she and her mother had scraped together in those days between the shooting and buying the house. When they didn't have any place of their own and scraped through on what fast food and convenience store junk they could manage.

She would have gone back to eating dry salads if it would have brought Gunter back to her. But she pretended she liked the burritos for John. Chloe ate half of a burrito and gave the rest to John to eat, claiming that she was full. She would eat whatever he wanted her to.

"I have a surprise for you," John said.

Chloe's heart sank. It was time for her to go. The surprise was that he was giving her her freedom, even though Chloe didn't want it. No more than she had wanted it when Bill took her away from her mother. Or when Mr. Clive had tried to take her away from her home after the shooting.

"Oh... what is it?" Chloe asked, her heart pounding and her eyes stinging.

"In the bedroom. Come on."

She dragged her feet behind him. Why did they need to go into the bedroom for him to tell her?

There were clothes laid out on the bed, and for a moment, Chloe had the illogical thought that he was packing her bags. But her back-pack was already packed, as it always was. She had dropped it in the living room when she got in. And the clothes on the bed weren't hers.

But they weren't John's either. They were women's clothes. Did he have a new girlfriend, then? Was that it? Did they belong to Chloe's replacement?

John was looking at her expectantly. Chloe didn't know what to say.

"Your clothes are getting worn and dingy," John said. "So I got you these. I want you to wear them."

Chloe crept up to the bed and picked up a shirt, and held it up to her body. "Wow... thank you, John. These are wonderful." Even if she didn't like them a bit, even if they didn't fit her or were scratchy or tight, Chloe would have been grateful. Because they meant that he still wanted her around. He wasn't kicking her out. If he were kicking her out, he wouldn't care what she looked like.

"No reason to walk around looking like an orphan," John said jovially. "I want you to take better care of these. Don't just put them in your backpack. Hang them in the closet. And wash them with my laundry." Chloe normally just hand washed her clothes in the sink, but she had to admit that they weren't looking too good.

"Put this on now," John suggested, handing her a shirt and pair of pants. "I want to see them on you."

Claiming her. Marking his territory. Making sure that she wore what he wanted her to wear. Chloe's whole body got warm, head to toes. She was his. He still wanted her.

~

Chloe shifted, her body sore from sitting in one place for too long. She looked up and down the street at the foot traffic. The afternoon rush was over and it was probably time for her to find another location. She didn't want to stay too long in one location and attract the attention of the cops. Too long in one place, and the store owners might call the cops, or a patrol might roll by once too often.

Her gaze caught on a small group of boys about a block down. Toughs. She had run into them before and wasn't in any hurry to have to face them again. So she quickly settled her guitar into the case and retreated down the nearest alley, hoping to be out of sight by the time they reached where she had been sitting.

Probably they hadn't identified her as a target. She'd been too far away. But there was no guarantee. Better safe than sorry. She reached a cross-street, turned again, and then again into another alley. She knew the neighborhood pretty well now, even the alleys; which ones were dead ends and which ones had several escape routes. Chloe approached a security fence that she had jumped a couple of times before. But as soon as she put her hand on it, there was a loud snarl. Chloe jumped back, shocked. A dog jumped toward her. Big, black, lean, his teeth bared threateningly. Chloe backed away more, even though the dog was on the other side of the fence.

"Shhh..." she tried to calm it down before the owner opened the door to see who was back there. "Shhh, boy. It's okay. No danger. It's okay."

Her voice didn't calm him. He continued to strain at her, growling and snarling fiercely.

"Sit," Chloe tried in a firm voice. "Get down. Sit. Stay."

He didn't obey. Her words had no impact on him. Maybe he was trained with German commands. Or code words. Something that she wouldn't know and be able to use against him. Her firm commands didn't change his demeanor. He still threatened her, getting more and more frantic.

"Shut up!" There was a yell from inside the building. Chloe ducked back and hid behind a dumpster, peeking out to watch. "I said shut up!" The owner of the voice poked his head out the door. A man. Broad, with a beer gut and stained shirt. He picked something up and threw it at the dog, hitting him and provoking a yelp. The dog danced around, turning on the man growling viciously.

They faced off against each other. Owner and beast. The man bent down to pick up another rock or piece of garbage and drew back his arm. The dog cringed back, watching his throwing hand, teeth still bared.

"You stupid beast! There's no one out here, quit your racket. I don't want you barking and growling at every rat and bird! Shut up!"

He released the projectile. The dog jumped aside, managing to avoid it, and trying to attack while the man was rearming himself. But he was on a chain, and it apparently didn't reach all the way to the door. The man wasn't in any danger. He was master of the situation. He threw again, managing to hit his target a second time. The dog yelped and ran at him, standing up on his two hind legs as he strained to reach beyond the chain to get at his tormentor.

The man laughed nastily. He reached back inside the door and brought out a metal baseball bat.

"You're not going to shut up?" he asked. "You think you can argue with me?"

As he approached, the dog backed away, getting back down on all fours. His ears and tail were down, pressing into his body. He still bared his teeth, but he didn't growl again.

"If I tell you to shut up, you shut up!" the man yelled. He swung the bat, and Chloe gasped at the sound of the bat hitting the dog's head. The yip was heart-breaking. It was all Chloe could do to hold herself back and not try to go to his rescue. If she got close, the dog would attack her, not knowing the difference between someone who would be kind to him and someone who would hit him. And the man might not think there was much difference between a recalcitrant dog and a homeless girl.

The man got a couple more whacks in, body blows, and then stepped back. The dog was making a high-pitched whine but did not growl or lunge at the man anymore.

"That's right," the man gloated. "You listen to me, or you're going to get beat a lot worse than that."

He went back into the building and pulled the door shut behind him. Chloe waited for a minute to make sure that the dog wasn't going to start growling again, and the man wasn't going to come back out again, then she emerged from behind the dumpster and made a run for it.

"Chloe."

Chloe's mind was far from the dinner table conversation, and she didn't even hear John calling her at first.

"Chloe. Earth to Chloe."

He touched her arm lightly, and Chloe dropped her fork with a clatter.

"Oh! What? I didn't hear what you said."

He shook his head. "You're off in a trance again. What are you thinking about?"

"Nothing. I'm sorry. I was just off in my own little world. Were you talking about work?"

"Well, I was for a while. Then I kind of lost you. I also asked if you wanted to go to a movie this weekend. There's a new release I want to see."

"Oh, yeah. Sure. That sounds good."

"What were you thinking of?"

"Just something I saw today. Nothing important. Didn't mean to go off like that."

He studied her for a few minutes, then nodded and continued talking about his day. It was only a few seconds before Chloe had tuned him out again and was thinking about the dog.

For the next few days, she dreamt about the dog, tossing and turning with nightmares. Sometimes crying out in the night. John suggested maybe she should try sleeping pills. He even went so far as to buy some for her. But Chloe couldn't bring herself to take them voluntarily. If he told her that she had to, then she would, but those little blue pills brought nightmares of their own.

As much as she kept trying to push all thoughts of the dog away and to bury the memory of the baseball bat connecting with the poor beast's skull, Chloe couldn't do it.

Eventually, no matter how much she feared running into the irate owner again, she had to go back to make sure that the dog was okay. She crept up on the fenced area. The dog slunk around behind a barrel, growling softly at her. She was glad to see that he wasn't dead or lying on his side, injured.

"Hey, boy," she said. "I'm not going to hurt you. Are you okay?"

He growled, watching her around the edge of the barrel.

"I know what it's like," Chloe whispered, sitting down beside the fence. "I know what it's like to be chained up and beaten."

For a long time, she just sat there. He watched her, sides quivering, teeth bared, waiting for her to make a move. Chloe whispered to him every now and then.

Eventually, he started to creep out from behind the barrel, sniffing the breeze to get her scent. She could see a mess of dried blood on his head where he had been hit. The blow had split the skin, and she guessed scalp wounds must bleed just as profusely in dogs as they did in humans.

He combat-crawled toward her, belly pressed against the ground while he studied her with wide brown eyes, showing white all around the edge.

"You look half crazy," she told him. She thought about it for a few minutes. "Just like me, I guess. Scared of everything that moves."

She could see his heaving sides more clearly now. He was excruciatingly thin. The man was starving his dog as well as abusing it. The dog's fur was matted, and she could see bugs crawling in his ears. Why would the man have a dog if he wasn't going to take care of it? He didn't even seem to want the dog for a guard dog, beating it when it barked or growled too much, raising the alarm.

"I'm gonna get you out of there," Chloe said. "I'm gonna find a way to get you out. Okay?"

He watched her, still scared, shying or growling at every movement. Chloe moved a hand toward her backpack, trying not to startle him. When her fingers touched crinkling plastic, his ears perked up for the first time. He watched her hand intently to see what she was doing.

Chloe removed the wrapper from the beef jerky. She shredded a few small pieces off of it and tossed them over to him. He smelled the meat and gobbled it up in an instant. He looked back at Chloe for more. She made the pieces as small as possible and kept tossing them just a little bit closer to herself, so that he had to move forward an inch at a time to get them. He decided he was too close to her and moved a couple of feet back again. Chloe waited for a long time before tossing the next piece in, closer to her than before.

It was too far away, and for a long time, the dog stared at it, far out of his reach, too close to the stranger who could be dangerous. He crawled forward on his stomach, inching closer and closer. Chloe didn't make a movement or a sound. He finally was close enough to snatch the piece of jerky up, and he stared at her.

They faced each other silently, both unmoving, analyzing each other.

The dog was suddenly barking and growling, making Chloe jump back. She realized that he wasn't barking at her, but had rushed toward the door of the building, which was opening. She grabbed her backpack and ran down the alley away from the danger while the man was focused on the barking dog and before he could realize there was somebody else in the alley.

CHAPTER
Twenty-Five

S he kept going back. The dog recognized her and stopped growling whenever she approached. He sat and waited for the treats she brought instead. A bit of jerky. The remains of a hamburger she found in the garbage. Sandwiches that people gave to her instead of giving her change, because she looked like a junkie and they thought she would just buy drugs instead of food.

Each day, he was more comfortable coming closer to her. Until he was coming as close to her as the chain would allow, and she was as close to him as the fence would allow. When she was done feeding him, he would lie down and watch her. She couldn't reach him through the fence, not even with one finger. But she longed to touch him. To stroke his soft fur and give him the attention that he deserved. He wasn't a bad dog. But he'd been horribly mistreated.

Then came the final day. Chloe had managed to borrow a set of bolt cutters and was determined to free him. He came to the end of his chain, and she fed him a little, and then put the bolt cutters to the first few links of the fence. The dog backed off, growling a little. He didn't know what the strange sounds meant. Chloe had never made them before.

"Shh, it's okay," she assured him. She kept going, clipping a link at a time to make a hole big enough that she could get in. The dog started barking, a volley of angry barks and growls that just about knocked her over backward. Chloe heard the door start to open, and she ran and hid behind the dumpster.

She crouched there, hiding as the door swung open and the man cursed and shouted at his dog. He reached for the baseball bat.

"No," Chloe whimpered. She closed her eyes. "No, no, no…"

But her quiet pleading made no difference. The man hit the dog and kept hitting until the poor thing was quiet and still. Chloe bit her knuckle, tears springing up in her eyes. How could anyone be so cruel? The dog had done nothing to hurt anyone. He was only doing what came naturally to him. Chloe knew he wasn't bad by nature. The man shouted at the dog a couple more times, then retreated into the building and closed the door again. He hadn't seen the gaping hole in the fence.

After waiting as long as she felt she could, Chloe crept out from behind the dumpster again. She looked in on the dog. He wasn't unconscious but was lying on his side, eyes rolling back as he watched her. Chloe swallowed.

"It's okay, boy. I'm gonna get you out of there. I'm going to help you. You did good, not letting him see the hole. You protected me." She couldn't stop a tear from running down her cheek. "You didn't let him come out and catch me at it. I'm going to take you out, so he can never do that again."

The dog was panting, its sides shuddering.

"It's okay."

Chloe looked at the door, frightened that the man would come out again. Then she put the bolt cutters to the links and continued to cut a hole up the side of the fence.

When she was sure that it was big enough for her to fit through without having to push her way through or risk getting snagged on it, Chloe went through the opening. The dog rolled onto its belly and watched her approach. Chloe waited anxiously to see if he would attack as she got closer.

"It's okay. You'll let me get close to you, won't you? You're not going to do anything to hurt me, because I bring you treats."

His ears twitched at the word treats, and he continued to watch her intently.

"I'm gonna have to get really close to you to cut the chain," Chloe told him. "Will you let me get close to you?"

She was worried that once she was that close, he would attack. He wasn't a bad dog. He was just scared. He had been brutalized. She stopped, putting the bolt cutters down for a minute to shake a few dog treats into her hand. She reached out tentatively toward him. "Come on. You'd like some treats, wouldn't you?"

He watched her, not moving, but his nose sniffing the breeze and his ears pointed directly at her hand. Chloe moved until she was just a couple of feet away from him. She knew that she was within the confines of the chain. If he decided to attack, she had a long way to retreat to get out of reach. He would bite her.

She held her hand out toward him, offering the treats. The dog's eyes rolled back, looking at her, still frightened.

"It's for you. You're still hungry, aren't you?"

His scrawny sides hadn't filled in, even with her bringing him extra food each day. She wondered if the man was feeding him anything at all. Maybe he was wondering why the dog hadn't starved to death yet. How he could still be alive when he wasn't being given anything at all to eat.

The dog moved too quickly for Chloe to react. Like lightning, he had jumped forward and snatched the treats from her hand. Not too injured to move. Chloe put a few more treats in her hand.

"Here. Have some more. I know you're hungry."

As she waited for him to take them from her, Chloe remembered Bill taking her into the kitchen after coaxing her out of her bed, feeding her two chicken strips from the pan on the stove. How her mouth had watered over them. They had tasted so good. Like ambrosia.

"I know..." she crooned.

This time, the dog didn't snatch at the treats, but licked them up from her hand, looking at her. When he had eaten them, he licked her hand. Not because he was hungry for more, but to thank her and show her affection.

"I'm going to cut the chain now. You have to be still and not bark. If he comes out here again, he'll beat us both. You have to keep very quiet."

She positioned the bolt cutters around one of the links that encircled his neck. It was thicker than the fence links and she had to bear down harder on the bolt cutters, but eventually there was a soft ping as the bolt cutters cut through the chain. It fell to the pavement with a rattle, and the dog danced back, startled.

"Shh. It's okay. You're free now. It's okay."

He didn't bare his teeth at her. Chloe moved back to the hole in the fence and pushed her way through it. She held the hole open for the dog.

"Come on, boy. Come on out. You're free now. He won't hurt you anymore."

He cocked his head slightly, looking at her.

"Come on," Chloe encouraged.

He still didn't move. Chloe let go of the fence to get some more treats out for him. Then she opened the hole again, holding the treats out.

"Here you go. Treats."

His ears pointed toward Chloe's hand. He crept forward, an inch at a time, waiting for the chain to stop him. When it didn't, he stopped anyway, his ears turning around all directions, confused.

"Come on." Chloe wiggled her fingers, trying to call him and to spread the smell of the treats on the breeze so that he would follow the scent to her.

He started again, inching toward Chloe. At the hole in the fence, he stepped gingerly through.

"There!" Chloe let him eat the treats out of her hand. She wanted to touch him, to feel his soft fur and scratch his ears, but she didn't dare. He was so scared and traumatized; he would probably take her hand off. She realized she should have cut the chain further up, leaving a loop around his neck that she could use as a collar, to direct him and keep him with her. What if he ran away? What if something scared him and he attacked someone?

"You going to come with me?" she asked him. "You going to stay here with me?"

He stared up at her as if he was trying to understand her words. Chloe let go of the fence so that it fell back into place. When she took a few steps away, the dog stayed still, watching her go.

"Come on. Come with me. Come on, boy."

He hesitated, looking back at the door where the man would come out. Chloe tried to whistle for him, but she had never learned how to whistle properly. Justin used to tease her, laughing at her weak attempts. He and June could both whistle like canaries.

"Come on, boy."

He followed slowly. He wouldn't come right up to her, but trailed several feet behind her. She kept speaking soothingly to him, giving him a treat every now and then to keep him coming.

When they got to the sidewalk, the dog balked and withdrew a few steps back into the shelter of the alley.

"It's okay," Chloe reassured him. "I'm not going to let anyone hurt you. Don't worry about the people. It's okay. Just stay with me."

He approached her tentatively, looking almost as if he was walking on tiptoes. Chloe hadn't offered him another treat, but he snuffled the hand she'd been feeding him with, and then thrust his snout into her palm and pushed her hand up until it was resting on his head. Chloe's heart beat faster. She stroked the short fur on the top of his head very gently, avoiding the clotted blood and splits in his skin. She had a little thrill of pleasure that sent goosebumps over her skin. She scratched his ears, and he leaned into her hand, making a short little whine.

"That feel good? You're a good boy. Good dog..."

When she was ready to try taking him onto the city sidewalk again, she kept one hand on his neck to guide him and keep him calm. He tensed when he saw all the people walking up and down the street, but Chloe scratched his neck.

"I know... all those people... it's a little scary at first," she agreed. "It's okay. I'll stay with you. They won't hurt you."

She stuck to the quieter streets as much as she could. She didn't want him running away or snapping at someone.

"Mommy! The guitar lady!"

Chloe looked around and saw Babe running toward her. The dog tensed, baring his teeth.

"Stay back!" Chloe shouted, stopping Babe in her tracks. She looked hurt by Chloe's sharp tone, wanting to give her a hug and see the new dog. "He's too aggressive," Chloe warned, as the dog growled beside her. She could feel his body coiled for action. "He'll bite."

Babe started to cry, suddenly frightened. Jenny hurried over, grabbing Babe and jerking her back hard. "You don't run up to a strange dog! How many times have I told you that? He could tear you to shreds!"

Babe cried harder at that, clinging to Jenny's leg.

"Why isn't he leashed and muzzled?" Jenny demanded from Chloe. "You can't walk around with a dangerous dog like that! What are you thinking?"

"I just rescued him," Chloe protested. "I don't have a leash yet, but I'll get one!"

"You shoulda thought of that before you rescued him!" Jenny held Babe close, rubbing her back.

"I... I should've," Chloe agreed. "I didn't think of it."

They both just stood there, looking at each other. Chloe was glad to see her. She hadn't seen Jenny and Babe all winter. Last time they had talked, Jenny had thought she was going to lose Babe. That obviously hadn't happened.

"Enough waterworks," Jenny told Babe. "You're such a crybaby. He didn't bite you, so you don't have anything to cry about."

Babe gasped and sobbed, trying to quell her tears.

"How are you?" Chloe asked. "I haven't seen you in ages."

"Been worse." Jenny continued to rub Babe's back. "We finally got a place to take us for the winter. It was nice to have our own little room for a while. But, weather's warming up, and they shut it down. Back to trying to get into shelters every night." She sighed. "Life ain't easy for little kids on the street. I wish I could give her better."

"Maybe something will come up."

Jenny stared away from Chloe. "I'm not counting on it."

Neither of them said anything. The dog was still sniffing the air, trying to gather all the information he could about Jenny and Babe. His teeth were no longer bared, and he didn't growl. But he was still tightly-wound. Chloe wouldn't be inviting Babe to come over and pat him.

"You're not looking too bad," Jenny observed. Her eyes moved over Chloe. "You're getting some flesh on you. Nice clothes."

Chloe's cheeks heated. She smiled, embarrassed. "Yeah. I'm doing pretty well. Had a job for a bit, but that didn't work out."

"Never does. So you must have finally shacked up with that boyfriend of yours, huh?"

"No... not with Jozef... another guy."

"Why didn't you move in with Mr. Nice Guy? He wouldn't give you a black eye."

Chloe's hand flew to her eye. She had disguised it well with makeup, but of course, Jenny could see through the camouflage job. Chloe could hide the color of the bruise, but not the puffy, swollen tissue.

"That's nothing," she protested. "I just—"

"Walked into a door? I've heard it all, girl. Why are you putting up with that? Nice Guy got tired of waiting?"

"No. He never asked me."

Jenny shook her head and clicked her tongue. "You gotta put it in his head. Tell him how cold it is at night. How you wish you had a warm bed. You wish there were somewhere you could go, just to get warm... he'd come around soon enough."

"I don't like to take anything from him. He doesn't like me that way."

"What does it matter? A bed is a bed. He'd take you."

"He got me a job, and I screwed that all up."

Jenny stared at her. "What does that have to do with it? Honey, you gotta wake up. If you want something, you gotta go after it."

"I got what I wanted," Chloe insisted. "I didn't want Jozef. I got someone who takes care of me. Who gives me a bed, and food, and clothes. Jozef doesn't care about me."

"Okay..." Jenny drew the word out. "But I still say you should've gone with Nice Guy."

Chloe shrugged. She scratched the dog's neck. "Guess I'd better get this boy home."

Jenny wrinkled her nose, looking down at the dog's matted, bloody fur.

"Don't know what you're doing picking up stray dogs. It's disgusting and probably has worms."

"If I left him there, he would've died."

"What does it matter to you? It's not your dog." She shook her head. "Get rid of it. Call the pound; they'll come get him."

"They'll put him down. I'm not letting them put him down."

"What are you going to do?"

Chloe blinked at Jenny. "Take him home."

"To *this* guy?" Jenny gestured at Chloe's black eye. "How do you think he's going to react?"

Chloe looked down at the dog. "He won't care."

~

Chloe hadn't thought about how John was going to react to the dog. She had known she had to rescue him; that was all. She had been focused on nothing else. Her stomach tied in knots as she left Jenny and Babe behind. She had to get a leash. And dog food. She had to give the dog a bath and find out how to get rid of worms. John wouldn't be upset about the dog, would he?

She made it to the apartment without incident. The first thing to do was to get him cleaned up. John wouldn't like it if he thought the dog was going to get dirt and fleas all over everything.

The dog jumped when she shut the apartment door and started to skitter around the apartment, looking for escape. Chloe tried to shush him and calm him down, but he just seemed to get more frantic. She went into the kitchen and got out a couple of big bowls. One she filled with water, and the other she sprinkled a few treats into. She was afraid that the dog would be getting full, and that food wouldn't have any effect on him. But the noise he was making running around the apartment ceased, and he was still, listening.

Chloe put the bowls down on the floor. "Here, boy! Dinner. Come have treats."

He was just outside the doorway, looking in at Chloe, ears alert. She encouraged him some more, and eventually he crept into the kitchen and walked closer to the bowls, nose quivering.

"Yeah. Come on. Come and have some treats and some water," Chloe urged. She sat on the floor against the wall, non-threatening.

He went for the water bowl before the food. Chloe realized that she had never seen a water bowl in the dog's fenced-in area. She had fed him little bits, but had never given him any water.

He started to lap the water. Chloe spoke softly to him and reached over to touch his side. He growled, and Chloe withdrew her hand again. She knew you weren't supposed to bother dogs while they were eating. If the dog through that she was going to take away his food and water, he could attack her.

He drank for a long time. Then he moved to the food and ate the few treats that she had sprinkled into the bowl. He sat back on his haunches and looked at her as if to ask what was next. His panic over being closed in seemed to have subsided, at least temporarily.

"There. Bet that feels good now, huh?" She extended her hand toward him and he came over and sniffed it, looking for treats. Then he nudged her hand so that she would pat him and scratch his ears. He got gradually closer to her until he was cuddled right up to her. He rested his head on her leg, and breathed slowly, gazing up at her face. Chloe continued to pat and scratch where he didn't appear to be hurt.

CHAPTER
Twenty-Six

W hat the hell is this?"

Chloe awoke with a start. The dog awoke too, jumping to his feet and snarling like a tiger at John. John backed out of the kitchen.

"What are you doing with that filthy animal in my house?" John demanded, looking around for a weapon to fight the dog off with.

"I'm sorry," Chloe said. "I was going to bath him before you got home, but I fell asleep."

"That still doesn't explain what he's doing in my house!" John shouted. He digressed to calling her names. The dog was inching forward, teeth bared, saliva dripping from his mouth. John grasped the lamp on the side table, raising it up defensively.

"No," Chloe pleaded, getting to her feet. "He won't hurt you. I'll make sure. Don't hit him!"

"Keep it away from me."

Chloe tried to soothe the dog. "It's okay, boy," she said in a soft voice, reaching out a hand to him. "He's not going to hurt you. You're safe. I won't let you get hurt."

"It's a dog, not a baby. Get a leash on it and get it out of here!"

"He'll calm down in a minute when he sees that you're not going to hurt him," Chloe promised. "He was hurt where he was. He thinks you're going to hurt him again. Won't you put the lamp down? He's afraid you're going to beat him."

"I am!"

"No! He's not doing anything wrong. You can't hit him for no reason."

"The hell I can't. He's threatening me. I'll *kill* him if I have to!"

"No, no," Chloe knelt next to the dog and touched it tentatively, worried that it would turn on her if she startled it. "Shh, boy. Calm down."

The dog didn't snap at her or pull away. Chloe put her arms around its body. "Shh. It's okay. It's okay..."

It gradually lost the aggressive stance and stopped snarling at John.

"I'll go wash him," Chloe said. "I know you won't want him getting dirt on everything."

John opened his mouth to retort, and then closed it, watching her encouraging the dog past him, through the bedroom, and into the bathroom. John folded his arms across his chest, and Chloe shut the door.

Chloe hadn't considered how difficult bathing the dog might be. It was cats that didn't like water, dogs loved to swim, so it should have been easy.

But the dog freaked out when she turned the water on, growling and throwing himself against the door, trying to escape. Chloe quickly turned the tap down to a trickle. Once the noise quieted, the dog calmed down and stopped trying to escape the room. His ears tracked the noise of the trickle, and he went over to the tub and watched the faucet, apparently fascinated. He put his front paws on the edge of the tub and leaned over to lick at the flowing water. He put his nose down to the water starting to collect in the tub and lapped at it. He was already halfway into the tub, so Chloe lifted his hind end and pushed him the rest of the way in.

The dog rocketed back out of the tub with a yelp and again crashed around the room looking for escape.

"I'm sorry. I'm sorry, I thought you were ready," Chloe apologized quickly, her voice high. "I didn't know you'd be scared. I'm sorry."

It took a while before he started to calm down again. Chloe

swished a washcloth in the tub to soak it, and squeezed it out before touching it to the dog's head to try to wipe away some of the filth and encrusted blood.

"You need a bath. You're all dirty, and you're hurt. You'll feel better when I clean you up."

He didn't flinch away when she dabbed carefully at the wound in his head where the blow of the bat had caused the skin to split. He stood still as a statue, except for his tail, which waved slowly back and forth. It looked like a question mark to Chloe. He wanted to know what she was doing. It felt good, so he didn't pull away, just gazed up at her in puzzlement.

The clotted blood broke up a little, and Chloe rinsed the washcloth in the bathtub and continued. It was long, tedious work, but the dog stood patiently for her. Chloe put an older, worn towel under him to catch any drips of dirty water and blood that trickled down from his body. He stayed there as she did her best to wash out the dirt and break up the mats and knots. She needed a brush. One more item to add to her list. She couldn't exactly use John's brush on the dog. Especially if the dog had fleas or lice or other parasites.

As she worked on the dog's fur, she remembered trying to work out the knots in her own hair after her imprisonment. They had wanted to just shave off all of Chloe's hair, but she had worked for hours to save what she could, loosening the knots. It had been pretty thin when she was done, but she could run a comb through it without snarls.

Chloe started humming as she worked on the dog's fur. The only tools she had were her fingers, but she did her best with those.

Her stomach growled, but she ignored it. The dog was probably hungry too. But they had both lived for long periods without food, so missing supper didn't really matter. With the tap off, she could hear John's TV if she put her ear to the door. Canned laughter. A sitcom. At least he wasn't banging on the door telling her to hurry up. Or that he needed to use it. If he bought or made supper, he didn't offer Chloe any. She supposed she'd wasted enough of his food the last few days, taking what food she could to the dog.

Eventually, she had done all that she could. She wished that she could soak his ears under the water to make sure that all the bugs were gone, but he wasn't going to be getting into the tub on his own anytime soon. She rubbed him dry with a towel, and he shook his head and body. Chloe drained the tub of the black water and washed and rinsed it until it came clean.

"Well, how's that feel?" Chloe asked, looking down at him. He pushed his nose into her hand to get her to scratch his ears.

∿

John didn't say anything when she got out of the bathroom with the dog. He didn't admire how much better the dog looked or how soft and smooth its fur was. He brushed by her into the bathroom to relieve himself.

Chloe refilled the dog's water bowl and threw a few scraps of John's leftover dinner into the food dish. John returned and stood in the doorway, watching the dog wolf down the food.

"You can't keep it," he said.

She walked over close to John. "He won't get in the way. I'll take good care of him; you won't have to do a thing. You won't even know he's here."

"I'll know when I'm scratching fleas in the bed. No. It can't stay here."

Chloe looked back at the dog, puzzling out the problem.

"I won't let him in the bed. He can sleep in the kitchen. I'll put down a towel for him, and he'll stay there."

"Except for one thing. He's not staying here."

"But... why not?"

John's hand caught her across the cheekbone, snapping her head back. "This is my house, and I said no dog! I don't need to give you a reason. My house. My rules. I can't believe you would even think to bring a dog here without asking for permission in the first place!"

Chloe's chest hurt. She hadn't meant to challenge him in his rights to set his own rules in his own house. She felt immediately sick and guilty for the affront.

"I'm sorry! I'm sorry, I shouldn't have done that. I just wasn't thinking!"

"I want it out of here."

"I can't take him anywhere tonight... can I figure it out in the morning? Figure out what to do with him?"

She stared down at the floor, hoping that it was a reasonable request. He couldn't expect her just to turn the dog loose on the street, could he? That could be dangerous to the dog and to people who approached him without realizing how frightened and traumatized he was.

John didn't answer right away. But he didn't hit her again either, which Chloe thought was a good sign.

"You can take it to the pound in the morning," he said finally. His voice was iron. It wasn't a request; it was an order.

Chloe blinked her eyes, holding back tears. She would have to find a better solution. But that could be done in the morning. The dog would be safe for the night.

~

"Wake up!"

Chloe tensed, fighting the hand that shook her. "No! Please..."

"Chloe, wake up. Come on." He shook her and poked her roughly. "It's a dream. Wake up!"

Chloe tried to feel his grip on her. Tried to swim out of the dream toward reality. But it was all so insubstantial. Reality was getting smaller and smaller. Harder and harder to see and feel things as they really were. Every day things happened to make her feel even farther away and more alien than ever before. And only now and then did she find something that made her feel human again. Like the Chloe that existed before she had dissociated the first time. The Chloe that was whole instead of divided and kept separate from the things that hurt.

"Chloe. Stop it. Wake up."

"No..."

"I'm not going to get any sleep with you thrashing around. Wake up or I'm going to push you right off the bed."

Chloe held the pillow against her body. She sat up, blinking her eyes, trying to recover herself from the dream. It had been a dark, dread-filled nightmare and she wasn't sure she could shake the residual feelings off.

"John?"

"Let me sleep, Chloe."

She looked down at the pillow. In her dream, a dying baby. Now it was gone. She felt the loss keenly. Would her arms always be empty?

"Hold me?" she begged.

John groaned, but he squirmed over and pulled her down into his arms. "Now shush. Go back to sleep. I need to work tomorrow."

Chloe tried to be still and to force herself to go back to sleep. Once the dream had fled, she was no longer tired. Sleep had fled, but the feelings of isolation and loss stayed with her. In a few minutes, John's breathing had lengthened and turned into quiet snores.

She couldn't go back to sleep, but she didn't want to chance waking him up again, so Chloe slipped out of bed and tiptoed out of the bedroom.

She was momentarily startled by the ghostly shape of the dog flitting across the doorway of the kitchen. She went in to see him, whispering softly to make sure that she didn't startle him.

"Hey, boy. Couldn't you sleep either? Do dogs have nightmares?"

Even though it was dark, she checked his water bowl to make sure that it wasn't empty. He nosed at her, his wet nose much colder than she expected it to be on her bare leg. Chloe giggled.

"You silly. Do you want hugs too? Do you want someone to hold you and make you feel better?"

She went over to where she had put down the towel for him, and sat down beside it, patting the towel for him to lie down. The dog came over and sniffed at the towel and at Chloe's hand, then lay down with a grunt.

Chloe ran his fingers through his fur, now soft and dry and downy like rabbit's fur. And suddenly she was *there*. She wasn't watching herself. She wasn't numb. She wasn't like an alien observer, trying to make sense of a world that shifted in and out around her. She was fully present and experiencing the moment with all her senses. Everything was crisp and clear in a way she couldn't remember it being since childhood. She caught her breath in wonder and was reluctant to start breathing again in case it shattered her new-found sense of herself.

The dog nudged her. Chloe breathed in slowly, feeling the air streaming into her lungs. She continued to pat the dog, feeling the soft, downy fur, and his breath and his heartbeat through his body.

~

In the morning, Chloe took the dog out early, before John was up. The dog was pacing around uncomfortably, and although he didn't scratch at the door, Chloe realized that he needed to take care of his business, so she put on her shoes, grabbed her things, and went out for a walk.

She had enough money when she counted up her change, to buy some things for him at the pet store. The woman at the counter looked Chloe over, and looked the dog over, and announced that everything she had selected for purchase was on sale.

Chloe smiled shyly at her, and although she didn't like charity, she needed those things to take care of her dog, so she accepted the manager's discount and got what she needed.

She felt a lot better once the dog had a collar and leash on. He didn't seem to mind them or think that he was trapped. He'd obviously had some owner in the past who had trained him to a leash.

"Who's your friend?"

Chloe had been lost in thought, standing at the corner waiting for the light to change. She turned to look behind her and saw Jozef.

"Oh! I didn't see you."

Jozef smiled. He held his hand out toward the dog, who bared his teeth and growled menacingly. Jozef's smile disappeared, and he withdrew his hand.

"Shh, it's okay," Chloe rubbed the dog's neck. "He's been hurt," she explained to Jozef. "He's just scared."

"Sorry."

She shrugged. "It's okay. You didn't do anything."

"Where did you find him?"

The light changed, and Chloe stepped out into the street. Jozef followed her. "He needed me," she said, not exactly answering his question. Jozef didn't pursue it further.

"What's his name?"

All along, Chloe had just been thinking about him as 'the dog.' As if he were the only dog in the world.

"Uh... I don't know. I haven't given him a name."

"Well, he'll need a name," Jozef pointed out.

"Yeah... I didn't think about that."

"Midnight?" Jozef suggested, looking the dog over. "Shadow?"

"No." Chloe didn't want anything referencing the dark. Not when he brought her such light.

"Bob? Andrew?"

Chloe laughed. "No!"

"You want to go for a coffee?"

Chloe was confused at the sudden change of subject and her mind went immediately to the campus coffee shop, dampening her mood. "Uh… I don't want to go back there."

"Back where?" Jozef said blankly. "Oh, Adrian's? I meant somewhere closer." He considered and reached to take Chloe by the arm. The dog immediately snarled, facing off against Jozef. Jozef dropped her arm as if it was hot and took a step back. "A little protective there!" he observed, sounding short of breath.

He and Chloe looked at each other for a minute. While Chloe rubbed the dog's ears, she made no attempt to reprimand him. He wasn't doing anything wrong. Just protecting her, like Jozef had said. Chloe knew that Jozef wasn't going to do anything to hurt her, but how was the dog to know that?

"How about Mindy's?" Jozef suggested. "We can sit outside, with your guardian. I have a feeling you don't want to leave him alone tied up on the street."

"No," Chloe agreed. That wouldn't be a good idea. Not for the dog, and not for anyone who approached him to try to make friends.

She and Jozef headed for Mindy's, a nice little place with an outside porch. It wouldn't be hard for them to find a table outside like it sometimes was; it was still too cool outside for most people.

The dog lay down beside her chair when Chloe sat, and Jozef went inside to get them their coffees. He came back out with two coffees, a couple of muffins, and a biscotti cookie.

"I know you're not supposed to give dogs people food, but I didn't think it would hurt. He's pretty thin, and it's just like a dog biscuit, right? Not too sweet or chocolate…"

Chloe was touched that Jozef would think to get something for the dog. Especially when the dog hadn't been particularly friendly toward him.

"Sure, that's really nice. Do you want to try giving it to him?"

Jozef settled himself into his seat, pulling his overcoat closer to him. "I don't know. You don't think he'll take my hand off?"

"No… I don't think so."

Jozef didn't look reassured. He broke off the end of the biscotti and held it in his fingertips toward the dog.

"Here you go, boy. You want a cookie?"

The dog stared at Jozef, growling. Jozef dropped the biscotti on the ground in front of him and pulled back quickly. The dog looked at it, not moving.

"It's okay," Chloe told him. She nudged the treat closer to him. "Jozef brought you a nice treat. Have a bite."

The dog sniffed at it suspiciously. He looked at Jozef, looked at Chloe one more time, and then ate it up.

"I don't think he trusts me," Jozef observed with a chuckle.

"No." Chloe scratched his ears. It made sense that he wouldn't trust a man like he did Chloe. Not when he'd been abused and neglected like he had been by a man.

Jozef picked up his coffee and had a sip. He winced at the heat or bitterness, but continued to drink it anyway.

"So, how have you been?" he asked. "You okay?"

"I'm fine." Chloe shrugged. "I get along."

"You're looking good."

She wondered if it was her new clothes. Or was it that she'd been able to put on a little weight? She was never sure what people meant when they said that.

"Uh, thanks."

"Have you got another job?"

"No. Just busking."

He nodded. She thought at first he was going to bring up the job at the coffee shop again, but he didn't.

"How is the dog about that?" he asked instead. "He doesn't get upset about people getting close or putting money in your case?"

Chloe bit her lip. "He'll be just fine. And he'll make sure no one bugs me."

Jozef frowned. "Do people harass you a lot?"

"No… not a lot. As long as I'm careful and I don't stay in one place for too long."

"I worry about you. You'll be careful, won't you?" He looked at the dog. "You take care of her for me."

The dog's nose quivered as he looked at Jozef, his eyes intent as if he understood what Jozef was saying.

～

Chloe was pleasantly tired at the end of the day. She felt good having the dog with her while she played her guitar. She hadn't realized how much she had always worried about people approaching her that intended harm. Cops, youth gangs, other homeless people, or just bullies looking for someone to kick around. She always had to be on the alert, and it was exhausting. With the dog with her, she didn't have to worry so much. Even though he was skinny and frail, people gave him a wide berth.

As Jozef had predicted, the dog didn't like the people who listened to Chloe's music and tossed money into her guitar case. He growled and threatened, and for the first little while, was on high alert the whole time. But as the day wore on, he started to settle down. None of these people acted aggressively toward Chloe, and Chloe didn't seem to mind the money they threw at her, so eventually he lay down and just watched her.

"Yeah, it's okay," Chloe murmured to him as she played and he lay quietly. He raised his head to look at her, then rested it back down again.

The dog garnered a little extra attention from the citizens walking by on the sidewalk as well. Chloe supposed it was like the men who would take a young niece or nephew to the park to attract girls. Because what girl could resist a man with little children? People were attracted to the dog, even though he wasn't friendly, and often stopped to say a few words to him, to ask Chloe if they could pat him, or to ask his name.

She needed a name for him. But it had to be just right. She was pondering on it when she got back to the apartment. John was already home, on the couch in front of the TV. He watched her come in.

"I thought we agreed you would find a new home for the dog," he said.

Chloe looked down at the dog. *Find him a new home?*

"No... I can't do that," she protested.

"I told you I won't have it here. You said you would take care of it."

"But I... I got him a leash, and flea shampoo, and worm pills. So you don't have to worry about any of that stuff. And I got a brush, so I won't use yours."

"Chloe... do you think I'm kidding?"

"No."

"No dog."

"But he won't be in the way. Where do you want to be? You want me to shut him in the bathroom?"

"No. I want it out of here. Is that so hard to understand?"

Chloe was still looking for a way to appease him. Obviously, she couldn't get rid of the dog. He needed her. And she needed him. The way that he made her feel so present and alive. His protection when she was on the street. His companionship. Surely John could under-stand that.

"Out of here," John said again.

"But..."

"Get him out. He can't stay here. I can't believe you brought him back after what I told you yesterday."

Chloe stared at John in dismay. He would really sooner turn her out on the street than put up with a dog in the apartment. One little dog that wouldn't cause anyone any trouble.

"I can't. I need him."

"Need him?" John scoffed. "You didn't need him a few days ago. All winter while I was looking after you. Nobody *needs* a dog. You felt sorry for him. You rescued him. That's fine. But you can't keep him. Call the pound; they'll find a new home for him. Somewhere he'll be happy. Maybe an acreage where he can run around outside. Wouldn't he like that?"

She was sure he would. But Chloe needed him. It wasn't a matter of him living happily on a farm instead of on the city streets. It was a matter of Chloe's survival.

"He looks after me out there," Chloe explained. "He'll make sure I don't get hurt."

"You didn't need him before," John repeated. "You survived just fine with me looking after you. You don't want my help anymore? You don't want a warm bed and a roof over your head? All I've done for you, and you're going to forget all of it for a mangy mutt?"

"He's not mangy!" Though truth be told, Chloe had no idea what mange was. "I appreciate all you've done... but... I can't..."

Guilt wrung at Chloe's insides. John had taken care of her all winter. And now she was acting like it was nothing. Like she could just go off on her own again and forget about him. But she couldn't abandon the dog. She couldn't just let go the creature who could bring focus and belonging back to her existence. That was more important. Who she was was more important than food, clothing, or a roof over her head. Even with all those things, she could still cease to exist. Chloe dug her fingers into the dog's dark fur. All at once, she felt that focus again. The clarity of knowing who and where she was, and feeling everything. The light and colors of the room became clear. She could hear every word on the TV. She could smell John's sweaty, musky scent. She even felt hunger, something she hadn't been aware of until that moment.

"I can't give him away," she said firmly. She had to stand by that. John could push or bully her into almost anything else, but there was a line.

John stared at her in disbelief. "That's it? Just like that? We're done because you found a dog?"

Chloe shrugged. Yes. They were done. Because she had found the dog and John wouldn't have it in his house. She waited to see if he would change his mind, having discovered the line that she would not cross. It was just a dog. And she would keep it out of his way. John could have everything else he wanted and the apartment was big enough for all three of them.

John's face grew dark. Flushed red, hard as flint. An ugly, brutal scowl.

"Get out of here, then. You and that beast just get out of my house."

Chloe nodded her head. She turned toward the door. She hesitated as she touched the door handle. Not because she thought he would change his mind and call her back, but because she was thinking of the clothes hanging in his closet. He had insisted she hang them up instead of carrying them in her backpack, so she only had a hoodie and some odds and ends in her backpack. At least she had the dog's things. She opened the door and walked out.

Chloe didn't go to a shelter. It was far too late in the day to get into one. It was warm enough that she didn't need to walk all night to keep from freezing. Though it was uncomfortable, she had her coat on, and she found a place to curl up to sleep. The dog moved around restlessly for a few minutes, then lay down with her, cuddling up close. He was warm. Chloe put her arms around him and tucked her face into his neck to keep herself warm. He didn't pull away from her cuddling.

Morning came too fast. Chloe gave the dog what food she had and brushed his coat until it was silky smooth and snapping with static electricity. She knew it was too early for the library to be open. She took him for a walk and cleaned up after him.

When she went around to the library, she was faced with another roadblock. A security guard moved in to intercept her.

"You can't bring a dog in here," he said.

"He's clean, and he'll behave," Chloe promised.

"No dogs. Sorry."

"I can't leave him alone outside."

"Then you can't go in."

"But I need him. He... helps me."

His mouth twitched. He shook his head. "I've seen you before without him. He's not a service dog. Doesn't have any harness or designation. He's not allowed in."

Chloe looked for a way to persuade him, but he folded his arms across his chest stubbornly.

"You want me to call the police to send you on your way?"

"No." Chloe dropped her eyes. The dog looked up at her with his ears cocked, wanting to know what was wrong.

"It's okay, boy," Chloe told him and scratched his ears. He licked her fingers.

Chloe put her head down and walked away. She wasn't going to be able to study the videos of guitar tutorials and songs anymore. But she had been through most of them already. It was getting difficult to find any more advanced tutorials, and she could pick out most songs by ear if she listened carefully. She didn't really need to go to the library anymore. It was just a comfortable routine.

She and the dog walked over to one of the benches that Chloe liked to sit on and played for the morning commuters. People were sleepy, few digging into their pockets to give her anything. She played quietly, not wanting to irritate them with loud, discordant noises. She could play something more lively at noon and at the end of the day. The dog settled at her feet, mostly under the bench where people couldn't approach him. Chloe had been playing for over an hour and was thinking it was time to move when a police car pulled up. Chloe hurried to put her guitar away and to leave before he confronted her. A city van pulled up behind the police car. It appeared that they were up to something other than harassing her to move on or shaking her down.

"Stay there, please, miss," the policeman said, climbing out of his car and approaching her, one hand on his sidearm.

Chloe snapped shut the latches on her guitar case. "I'm moving on. I was already going to leave."

"Don't move. Stay where you are."

Chloe froze at the snap in his voice. She pulled her hands back from her guitar case, holding them nervously at shoulder level. "What's wrong?"

"There's been a complaint about your dog."

"My dog? What kind of complaint?"

"A complaint that he's aggressive. That he bit someone."

Chloe was baffled. "He never bit anyone!"

The man from the city truck was moving toward them. A dog catcher, with a loop on a rod.

The dog growled, not liking the two men approaching Chloe, pincering her between them. He bared his teeth and snarled, then barked when they got still closer.

"He's scared," Chloe said. "He's been abused, and he thinks you're going to hurt him. Or hurt me. He's not dangerous!"

"Looks pretty aggressive to me," the dog catcher observed.

"That's because you're getting too close to him. If you just left him alone, he wouldn't do anything. You can't take him when he's just lying there, not hurting anyone!"

"There's been a complaint, miss. We need to follow up and have him assessed." The cop took a couple more steps toward her.

"Does that mean you'll give him back?"

"If the assessment says that he doesn't need to be put down, then you can pay a fine and get him back. If you can't pay the fines, he'll be adopted out or destroyed."

"You can't do that!"

The dog was going nuts with the two of them closing steadily in. He barked frantically, his body pressed against Chloe's leg, snarling and drooling and looking like a mad wolf.

"Please don't upset him," Chloe pleaded. "You're making it worse!"

"I suggest you get out of the way," the dog catcher said. "This could get dangerous."

"No, please. Just back off. It's because you're threatening." She tightened her hold on the dog's leash, taking up the slack. "I'm holding him back. He's not going to attack anyone!"

She didn't like the way that the policeman was fingering his gun. He'd already unsnapped it. The dog catcher didn't look happy about the situation.

"Let me get the loop over him so I can put him in the truck. We don't want anything to happen to him or anyone else."

Chloe blinked back tears. "Please…"

"We need to get him in the truck," the dog catcher repeated.

Chloe sniffled. "Then let me put him in. You don't need to treat him like… a wild animal. He's not a bad dog."

"You'll put him in?"

"Yes."

They both backed off a little. Chloe bent down over the dog and whispered to him, scratching his ears and trying to calm him down.

"I'm sorry… I'm so sorry… I'm only doing this so that you'll be safe. I'll come to the pound, and I'll get you back… somehow."

He calmed a little and Chloe walked him over to the back of the truck, where the dog catcher indicated one of the large kennels. "If you can get him in there. Otherwise, I'm going to have to force him."

"Come on. Jump up." Chloe patted the floor of the truck, inviting him. He bared his teeth at the dog catcher, but when the man backed up a couple more steps, he jumped up into the truck. "In here." Chloe patted the inside of the cage. "Come on, boy. I'm sorry. I don't want you to be locked up again. But they won't hurt you. They won't beat you or starve you."

Tears were running down her cheeks now. It was a betrayal of the dog, and she was afraid that if she let him go, she would never be able to feel again. Everything would be numbness and alien for the rest of her life. If that was what she was doomed to... her life might not be very long.

The dog kept looking at her and did not want to enter the cage. She petted and encouraged him. "Come on, boy. Just do this for me. I know you don't understand, but I'll come and get you again. I won't let you stay in a cage."

He slunk into the kennel, his tail between his legs. He turned around inside it and lay down with his nose pointing out the door, looking miserable. Chloe was sure that she saw tears in his eyes too.

"I promise, I'll come get you."

She unhooked the leash from his collar, and closed the door of the cage and latched it so that he couldn't push back out.

Chloe turned back toward the dog catcher and the cop.

"Thank you, ma'am," the dog catcher said, touching his cap in a little salute. He closed the back of the truck and then climbed into the truck cab. "You know where to find him."

He drove away. Chloe watched the truck until it turned and was out of sight. Chloe held her palms to her eyes, trying not to break down.

"I'm sorry, miss," the police officer said. He no longer sounded steely and angry. Now that the danger was past, he could afford to show some humanity. "I can see you love him very much, and he loves you too. He wouldn't have gotten into that cage for anyone else."

"I have to go get him. I don't know how I'm going to pay the fine. I don't have any money."

"Is he licensed?"

Chloe shook her head. "No. I just got him. I only got the leash yesterday. I spent all the money I had. I couldn't stay where I was because he wouldn't allow any dogs. And now I don't have any money, anywhere to live, and my dog is gone!"

"You understand that having an unlicensed dog on the street is illegal?" he said, staring down at his ticket book. "You have to get it licensed. Your name is Chloe?"

She was surprised. She hadn't told him her name.

"Yes."

"Last name?"

"Simpson."

He wrote it down. Not in a notebook, to make a report. In the ticket book. Not only was she going to have to pay the impound fees, but she was also going to have to pay for a ticket. And a license, if she ever got him out. Chloe sat back down on the bench where her backpack and guitar case were and covered her face. She sobbed silently, trying to keep the tears from flooding down her face.

She continued to answer the cop's questions in as calm a voice as she could manage. As she sat there, she separated from herself and from the pain and despair. She floated up away, so far that she could barely hear the cop anymore.

CHAPTER

Twenty-Seven

Chloe sat there for a long time after the cop had left, numb. She knew that she had been there for too long, but she couldn't make herself move from the spot. It would take too much energy. Too much thought.

Eventually, another cop rousted her, and she walked on down the street to escape his harassment. Her feet moved without her instructions and eventually Chloe found herself again in front of the door of John's apartment.

She wasn't sure what she was doing there, but it had been home for weeks, and she had returned there without thought. John wasn't home. Chloe lay down on the bed and closed her eyes, shutting everything out.

Time passed. She continued to sleep, or to lie there all shut up inside herself and pretend that it was where she belonged. When John got home, something must have tipped him off to her presence. He walked into the bedroom.

"Well, sleeping beauty," he observed. "And it looks like you got rid of the dog. I knew you'd come to your senses."

He leaned over her on the bed and kissed her. He lay down beside her and took her in his arms, his kisses becoming more insistent. Chloe pulled away from him, irritated at being touched. John closed his hand tightly around her arm and didn't let her go.

"I need your help," Chloe told him.

"My help? You don't think I've done enough for you?"

"I know you don't like the dog, but he got taken away. They took him to the pound. I need money to get him out. I know that usually..." she made a gestured to indicate each of them. "We just... exchange favors. But I... I really need cash, now."

He chuckled. "You think I'm going to spring that dog? Not likely! Once I got him out of the way, I'm not likely to pay for him to come back here, am I?"

Chloe processed his words. "*You* got him out of the way?"

He smiled, showing his crooked teeth. "I got him out of the way," he agreed.

Chloe tried to jerk away from him, but he wouldn't let her go. He pulled her closer, against his body. "One more time, for old time's sake. Since you're not likely to be coming around here anymore."

"No!"

John was much stronger than her, several times her weight. Chloe was stronger than she had been, but still frail, her bones still weak from malnutrition. He was going to have his way, whether she fought him or not.

It was best not to fight and just to go somewhere far, far away.

When Chloe awoke in the morning, she was sore and cold. She had been through so much over the previous twenty-four hours; she didn't know where to start in itemizing the abuse her body had taken. And it seemed like just when she had gotten to sleep, someone was shaking her awake again.

"Get up. Move on. You can't be sleeping here!" The rough hand shook her shoulder. Chloe opened her eyes and saw a woman. Not much taller than Chloe. Stout, but not fat like Mim. Her dark eyes snapped, and she was wearing a hat with furry earflaps and a checkered jacket. Like a lumberjack. "You don't want me to have to call the cops to get you to move, do you? Just get up and move on. There's nothing here for you."

Chloe looked around, trying to remember everything that had happened and where she was. Her hand was pressed against a chain link fence, and as Chloe's fingers pushed through the links, she remembered.

She rubbed the fur of the dark dog lying on the other side of the fence. Indoor dog cages at the Humane Society had flap doors that allowed the animals to move into the outside runs at will. And her dog had come outside at her call and lay on the other side of the fence, where she could touch him through the links. They lay sleeping against each other as they had throughout the night, only separated by the wire of the fence.

He roused a little at Chloe's touch, whining and turning his head to look around at her. When he saw the other woman standing there towering over Chloe, he went wild. He barked and snarled and jumped up against the fence, threatening the woman and trying to get at her.

Although the woman startled initially at his violent reaction, she had no concern that he was going to break out and hurt her. She just chuckled at his frantic growling.

"Settle down, black," she said in good humor. "Nobody's listening to your threats."

The dog gradually settled, but as soon as the woman moved a muscle, he was at it again, jumping and barking and snarling like he would rip her to shreds.

"Here, you'd better get on your way," the woman told Chloe. "Us being here is just getting him more riled up. He'll settle down once we're back from the cage."

Chloe poked her fingers through the links at him. "He's my dog."

"Your dog." The woman's manner changed. "Is he really? Well, I think you've got some questions to answer, then."

She watched as Chloe touched the dog's muzzle through the fence and rubbed the short fur over his nose. He relaxed a little under her touch.

"I told you I wouldn't let you go," Chloe whispered.

"Come with me. Into the office."

Chloe looked at the woman and considered the barked order. She didn't have to go in. She could just run. But she would need to come back and see the dog again. Would need to find a way to get him out eventually. So it was best to be cooperative when she was first asked.

Chloe followed her into the Humane Society through the back door. Chloe could smell the animals as soon as they walked in the door. Along with an assault of bleach and other disinfectants, a ruckus raised by the dogs who heard them enter, and florescent lights that hurt Chloe's eyes.

The woman motioned to a chair in front of a messy desk in a tiny office that held three desks but was only made for one.

"There's coffee. You want one?"

Chloe couldn't remember the last time she had eaten or had anything to drink. "Yes. Please. That would be great."

The woman left the office momentarily and came back with two mismatched mugs, one of which she set in front of Chloe. It had a picture of a cat on it. The woman took off her gloves and her ear-flap hat, which liberated a messy cap of curly hair. She fell into her office chair.

"I'm Wanda," she introduced herself. She pushed through the files on her desk and pulled one out. "And you claim to be the owner. Chloe?"

Chloe nodded. "Yes."

"Tell me about the black."

Chloe stared at her coffee mug. "He's not vicious," she explained. "He's just scared."

"It all comes out to the same. If he's going to be aggressive and bite, then he's not safe."

"He didn't bite anyone. My... the guy I was with... didn't want him around, so he called in a fake report. The dog never bit anyone. Just growled."

"You can't deny that he's aggressive. And more than aggressive, he's been abused and neglected." Her eyes were fixed on Chloe. "Explain that."

Did Wanda really think that Chloe had hurt him?

"The man I rescued him from had him locked up. No water and hardly any food, except for what I started bringing him. He was chained and fenced, and if he made too much noise, then the man would come out and beat him." Chloe closed her eyes, feeling tears threaten. She saw it all replaying in front of her again, even though she had tried to hide her face and close her eyes when it had happened. The man coming out with his baseball bat and hitting the dog over and over again. "He beat him with a bat."

"He's got broken ribs, and a fractured skull. He's so undernourished, if he'd been brought in as a stray, we would have just put him down."

Chloe nodded. "I've only had him for a few days. I washed him. Got him a collar and leash, so that he wouldn't be able to attack anyone while we were out. He was under control, and he never bit anyone."

"Did you think to get a muzzle?"

"No... I had to spend all my money just to get the collar and leash. A muzzle would be too much. And he never bit anyone. He never snapped at anyone. He's a good dog. He's just scared."

"And that makes him dangerous. I'm sorry, but I can't release him in the condition he's in."

"Because he's hurt."

"Because he's aggressive. Because we don't have any proof as to who it was that beat him. We don't know whether he is trainable. Whether he can be turned around again. Some dogs, once they're traumatized like that, it's a lost cause. They're always going to be aggressive and unpredictable."

"No, not him. You haven't seen how much better he is now than he was before. He doesn't get aggressive when it's just him and me. He trusts me. I can train him to be around other people again. I know how he feels."

The last words slipped out. Chloe hadn't meant them to.

"Nobody can know how he feels," Wanda disagreed. "No one who hasn't been through the same thing."

Chloe didn't argue with her.

Wanda was insistent that Chloe couldn't stay at the Humane Society. She had to go away. So eventually, Chloe obeyed, heading back to her own familiar neighborhood. She would need money to get the dog out. Somehow, she had to raise enough to do it, so that when they finished evaluating him and decided that he could be retrained and not be a dangerous dog, she could get him back again.

She had played several different places throughout the day and was taking a break at a coffee shop when Jozef showed up.

"Fancy meeting you here," he said cheerfully.

Chloe nodded.

"Mind if I join you?"

She considered him for a long moment and then nodded again. "Yeah, sure. Of course."

"Great. Let me just get my fix, and I'll be right with you."

Chloe's coffee was only lukewarm. She'd been sitting there too long. The manager would probably have kicked her out before too long, but with Jozef joining her and buying a fresh cup, they would let Chloe stay for longer.

She rubbed the tight band of muscle around her forehead. She was so worried about the dog that she could barely think of anything else. He needed her, and she needed him.

Jozef returned with his coffee. No muffin today, but Chloe supposed he'd had one for breakfast.

"You look sadder than usual," Jozef observed. "What's going on?"

"Things... aren't going so great."

Jozef sipped his coffee, looking serious. "What things?"

For once, he didn't jump in offering to help her with whatever she needed. It was easier that way. She didn't have to fend off his attention. She could just think about the problem at hand.

"The guy I was living with... he kicked me out. Because of the dog."

Jozef looked around, eyebrows up. "I forgot about the dog. Where is he? Outside?"

"No... at the pound."

"Oh. I'm sorry to hear that."

"They think that he's vicious. That he's dangerous. They say they might have to put him down."

"Oh, no! Really? Are you all right?"

"I am... I guess. But they can't put him to sleep. I need him. They can't... they can't just kill him because he's afraid. Because somebody abused him."

"Mmm," Jozef made a noncommittal noise in his throat. "You can see their point, though, can't you? It's not like he's a person. You can't reason with him. Get inside his head. If they think that he might hurt someone... he could do real damage, especially to a little kid. You'd hate for that to happen."

"It's not going to happen. I was taking care of him. I wouldn't have let him hurt anyone."

He shrugged and didn't try to argue it further. His eyes went away for a few moments, and then back at her.

"Your boyfriend kicked you out? So where are you living now?"

"Nowhere. It's okay. It's warm enough now... I can sleep outside without freezing."

"That's no good. Why don't you go to a shelter? Get into some kind of program where you can get an apartment? There are subsidies, aren't there? Special programs?"

"I don't know. I don't like shelters. There's too many people." Babies crying.

"You can't just sleep outside. What about when it rains? What if someone mugs you?"

"I don't have anything for anyone to steal." Not that night-time attackers were always after valuables. "It's okay."

Jozef's mouth twisted up. "I could... I have a spare room. You could stay there for a while until you can come up with something else."

Chloe looked at him. The offer surprised her. But it seemed forced. He was offering because he thought he should, not because he really wanted her there. And what would he expect in return?

"This other guy," she said slowly, "we had an... arrangement."

"What kind of... oh. I'm not saying that! I'm just offering you the room, no strings. So you have somewhere safe."

Chloe shook her head. "No. I'm not taking it without giving something back."

"Why not? I'm not asking for anything."

"I'm not a freeloader."

"Chloe..." His voice was firm.

"No."

"I can't just let you sleep on the street. You're my friend."

"I'll be fine."

He let out a long sigh. "It's not safe. You're not going to be fine. Not for long."

"I can take care of myself. And when I get the dog out, he'll keep me safe."

"What are the fees to get him out? I could help you pay for that."

Chloe was sorely tempted. She didn't know how she was going to raise the money otherwise. She hesitated.

"Maybe... I don't know how much it's going to be. They won't release him yet. Not until they've decided he's safe." She shook her head. "I don't know how they're going to make him safe by locking him up again. He'll just be more scared, like he was... before."

"Okay... but would you let me know when they decide, and I can help you get him out? Or maybe... if you can't get him... you can choose another dog."

Chloe's eyes misted up immediately before she was aware of the emotion. She blinked rapidly. "I don't want another dog. I have to have him."

As it started to get late, Chloe returned to the Humane Society. She settled down a distance away and watched for people to leave and for the lights to go out. Once it looked as if everyone had gone home, she went around the back of the building and to the outdoor dog runs, as before.

"Here, boy... come on out," she called softly. "Come on."

She really did have to give him a name. 'Here, boy' could have been intended for any of the dogs within earshot. Several of them poked their noses out their door flaps, but only her dog came out and walked up to the fence, tail swinging slowly back and forth.

"Come on," Chloe repeated.

He came right up to the fence. Chloe poked her fingers through the links and he licked her and pushed up against the fence for her to scratch his ears, performing several contortions to get her to scratch the best places. Chloe chuckled softly at this. She breathed in the cool night air, feeling it flowing all the way into her lungs and spreading a feeling of well-being through her body. The stars seemed brighter and everything around her more clear and crisp. The dog's fur was soft under her fingers.

After a few minutes, she sat down on the grass and dug into her backpack to give him a few treats. For a long time, they sat and communed with each other, just feeling the other's closeness.

Eventually, Chloe lay down against the fence, and he cuddled up to her the best that he could.

~

"Chloe! Chloe, wake up. You can't keep doing this. You're trespassing. Come on. Get up."

Chloe awoke to Wanda's voice, shaking, and light kicks. She rubbed her eyes and sat up, sweeping her hair out of her face and back over her shoulders.

"This isn't a campsite," Wanda growled. "Now move on."

"He's my dog."

Wanda let out a puff of breath, making a cloud of smoke in the chilly air. "Not according to the report filed by the man who tattooed him," she said.

"What?"

"He has an identification tattoo. And the registration is not to you."

"You can't give him back to that man! He's the one who beat the dog!"

"Where's the proof? You're the last one who had possession of him, and his most recent injuries are pretty fresh. How do I know you're not the one who beat him?"

Chloe looked at the dog, yawning and stretching and sticking close to the fence where Chloe sat. He bumped his nose against the links, trying to rub against her.

"Does it look like I'm the one who hurt him?"

"No," Wanda admitted. "It doesn't. But that's not proof. You'd better scram if you don't want to get in any trouble."

Chloe got rustily to her feet. She put her fingers through the links of the fence so that she could touch the dog again and scratch his nose. "Okay. But I'm not abandoning him. When you decide he can be released, I'm bailing him out."

Wanda shook her head. "Don't set your heart on it," she warned.

~

Chloe didn't raise much money from playing guitar, but she didn't eat, so she kept all the money to put toward the dog's impound fees. She went back to the Humane Society, as she had the previous two nights, once the lights went out.

As she called the dog and then crouched down to his level to greet him, whispering to him and warming at the touch of his tongue, there were footsteps behind her.

The dog growled, and Chloe whirled around to face the intruder. It was a cop. A big one. Not that Chloe would have fought even a small cop.

"Chloe Simpson?" he asked.

"I didn't do anything," Chloe said. Although Wanda had accused her of trespassing, it wasn't like Chloe had broken in or stolen anything. She had just walked up to talk to her dog. That wasn't against the law.

"You're under arrest for theft. Turn around please, hands on your head."

Chloe's mouth fell open. "Theft? I haven't stolen anything!"

"Turn around, please."

She obeyed his instructions. The dog growled and snarled as the policeman patted her down and then pulled her hands around behind her back and ratcheted handcuffs closed around them.

"Come with me, please."

He picked up her backpack and escorted her back around the building to his car, which was parked in a dark corner of the parking lot where Chloe hadn't noticed it.

"I didn't steal anything," Chloe asserted.

"That dog was in your possession when it was apprehended."

"Yes."

"Where did you get it?"

Chloe couldn't think of a lie that made sense. She'd already told Wanda that the previous owner had beaten the dog. How would she know that if she'd just picked up the dog wandering on the street? And the vicious man wasn't going to say that he had given it to Chloe. They both knew better.

"I... I rescued him. He was chained up and starving. So I rescued him."

He reminded her of her rights, including the right to shut up and not incriminate herself. He put Chloe into the back seat of the car, pushing her head down to make sure she didn't bump it on the car's doorframe. Chloe sat in silence all the way to the police station. They couldn't arrest her for rescuing the dog. Not when they knew the truth about how he was being abused.

She was fingerprinted and photographed and taken to a small, airless room to be questioned. Chloe remembered the nice room that Bill had talked to her in after she was taken from her home. This time, she was obviously not the victim, she was the suspect.

"So, the way you see it, you rescued this dog," said the police officer, who had tersely introduced himself as Baker.

Chloe nodded. "He was chained up outside. He wasn't being given any food or water. If I'd left him there, he would just have died."

"How do you know he wasn't being given any food or water?"

"He didn't have any dishes. I watched him for a long time. He didn't get anything to eat."

"He could have been fed while you weren't there to see."

"Have you seen him? His belly's just about sticking to his spine. He was starving to death."

"So you saw him and decided it was up to you to rescue him."

"Yeah. Nobody else was doing anything to help him."

"You don't know that."

"I went and fed him for a few days. I never saw anyone else trying to help."

He scratched something into his notepad. "So then you decided to steal him."

"I decided to rescue him! Somebody had to do it! That guy was going to kill him otherwise."

"So... you did see his owner. You knew that the dog hadn't been abandoned."

Chloe examined the question from several angles. She couldn't deny that she had known the dog belonged to someone. That she had seen the owner.

"I saw that guy beat him with a baseball bat. Break his skull and ribs."

Baker gave her a long, thoughtful look. He looked back down at his notepad and made more notes.

"Describe this guy who beat him."

Chloe was happy to do so. If she could get that beast put behind bars, where he couldn't hurt any other animals, it would make her happy. She never wanted him to have the dog again. Or any dog. She gave all the details she could remember to Baker.

"How do I know that you're not the one who beat and starved him? It's easy to blame someone else, but you don't have any proof, do you?"

"What am I supposed to do? Take his picture?"

"Well, you could have called the police or Animal Control when he was still there so that we could investigate and lay charges. We could have rescued the dog. That's what Animal Control does, you know. Rescues animals. That's not up to random teenagers."

Chloe stared at him. Calling the police to rescue the dog had never even crossed her mind. The dog was there in front of her. He needed to be rescued. She had rescued him.

"Um... I didn't think..."

"No, you didn't, did you? Instead, you went and got yourself mixed up in something. You can't just steal from someone and then try to justify it. It's still stealing. Call the police. Get the professionals involved."

"Yeah... I guess."

"I don't like to see an animal abused any more than you do. I want to get this guy. But citizens getting in the way like you did, you make it impossible for me to do my job. I can't arrest him now, because he's just going to turn around and say that you're the one who abused the dog. And I can't prove otherwise."

"You can't give the dog back to him."

"I have my doubts that that dog is ever going to be released to anyone. He's too aggressive."

"Not to me."

"You can't guarantee that he's never going to hurt anyone. You can't even tell me that you'll keep him inside your house, can you?"

"I don't have a house."

Baker nodded.

"You can't let them put him to sleep; you know the only reason he's aggressive is because he's been abused."

"But it doesn't matter why he's aggressive. It only matters that he is." He closed his notepad. "I don't have anything to do with the decision. That's up to the Humane Society, not to me."

"You won't try to help him?"

"Right now I'm trying to help you."

"You can't help me."

"I'll recommend that charges not be pursued against you, but I don't have any control over the outcome. And if the owner decides to file against you civilly, there's nothing I can do about it."

Chloe folded her arms across her chest and shook her head. "Let him try," she challenged. "I'll testify I saw him beat the dog."

"Good for you." Baker stood up, motioning for Chloe to stand. He handcuffed her wrists again.

"What now?" Chloe asked.

"Now, you get a cell you for the night. I can't tell what will happen after that; it's out of my hands."

"Least it will be warm."

"And it comes with breakfast," Baker added, with a hint of a smile.

Chloe rolled her eyes. But she had to admit that she was looking forward to it. She wasn't big on breakfast, but she hadn't eaten for more than a day, so she would eat all of the reconstituted eggs they fed her.

CHAPTER
Twenty-Eight

Chloe went to the Humane Society in the afternoon, as soon as she was released. There were still charges pending against her, but the judge didn't see any reason to keep her behind bars over a petty theft. They needed the space for more dangerous criminals. Chloe didn't want the dog to think that she had forgotten him or abandoned him. It was important to see him and reassure him that she was still around and would be getting him out as soon as she was able.

She didn't go around back to the dog run, but in through the front doors of the building, where an employee or volunteer happily showed her the dog room and left her alone to have a look around. Chloe went immediately to the black dog. He nosed her through the bars, whining.

"Hi, boy. Did you miss me? I'm sorry I couldn't sleep here last night. I was in jail. In a cage like this. But they let me out this afternoon."

He didn't seem to hold it against her, sucking up all the attention she could give him. The volunteer who had shown Chloe in was back a little while later and looked at the dog.

"Wow, that's the first time I've seen him happy and not growling at anyone. You've got a real connection with him," the girl noted.

Chloe nodded.

"Do you want to see how he'll behave on leash for you? I'm sure he'd like to get out and stretch his legs a little. He hasn't been able to go anywhere but his run, and he must be tired of the scenery."

"Yeah. That'd be nice." Chloe's spirits lifted. Was there a chance they would let her just walk out with him?

"I'll go arrange it," the girl chirped, and headed toward the offices in the back.

Chloe pretty much expected what happened next. They weren't going to just let her walk him out of there. The girl returned, another figure behind her.

"That dog is still on hold. He's too unpredictable to let anyone take him out yet."

"But he was acting real nice and quiet—"

"Oh, it's you." Wanda looked Chloe over and shook her head. "You know I can't give him to you."

"I just came to say hi."

"This is Chloe," Wanda told the girl. "This is who the dog was apprehended from."

The girl frowned. "But he doesn't act afraid or aggressive around her. Look how calm he is."

Wanda looked into the cage. "I know. But we have to go through the appropriate channels. We can't just decide that he's fine around her and he can go back to her. We have to make inquiries. Test his behavior with others. Make sure that he's properly trained so that he's not going to freak out when someone yells, moves too fast, or picks up a baseball bat." Her mouth twisted in an ironic smile.

"I dunno. He seems really good with her," the volunteer said.

Wanda nodded.

"Can't she go in there?" the girl asked. "Interact with him directly?"

"It's not safe."

"It is for me," Chloe said. "He's not going to hurt me."

Wanda's expression was closed. The dog nuzzled Chloe's hand, making a high-pitched noise that was barely audible.

"Please," begged Chloe, not afraid to grovel for what she wanted. "Please just let me go in and touch him."

Wanda didn't answer right away, which was a good sign. Chloe waited, letting her think about it. Finally, Wanda nodded.

"Okay, you can go in there. You can't take him out for a walk and you have to be supervised. And you have to sign a waiver that you won't sue us if he bites you."

"Oh, thank you! Thank you, thank you!" Chloe was so happy she felt like she would burst. Finally, some progress in the right direction.

Wanda took her back to the office, where Chloe scrawled her babyish signature on the waiver form. Wanda insisted that she take off her coat and backpack and not take anything into the cage.

"Can't I take his brush?" Chloe asked. "I want to keep his coat from getting matted again, and no one else can get close enough to do it for him. It gets him used to being touched."

"Just the brush," Wanda agreed. "Anything in your pockets?"

Chloe cleaned out what change she had. She put it into her backpack and left her coat and pack in Wanda's office. Wanda took her back out to the cage and Chloe waited impatiently, her heart thumping fast, while Wanda seemed to take forever to find the right key and get the door open. The dog was pushing on the door, trying to nose his way out to Chloe.

"Shh... get back," Chloe told him, grabbing his collar and directing him back into the cage as she pushed her way through the door. "I'm coming in. Settle down."

He let her into the little room and pranced around her excitedly. Chloe dropped to her knees and put her arms around him, burying her face in his fur. All her worry and anxiety receded, but it wasn't like when she disassociated. She was still aware of everything around her, still in full possession of all her senses, but the worry and frustration just all melted away. She was with the dog. In the present. She shared his time and space and hadn't withdrawn from anything.

"That's all right, boy," she murmured. "That's all right. I'm here."

"Be careful," Wanda warned. "He has broken ribs. You put pressure on them, and he may go after you."

"I know. I'm not going to hurt him. And he's not going to hurt me."

"He's unpredictable and very aggressive."

Chloe looked up from the dog. "Is that what you see?" she demanded.

"Well, I have to admit, I haven't seen him this mellow before."

"He's my dog," Chloe said firmly. "One hundred percent mine."

Wanda didn't answer. She stood there watching for a few more minutes, then passed responsibility off to the volunteer. "You give me a shout if anything concerns you."

Chloe sat on the hard concrete floor and ran the brush bristles lightly over the dog's fur. He sniffed at it curiously but didn't nip at her. In a few minutes he was rubbing his face and body against it, and if he'd been a cat, he would have been purring. Chloe laughed and continued to brush him for a long time. Eventually, he crawled into her lap and curled up there like a kitten. He was much too big for Chloe's thin lap, but she hugged him close to her, kissing the wound at the top of his head and stroking him gently.

When Jozef asked Chloe if she would go to a movie with him, she had been surprised and didn't know what to do about it. The last time she had been to a movie theater was when she was just a kid, and Mim had taken her and the younger children to some popular animated movie. Gunter had never offered to take her, and certainly, none of the other boyfriends had. John had suggested going to a movie, but they never actually went. He seemed to prefer staying in with Chloe, relying on takeout and rented movies or just whatever was on TV.

Jozef laughed at Chloe's expression. "Don't tell me you've never been asked to a movie before," he teased.

"Of course I have," Chloe retorted. "I've been to lots of movies. With lots of guys."

It was a bald-faced lie, but she didn't know what else to say. She couldn't very well admit that no one had ever taken her out on a real date.

"Okay, then. Will you go to one with me?"

"What movie?" Chloe asked, stalling for time. She couldn't put her finger on why she was so panicked about his question. But it was disorienting. She had repeatedly told herself that Jozef didn't have any interest in her. And if he didn't have any interest in her, then why would he offer to take her out? It was different than offering her a bed or money to bail out the dog. Those were practical things. Sometimes people gave away money or let someone stay at their house for a day or two without expecting anything back. The people who put money in Chloe's guitar case didn't get anything in return. They just listened to her music.

But taking Chloe to a movie was different. People didn't just take homeless people to movies to make them feel better about themselves or to get them off the streets. They took them to movies because they had a romantic attachment to them, or because they were little kids.

"I'm not sure what is showing," Jozef said. "We could look at the listings and find something that you like."

"I guess."

"Does that mean you guess we could find something you liked, or you guess you'll come with me?"

Chloe frowned, scratching at a bit of dried food on her pants. "I guess… I could go with you."

"Great! I suppose I should find out what kind of movies you like. I don't like horror, so I'm hoping that's not all you like."

"No. I don't know… maybe comedy or adventure."

"That sounds good. I'm sure we can find something. Have you seen any previews of what's showing?"

"No." She didn't exactly have a TV to watch, so she wasn't sure how he thought she would have seen any commercials.

They met up in the evening, at the theater that Jozef directed her to. Chloe was afraid she was going to have to stand around waiting for him, but he was there ahead of her and put his arm protectively around her so that the single guys standing around without dates scoping out the girls would know that she was taken and wouldn't harass her.

"You found it okay?" he asked.

"Yeah. I know my way around pretty well now."

"Good. Let's look at the posters and see what we want to watch."

They walked around looking at the posters on the wall, but Jozef dropped his arm from Chloe and stood and walked with her without touching her. Chloe puzzled, trying to sort out the mixed message. Was she wrong and they were only there as friends? Maybe there was some new trend of taking homeless people to movies. She stood close to him as they picked out a movie, Chloe settling on a romantic comedy as the best opportunity to test out the parameters of their relationship. She just about bumped into him; she was standing so close as he purchased popcorn and drinks for them. He bought Chloe a huge drink that she knew she'd never be able to get down. Particularly not without having to pee halfway through the movie. And an enormous popcorn for them both to share. That was good; better than him buying them separate popcorns so their hands would never happen to touch each other as they both reached for the bag at the same time.

They sat in the middle of the theater, not the back where no one would be looking at them during the movie, so she assumed that Jozef wasn't interested in any fooling around. She looked around at the people who were arriving and finding their seats. She pointed to a young man who was standing by himself, trying to decide where to sit.

"He's cute. I wonder why he's not with anyone."

Jozef frowned. "What?"

"We should tell him to sit with us. He looks lonely." Chloe waved at the boy. He looked startled and turned to see if there was someone standing behind him.

"No, you!" Chloe said. "You want to come sit with us? Come on over."

He approached tentatively. "I don't want to be in the way," he said.

"No, we're just friends," Chloe said. She patted the seat next to her. "Come on over here."

Jozef said nothing. He put on a strained smile when the young man sat down on Chloe's other side. But he didn't get after Chloe for bringing in a third wheel and didn't tell the young man that they were on a date and wanted some privacy. He didn't even grab Chloe's hand to show his possession of her. He did nothing to indicate that he was angry or upset about the situation.

"What's your name?" Chloe asked the young man, touching his leg for an instant.

"Uh, Harvey."

"You don't have a date tonight?"

Harvey shook his head. Chloe looked back at Jozef. He was staring at her, his face a little pink, his expression hurt. She returned his gaze, waiting for him to do something about it.

But he still did nothing. Chloe let her body slump into the soft cushions of the theater chairs. She took a sip of her pop. Apparently, it must have been 'take a homeless person to the theater' day. Because Jozef still had no interest in a relationship with her.

❧

"Chloe, I have a proposal for you."

Chloe looked at Wanda as the woman locked the dog's cage, following Chloe's latest session with him.

"Yeah, what?" she asked.

"You don't have the money to pay for the dog's impound fees."

"No. Not yet. But I'm saving up as much as I can."

"Except that they get bigger the longer he's kept here. And you're not his actual owner."

"I would take care of him. That other guy doesn't want him back, does he?"

"I don't know if he'll take any action. So here's my thought… you help out with other jobs around here, cleaning out cages, taking dogs for walks, and so on, and earn the money that you'll need to get him out."

Chloe felt her eyes widen in her surprise. "Really?"

"You like animals, right? So it wouldn't be a job you'd hate."

"Sure. I like animals. Taking care of them."

"We could involve you in the dog's retraining, since you're the only one who can really reach him. I'll teach you what to do. You can work with me in trying to get him to the point where he can be in public again."

"I can do that!"

"There's no guarantee, okay? I'm not the one who will make the final call about whether he can be reintegrated or needs to be put down. So I'm not making any promises that he'll even be released."

"But if he is, I'll be able to bail him out, and I can take him with me, right?"

"I don't know what's going to happen with his owner. He hasn't relinquished. He says the dog was stolen from him; he didn't give up his ownership rights."

"But you know he can't go back there! That guy will beat him to death next time!"

"I'll do everything I can to prevent that. But again... I can't make you any promises. I don't know what's going to happen, or in the end, if you'll get the dog. I can't tell you it will work out. Because it might not. There are lots of other things that could happen."

"But if I don't do it," Chloe said, "then he's never going to be retrained right, and I won't have enough money to get him."

Wanda nodded.

"I'm going to do it, then. I have to."

"Are you sure? Do you want to sleep on it? Talk it over with a friend?"

"No. When do you want me to start?"

Wanda gave her a wide smile. "Why don't you start by cleaning out the black's cage?"

Chloe nodded. "Sure."

"I'll show you where everything is—"

"You don't need to. I know." Chloe had been around the Humane Society enough over the preceding days to know where everything was. She went to the supply closet and helped herself.

Chloe was awake and waiting for Wanda by the back door when Wanda got there in the morning. Wanda looked Chloe over, reaching up to brush a piece of grass out of her hair.

"I keep telling you; you're not allowed to sleep here," she said. "It's trespassing. You need to find somewhere else to sleep."

"I work here," Chloe asserted. "It's not trespassing."

"You're not supposed to be here after closing. Go find a shelter or something. It doesn't do either of you any good to be sleeping out there on the ground. Isn't it cold?"

"Not so much anymore. I can stay warm."

"Change your clothes before you start." Wanda's mouth tightened. "Can you wash those in the sink and hang them up in the bathroom to dry?"

Chloe nodded. She didn't think that she smelled offensive. Especially not in a place like the Humane Society, filled with the smells of animals, feces, urine, bleach, and other cleaning agents. How bad could Chloe's sweat be? But she followed Wanda's instructions, scrubbing her clothes with soap, rinsing, wringing, and hanging them up to dry. She didn't think anyone would steal them from the staff bathroom. It was too bad the Humane Society didn't have uniforms. Then she'd have another set of clothes.

"Okay, where do you want me to start?" she asked Wanda, after getting herself a cup of coffee for breakfast.

"Rodent and ferret cages, and then on to the cats."

"Okay."

"You okay around rodents? You're not going to freak out and let them get loose?"

Chloe frowned at this. "No, why would I do that?"

"Let's just say it wouldn't be the first time it happened. Tux might not mind, but I'd rather rehome the rodents than make dinner of them."

Chloe grinned. Tux was the one-eyed black cat with a white bib that roamed free around the Humane Society. A pet or mascot, he wasn't up for adoption. He was friendly to everyone and so mellow around any of the animals that were brought in, he never turned a hair. Chloe went to see him before starting on the rodent cages, explaining that she wouldn't be providing him with a mousie breakfast or lunch and he'd just have to make do with kibble.

He rubbed against her, his purr rasping loudly. Chloe gave him one last chin-scratch and went to do her job.

Chloe had been occupied by her work and hadn't been paying attention to any of the comings or goings around the Humane Society. But then she heard the dog start to bark and snarl. He'd been pretty good around the staff members lately, used to them and hopefully understanding that they would feed and care for him and wouldn't hurt him. Chloe worked with him every day, trying to introduce him to new people and get him used to the various changes and distractions that he would have to take in stride if he was ever to leave the Humane Society with her.

Chloe immediately straightened up and went to see what was the matter. Had something spooked him? Had a visitor gotten too close to his cage or made some unexpected movement that had upset him? Chloe froze when she got into the dog room. Wanda stood in front of the dog's cage, the dog's former owner at her side.

Chloe wanted to rush in and settle the dog down, but she couldn't approach him while his legitimate owner was there. Then the horrible man would know who had taken his dog and might come after her. He had already laid theft charges against her. She didn't want to have to face him in person.

"Shut up, dog!" the man growled. "You know better than to make that kind of noise! Just lay off!"

Chloe swallowed a protest and just stood there with a lump in her throat.

"Open up the door," the man told Wanda. "I want to see him. He knows me."

"I can't do that, sir. He's too aggressive."

"He won't bite me. He knows better than that."

"This dog is not allowed out of his cage. We're doing our best to retrain him, but he is not safe to be around the general public right now."

"I'm not the general public. I'm his owner! He's my dog! You know that."

"He may have belonged to you. But he is acting too aggressively for me to allow you to get close to him."

"It's that girl who stole him. I don't know what she did to him. He was never like this when he was with me."

"Did you ever hit this dog?"

"Hit him? Maybe a smack on the rump when he was a puppy and made a mess."

"You didn't starve him?"

The man looked at the dog's lean figure. "He must have worms or something, for him to have lost weight like that. Don't you people deworm them?"

"Yes, he has been treated."

"Then he's getting better, right? Starting to put weight back on?"

Wanda nodded. "Yes, he is."

"You see? Must have been the worms."

"And you never hit him?" The man was shaking his head vigorously. "With a baseball bat?"

His jaw dropped, and for a moment he stopped shaking his head.

Chloe could see the question that went through his mind clearly. *How did you know that?* But the words did not pass his lips.

"I wouldn't abuse an animal," he said. "Not even a stupid, ungrateful one like this."

He moved closer to the bars and the dog set up another volley of barks and growls.

"Shut up!" the man bellowed.

The dog backed away, eyeing the man warily. The man banged the bars of the cage, and the dog backed still further away, teeth still bared, but not making a sound.

The man turned abruptly to Wanda. "I'm not paying hundreds of dollars to get him out of impound when I wasn't the one who brought him here. He was stolen from my fenced yard. That's not my fault, so why should I pay anything?"

"We've spent money taking care of him and putting time into retraining him. He's had to have medical treatment and his bones are still healing. The impound fees help to cover what we've sunk into him."

"Why would I pay to get a damaged dog back?"

"Does that mean you are relinquishing your rights?"

"What will happen if I do that?"

"He'll likely be put down," Wanda said. "You can see how aggressive he is. We can't adopt him out to a family like that."

The man nodded. "Good. Put him down, then," he agreed. "You need me to sign something?"

"Yes. I'll get you the form."

Wanda took him to the back office. Her eyes flicked toward Chloe as she left, seeing her there for the first time. Her expression was a warning. *Don't interfere.* Chloe let them walk by her without a word.

Chloe was supposed to be cleaning the cat cages, but she didn't move to the cat room. She wanted to be with her dog and make sure that nothing happened to him. Her chest was tight and her eyes stung with tears. Wanda had promised to do what she could so that Chloe could get the dog, but now she was saying that he was going to be put down. They were going to destroy him because of the trauma that the evil man had put him through.

Chloe didn't start with the black dog's cage. He was all worked up and she was too. They both needed time to cool down. She started at the other end, entering each cage, interacting with each dog for a few minutes and then cleaning the cage out. It seemed like a long time before she heard Wanda showing the man out. Then she came back looking for Chloe.

"You can't put him down!" Chloe burst out. "He's doing so much better! You know the only reason he was upset was because that was the man who beat him. How would you feel, if someone who hurt you acted like they were going to do it again? It's not the dog's fault!"

Wanda held up her hands. "Whoa. You need to calm down, Chloe."

"You said you're going to put him down!"

"I told that vile man that he would *likely* be put down. I never said it was for sure."

"But you can't do that! He's making progress. Please—"

"Do you think that he would have relinquished ownership if I said that *you* were going to take him?" Wanda demanded.

Chloe stopped short. "No."

"No. But when I said that the dog would likely be put down, he relinquished. He doesn't own that dog anymore. We do."

"You do," Chloe echoed.

"That's right. So he won't be coming back here and upsetting the black. And he won't be demanding the dog back when it's recovered. He's gone and he won't be coming back. And he will not be approved to adopt any other dogs, in case you're wondering."

A smile slowly crept onto Chloe's face. "He won't be coming back here again."

"And now that I've seen him with the dog, and you with the dog, if you have to go to court, I can testify that without doubt, he is the one that beat that dog, not you. And that while you might have taken him away unlawfully, you were justified in doing it to save his life."

Chloe breathed out a long sigh of relief. "Really?"

"Really. Now are you calmed down enough to go have a talk with your dog and make sure he's okay?"

Chloe nodded and started toward the cage. "*My* dog?" she repeated.

"If he continues to show the same improvement that he has, I think I can pretty confidently say *your* dog."

Chloe unlocked the lock on the cage. Unlike most of the dog

cages, the door wasn't just latched but was securely padlocked to make sure that no one could be hurt by approaching him without knowing his temperament.

The dog came to the gate and whined, eager for Chloe to come in. After pulling the door shut behind her, Chloe immediately dropped to her knees and gave him a big hug.

"It's okay," she told him. "That horrible man will never be coming back. You never have to see him again. He's not going to hurt you anymore."

The dog licked her face. Chloe laughed and tried to wipe off the dog slobber, while he continued to try to lick away her salty tears.

"Shh, stop that!" she giggled.

"It's about time that dog had a name, don't you think?" Wanda suggested.

Chloe nodded.

"Do you have something in mind? Black Beauty? Coal?"

Chloe shook her head. She had put a lot of thought into it, but the name had not come to her until the man had left, gone from their lives forever. She pressed her face into the dog's dark fur, feeling the thrum of his heart and totally aware of everything around her. She felt centered and whole. And then she named his name.

"Triumph."

CHAPTER
Twenty~Nine

"Y ou're looking happy today," Jozef observed.

Chloe looked up at him and gestured for him to sit with her as she worked her way through a sandwich for supper.

She hadn't seen him much since the failed movie date. Rather than being provoked into fighting for her, he had apparently given up. Or he had never actually been interested in a relationship, as she had suspected.

But then, Chloe hadn't been a lot of the usual places since then. She'd been at the Humane Society. Working there, sleeping, living mostly on coffee and the occasional doughnut or muffin. She didn't like to leave Triumph alone for too long. Every time she left the Humane Society, she felt like he might not be there when she got back. Wanda reassured Chloe that she wasn't going to let someone else adopt Triumph, but so many of the visitors seemed attracted to him that Chloe feared one day one of them would succeed in talking Wanda into it. After all, what kind of a life could Chloe give him? Like Jenny with Babe, Chloe couldn't give him a roof over his head, a warm bed at night, or guarantee food to eat. She didn't know if Wanda would let her continue to work at the Humane Society after they let Triumph out, or whether her employment would then be up and she would have to go back to busking for loose change. It made a lot more sense for Wanda to give Triumph to a family who could provide for him. People who could afford the best food, had grounds for him to run on, and could afford a trainer or dog psychologist if Triumph had any lingering issues.

"How have you been?" Jozef asked.

"Good. I'm going to get my dog out soon. He's doing really well."

"That's great. I'm glad to hear it. How much money will you need? I told you I would help."

"I'm not sure how much it will be," Chloe confessed. "But it's covered."

"It's covered?"

"I got a job."

"Really?" Jozef's smile was broad. "I'm so happy for you, Chloe! And it's working out? No trouble this time?"

"Well... mostly. I still mess up sometimes. But I don't have to rush, and I don't have to deal with customers. I work at the Humane Society, helping to take care of Triumph and the other animals."

"Triumph is what you named your dog?"

Chloe nodded. "Uh-huh."

"That's a great name."

They were both quiet for a while. Jozef had bought a sandwich as well, and they both ate their sandwiches and drank their coffee. Chloe was awkward. She had thought that after the movie, he wouldn't talk to her anymore. He'd obviously been angry, but he hadn't fought for her or confronted her about it. Didn't that mean that he wasn't going to pursue a relationship?

But here he was again, seeking her out, sitting with her and chatting as if nothing had happened.

"Chloe."

Chloe looked at him. "Yeah?"

"I want to talk... about us."

Chloe took a bite of her sandwich and didn't say anything at first. Let him talk, then. *Us? Was there an us?* She wasn't sure if there ever had been or if there ever would be.

"Chloe... when I took you to the movie, you were behaving sort of... I don't know. Bizarre. Just what were you doing?"

Chloe traced a burn scar on the table with her fingertip. "I dunno. Trying to see..."

She closed her eyes, unable to explain.

"Trying to see what? How far away you could push me? Are you so afraid of a relationship that you'll resort to anything to keep me away?"

Chloe shrugged. "Do you want... a relationship?"

"Of course I do!"

Jozef's voice was loud enough to attract the attention of other patrons. There was a lull in the conversations around them as people looked over to see what was going on. Chloe kept her head down.

"You don't act like it," she said.

"What does that mean? I see you whenever I can. Try to help you with anything that you need. Buy you food. Take you on a date. What exactly are you expecting me to do?"

"Take control. Say what *you* want. Tell me... tell me what you want me to do." Chloe shook her head. "Because I can't figure it out."

Jozef stared at her. "You want me to tell you what I want?"

Chloe nodded.

"Isn't it obvious?"

"No."

Jozef sat back in his seat, looking at her as if his whole perspective had changed.

"I want you to be yourself. To hang out with me because you like me. To enjoy being with me."

"But... what do you want me to *do*?"

"I just want to take it one step at a time. To learn about each other... see if we are compatible."

Chloe chewed on her sandwich.

"How do we know that? Other guys I've been with... I've never done that. I don't know what that means."

Jozef stared off into space, somewhere past Chloe's head.

"You've never told me anything about yourself. About your past, and how you became homeless, and how you became the person you are."

Chloe shifted uncomfortably. Talk to him about her past? Talk about herself? None of the other men had ever needed that information.

"Why does that matter?"

"Well... think about your dog. Triumph. Why did you choose him over any other dog? There are hundreds of dogs in the city. You must have seen plenty of others. Maybe strays wandering around loose. What was it about Triumph that made you pick him out? Made you want to rescue him and take care of him?"

"He needed my help," Chloe said. "He was being hurt... and neglected... and I just had to help him."

"And after you rescued him... why go to all the work to get him out of the pound? He was safe. He didn't need to be rescued from there."

Chloe rubbed her sweaty palms on her pants. She didn't want to tell Jozef about the way that Triumph made her feel. She didn't know how to describe it. She needed Triumph as much as he needed her. But she couldn't explain that to Jozef. Not without explaining a lot of other things.

"Does knowing what Triumph went through help you understand his behavior?" Jozef said, changing direction.

Chloe nodded immediately. "Of course! I understand why he's more scared of men than women or children. And why he gets aggressive the way he does, when he gets scared. He's not a mean dog. He's scared. Traumatized."

"So maybe if I knew more about you, I'd understand better why you act the way you do. Things that don't make sense to me, maybe I could make sense out of them."

Chloe pondered over this. She and Jozef came from very different backgrounds. She didn't know a lot about the way that he had grown up and whether he had many challenges in his life like she had. But he seemed to come from a comfortable background. Not poverty-stricken like Chloe and Mim. He had spoken in the past about both his father and his mother, as if he had grown up with both of them and they were still together. He had a religious background, though she had never asked him what it was. He was educated. A college professor. In fact, it seemed like he was opposite to her in just about everything. And maybe he found her behavior just as puzzling as she found his.

"Okay... so what do you want me to tell you?"

"What do you want to tell me? I don't want to pry. I don't want to know all your secrets. I just want to understand a little bit more about you. Just... something."

Chloe thought back. She understood Triumph because she knew how he had been caged, neglected, and beaten. She wasn't ready to reveal that much yet to Jozef. But if he knew just a little bit about her background... just the barest essential...

"When I was thirteen," she said, "my brother killed my father."

Jozef's eyes widened. He swore in disbelief. "Really, Chloe? That's horrible!"

Chloe shredded the crusts that were left of the sandwich. "It was awful," she admitted. "I was scared... but I wasn't sad. I felt... relieved. And when it was just me and my mom, that was the best. When it was just her and me... I felt... safer."

She didn't tell him about Gunter. Leave him out of it to start out with. Jozef had enough to think about.

"We didn't have much money. Not when Daddy was alive, and not after. We had insurance money so that we could get a place, but not much left over after that."

"What happened to your mom? Is she still around?"

Chloe hesitated. "She's in jail," she said finally. "That's why I had to go to the group home. Why I don't have any home anymore."

"What did she go to jail for?"

Chloe shook her head, closing her eyes. "Not yet."

"Okay. I told you I'm not trying to pry all your secrets out of you."

They were both done their sandwiches. Jozef reached across the table and put his hand over Chloe's bony one.

"Thank you for trusting me with that. I really appreciate it. I do want to see if we can work things out together. We'll just go one step at a time."

Chloe had barely slept. Any sleep that she did get was restless and full of nightmares that she wouldn't ever get Triumph out. The weather was pleasant, but her joints still ached from lying on the ground. When she moved around and Triumph's eyes opened, she tried to explain to him what was going on.

"I just can't wait until morning," she told him.

When Wanda arrived to open up the Humane Society, Chloe was waiting impatiently at the door, feeling like a child at Christmas, barely able to stand still with the excitement of seeing what was under the tree.

"You didn't forget?" Wanda teased.

Chloe laughed. It had been a long time since she could laugh so easily. Since she could feel lighthearted at all.

"I didn't forget!"

"Well, come in, then. I'll get coffee on, and we'll get started on the paperwork."

"I'll put the coffee on for you."

"Well, that should shave about twenty seconds off."

"Good!"

They smiled at each other. Chloe put on the coffee, went around and turned on all the lights, and went by Triumph's cage to give him a quick scratch behind the ears and to tell him that she would be back to see him again soon. The scars on the top of his head were healed. Wanda said that the bones were knitting well, and hopefully weren't causing Triumph pain anymore.

She went to the back office where Wanda was just sorting through the paperwork that had to be filled out.

"The director filed the paperwork yesterday to say that Triumph can be reintegrated," Wanda said. "So we'll process him to free him for adoption today. Calculate the impound fees, which you've promised to pay, and cut you a paycheck. Then... we'll fill out the paperwork to transfer ownership to you."

Chloe couldn't shut down the silly grin on her face. "And then he'll be mine. Forever!"

Wanda sighed. "Dogs don't live forever, unfortunately. And we don't know how much the abuse that he's gone through will affect his lifespan or quality of life. You'll have him for a few years."

Chloe nodded. "I'll have him for however long I can."

The paperwork was long and tedious, and they both rolled their eyes over all the warnings and advice that Wanda was required to give on Triumph's care and on being a responsible pet owner. Chloe signed and initialed all the forms where Wanda indicated, and eventually they got to the end of the stack.

"Let's go get your dog!"

Chloe jumped to her feet. As they walked to the cages, she asked, "Can he stay out, like Tux, while I'm working?"

Wanda looked at her, raising an eyebrow. "Are you thinking of staying on, now that you've got him out?"

Chloe stopped short.

"I... was hoping to... don't you still need someone to help?"

"You're good with the animals. I'm happy to keep you on if you want to stay. I just assumed that as soon as you got Triumph, you would be out of here."

"No, I'd like to keep my job. It's the best one I've had."

"Okay." They continued down the hall on the way to the dog room. "On one condition."

"What?" Chloe's stomach tied in a knot. She couldn't bring Triumph in to work? She would be expected to take up other duties?

"You can't sleep here."

Chloe laughed, relieved. "I don't need to if Triumph isn't."

"I'd better not find you here, then."

"Maybe I'll be able to get a place of my own." Now that she didn't have to save every penny for Triumph's impound fees, maybe she could find something that she could afford. She knew it would be no more than a room, but if she could at least get a place to call her own... Or maybe at some point, she would be moving in with Jozef, if they decided that they were compatible. It was a strange concept that Chloe was still trying to wrap her mind around. Jozef's concept of compatibility seemed to involve some kind of shared consciousness, and Chloe wasn't quite sure she understood it yet. They didn't have any experiences in common, but somehow in spite of that he still expected them to fit together... somehow.

"That would be good for you," Wanda said. "I hope you find a place that will take a dog."

At Chloe's expression, she cocked her head to the side. "What's wrong?"

Chloe unlocked the cage to get Triumph out. He pushed the gate with his nose, and she didn't stop him. Triumph immediately wanted cuddles, pushing against Chloe's hand and her leg, and whining for her attention. She knelt down to hug him and to snap his leash on.

"What a little wuss you are," she told him. "No one would believe that you are a vicious dog now."

"Chloe...? Did I say something that upset you?" Wanda asked.

Chloe looked at her for a moment. "When I first rescued Triumph, the guy I was living with kicked me out. And he's the one that called Animal Control to get him apprehended. That... wasn't such a great experience."

"That sounds like an understatement!" Wanda offered her hand to Triumph, who pushed his head against it for her to scratch his ears. "But... in the end, it was probably good for both of you. Triumph got the medical attention and retraining that he needed. You got a job. You're better off without a boyfriend like that."

Chloe smiled. "Yeah, you're right. Probably a good thing after all."

"Young lady here to see you, Maynard."

Bill shut off his computer screen and sat back for a moment to rub his burning eyes and get his perspective back. Sometimes it seemed like he was caught in a tunnel, spreading in either direction as far as the eye could see, with no way out. He knew he had only to step back and turn off the screen. He knew that the task force offered counseling to their members at any time, night or day, to help them to deal with the horrific images that they saw all day long. But sometimes, he still felt alone with no way out.

"She's in Room B," Cotter advised, still standing by, waiting for Bill to get up and take care of it.

"Yeah. Thanks. I just need a minute."

"Sure, of course."

More time passed. Eventually, Bill rubbed his eyes again and got to his feet. He wasn't sure who the unscheduled visitor was, but a young lady could have information about new victims, or identifying information about old ones. She was waiting for him while he was just sitting around feeling sorry for himself.

Bill walked into Visitor Room B and smiled expectantly at the young blond bending over talking to a coal-black dog. When he entered, she looked up. Her fingers dug into the dog's fur, disappearing into it.

"Uh... hi, Bill."

Her voice was very tentative. Bill stared at her, trying to place her.

It took longer than it should have. She was still young, thin, and blond. No longer bruised and disheveled, though, wearing makeup and clean, tidy clothes, she seemed like a different person.

"Is it... it's not Chloe Simpson, is it?"

She gave him a bright smile. Bill felt for a moment like he couldn't breathe. She hadn't smiled after the arrests. Even though the rescue was a success, she had considered him the enemy for taking her mother and her home away and had never smiled at him once. It bowled him right over.

Bill dropped into the chair across from her. "How are you? You're looking great!"

He didn't know if it was appropriate to shake her hand or to give her a hug. He wanted to do something to express how happy he was to see her. Chloe reached over to him to squeeze his hand for an instant. Not a handshake, just a warm, personal gesture.

"I'm doing better," she said. "Things are... things are getting better."

"Tell me about it." Bill settled into the chair, waiting for her story. He didn't know why she had come, but he was glad that she had. Any time he could see any of his rescued kids was a good day. Especially if they could smile at him like Chloe had.

"Umm... I don't really know what to say. I guess you probably know I didn't exactly stay at the group home."

"If by 'didn't exactly stay,' you mean flew out of there like a bat out of hell," Bill said, smiling.

Chloe laughed. "Uh... yeah. It wasn't for me."

"So what was for you? What are you doing now?"

"I'm trying to get my own place. I'm working now, so I want to get a room somewhere..."

"So... you're currently homeless? That's not good."

Chloe waved his concern away.

"Better than some of the places I've been. And Triumph keeps me safe." Her gaze dropped to the dog.

"That's a beautiful name for a dog. What made you choose it?"

Chloe didn't answer directly.

"I rescued him," she said. "He was chained up, and his owner was starving him and beating him."

"I heard something about that," Bill remembered. "The officer

who arrested you saw my name on your file and came to talk to me."
He met Chloe's gaze. "No way you could have left a dog to suffer
through that."

Chloe shook her head. Her eyes brimmed with tears.

"How could anyone do something like that?" she asked Bill. "How
could someone do that to a poor, defenseless dog? He never did
anything to deserve that!"

"No," Bill agreed. "And neither did you."

Her eyes moved away from him. "He didn't choose to stay there.
I... I did."

"Chloe, you were just as much an innocent victim and a prisoner
as that dog was. You didn't choose to be abused. You chose to
survive."

"I couldn't leave my mom. I couldn't leave..." She stopped,
trailing off.

"The babies?" Bill suggested.

She sat there staring off into space, her mind obviously far away
in the past. After a few minutes, the dog nudged her hands, whining. Chloe startled and looked down at him. She buried her fingers
in the dog's fur again, kneading his body. Her face was a grimace of
pain.

"I did everything I could for the babies," she said. "I wanted so
badly for them to survive. All of them. Any of them. Just one... but I
couldn't save them. No matter how hard I tried." She wiped at one
eye with the back of her wrist to avoid getting dog hair in it. "I
swear... I would have died to save those babies. But I couldn't."

"They weren't yours, were they?" Bill asked gently. "They were
your mother's."

"I don't understand what was wrong with her. Why she had to
hide them, and wouldn't go to the hospital. I understood about
Gunter, but the others... it was so sick, her giving them to me.
Refusing to take care of them."

Bill was silent, listening to the story, trying to glean as much as he
could from her words without planting any new ideas or interrupting
the flow.

Chloe made a motion like she was handing something to Bill, her
hands empty.

"'Take care of it,' she said. 'Just get rid of it.'" Chloe's voice was breaking, tears escaping her eyes. Bill was sickened by the words. "She told me once... 'babies are fragile. It only takes a few seconds.'"

Bill swore, his voice low and rough. "Infanticide as a means of birth control. Between that and what she allowed to happen to you... there's something wrong with her, Chloe. No normal person would behave like that."

"But I loved her," Chloe said. "No matter how bad she whipped me, I never wanted to leave. I never wanted to do anything to hurt her. She's my mom. I loved her, and I just wanted... I wanted her to love me too. I did everything she said. I always obeyed her... and she never told me she loved me."

Bill couldn't resist touching Chloe's hand, trying to comfort her. How she could love a monster like Mim Simpson, he didn't know. He'd read through the news articles, Social Services reports, and court documents detailing how Mim had allowed the other girls to be abused. How she had been complicit in it. And poor little Chloe, who had stayed loyally by her side all those years, had been hurt the worst of all.

"That's not how a normal mother behaves," he told Chloe. "Any mother would have been lucky to have you as her daughter."

Chloe nodded and sniffled, but Bill doubted if she believed it. She was still beating herself up for everything that her mother told her she had done wrong. For everything that had gone wrong in Mim's life.

"She beat you too?" Bill asked gently, as Chloe seemed to have talked herself out.

Chloe sniffled and looked at him. "I can't. I can't talk to you about it."

"Okay. Not yet. I understand. Do you want to tell me about the babies? Tell me what happened?"

Chloe rested her face in her palms. For a few minutes, she just sobbed, choking, heartbreaking sounds. He didn't know how to comfort her. He knew that nothing he said could erase the damage that had already been done. So he just waited, hoping she would calm on her own.

The dog thrust his face in Chloe's and licked at the tears. Chloe made a snorting sound and pushed him away. Triumph kept trying to get at her face, and she held him close, wiping her face in his fur. She rubbed her nose with the back of her hand.

"Dog fur up my nose!"

Bill gave a little chuckle. Chloe took a few deep breaths to steady herself and began to talk in a calm, even tone.

"The first one was while Gunter was with us," she said, taking long breaths between each phrase as she explained. "He was my guidance counselor from school, and he... liked junior high girls. Mom said I had to hide the baby, to get rid of it, so that Gunter wouldn't find out."

"Why wouldn't Gunter have wanted her to have his baby?"

"It wasn't his. He didn't... him and my mom didn't... he knew they'd never... gotten together."

This was news to Bill. "Oh. I see."

"He didn't want Mom. He only... wanted me." She swallowed and looked at Bill for a fleeting moment. "You should get him out of that school. Don't let him... don't let him go after girls..."

"He's not there anymore," Bill assured her.

"He's not? You arrested him?"

Bill wasn't sure how much to say. He still wanted her to tell him more about the babies and the men who had abused her. But anything he told her might be enough to dissuade her from talking to him.

"We... started an investigation into him..."

Chloe's eyes were wide. "Did he run away? You have to find him because he'll just do it again."

Bill shook his head. "He took his own life."

"Oh." There was pain in her features. But maybe relief too. Gunter Gnatsky would never hurt her again, or any other young innocent girls. He was gone from the earth.

"So the first baby wasn't Gnatsky's," Bill said, trying to circle back to the original topic. "Do you know whose it was?"

"No. It was... too long to have been my dad's. And it wasn't Gunter's. I don't know who she was with. Maybe someone she worked for. I never asked."

"What happened?"

"I named him Joshua. I don't know what happened. Why he died. I gave him milk... but it was just cow's milk, not baby formula. Maybe he didn't get enough, or it wasn't the right thing for a baby. Or maybe there was something else wrong with him. Mom wouldn't take him to the doctor."

"Did you know he was sick?"

"No…" She kneaded the dog's fur. "Well, not really. He wasn't looking like a healthy, happy baby. His eyes got dark. And his skin got dry. He was snoring, and I thought it was just a cute little noise. But then… he stopped."

"I'm so sorry, Chloe."

She nodded and wiped away more tears for baby Joshua.

"The next one was premature," Bill remembered. "Was he still-born? Or was he born alive?"

"She," Chloe corrected. "That one was a girl. She didn't live for long… just a few minutes…"

"She was just too early," Bill deduced.

"She came early because Walter was beating on Mom," Chloe said. "She had awful bruises on her back. That's why she went into labor. I think."

"Walter?" This was a new name to Bill.

Chloe rolled her eyes up toward the ceiling. "Walter… Bose," she said after a few minutes of thinking. "He went to jail. Drugs."

"I remember," Bill said. "There was a Social Services investigation. But they left you there."

"He was gone," Chloe said with a shrug. "So why would they take me away?"

Bill refrained from pointing out that Mim was still abusive as well. "The next baby, was it Walter's? Or Sal's? Or was there another boyfriend in between?"

"He was the twin," Chloe explained. "Of the baby girl. Mom lost the girl, but then the labor stopped, and the boy kept growing."

"So he was Walter's."

Chloe nodded.

"Was he injured in utero?" Bill probed, remembering the baby's injuries. Perhaps even though he'd been born later, he had still carried injuries from the same beating that had made Mim miscarry the girl twin.

Chloe rubbed her dog's face and ears and kissed him on the nose. Bill waited.

"He was born okay," she said softly. "And I got a bottle and formula for him." She blinked tears away. "Phillip."

"That's a nice name." Bill waited, not pushing for more details.

"He was sick. Just like Joshua. He was strong for a few days, but then he got hot, and his eyes got dark. I wanted to take him to the hospital."

"He didn't die of a fever."

Chloe gulped. "She's bigger than me! I covered him up. I tried to protect him. But she's bigger and stronger."

Bill's heart wrenched at the pain and despair in her voice. "Your mother took him away from you?"

Chloe nodded.

"Because she didn't want you to take him to the hospital or get help."

"Yes." She sobbed.

"And she killed him."

Chloe just cried silently.

Bill took several long, deep breaths. "You're not responsible, Chloe. It's not your fault. You did your best. Saving those babies wasn't within your power."

"I should have... I should have taken him to someone without her knowing. I should have done it the day he was born when she was still too weak. I waited until she was strong. Too strong for me."

"It's still not your fault. Your mother was responsible for those deaths. Not you."

"I wanted them to live. I wanted so bad."

Bill touched her shoulder gently. Triumph watched Bill; not threatening, but alert to every movement.

"And the last one, he died from an infection before we could rescue you."

"Why couldn't he have lasted just one more day?" Chloe agonized. "Why couldn't I have saved just one of them? My baby brothers. I don't have any brothers. Not after Justin shot my daddy. If she would just have gone to the hospital to have them... nursed them... I would have changed all the diapers. Done all the hard stuff. If she had just let them live."

"Oh, sweetheart," Bill murmured. "I wish I could change it all."

"I can't hear babies cry. It makes me crazy. I'm afraid they'll be found... and hurt... and when they stop crying, I think they're dead..."

"Someday... one day you'll have a baby of your own. And he'll live."

Chloe wiped at her eyes. She shook her head. "I could never have a baby. I'd be too scared."

"I think you'd make a good mom."

"No. They would just die. Like my baby brothers."

Bill held her hand in his.

CHAPTER
Thirty

Chloe looked over the courtroom. She remembered going to Justin's trial. Now Mim was sitting in his place. And Blue Jeans. Sal, no longer in blue jeans, but in an orange prison jumpsuit. He looked smaller than Chloe remembered. Mim's bulk overlapped the edges of the chair. Chloe found herself studying Mim's body, looking for any sign that she was pregnant. But there was no way that Chloe could redeem herself now. There would be no more babies for Chloe to take care of. For her to try to save, to make up for the ones she had lost. Even if Mim got pregnant again, no one would be bringing Chloe the helpless baby, telling her to take care of it. Or to get rid of it.

Mim looked at Chloe across the courtroom. Her eyes were full of hate. Chloe's blood froze in her veins. She felt sick to her stomach.

What was she doing there?

She couldn't testify against Mim.

She was the obedient daughter. She was the one who always did what she was told. Chloe couldn't testify against Mim.

"Chloe."

The voice called her from a distance. Chloe was too far away to respond; she could barely even hear the words.

"Chloe, are you okay?"

She couldn't feel the hand on her arm. Looking down on herself from above, Chloe could see the lawyer shaking her, but she couldn't feel it. A little nudge couldn't pull her out of the trance. She could get through broken bones without even feeling them. The worse the trauma, the easier it was to slip away. And facing her mother again was just too much.

"Get the dog."

The guard the prosecutor spoke to left the courtroom through a side door that Chloe knew led to the little antechamber where she had left Triumph. And when he returned a couple of minutes later, he had Triumph with him. He led the dog up to Chloe. Triumph nudged Chloe's leg. She put her hand down and laid it on his back.

All at once, she was back in her body again. She sucked in air like she was drowning. All of the sensory inputs rushed back, overwhelming her. The lights and noise of the courtroom. The guilt and worry that Mim's gaze inspired. Chloe's stomach boiled and bubbled so much she was afraid she was going to throw up.

"You're okay," Temple murmured. "Just take a few deep breaths. Triumph is here to help."

The psychiatrist had gotten Triumph declared an emotional support animal, certifying to the court that Chloe would need him if she were going to testify. Triumph whined and nudged Chloe. He licked her face when she leaned forward, sliding her fingers deeper into his glossy black fur.

He was fatter now. No longer emaciated like when she had rescued him. Wanda said that Chloe gave him too many treats, and if she wasn't careful, she was going to make him overweight. But he was just right. Not too skinny. Not too fat.

Unlike Chloe, who remained too skinny. The psychiatrist said that she needed to take care of herself, and Chloe tried. But skipping meals was easy, and when she did eat, she got full easily. The psychiatrist said that she was still trying to please Gunter by not eating, constantly keeping herself on the brink of starvation. He talked about an eating disorder clinic that would help her to put on weight more quickly. But Chloe was winning. Gaining weight was difficult, but she was putting it back on, an ounce at a time. She never wanted to look like Mim. Or like Chloe had back in the days before Gunter. Chloe heard his criticisms whenever she weighed herself. And remembered his loving approval when she had slimmed down and become more attractive to him.

"Better?" the lawyer asked worriedly.

Chloe nodded. "Yeah. I'm okay."

"I didn't think you'd need him until you were up on the stand."

Chloe wished he wouldn't talk about her testifying. She looked up at the witness chair, and another wave of nausea rolled through her. She hugged Triumph. She wanted to sit down on the floor and bury her face in his fur. But for now, she would have to settle for patting him and scratching his ears. She had to maintain some appearance of emotional stability.

The judge wasn't there yet. There was a lot of activity in the court-room as everyone got ready. Someone put a folded piece of paper on the table in front of Chloe. She looked at it in confusion. Torn from a yellow legal pad, it was folded into eighths and had her name printed on the front in pencil. She knew that untidy scrawl. Temple was turned the other direction, talking to his paralegal, and hadn't seen it. Chloe picked up the paper and unfolded it. The message was brief and to the point.

You will not do this.

It wasn't signed, but Mim didn't need to sign it for Chloe to know who had written it. Chloe looked at her mother. Mim stared back at her, beady eyes intense and furious. She gave Chloe a firm nod.

"I—I can't," Chloe blurted. She got to her feet. "Bathroom," she gasped, and she staggered back down the aisle the way she had come in. She had seen the sign for the restrooms before entering the court-room. Triumph's collar jingling, he trotted beside her, unworried by the people they pushed past.

Chloe rushed into a toilet stall, and for three seconds thought that maybe she had misjudged, and she wasn't going to be physically sick after all. Then her stomach wrenched inside out, and she hung over the porcelain bowl, ridding her body of her morning coffee and burning yellow acid.

Triumph whined, bumping his head against her. Chloe knelt on the hard tiled floor, Mim's angry face still in front of her eyes. Memories of vicious beatings and burning insults played through her mind.

It wasn't long before someone was there looking for Chloe. The paralegal.

"Chloe? Are you okay?"

Chloe cleared her throat, burning from the acid. "I'm... I'm not feeling good. I don't think I can do this. I'd better go home."

Even though she had no home to go to.

"You're just a little nervous. You'll feel much better once it's over."

"I don't think I can."

"You can do it," the woman said firmly. "You need to do this. Make sure they can never hurt anyone again. Move forward in your life."

"I... I can't."

"Don't let her win. Come on. Come out and talk to Mr. Temple."

Chloe wiped her mouth and flushed the toilet. At the sink, she rinsed her mouth and soaked a wad of paper towels to sponge her hot face and the back of her neck.

"You can do this," the paralegal said. "You're strong."

They went back to the courtroom, which was even more chaotic than it had been. Mr. Temple was waving the yellow paper and talking angrily to a man in a court uniform. The other lawyer, for Mim and Blue Jeans, was shrugging and making placating gestures, not managing to hide a smirk at the corner of his mouth. Mr. Temple looked over to see Chloe standing in the aisle. He motioned her back to the table, but Chloe shook her head.

Temple said a few more words to the court clerk and approached Chloe.

"I'm sorry, Chloe. That should never have happened. But she can't do anything to you. You're safe. Please come sit back down."

"I can't do it."

"You can, Chloe. I know it's hard. But you've got Triumph to help you through it. You don't have to look at your mom. Just look at me, or at the dog."

Chloe stood there, unwilling to move and to go sit back down at the table.

"Can I sit on the other side?"

He raised his brows. "What?" He looked over at Mim.

Chloe indicated the chair that the paralegal had been sitting in. "On your other side, so that you're between me and... them."

"Oh, of course. Come on over."

He escorted her over to the chair, and they shuffled briefcases and folders around so that Chloe could sit down as far away from her mother, with as big a buffer as possible.

She sat patting Triumph, trying to calm her body down and stay present at the same time, a mental juggling act that took massive effort.

The judge came in, and everyone stood up while the bailiff read the docket. Everyone stood. The judge looked the courtroom over, giving Chloe a reassuring smile, and scowling at the table Mim and Blue Jeans sat at.

"There will be no more nonsense here today, counsel. You are expected to keep the accused in line. They are not to communicate with any witnesses directly."

The lawyer stood and nodded his agreement.

"Fine," the judge said grumpily. "How do the accused plead?"

Chloe put her elbows on the table and her forehead in her hands. There was no immediate answer. She peeked over at the other table to see what was going on. The lawyer was leaning over, whispering with Mim and Blue Jeans.

"What's going on?" Chloe asked.

"I don't know," Temple said with a frown, waiting for them to finish.

There was a murmur of talk running through the spectators in the courtroom, as they speculated on what was happening.

"Your honor... the accused would both like to enter a plea of guilty."

There was an immediate uproar in the audience. Chloe looked at Temple in disbelief.

"What? That means I don't have to testify?"

"Hold on..." Temple turned, consulting with the paralegal. "There's no deal on the table. So they're not pleading to a lesser charge. What are they up to?"

"They know Chloe's testimony would be devastating. They're worried that if she takes the stand, they'll get a longer sentence than if they enter a guilty verdict."

Temple nodded agreement.

The judge was pounding his gavel to quiet everyone down. He looked at Temple.

"Mr. Temple, any comment?"

"We would like to request a victim impact statement."

The judge nodded his approval. "Jury is dismissed." He gazed out at the spectators. "And I'm going to close the courtroom."

There was a lot of noise as people got up and headed for the doors. Chloe looked at Temple.

"What does that mean? Victim statement?"

Temple looked away from her, grimacing. "It means you've still got a job to do, Chloe. I can't do this. I can emphasize the brutality of what they have done and ask for heavy sentences, but it's not going to have nearly the impact of what you have to say."

"But I don't need to testify. They pled guilty."

"A victim impact statement means that you can describe what happened to you and how it affects your life every day. The judge will take it into account when he decides how much to sentence them with."

"But he's going to put them in prison even if I don't say anything."

"Yes. But do you want them to argue that they didn't understand what they were doing, and that they regret it and are reformed? Do you want them to serve five years and get out, so they can victimize other children?"

"That wouldn't happen. And there are no other children, there was just me, and I won't go back to them. I'll be an adult."

Chloe rubbed her hands in Triumph's fur. He was distracted with so many people getting up and moving around, but she wasn't doing it to calm him; not really.

"Couples like this don't stop," Temple said. "They egg each other on. If they can't have you, and they don't decide to have more children of their own, they'll go out and kidnap one. Or more. I've seen it happen. I'm sure you've seen stories in the news too. They're not going to quit because they were caught, and they're not going to quit because they don't have access to you anymore. If they only go away for a few years, they'll be right back at it as soon as they're out."

Temple watched her rubbing Triumph's fur. Chloe was barely holding it together. Even touching Triumph, she could feel her brain trying to disengage, trying to take her away from her body. Temple's words wouldn't let her stop thinking about Mim and Blue Jeans and all that they had done. She pictured what Temple said, the two of them rolling up in a van beside a little kid, pulling her in and chaining her up in another basement in another house.

Chloe said nothing while she watched the courtroom empty. She felt the heavy burden on her shoulders. Tell what they had done to her. Tell how it still affected her. Somehow convince the judge that he had to put them away for a long, long time.

Her mind went back to Mim's note. *You will not do this.* An unmistakable command. And Chloe had always been the obedient daughter. But obedience had not protected Chloe, had not brought her closer to her mother, and had not protected the other children.

The room quieted. Chloe looked up at the judge.

"Counselor, does your witness need more time to prepare?" he asked sympathetically.

Temple looked at Chloe, raising one eyebrow. Chloe shook her head.

"No… let's just get this over with," she said, loud enough for both to hear.

The judge and Temple nodded.

"So… what do I do?"

"Come on up to the front," the judge invited.

Chloe's legs were weak and wobbly. She took a shaky step toward the witness box. She looked back at Temple, with a small gesture toward Triumph. Was she allowed to take him up to the front?

Temple nodded. Chloe tugged on the leash and Triumph escorted her up to the front. Chloe sat down in the witness chair, and he cuddled up protectively against her. Chloe turned her eyes toward the judge.

"Do I have to swear to tell the truth?"

"This isn't sworn testimony. This is just your thoughts and feelings."

"How do I do this?"

"You can talk to me. Or you can talk to your mother directly. If you need some guidance, Mr. Temple can ask you some questions and get you going."

Chloe nodded. She darted a glance toward the other table, but she knew she couldn't look at her mother. Chloe couldn't address her directly. She would just break down. Maybe she wouldn't be able to continue on. And she had to do it. She had to keep them in prison for as long as possible.

She blew out her breath and took a deep lungful of air that seemed too thin.

"They locked me up," she said awkwardly, not knowing how to start. "I guess it was two years, but I lost track... Sometimes I was chained and sometimes just locked in." Her mouth twisted into a frown, and she knew she wasn't being completely honest. She had to be completely honest with the judge, or he wouldn't believe her and wouldn't do the right thing. "I wasn't always locked in," she confessed. "After a while... it didn't really matter whether the door was locked or not. I never tried to escape."

The judge nodded. "That's okay, Chloe. It's not your fault."

"I'm trying to tell you everything."

He gave an encouraging nod, but didn't say anything else, just waiting for her to go on.

"It wasn't nice. It was cold and pretty dark. Except for the beginning, I didn't have food or clothes most of the time. I got really hungry and really skinny." Chloe looked down at her bony arms and rubbed them, chilled just thinking of the basement. "Worse than this. A lot worse."

Triumph pawed at Chloe's lap. She pulled his head close and cuddled him and kissed the scars on his head where the fur hadn't grown back. He had been hurt too. Chloe would have told them everything if Triumph had been the one Mim and Blue Jeans had tortured. So why wouldn't Chloe do the same for the child she herself had been?

"They tortured her—me. Beat me and... did unspeakable things to me. And he videoed himself doing them." She glanced toward Blue Jeans. She couldn't look at his face. She saw instead the waist chain around the orange jumper. No more big belt buckle and blue jeans for him. Not for a long time. "That was evil. And he uploaded them so that... they'll always be out there. I can't ever erase them. The police can't. Because people with downloaded copies will just upload them again."

The judge nodded. His brows were down, his eyes a little red around the rims.

"Was your mother a part of this? Did she participate? Did she know what was going on?"

Chloe breathed hard. She bent over to give Triumph a hug all the way around his chest and back. He licked her face.

"She beat me plenty of times. Even before Blue—before Sal. Bad. Black and blue. Broken bones sometimes. Before my daddy died, I tried to take care of the younger kids. Take responsibility and make sure they didn't do anything wrong, to protect them. So she'd hit me and not them." Chloe swallowed. She thought about the judge's question. "Then with Sal… and the others, Gunter and Walter. She knew when they were with me. What they were doing. She said so right in front of me."

Chloe felt fresh the betrayal in realizing that her mother knew exactly what was going on. They weren't keep anything from her. She was allowing or even encouraging it. Chloe looked at Temple.

"Do I tell him about the babies too? Is that part of this?"

Temple nodded. "Tell him everything you can."

"She kept getting pregnant. And then she would give the baby to me, and tell me to get rid of it. I never did. I always tried to save them. But they would get infections and die in a few days. No matter what I did. And Phillip…" Chloe's voice cracked. "I was begging her. Pleading with her to take him to the hospital. To let me leave him somewhere that someone would find him and take care of him."

Mim knew what was coming. She bolted to her feet. "This is a travesty! You're just going to sit there and let that little liar make up stories about me? She's not allowed to testify! I pleaded guilty!"

"Counselor, restrain the accused or she will be removed."

"Chloe *is* testifying," the attorney pointed out desperately. "No groundwork has been lain. I don't have the opportunity for cross-examination. It could all be spurious lies."

"I'll be the judge of that," the judge said. He watched them for a minute to be sure that they were going to stay quiet and then nodded to Chloe. "Continue. What happened when you asked her to let you get help?"

"She had a bottle. Not a baby bottle, a wine bottle. She hit me over the head and kept hitting me when I was on the ground. I was holding Phillip. Trying to protect him. But I was blacking out…"

Tears overcame Chloe. She couldn't go on. She sat there in the witness chair, her whole body shaking. Triumph tried to comfort her, whining and licking her and pawing and nosing at her.

"Your honor..." Temple was on his feet. "The coroner's report indicates that baby number three, the one Chloe calls Phillip, sustained multiple skull fractures. He died of massive head trauma."

"Okay," the judge said quietly. "Let's take a short recess while Miss Simpson collects herself. When you come back," he spoke to Chloe, "I want to hear about your life now. The lasting effects of the abuse and trauma in your life."

Chloe nodded.

Temple took her for a walk up and down the corridors of the courthouse, got her a drink of ice water, and had her splash cold water on her face.

"Just about done," he assured Chloe. "You don't have to go back to those experiences anymore. Just tell him about your life now. How it's affecting you now."

Chloe shook her head. "I don't know what to say."

"You've done a good job so far. And the judge or I will prompt you if you get stuck. Not much longer now."

Once back in the witness chair, composed as much as she could be, Chloe breathed deeply and gave a brief outline of what her life was like.

"I... I don't have a home anymore. I'm homeless. I can't sleep at a shelter, with all of the people and with babies crying. I have a job... at the animal shelter..." She looked down at Triumph and gave him a little smile. "It's better than other jobs I tried, but it doesn't pay enough to live on. And I still screw things up, because I forget what I'm doing, get all stuck in flashbacks or go into sort of a trance when something scares me. The psychiatrist had a long name for it, but it's just like... I'm not there anymore. I go somewhere else where no one can hurt me anymore." She dug her fingers into Triumph's fur. "That's where Triumph helps me. When I touch him... I feel real. Present. He keeps me grounded, keeps me from going away."

The judge nodded.

"My feelings are all mixed up... I want to go back to my mom, even though I know how she hurt me. I feel... guilty. For everything that happened to her. And to me. I feel guilty about the younger kids, when we all lived at home still... I tried to look after them and keep them out of trouble... so it would be my fault, if they ever got in trouble. I would take the punishment if I could. I tried to make everyone do everything Mom and Dad said... but they still got hurt. Ronnie and then June. And Justin, in a different way. I even testified against him in court. Tried to make Mommy happy. And when she got hurt... I blamed myself. It was my fault for not taking care of her, or not being able to keep her men happy... I want to be able to have friends. Maybe even a boyfriend of my own someday. Not someone I'm just with to put a roof over my head. Someone who cares about me, and I can care about him. But... I don't think I ever can." Chloe scratched at a worn, frayed spot on her pants. They seemed to wear out quickly, always getting snagged on cats' or dogs' claws. "I don't know how to have a   boyfriend." She glanced in the direction of her mother. "Because *that's* all I ever saw."

The judge thanked Chloe and excused her. She wobbled back to the other table and sat down beside Temple. Temple gave her a nod and a tentative pat on the hand.

"You did good," he mouthed.

The judge looked at his files, readjusting papers here and there as he considered his course of action.

"I was planning to adjourn until tomorrow to consider sentencing. But I don't want to draw this out any longer. I want to end the suffering of Miss Simpson so that she can have closure and move on however she can." More paper shuffling. "I see no reason not to impose the maximum penalty for each charge against Mim Simpson and Sal Durrant. By my count, that is at least three life sentences against each. Plus another fifty or sixty years. All to be served consecutively. I'll draw up the totals and publish the judgment tomorrow. In the meantime..." He fixed his gaze on Mim and Blue Jeans. "Suffice to say that you will be in prison for the rest of your natural lives."

Mim turned to her lawyer to make some objection, and he motioned her to silence. The judge rapped his gavel once, stood up, and disappeared through a door that opened up behind him.

"You did it," Temple told Chloe, beaming. "You did a wonderful job. And now it's done. You never have to go through that again."

"What if they apply for parole? Or they appeal, and it has to go to court again?"

Temple patted her shoulder. "Not going to happen. Sure, they'll appeal, but it won't ever go anywhere. You're safe. You can move on with your life."

Chloe stood up. She bent down to give Triumph another hug. "All done," she whispered to him. "Now we're both safe."

~

Chloe walked out of the courthouse and took a deep breath of the fresh air. She could breathe again. It was all over.

None of those feelings she had talked to the judge about were going to go away. She knew she was going to be fighting against them for the rest of her life. Mim was in prison, but so was Chloe. She had done what she was required to do, and maybe it was time to consider her own final release.

There was a familiar figure at the bottom of the concrete stairs. Chloe walked toward it. She frowned, shaking her head at Jozef.

"What are you doing here?"

Jozef gave her a smile. "I was in the courtroom to give you moral support. But as it turned out, you didn't need me. They pleaded guilty."

Chloe nodded. She hadn't realized that there were any friendly faces in the crowd of spectators in the courtroom. She had only seen strangers. The bored and the curious. A few people with pads of paper that she thought might be reporters, looking for a good story.

"How did your statement go after the judge closed the court-room?" Jozef asked. "Everything okay?"

It seemed like it had taken days to get through her witness state-ment, but Chloe realized that it hadn't even been an hour.

"Uh... it was pretty hard. But it went okay." He didn't ask, but she told him anyway. "The judge gave them both maximum sentences on everything."

"Wow. That doesn't happen often. You must have done a really good job."

Chloe nodded, exhausted.

"You look really beat," Jozef observed. "Can I make a suggestion, and you promise you won't freak out over it? I just want to do what I can to help."

Chloe studied him suspiciously. "What?"

"Come home with me. There's a spare room. Or the couch, if you prefer. Just lay down, have a nap. I can't imagine you sleep very well on the street and today you really need it. Don't you?"

The idea of lying down on a couch or bed sounded heavenly. Chloe was wary of what would be expected in return. But did she care? Did it matter?

Jozef saw her hesitation. "Chloe, please trust me. I just want you to be well and happy. Have I ever done anything to hurt you?"

"Trusting is hard for me."

"I know. I can't imagine everything you've had to go through." As much as she had tried to keep the details from Jozef, she couldn't keep the trial and many of the details of the charges from him. Even though the papers had been banned from mentioning her name, he knew the articles were about her, so he knew much more than she would have liked. "Tell you what; you tell Triumph to guard you. He wouldn't let me do anything to hurt you."

Chloe looked down at her dog, and he stared back up at her, his eyes deep and adoring. He gave a little whine.

Chloe supposed that he could use a nice soft bed to sleep on just as much as she could. So she nodded.

"Okay. Thanks."

Epilogue

Chloe didn't recognize the number on the caller ID. But it didn't look like a telemarketer number; it was local. She considered for a moment before deciding that she could handle answering it without knowing who was calling. If it were a wrong number or telemarketer, she would just hang up.

"Hello?"

"Is this Chloe Simpson?"

Chloe breathed out slowly, her stomach tightening with anxiety. "Chloe Gould," she corrected. "I don't go by Simpson."

The female caller didn't speak for a few long seconds. "But... did you used to be Chloe Simpson?" she asked tentatively.

"Who is this?"

The last thing Chloe needed was some reporter doing a 'Where Are They Twenty Years Later?' story.

"It's... Ronnie."

Chloe looked down at the number on the phone again. It was a local number. Probably right in the city. After so long without any contact with any of her family, Chloe didn't know what to say.

"Your sister," Ronnie said, in case Chloe hadn't understood.

"Ronnie?" Chloe couldn't think of what to say. "Where are you? Are you okay?"

"I'm... I'm fine. I just wondered... I wanted to talk to you. To try to reconnect."

"Wow. Is it really you? It's been so long!"

"I know. I should have kept in touch... but it was hard."

"Yeah... you probably wouldn't have been able to keep in touch with me even if you'd tried. I was... unreachable for a lot of years."

"I read the court file and newspaper articles about what happened to you... I'm sorry..."

"That was a long time ago. I try not to think about it too much."

"Yeah." A bleak laugh from Ronnie. "Been there!"

Chloe remembered how Ronnie had refused to even acknowledge what had happened to her until she had been forced to testify at Justin's trial. Chloe had been in denial about it herself. They had all been conditioned to say nothing. Admit nothing. Deny that anything had ever happened, and it would all just go away.

"So... how are you?" Chloe asked. "I suppose you're married with ten kids."

"Well... not exactly. It's complicated."

"Oh." Ronnie's tone hadn't been light-hearted. She didn't have a funny story about how she had married her best friend's ex. More likely four marriages, three divorces, and six kids with different fathers. "I'm sorry."

"It's okay. I've... had to work through some things."

"Sure. I guess we've all had a lot to work through."

"I think yours was the worst," Ronnie confided. "We all just always thought you were the best off. The one who escaped the abuse. And then... reading about what happened to you..."

"All of us?" Chloe said. "Have you talked to the others?"

"Yeah. You were really hard to track down. Everyone else kept their names. Other than you and me, I mean."

"How... is everyone...?"

"Well... okay, I guess. None of them had kept in touch until about two years ago, when they reconnected. They want to meet with me. And you."

Chloe frowned, considering her conflicting emotions. She had never thought that she would see any of them again. Of course, she had wondered what had happened to them, how they all were. But the way that everything had ended, with her testifying on the wrong side of Justin's trial, she figured there would be some pretty hard feelings. Justin had not had to go to prison as a result, but none of them had ever reached out to her. Chloe had stayed with her mom, and that again put her on the wrong side. Everybody hated Mim.

"Would you be okay to meet with us?" Ronnie asked tentatively.

"I dunno," Chloe said cautiously. "Could I just... meet with you, to start with?"

"Sure," Ronnie agreed, her tone brighter. "I'd love that."

"What's up? Is everything okay?" Jozef asked.

Chloe tore herself away from her thoughts. "What...?" She looked down at her dinner plate, where she had been absently shredding a piece of lasagna.

"Are you worrying about the animals?"

"No... I had sort of a strange call today."

"What about? A dog?"

"No... it was Ronnie."

Jozef gave her a blank look. Chloe bit her lip.

"My sister."

"Your sister?" His eyes widened in shock. "That's fantastic, hon! What did she have to say? How did she find you?"

"I'm not sure how she found me. I don't have my name listed as Simpson anywhere." Chloe looked at his face. "She wants to meet me."

"Great!" Jozef's eyes crinkled up in the corners. "When are you going to see her?"

"Next weekend. I need a little time... to prepare myself."

"You'll do just fine. You'll have a blast with her, I'm sure."

"I'm not so sure," Chloe disagreed. "I testified against her at Justin's trial. Against all of them. And I stayed with Mom and didn't believe any of what Ronnie said." Chloe swallowed hard. "She can't be happy about all that."

"Twenty years is a long time to hold a grudge. I'm sure she'll be very excited to see you. Aren't you excited about it?"

"No."

Chloe went back to picking at her dinner.

"She wouldn't seek you out if she was mad at you for what

happened when you were kids," Jozef said logically. "She's the only one you know how to reach, so you should take the opportunity."

"I am... but she wanted me to meet the others, too."

"The others?"

"All of them. She's talked to everyone."

"Wow." Jozef took a couple of large bites of his pasta, chewing thoughtfully. "This is really big. No wonder you're feeling so anxious."

"Yeah, thanks for that."

Jozef laughed. "I'm not trying to make you feel worse, just saying I see why you're feeling so overwhelmed. Are you meeting them all, then?"

"No, just Ronnie. I couldn't... I couldn't meet them all at the same time. Not yet."

He nodded understandingly. Chloe sighed and pushed her plate away, her meal barely touched. She liked lasagna, but she felt too squirmy and unsettled to get anything down. Jozef looked at her full plate but didn't censure her.

"I'm going to go check the kennels, make sure everyone is settled," Chloe offered.

Jozef grinned and didn't object to her leaving the table so abruptly.

She wasn't fooling Jozef. He knew that Chloe wasn't really concerned about whether the dogs were properly settled for the night. She had seen to all their needs before her own, as she always did. She needed the contact with the dogs for herself.

Chloe walked along the line of kennels, looking in on each dog. She missed Triumph so much at times like this. He had been with her for twelve years, and that was pretty good for a dog who had been so badly neglected and abused. But no other dog had ever touched her in exactly the same way as Triumph had. Other dogs helped her, but none of them had the same intuition as Triumph. Their shared experiences had created a bond between them that Chloe had never replicated with another animal.

The new Bassett hound was moving around restlessly. When

Chloe stood by his kennel, he walked up to the bars, snuffling at her. Chloe loved his sad-looking face. He was slow and solemn, and she thought that he would be especially good at working with traumatized children.

"Can't get settled?" Chloe asked the hound in a low voice.

He looked up at her with his sad brown eyes. He didn't whine or paw at the gate; he just looked at her. Chloe lifted the latch on the gate and opened it. She stooped to give his droopy ears and jowls a scratch. Her connection with him wasn't nearly as strong as it had been with Triumph, but she immediately felt the sharpening of her senses, the grounding and centering that she always got from sympathetic animals.

"You're a nice boy," she murmured. "What do you think, huh? Will it be okay? I haven't seen Ronnie in twenty years. I have no idea what she'll be like."

But that wasn't true. She had talked to Ronnie on the phone. Heard her tone of voice and the tentativeness in her manner. Chloe could trust her intuition. Ronnie hadn't sounded angry or cruel. Surely she wouldn't track Chloe down just to hurt her twenty years later.

Jozef was grading papers in front of the TV. It was something he had resolved to stop, but he couldn't seem to break the habit. He looked up at Chloe as she walked back in, adjusting his glasses slightly and looking at her and then down at the hound.

"Company tonight?" he asked. "Everyone else settled?"

"Yeah. You don't mind?"

He looked back down at his papers, shaking his head. "Why would I start minding now?"

Chloe sat down on the couch and pulled a blanket around herself. The dog snuffled around the couch and their feet for a while, then with a deep sigh, he lay down right on top of Chloe's feet. Chloe laughed and wiggled her toes.

"Comfy?" she asked him.

He looked up at her with sad eyes and made no sign he planned to move. Chloe closed her eyes for a minute, just focusing on his warm body on her feet and the clarity of all of her senses. She was there with Jozef. And a dog.

And as far as she could see in the future, she would be there with Jozef.

And a dog.

Did you enjoy this book? Reviews and recommendations are vital
to making a book successful.

Please leave a review at your favorite book store or review site
and share it with your friends.

Don't miss the following bonus material:
Sign up for mailing list to get a free ebook
Read a sneak preview chapter
Other books by P.D. Workman
Learn more about the author

DON'T MISS A THING! GET THE LATEST NEWS AND A FREE EBOOK

PDWORKMAN.COM/SIGNUP

Preview of Ronnie

CHAPTER
One

(I)

Dusty Coleman came home from work to an empty house. It was odd for Ronnie and the children to be gone when he got home, but there might have been something on the family calendar that he had failed to notice. A piano recital or Little League game. Maybe a birthday party. He showered and changed. When the house was still empty when he finished, he went down to the kitchen and looked at the dry-erase calendar on the wall. There was nothing indicating a scheduled activity.

He tried Ronnie's cell-phone, but she was notorious for not answering it, so he didn't panic when there was no answer. She was having a conversation and it was buzzing away in her purse, or she was driving and the hands-free wasn't kicking in, or one of the kids was crying and she just wasn't available.

Dusty popped a couple of frozen waffles in the toaster and got himself a beer. Maybe he should put some macaroni on to boil so that there would be something for the kids to eat when they got home, heading off the hungry-grumpies at the end of what had probably been a stressful day for Ronnie.

But if they had gone to a birthday party or stopped at the food court in the mall, they wouldn't be hungry and it would be a waste of his time.

At six o'clock, he was starting to worry. He called and messaged Ronnie several times. He tried Margret, a friend from work, to see if Ronnie had talked to her.

"I haven't heard from Ronnie in a few days," Margret said, a frown in her voice. "You don't think something has happened to her...?"

"No... no, nothing has happened. I'm sure it's nothing. She probably told me where she was going and I just forgot."

"Have you called the hospital? Maybe one of the kids had an accident. You're not allowed to keep your phone on, so she wouldn't be able to answer you."

"It's nothing," Dusty said. "She's fine."

But he made a call to the hospital just to be sure. None of their names was on the admissions list. He started calling the names from the list Ronnie kept on the fridge. A quick reference of numbers of her friends and the children's little friends. She didn't trust the cell-phone directories and complained that they always ended up losing numbers.

He looked out the window for the car, hoping to see her pulling up. He paced, regretting the waffles now sitting like a lead weight in his stomach.

Finally, he called the police.

"I feel a little silly," he explained, "but I think my wife and my kids are missing... I can't reach her, I've called all of her friends. They're always home by now..."

"What's your name, sir?" the police dispatcher asked calmly.

"Dusty Coleman."

"What is your address?"

He gave it. He knew his tone was terse. He was worried and he wanted to tell his story, not to have to give them all of the routine details.

"What is your wife's name, and how old are the children?"

"Ronnie Coleman. The kids are Mandi, she's four, and Dane, just about six."

"Has anything happened to indicate that they might be in danger?"

"No. Just that they're not home. I called the hospital, but they haven't been admitted."

There was a long pause as the dispatcher typed information into her computer. Dusty had an uneasy feeling that she knew something, but he brushed it off. What could the dispatcher possibly know that he didn't, when he had just called the information in?

"I am dispatching a police unit to come and talk to you," she told him, giving nothing away. "ETA is about... ten minutes. When is the last time you saw or talked to your wife, sir?"

"Not since this morning. She often calls me over lunch, but not today..."

"Have you had an argument recently? Any domestic problems?"

"No, nothing like that."

Dusty paced, answering more routine questions, until he finally saw the police car pull up in front of the house.

"They're here," he told the dispatcher.

"Thank you, sir. I hope everything turns out all right."

Dusty Coleman looked pretty much like Omar had imagined him while listening to a replay of his phone call. A thirty-something blue collar worker. Medium height, muscular build, hair that was close-cropped but not shaved. He had five o'clock shadow, but was clean and smelled of soap.

"Mr. Coleman? I'm Omar Bluff. I'll be heading up this investigation." Omar held out his hand and Dusty shook it. Good firm grip. Fleeting eye contact. Dusty turned and looked out the window as if expecting his wife to roll up any minute.

"Dusty. Just call me Dusty."

"Fine. Can we sit down, Mr. Coleman?"

Dusty was too restless to sit down. He circled the living room, looking for a place to settle, but couldn't select a seat. Omar sat down anyway, powering on his tablet and flipping through the files that Jane Withers had sent to him, arranging them so that he could put his fingers on whichever one he wanted in an instant.

"Please walk me through your day today," he told Dusty, touching the record button on the tablet app. "From the time you woke up this morning, anything that you can remember, whether it seems significant or not."

"I was worried that you were going to tell me I had to wait twenty-four or forty-eight hours before I could report them missing," Dusty confessed. "I don't know how I could have gotten through the night, let alone a whole day or two."

"Where children are involved, we don't wait," Omar said. "The two of you haven't had any custody issues? You are both custodial parents? No separation, the kids are both of yours?"

"Yes, nothing like that. Everything has been fine."

"Right. If you could tell me about your day, then...?"

Dusty did his best, attempting a chronological narrative. But he kept jumping forward to coming home and discovering that they were gone. Omar had to keep directing him backward, making him go through his day a step at a time, listening for anything that sounded off, considering Dusty's alibis, and analyzing his emotion and the words that he used.

"You haven't had a fight recently?"

"No, nothing. I mean, nothing serious. Worries about finances, chores getting done, normal stuff like that. Nothing... we don't have any big issues. We're a happy family."

"Neither of you were seeing someone else?"

Dusty looked floored. "Seeing someone else? Like, dating? An affair? No, certainly not. Ronnie had the kids all day, she couldn't exactly carry on an affair. And me... I'd never... I love Ronnie. I'd never cheat on her."

In Omar's experience, everyone who cheated said at some point that they never would. Everyone lied.

"Has anything unusual happened? Strange phone calls? Hang ups? People you don't know who recognize her?"

"No."

"How did the two of you meet?"

"Uh... at work, actually. Ronnie was hired on as a temp receptionist. I saw her every day... thought she was kind of cute... we went out a few times and it all just fell into place."

"Does Ronnie have any family? What do you know about her past?"

"No, she's on her own. I gather her parents were killed in some kind of car accident. She didn't have any siblings. We're her only family."

"You don't know the details of how her parents were killed?"

"It upsets her to talk about them, even casually. So, I don't know much. Just that they're dead."

"How about her childhood and her life before the two of you met? What can you tell me about that?"

Dusty shook his head, frowning. "I... don't know. She didn't talk about herself. It was just... we didn't really talk about it."

Omar paged restlessly through the reports on his tablet. "Mr. Coleman... your children were picked up at the park today. By themselves, no supervision."

He gaped. "They're safe? Why didn't you tell me you found them? Where's Ronnie?"

"Ronnie was not with them. They were alone."

"Well, what did they say? Where did she go?"

"She told them she would be right back and then never returned."

"That doesn't make any sense. She wouldn't leave them alone there, and she'd never leave and not come back again!"

Omar didn't give Dusty any of the other information available to him. As the spouse, Dusty was the most likely suspect in Ronnie Coleman's disappearance. They would give him no more information than necessary and then would wait for him to slip up.

"Where did she go?" Dusty demanded. "Someone else must have seen her. There are always people at that park. The other mothers must have seen her if she left the kids there."

"What park?" Omar said.

"The park over by the school. Isn't that where they were? You said the park, and that's the one that they go to..."

"No, that's not where they were."

Coleman looked baffled. "Why would she take them to a different park?"

"You don't have a guess?"

Dusty didn't come up with one. Omar watched the doubts fly across his face. Omar could think of plenty of reasons. The kids wanted to go somewhere new. It was near an errand that she wanted to run. She was meeting someone else and needed to do it away from people that she knew, who might slip up and say something to her husband. It was unusual behavior. When people who follow a routine suddenly break the routine and do something out of character, that was worth looking at.

"I want to see the kids. Where are they? I have to see them. They should be home, I'll need to put them to bed."

"The kids are being taken care of right now. You'll see them in time. Right now, we need to be concerned about your wife and what might have happened to her."

Dusty nodded. "You're right," he agreed. He looked out the window. Still, Ronnie didn't drive up to the house, full of explanations as to what had happened that made her abandon their children at the park and disappear for hours.

"What kind of car does Ronnie drive?"

Omar already knew this. They were way ahead of Dusty on the investigation. Let him flounder behind, trying to figure out what they knew and what was still a secret.

"A white Mazda, about ten years old." Coleman gave him the plate number.

"Any car trouble lately? Something that might have left her stranded?"

"No... not really... but finances have been tight. We haven't had it in for a while and there's a few things that needed to be checked out. We were just waiting, you know, until we had a bit more cash to get it fixed up..."

"Sure," Omar agreed. He tapped the tablet for a few minutes, letting Dusty sweat it out.

"You haven't found her car?" Dusty asked. "No sign of her anywhere?"

"I didn't say that," Omar said.

"What's that supposed to mean? Have you found her or not?"

"We have not found your wife, Mr. Coleman. Maybe you could help us with that."

"Help you?" Dusty's voice rose. He stared at Omar. "What do you think I'm trying to do? Why do you think I called you? I'm scared for her. I don't know where she is or what I can do. Don't you understand that?"

"You called the hospital. Why?"

"To see if something had happened to Ronnie or one of the kids. If one of them had gotten hurt, Ronnie would have to turn off her phone and wouldn't have been able to answer when I called. I just called there to... to be sure."

"What made you think that one of them might have been hurt?"

"I was just checking. Nothing made me think they might be, but they were missing. It was unusual. I was just checking."

"Right. How late was your wife getting home at that point? What time does she usually get home? She hasn't ever been that late before?"

"Sometimes she's later getting home, but I always know where she is and what she's doing. So, I don't worry. But today... there wasn't anything on the calendar. I couldn't remember her telling me she was going to be anywhere special. She's never that late without telling me why."

"What time is she usually home by?"

"Well, if Dane has Little League, or piano, then maybe five-thirty..."

"She wasn't even an hour late and you were calling the hospital."

"She's usually home before me. Other than when they have something scheduled. There wasn't anything scheduled, so she should have been home at four-thirty. She was almost two hours late getting home and I'd called everyone on the list. Everyone who might know where she was. I was getting scared. It was just to reassure myself that nothing had happened to them."

Omar said nothing.

"Did you find her car?" Dusty asked. "I don't understand what you're telling me."

"Yes. We found her car."

"But... Ronnie wasn't in it? So, where's Ronnie? Was it stolen? Carjacked?"

"No, it doesn't appear so."

"She just parked it and went shopping or something, and never came back?"

Ronnie Coleman hadn't gone shopping. Her wallet and purse were still in the car. There was no sign of any violence, but the lab boys would be checking for any minute drops of blood or other evidence of what had happened to her.

"Does that sound like your wife?" Omar asked.

"No... no, she would never leave the kids at the park, or leave her car and never come back. None of this makes any sense."

Dusty appealed to Omar.

"Do you know what happened? Can you explain it to me?"

"I'm afraid not, Mr. Coleman. Your wife is missing. It would appear she might have been the victim of a crime. At this point... we are just as confused as you are."

Dusty rubbed his eyes, suddenly looking exhausted. "Where are my kids? Mandi and Dane will need to go to bed, and someone will have to explain to them..."

"They are taken care of tonight," Omar said. "You don't need to worry about that right now."

"Taken care of?"

"They were turned over to Social Services when they were abandoned at the park. Once they have a chance to evaluate the situation they will be returned to you. But being abandoned like that triggers an investigation."

"But that was Ronnie, not me. I should be able to go and get them back."

"Not the way it works. They have to satisfy themselves that this is a safe environment. I'm sure they'll be talking to you tomorrow."

Jane Withers was ready for Omar when he returned. She sat expectantly with her fingers hovering over the keyboard, waiting for instructions.

"Background on Dusty Coleman is already started," she said. "So far, no red flags, but we've only just begun. *Ronnie* Coleman, however..."

"She has a record?" Omar guessed.

"No. She doesn't exist."

Omar lowered himself into the chair beside her so that he could see the reports that she brought up on the screen.

"She's a ghost?"

"Never existed until she started working at Starcan, the company that Dusty works at now. At that point, she applied for a social and started working."

"Birth certificate?"

"A Veronica Stern, born June first, twenty-three years old. Only problem is, Veronica Stern died at age two."

"She created a paper trail for herself. Professional?"

"Doesn't appear to be. Professionals usually develop an identity very thoroughly. Library card, gym, social, driver's, everything you can think of. Ronnie's trail is very low-key. Minimal. A social and a fake driver's. Nothing else. No credit cards, her name is not on the house or on the car registration. Her marriage license and children's birth certificates. Everything else kept below the radar. No store loyalty cards, library, gym."

"Phone, email, social networks?"

"Her cell is in Dusty's name. I can't find any email or social networks. We'll have to get her computer and take a look."

Omar studied the screen. "What was she running from? Criminal past? Abuser? Someone who just wanted to start fresh?"

"What did her husband say about her past and her family?"

"It upset her to discuss them, so he didn't. He thought that her parents were killed in a car accident."

"I'll check for car accidents six or seven years ago, just to be sure. Also any missing persons reports around the time that she assumed her new identity. She came from somewhere."

"But where? She could be from out of our jurisdiction."

She shrugged. "I'll keep it narrow to start with. We'll widen the net if nothing shows up."

Omar had watched the videos of the children's interviews with Mrs. Vital, the social worker. Mandi, age four, hadn't had much to say, other than that she wanted to go home to her mother. Dane was almost six and was more articulate in his interview.

"Where did Mommy go?" Mrs. Vital asked him.

"She went to the car."

"Why did she go to the car?"

Dane considered the question seriously. "Maybe she forgot something," he suggested.

"What do you think she forgot?"

"Snacks?"

"Were you guys hungry?" Vital asked.

"We were hungry when the police came."

"Yes, you were. But you'd been at the park for a long time, then. Were you hungry when your mom left you there and went back to the car?"

"No."

"What did Mommy say when she went back to the car? Did she say she was going to go get some snacks?"

He shook his head and looked around the room restlessly. Omar got the idea that he was normally a pretty active little boy and not used to having to sit still for long. But the interview room, although made to look cozy and furnished with toys and teddies, was an unfamiliar place and he stayed in his seat.

"She just said... 'I'll be right back,'" he reported.

"And did she come right back?"

He shook his head vigorously. "We played for a looong time. Usually we can't stay for a long time. But we got hungry, and Mandi got dirt in her eye, and my hands were cold."

"She just let you play there for the whole time? And then you got sad because she hadn't come back from the car?"

"Uh-huh," Dane agreed. "Where is she? Can we go home now?"

"I still need you to talk to me. Did you see your mom go back to the car?"

He nodded.

"I want you to think about it, Dane. Did she get into the car?"

He was hesitant. "Nooo..."

"Did she get anything out of the car?"

"I don't know."

"Did she have a bag or a suitcase in the car, like she was going to go on a trip?"

"No."

"Did she talk to anyone else at the park? Any of the grown-ups?"

Dane thought about it. "No."

"Did she usually talk to others?"

"My friends' moms. But they weren't there. It was a different park."

"Yes, it was, wasn't it? Did your mom say why you were going to a different park today?"

"No."

"She didn't say that there was something special about it?"

"No."

"Or that she wanted to meet someone there?"

Dane played with his sandy curls. He looked around the room, getting up on his chair to look around. Then he sat back down again.

"I want my mom. Is she coming here?"

"Where did she say she was going, Dane? She must have told you."

"No. She said, 'I'll be right back.'"

"Did your dad go to the park?"

"No," he shook his head, brows drawn down, at such an idea. "Daddy doesn't go to the park. Daddy goes to work."

"He never goes to the park?"

"No."

"You didn't see him at all today? He didn't go to the park to surprise your mom?"

"No."

"Did anybody go to the park to surprise your mom?"

"Uh-uh."

"A special friend? Did your mom have any special friends?"

Dane chewed on the end of his finger, this question apparently not prompting any memories. "No."

"When she went to the car, was there anyone else around watching her? Standing nearby? Did anyone talk to her?"

He gave a frustrated sigh, scowling. "No," he huffed.

"Where did she go after she went to the car?"

Dane shrugged. "I don't know."

"Did you see her walk away from the car?"

"No."

"Or get into someone else's car?"

"No."

"Was there anyone at the park who made you feel scared or icky?"

He arched his eyebrows and shook his head, scornful at the idea. "There were no *strangers* there."

"Did you know the other kids playing at the park?" Vital questioned in surprise.

"No."

"Or their parents?"

"No."

"Then they *were* strangers."

"No," Dane asserted. "They weren't strangers. You're not supposed to talk to strangers. But they were nice."

Vital nodded, understanding. Omar rolled his eyes at this, but was used to this common misconception among children. Strangers were scary monsters. People who tried to steal you or rip your clothes off. People who were nice to you were obviously not strangers. A stranger could be recognized by his scowling face or scary music that accompanied his entrance. Vital had obviously run into this situation before as well. She didn't try to force understanding, just continued to question him.

"And when you started to feel tired and cold and hungry, you talked to the adults and told them that you wanted your mom."

Dane agreed. "They helped us and gave us snacks and mittens. Then the police came to help and gave us a ride in their car."

"That was nice, wasn't it?"

"But they left Mommy's car there. Where is Mommy?"

"We're still looking for your mommy. Did she say she was going to visit a friend today?"

"No."

"Or to run errands? Maybe she had some shopping to do?"

"No. She went shopping *yesterday*."

"Maybe she forgot something."

Dane shook his head with all of the assurance a five-year-old could muster. He yawned widely, making no attempt to cover his mouth.

"Where is my mom? When can I go home?"

"We're going to let you sleep over at someone else's house tonight. Then we'll work on getting you back home once we know it is safe."

"It's safe. I want to go home."

"I know, sweetie," she agreed. But she didn't tell him that he could.

They had slept at a respite home, and went back to Dusty

Coleman the next day. Omar met up with them and Mrs. Vital at the respite home to observe the reunion and to see what he could divine from it.

Mandi and Dane were reticent with the social worker. No smiles. No childish chatter. Each clung to one of Mrs. Vital's hands, looking at Omar and then Mrs. Vital's unfamiliar car with nervousness. Omar followed the social worker's car in his own vehicle and stayed to the side, unobtrusive, when they got out at the house.

Dusty was watching for them and hurried out the door as soon as the social worker got out of the car to unbuckle the kids from their booster seats.

"Mandi! Dane!" He called to them and hurried down the sidewalk in stocking feet. "Oh, I'm so glad to see you!"

He didn't look like he had slept a wink the previous night. There were dark circles under his eyes and he hadn't bothered to shave that morning. He crouched down and gathered the kids into his arms, hugging them tightly, eyes brimming with tears.

"I'm so glad to see you. Are you guys okay? Are you all right?" He looked at their faces, and then hugged them again.

Mandi, who had been mostly silent during her interview and the intervening time, was noisy.

"Daddy, Daddy, Daddy!"

"What is it, Mandi?"

"Daddy!"

"Yes, Daddy's here. What do you want? Are you okay?"

"Daddy!"

He hugged her to him tightly, grinning at Dane over Mandi's shoulder.

"I missed you kids so much last night! Are you okay? Did you sleep okay last night?"

"We had to sleep at a lady's house," Dane announced. "A lady we didn't even know!"

"I know, Dane. But you are back home now. You can sleep back in your own bed tonight."

"I missed it!" Dane said with a dramatically weary sigh.

Dusty laughed. "How about you, princess? How did you sleep?"

Mandi was still pasted to Dusty, lying limply against him. Her eyes were glazed and far away, like she had just woken up.

"I want Mommy."

"I know, princess," Dusty agreed. "I do too."

Dane addressed his father in a stern tone. "Where is Mommy?"

Omar was interested to note that Dane assumed that his father knew exactly where Ronnie would be.

"Mommy didn't come home yesterday. We... we don't know where she is. I'm sure the police will find her, and they'll bring her home safe and sound. Okay?"

Dane scowled at this. He looked over his shoulder at Omar.

"That policeman came with us. Does *he* know where Mommy is?"

Dusty followed his gaze to Omar and stood back up, straightening from his crouch at the children's eye-level. He picked up Mandi with him, not shifting her from the spot where she had landed, her arms still around his neck.

"Do you know anything?" Dusty asked, as if nervous what the answer might be. He acted as if he believed that Omar knew more than he did about where Ronnie was. Whether that was true, or whether he knew exactly where Ronnie or her body now resided, Omar wasn't at all sure.

"We haven't found your wife yet," Omar said. "Have you heard anything from her? Had any phone calls? Any friends who have called you up to talk about it?"

"No," Dusty said flatly. "No one knows anything about where she could be."

"Unless you can give us something, we have very little to go on."

"There must be some clue of what happened to her... isn't there anything in her car? Something to suggest..." he trailed off, looking frightened by his own words.

"Mr. Coleman... I don't believe that your wife just walked off the face of the earth. Somebody did something. Somebody knows something. The most likely person is... you."

"You think I did something to my wife?" Dusty demanded, his voice rising in anger. "I was at work all day! You know that, didn't you check with the others? I was at work all day, I couldn't have done anything to her."

"You'd be surprised how many times we hear that line. Maybe you snuck off at some point. Or maybe you hired someone, or talked someone else into helping. There are ways around alibis. Nothing is ever ironclad."

"I didn't do anything to hurt my wife. You need to be out looking for her."

"Where?"

"I don't know. The hospital. Put out news announcements asking for help. Hand out flyers. Go door to door. Surely you have a protocol!"

"The protocol is to wait twenty-four hours. You really want me to do that?"

"I want you to do something!"

"I am. Right now I'm seeing that you get your kids back, which is the thing that you were most concerned about last night."

"I was concerned about getting the kids back and about my wife."

"You keep saying 'my wife' instead of Ronnie. Is there a reason you are having problems saying her name?"

"Ronnie. I don't have any problem saying Ronnie's name. I'm just trying to impress on you how important it is to me that you find her. She's not just a random woman. She is the woman I love. The mother of my children. Please find her."

"We're doing our best, Mr. Coleman. We will continue to work on it."

Dusty rubbed Mandi's back, his eyes misting over. He closed them for a moment. "Okay," he agreed. "Thank you."

"Anything?" Jane asked, coming upon Omar while he was rubbing his eyes, stinging and dry from staring at the computer screen for too long. "Looks like you need to take a break."

Omar sat back in his chair and looked up at the statuesque blond.

"It's got to be the husband," Omar said. "There's no indication of foul play. If it was a kidnapping, carjacking, or murder, her purse wouldn't still be sitting in the car with her wallet in it. It's like she just walked away."

"Wouldn't the husband know to take her purse and wallet if he wanted to make it look like a carjacking? Maybe whoever it was got interrupted."

"If he got interrupted, then where the hell is Ronnie Coleman?"

"Well... true."

"Have you had any luck tracking down her previous identity?"

"No, 'fraid not. I've checked back ten years, but generally, anything older than that has been archived and warehoused. Active cases should still be on the computer network, but that's going back to before everything was standardized and integrated into a single database. Not much we can do if it never made it onto the integrated database. Some jurisdictions are still working their way backward, adding old information onto the system. Others just have an arbitrary cut-off and only cases that were opened after that date are required to be entered into the system."

"Or there's the possibility that she was never reported missing. If her family thought they knew where she had gone, or she had no family, she may never have made it to the missing persons database at all."

Jane nodded, conceding this point.

"You're right, of course." Jane leaned on Omar's chair. "You know, though... if she's done this before, maybe it's not the husband. Maybe she just takes on a new identity every so often."

"You think she walked away from a four-year-old and a six-year-old? That's pretty cold for a mother."

"It's been known to happen. Mothers have been known to kill their children too. At least she didn't do that."

"She could have just walked away," Omar admitted. "But without even the cash in her wallet? If you were leaving your life behind, wouldn't you at least take the cash with you?"

"Yes... of course I would."

CHAPTER
Two

(I)

I t was a full year later, almost on the anniversary of Ronnie Coleman's disappearance, that the news story broke. Omar had stopped at a diner for a quick meal between interviews, and the television was set to a news channel with a running ticker at the bottom of the screen. Omar's eyes caught the words on the banner.

Woman who disappeared eleven years ago reunited with family.

That was an unusual story, but what happened next grabbed Omar by the throat and shook him. The picture of the woman tentatively approaching her teenage children for the first time in eleven years. It was Ronnie Coleman. He was sure of it. He'd studied her photo, he'd spread it across all the networks. He'd made sure it was posted in any forums where people might happen to see her.

"Can you turn this up?" Omar waved at a waitress. She looked grumpy, like she would argue about it, but a couple of the other patrons eating dinner made noises of agreement. It was a feel-good story. People wanted to see and hear the reunion. To hear how such a miraculous thing had happened.

The waitress turned it up.

The woman, who had to be either Ronnie Coleman or her twin, tentatively hugged each of the two teenage children, a boy and a girl, and greeted her ex-husband with a handshake and a kiss on the cheek, looking very awkward.

The television reporter pressed in close to Ronnie with the microphone.

"How does it feel to be reunited with your family?"

"Uh... good," Ronnie said in a low voice that was almost a whisper. "It's... really... nice."

"Can you explain to us what happened to you? You disappeared without a trace eleven years ago. Your family gave you up for dead. But here you are. You weren't murdered, you weren't kidnapped, so what happened?"

"I don't know," Ronnie said. "I don't remember."

"You don't remember? Do you have some kind of amnesia? Did you have a head injury?"

"I don't know. I'm trying to figure out what happened. I'm sorry, I just don't know."

"Do you remember your husband and children?"

There was a long moment of silence and then Ronnie shook her head. "No... this is all news to me. I didn't even know that I had been married, let alone that I had a family."

"What is the first thing that you can remember?" the reporter's tone was bullying. "Didn't you try to find out what had happened to you?"

"I... I'm sorry, I can't answer any more questions."

She turned away from the reporter, and walked away from the crowds toward a car that then whisked her and her family off to an undisclosed location.

"Didn't even know that she had a family!" Omar growled. "What about two families?"

The other patrons looked at him with confused, questioning looks. Omar dialed Jane Withers. It took him a while to get through. She was probably having supper at a similar diner on the other side of the state.

"Withers," she announced.

"Jane. Omar. Listen, there's a story on—"

"You talking about the mysterious reappearance eleven years later?" Jane demanded. "I'm on it. Did you catch her name?"

"No. I'm at a diner. Turned it on too late."

"Ronnie Plum."

Omar caught his breath. "No way."

"She kept the same first name. I'm seeing what information I can get."

"What about informing the Coleman family?"

"We're behind the eight ball on that one. He's the one who called the hotline number and put me onto it."

"Oh. Well, we can't be expected to know things before they happen, can we? How is he?"

"Pretty upset. She's claiming to be an amnesiac, so he has some solace in the possibility that she doesn't remember anything that happened in the past. The fact that she has abandoned not just one but two families... I've never heard of such a thing before, have you?"

"No. It's a first for me. Even doing it once... most people who claim that they left their families in some kind of fugue or amnesiac episode are later proven to be lying. So, I'm not expecting any different from her. I think it's a story."

Floyd Plum faced off against Adah Cruz, the police investigator who had not only had the gall to challenge his alibi and accuse him of having something to do with his wife's disappearance eleven years before, but had actually had him arrested for her murder a year into the investigation.

Floyd, once a reasonably handsome man, had been imprisoned for two years, had lost custody of the children for another two years beyond that, and his name had been blackened in the public eye forever. The prosecution had eventually been abandoned when they decided they didn't have enough to go to trial. He could no longer get employment as a CPA and ended up working a string of short-term contractor jobs. Not something that supported his family very well. The instability of the employment always left him on the brink of homelessness and having to give the children up again. He hadn't aged well. He had lost much of his blond hair, become a little paunchy, and gained a stoop, losing an inch or two off of his height.

"Mr. Plum," Adah started awkwardly. "Floyd... this has taken us all completely by surprise."

"I should think so," Floyd growled. "Since you accused me of murdering my wife. It is somewhat surprising to have her suddenly show up alive ten years later."

"You have to admit, things looked bad. Ronnie just disappearing without a trace like that. You claiming that you had come home to find your children abandoned, wife missing. It's a very unusual case."

"I told you all along that something had happened to her. I told you that she wouldn't just have abandoned me and the children. And that I didn't have anything to do with her disappearance. I told you over and over again."

"You did," Adah acknowledged. "But it was a very unusual case. Women don't usually just disappear like that. There is usually a reason. Someone has abducted or murdered them. And the prime suspect is always the husband or boyfriend."

"That's profiling."

"That's investigating. Going by the numbers and identifying the most likely suspect. And in ninety-nine percent of the cases, I would have been right."

He stared at her, waiting. Adah cleared her throat and fidgeted with her computer, running a finger along the smooth edge.

"I want to apologize, Mr. Plum. We were wrong, and I acknowledge that. Your life has been changed by our investigation as much as by your wife's disappearance. Maybe more so. And... for that I apologize. But we were not wrong in pursuing you as a suspect, given the circumstances."

Floyd folded his arms across his chest. "So, here we all are. Has Ronnie been able to give you any details, to explain what happened?"

"Unfortunately, not much. She claims not to remember her life here. Not her own childhood, you, or the children. Not her parents or any of her friends. Of course, we're having a psychiatrist interview her, trying to determine whether she is telling the truth. She's scheduled to go to the hospital for x-rays and a scan of her brain. See whether there is any sign that she was the victim of violence eleven years ago, or if there's any organic explanation for why she can't remember her former life. You do hear of these things happening sometimes… a head injury or extreme stress… the person wakes up with no memory and starts a new life…"

"Where has she been for eleven years?"

"For the last year, she has been here. As you know, Kent and a few old friends saw her and recognized her. When we started getting reports, we investigated. But the ten years before that… I'm afraid they're still a blank. Ronnie hasn't been able to tell us anything that happened during that time. We can only assume that she left town, or people would have seen her."

"She has no idea where she was for ten years."

"No. So she says."

"But she's going by the name Ronnie Kepler. So, she knows her name is Ronnie. She must remember something."

Adah nodded. "That's one of the inconsistencies that we are trying to reconcile."

"How long is the investigation going to take? When can she come home?"

"Floyd… she can go home whenever she wants to. We're not keeping her. She's cooperating with our investigation. She's not being detained."

"When I asked her to come home, she said she couldn't."

"We're not stopping her. If she can't, she's the one who is blocking it, not us. I assume that after all this time… she doesn't feel comfortable moving in with people that—she claims—she does not know."

"We're her family. Whether she remembers or not, that's where she belongs. She should be with us. Everything else… we'll sort it out. I'm sure if she was with us, she'd start to remember. She'd fall in love with the kids all over again, at least. They've been without a mother for most of their formative years. She has to come back."

"You'll need to address that with her."

He shook his head, scowling. "Can you give me her phone number? Her address? I have no idea how to reach her."

"We can't release private information."

"I'm her husband!"

"The same rules apply as would if you were an abusive husband trying to track his wife down at a shelter. We can't give you any personal information without Ronnie's permission."

"The children want her home."

"I understand that. But that is up to Ronnie, not up to me."

Adah watched Floyd Plum's departure. She felt bad for him. For all that he had suffered since his wife's disappearance, including his incarceration based on her own recommendation. She had been right to suspect him. All of the indicators were that he had killed and disposed of his wife, right down to the freshly muddy shovel in his car trunk. But she had been wrong.

Looking down at the transcribed messages on her phone screen, though, she realized that even more pain was in store for him. If the report from the neighboring town of Anchor was correct, then at least part of Ronnie's ten-year blank had been spent with another husband and another family.

She went back to her desk to put in a call to Omar Bluff.

Ronnie double-checked the house number and climbed reluctantly out of the car. She studied the house as she shut the car door, still hesitant to step off the road onto the property. She felt like Alice Though the Looking Glass, entering into another world. One where nothing made any sense.

Had she lived in this house? She hadn't thought to ask. Nothing about it was familiar to her. If she had lived there with this new family who claimed that she was a member of, she couldn't remember it. She had hoped that something would stir in her memory and she'd recognize the mailbox or the siding. That something about it would whisper 'home' to her. Then these people would start to emerge like ghosts from her memory, gradually gaining substance until she remembered everything about them. It would all come back, and she would remember her life with them and all that had happened since.

Floyd opened the front door and stood there, waiting for her to come up the walk. The children weren't with him. They weren't waiting excitedly for her return, clamoring to tell her everything that had happened since her departure. They had been reserved at the media event. As awkward as Ronnie was herself.

Ronnie pulled her hands back from the car, feeling like it would disappear as soon as she let it go. Or that *she* would. But nothing happened. The car and the house and her supposed ex-husband could all coexist in the same bubble of reality.

She walked up the cracked, uneven sidewalk to the front door.

"Hi," Floyd greeted, with a nod and a forced smile.

"Hi."

"Thanks for coming. I know it has to be pretty weird for you…"

"You too," Ronnie pointed out. For him to have his ex-wife return from the dead, that had to be a really weird feeling.

Ronnie stepped into the house. She didn't cease to exist. She didn't remember anything there. She looked around.

"This is very nice."

"It's a rental," Floyd said. "I can't afford to buy a house. All of the stuff that has happened since you disappeared… I don't have the same earning power as I did before that."

"Oh." Ronnie nodded politely. "What is it you do?"

Floyd studied her a moment. He motioned her into the living room and Ronnie selected a chair rather than the couch, so that he wouldn't sit down next to her. She perched on the edge of the seat, uncomfortable, not wanting to sink into it. She would feel trapped if she got too comfortable.

"I used to be a CPA," Floyd said. "Accounting. But I can't get work in that anymore. So, I'm working odd jobs… short term… contracting in home building. It's a little rocky in this market."

"Oh. Right."

The house was quiet. She wished that there were a stereo or TV on. The kids playing with their friends. Some kind of background noise that would cover up the awkwardness between them.

"Where are the children?" she asked.

"Kent went out to a friend's. Carrie is here. Reading or on her computer. But I figured… it might be too overwhelming if we were all here. The kids… don't quite know what to make of this whole thing."

Ronnie sighed. "Me too. I can't believe it's even possible for me to have kids that old. Teenagers. I don't feel like… what? Thirty-three?"

"By my calculation."

She shook her head. "That just doesn't seem possible."

"You were just eighteen when Kent was born. You were seventeen when we got married."

"Seventeen…" Ronnie shook her head. "That's really young to get married. Were we… was I already pregnant?"

"No. It wasn't like that. We just… we loved each other and we knew what we wanted. There was no point in waiting for years to formalize what we already knew and felt."

"What did your parents think? How old were you?"

He looked older than Ronnie. Older than thirty-three.

"I was twenty-five," he said. "So, I'm forty-one now."

Eight years older. His face was old for a forty-year-old. She supposed that the stress of losing her and being a single father had aged him prematurely.

"My parents were a little concerned," Floyd admitted. "Me getting married to such a young girl. Afraid that you were too immature. That you'd get older and realize that you'd made a big mistake."

He stopped, looking like he regretted what he had said. Maybe they had been right. Maybe at twenty-two, finding herself married and with two young children, Ronnie had just decided that it wasn't what she wanted, and left.

"Your parents were the ones that should have been worried," Floyd plowed on. "A seventeen-year-old marrying a twenty-five-year-old. You were just barely finished high school. You were so young."

"My parents?" Ronnie echoed. She hadn't reunited with them yet. The media had wanted Ronnie and her husband and children, and her parents hadn't pushed to see her on camera, so she had put it off. She couldn't remember anything about her parents. Meeting them was just one more chore the she would rather put off.

"They were over the moon about it," Floyd exclaimed. "Delighted. They said…" he flushed a little, and his eyes slid away from her. "They said I was a great catch and they were happy with your choice. I would give you stability and be a good breadwinner for you." He shrugged. "It wasn't an arranged marriage, but they were certainly happy with your choice."

Ronnie's stomach squeezed into a tight knot. She wasn't sure why his words made her so uncomfortable. She should be happy that she had made choices that made her family happy. Except, of course, she had later undone those choices in the worst possible way.

"I'm sorry," she said.

Floyd looked surprised. He didn't say anything at first.

"I know... you don't remember what happened," he said. "Probably, it wasn't anything that you made a conscious choice about. I think it was probably... an accident, or some kind of psychotic break or something. A psychiatrist that I talked to said that sometimes, when someone is having a stressful time... they can have a psychotic break, as a way of the brain just stopping all the stress..."

Ronnie stared down at the worn brown carpet.

"I don't think you have anything to apologize for," Floyd said. "Not if it wasn't a conscious choice."

It was an 'out' and a challenge. She could accept his olive branch, or she could repeat the apology, affirming that she couldn't remember what had happened and that it hadn't been a conscious choice to leave them. Ronnie didn't want to do either one. She didn't want to be forced into telling him any of her story. Her life was her own. Or it had been up until a couple of days ago when the police had landed on her doorstep. Every time she had to meet with Floyd, or a policeman, or a psychiatrist, she felt them pulling her life out of her hands. It was a tug-of-war, everyone else pulling on what she held in her hands, wanting a part of it, wanting to control a part of it.

So Ronnie just stared down, saying nothing. Floyd looked at her, wanting to ask her all of his questions. Wanting to know why she had left him and her two young children eleven years ago. Expecting her to be the same person as she had been before they left.

"Was there a lot of stress?" Ronnie asked.

"What?"

"If I had a psychotic break, then I must have been under stress... a lot of stress."

Floyd raised his eyebrows.

"I've talked to a psychiatrist too," Ronnie went on. "It would have to be more than normal stress, or people all over would be having psychotic breaks... running away from their lives... and they don't."

"I guess."

Ronnie didn't speak the question. What stress had they been under?

"We had the usual issues," Floyd said uncomfortably. "Arguments about finances. The stress of having two young kids. Intimacy." At Ronnie's change in expression, he hurried on. "Neither of us was having an affair, or anything like that. Just... recently married, two kids really close together... You were tired a lot. Not really... interested."

Ronnie felt her face flush. She looked away from him.

"It must have been hard after I disappeared," she observed. "Taking care of two little kids by yourself. You'd have to... get help."

"People were really good, that first year, volunteering to look after them without charging babysitting fees, taking them off my hands when I needed to talk to the police or take care of other issues. Then... your parents took custody when I..."

Ronnie looked at him, waiting for him to finish his sentence. Her parents took custody of the children. Why? He couldn't handle them anymore? He had remarried? He had been accused of being abusive and they were taken away?

Floyd sighed and stared off into space.

"It's been tough, Ronnie."

"Yeah, I know."

"No, you really don't. It's not just tough because my wife left me. I was arrested for your murder."

Ronnie's jaw dropped. "What? But I wasn't murdered!"

"Well, that's obvious to the police now," he said wryly, "but it wasn't then. In fact, they were pretty sure that I had murdered you, buried your body out in the woods somewhere, and then reported you missing. I was arrested and I was in prison pending trial. Your parents took custody of the kids."

"But... how long were you in prison? Not until now...?"

"No. Eventually, they decided that they didn't have enough evidence to prosecute it, so they had to let me go. After a couple of years. But your parents still had the kids. And I guess they still thought that I had killed you, so they didn't want me getting the kids back. We fought for two years, before Social Services finally returned custody to me. Your parents had been in the process of trying to adopt them. Even though I hadn't been convicted. They figured since I was out of the picture for an indefinite period, they'd be able to get the kids permanently."

"Oh." The thought made Ronnie anxious. Even though this man was a stranger to her, the thought of him having his children ripped from him and given to someone else, through no fault of his own, upset her. That shouldn't happen. Bubbling under the anxiety was something else. Something darker. Anger. Fury that her parents, who she couldn't even remember, would do such a thing. "I'm... I'm really sorry they did that."

He must have seen something in her expression, because he didn't argue with her this time. He just nodded, accepting it.

"It's good that you got them back. That was a really long time not to have them, though."

"Four years. Yeah. But they didn't have you for eleven."

Ronnie shook her head. "I really messed up your family."

"*Your* family," Floyd said.

Ronnie traced the pattern on the upholstered arm of the chair. There was a sound, and she looked up.

Carrie stood in the other doorway to the living room. Ronnie supposed that Carrie looked a little like she did. Shoulder length brown hair. Brown eyes. She didn't have much of Floyd in her face. It was a little like looking in the mirror. It wasn't just her features, there was something inside Carrie's eyes that Ronnie identified with. A sort of a sad, haunted look. Ronnie hadn't seen her smile yet, except for the plastic smile she had pasted on for the television reconciliation.

"Oh, hi," Ronnie said.

"Hi."

Carrie stood there. Waiting. Expecting more. Ronnie swallowed.

"You like to read?" she asked.

"What?"

"Your dad said you were probably reading. So, I thought... you must like to read."

"Yeah, I do."

Ronnie nodded.

"Do you like to read?" Carrie countered.

"Uh... not really. I'm usually doing other things. I can read okay, I just... I'm not big on books, I guess."

Carried shifted, leaning against the doorway as she looked in on Ronnie. "What *do* you like to do?"

"I don't know... watch TV. Go out."

"Go out where? To bars?" Carrie's tone rose accusingly.

"I don't know... sometimes, bars or clubs. Sometimes I want to be around other people. Where else would I go?"

"Is that why you left us? So you could go party?"

"Carrie," Floyd said in a warning voice.

"I want to know," Carrie insisted.

"I don't know," Ronnie said, hating to see them fighting with each other. "I don't remember what happened, why I left. I'm sorry. I don't know why I would ever have done such a thing. It's wrong. I just... I don't remember. I don't remember what happened."

"How could you forget your own children?"

Ronnie shook her head, tears welling up in her eyes. "I don't know. I keep feeling like... it's all a big mistake. That it must have happened to someone else, and you just think that I'm your mom. It doesn't make any sense to me. It's like it happened to someone else."

"Well, unless you have a clone, you're my mom."

Ronnie stared at the girl, trying to force her brain to recognize the child in front of her. Surely if she were Carrie's mother, she couldn't forget?

"Maybe I have a twin," Ronnie said, rubbing her aching temples. "Couldn't I have an identical twin?"

She had floated this theory with both the police and the psychiatrist, but neither one bought it.

"Then why wouldn't you remember?" Carrie demanded. "Wouldn't you remember your twin? And what happened to you in the last eleven years?"

Ronnie covered her eyes, resting her elbows on her knees.

"Carrie, let her alone," Floyd said. "You're upsetting her."

Ronnie swallowed, wiped her eyes, and forced herself to face the teen. "You were only two when I left? Do you remember me?"

"Kent does."

Ronnie nodded. She couldn't very well forget that Kent had recognized her. "Do you?"

"No. I don't remember anything from that far back. I remember living with Nana. That was after you were gone, when Daddy was in prison. I don't remember anything about you."

Ronnie must have nursed her, rocked her to sleep, taken care of her when she was sick. Watched her crawl and take her first steps.

She probably recorded all of those things in a baby book. Played with the children, took them to parks, made their meals every day. She tried to remember what their favorite meals were. Hot dogs? Macaroni and cheese? Chicken fingers? Why couldn't she remember any of those things that must have mattered so much when they were little?

"Do you still see them? Your Nana and...?"

"Nana and Papa. Yes, we go see them lots. We're really close."

Ronnie's skin crawled when she really comprehended that Carrie was talking about Ronnie's parents. Whom she hadn't met yet.

"Did they ever talk about me?"

"Yeah, all the time."

Ronnie scratched the back of her head. "That's weird. That kind of... creeps me out."

Floyd laughed, and they both looked at him.

"It creeps you out that your parents talk about you? That's ridiculous."

"It creeps me out that people I don't know talk about things that happened when I was a kid, that I can't remember happened. That *really* creeps me out!"

Floyd shook his head again over that. "We thought you were dead," he said. "How were we supposed to keep your memory alive, unless by talking about you?"

He had talked about her too, Ronnie realized. Told the children stories about when she had been alive. How he had met her. About their wedding, and the children's births, and dozens of other things that Ronnie had no memory of.

Everybody that she knew had talked about her.

And if she stayed in the community, there would always be talk going on around her, out of her hearing, about how she had disappeared and reappeared. About the person that she had been eleven years ago, and the person she was now.

They would always be talking about her.

She didn't see Kent again before she left Floyd's house. She couldn't think of it as her house, even though he had repeated the invitation that she was welcome to move in with them at any time. She could take the spare room while they rebuilt their family. He wouldn't insist on her taking up her place as his wife again, but she could at least reintegrate with the family.

Ronnie wondered what would happen if she tried, and then one day her brain just turned off again, and she walked away.

She wouldn't plan it that way, but she couldn't guarantee that it wouldn't happen. She couldn't imagine how devastating that would be to the children. Disappearing from their lives again a second time... They would never get over that.

They hadn't gotten over her leaving the first time. She couldn't get Kent's face out of her mind, the first time that she had seen him.

Ronnie had been walking home from the grocery store. He was riding his bike down the road and suddenly skidded to a stop, the bike nearly flying out from under him as he stopped and stared at her. Ronnie turned and looked behind her, thinking that he was looking at something beyond her, not at Ronnie herself. But there was nothing going on behind her, and when she looked at him, his eyes were riveted on her, wide with shock. Ronnie stood stock still, with a grocery bag in each hand, looking back at him.

"Mom?" he asked in astonishment. He had dark blond, spiky hair and a face that was just gaining definition as he changed from boy to man.

Ronnie was confused. She again looked around for someone else he might be talking to.

"Mom!" he repeated. He threw his bike down on the road and approached her. "Mom, it's me! It's Kent!"

She shook her head. "I don't know who you are. You've mixed me up with someone else. I don't have any kids."

"Yes, you do!" he insisted. "I'm Kent. Kent Plum. You're my mom. You're Ronnie Plum!"

It astonished her that he knew her first name. It was the one thing that kept her from just shaking her head and walking away from him.

"No... I'm Ronnie Kepler," she said. "I don't know anyone named Plum."

"You're my mom! You're Ronnie Plum! What are you trying to pull?"

"I'm sorry... you're mixed up. I don't know who you're talking about."

His mouth opened and closed like a fish. He stood there, his eyes so wide she wondered if he would ever blink again.

"I'm sorry," she repeated again. "I don't know who you are."

It was difficult to turn her back on the boy. He was somebody's son, and she knew he was hurt, but she couldn't help him. She couldn't pretend to be his mother. That wouldn't help him. It wouldn't fill the hole in his life. Pretending to be his mother when she wasn't would just be cruel.

"Mom!" he called after her, his voice breaking.

Ronnie blinked back tears, ignoring him. It would be cruelled to stop again and to build up his hopes. She had to just walk away and let him be.

She was relieved when she turned the corner and knew that she would be out of his sight. He could go and pick his bike back up and go back home. She felt bad for him, and for his confusion. Maybe he was mentally ill. She wondered if he often accosted women in the street, mistaking them for his mother.

When she got back to her apartment, she was shaking. She put her groceries in the fridge as calmly as she could. She didn't make anything to eat. Normally one of her favorite things was making something special to eat right after she got done a grocery shopping trip and had lots of good food in the fridge. Instead, she went to the couch, and turned on the TV, and just sat and tried to forget about Kent, the boy on the street.

It didn't last for long. Before she knew it, there was someone knocking on her door, and when she opened it, there were two uniformed police officers standing there.

"Ronnie Plum?" one of them asked.

"No. No, it's Ronnie Kepler."

He held up a picture of a young woman. "Is this you?"

Ronnie couldn't deny that it looked like her. The hair and clothing style were different. The makeup a little heavier. But it was her face looking back out of the picture at her. Ronnie frowned, studying her.

She couldn't remember ever seeing a picture of herself before. It was a weird feeling, seeing herself looking out of her picture just like she looked at herself in the mirror every day. It would be like turning on the TV and seeing herself talking.

"That... looks like me. But it isn't."

"Do you have a twin?"

"Uh... no..."

"Then I would say this is you."

"No."

"We'd like you to come in with us. Someone will need to talk to you, verify your identity."

"My name is Ronnie Kepler. I can show you my driver's license." Ronnie went into the kitchen and picked up her purse from where she had left it on the counter beside the empty grocery bags. She pulled out her wallet and removed the driver's license. She handed it to one of the officers. He examined it with interest, looking at her face and then back down at the license again.

"Where did you get this?"

"From... the DMV. Where else would I get a driver's license?"

"How did you get it?"

"I... took the driving test."

"What information did you give them? Birth certificate? Social?"

"Yes."

"Let's see them."

Ronnie retrieved the other pieces of identification. He looked over everything carefully.

"It's all issued in the last year."

Ronnie thought about that. "Well, yes..."

"What happened before that?"

"I... lost my wallet. I lost everything, and had to get everything reissued."

"Where was your previous driver's license issued?"

"I don't remember."

"What was your address before this one?"

She gave it to him, stumbling over the zip code but eventually remembering everything.

"And before that?"

"I don't remember the address..."

"You don't remember the address you lived at just a year ago? What city was it in? What neighborhood?"

"A lot has happened," Ronnie said anxiously "I don't remember everything."

"You don't remember what city you lived in?"

She swallowed and didn't answer.

"We'll need you to come in to the police station."

"I haven't done anything wrong."

"I think your identification is forged. That's enough to start with. You can come with us willingly, or I can put you in cuffs. Which is it going to be?"

Ronnie stared at him in disbelief. She knew that she hadn't done anything wrong. There was nothing wrong with her ID. There was no reason that she had to give him all of her previous residences. She had the right to privacy.

"I don't want to come in with you," she objected.

"Please put your hands behind your back, ma'am."

He moved around her, and his partner stood there in front of Ronnie, his hand on the butt of his gun.

"What...?"

He grabbed her hands roughly and pulled them behind her, where he clipped handcuffs over them.

"Do you have any weapons on you?"

"No."

"Anything sharp in your pockets?"

"No."

He patted her pockets. Turned them inside out.

"This is your purse?"

"Yes."

"Let's go, then."

He picked up her purse and they escorted her out of her apartment. The cop locked her door and put her keys back into her purse. In the car, he put the purse in the front seat, and Ronnie in the back seat, graciously helping her to sit down and warning her not to bump her head. Ronnie slid into the car, objecting.

"I didn't do anything. You can't arrest me for nothing. I don't have to go with you."

But she was already in the car, and she was going with them, whether she liked it or not.

~

The questions at the police station went by in a blur. She was shown pictures of a man and two children. More pictures of the young woman who looked like Ronnie. They fingerprinted her, and told her that her fingerprints matched those of Ronnie Plum.

"I'm not Ronnie Plum," Ronnie insisted. "I don't know who that is. I'm Ronnie Kepler."

"Well, you have Ronnie Plum's fingerprints," the cop told her. And he told her about her family. About the family that she had apparently walked away from eleven years ago. Part of a past that she couldn't remember anything about.

~

When Ronnie got back to her apartment after the visit with Floyd at his house, she was met by Adah Cruz.

Ronnie rolled her eyes and shook her head.

"I'm exhausted," she said. "I just met with Floyd and Carrie, and I can't take anymore. I can't answer your questions any more today than I could yesterday, or the day before that. I just don't remember any of it. Nothing is familiar."

"I know you were hoping that visiting the house would trigger something," Adah said with no sympathy in her voice. "As it happens... I have more information to show you. Maybe this will trigger something more."

Ronnie unlocked the door to her apartment. "I can't take it right now."

"You're going to have to."

Adah followed Ronnie into the apartment without an invitation. Ronnie looked at the couch in front of the TV. She would give anything to just be able to lie down and veg out in front of one of her favorite shows. She didn't want to have to think. Didn't want to have to go over anything else from her supposed past. She didn't want to be Ronnie Plum. She just wanted to be herself. Ronnie Kepler, the nobody.

"Maybe we could sit at the table," Adah suggested.

Ronnie looked longingly at the TV, then at the kitchen table, stacked with flyers and unopened mail. She sighed and went to the table. She tossed out the flyers and put the mail on the counter. She brushed toast crumbs into her hand and then emptied them into the garbage.

Sitting down on one of the thrift-store chairs, she put her elbows on the table and her head in her hands.

"Do we really have to do this?"

"Yes."

Adah sat in the other chair, directly across from Ronnie. She didn't make small talk about the weather or ask Ronnie how she was doing. It should have been pretty obvious how Ronnie was doing.

Adah put a picture of Ronnie on the table. Another missing poster. Ronnie didn't know why that should be news. Adah looked at her face for some change in expression. Then she put down a series of family pictures. Ronnie posing and smiling with Floyd, Kent, and Carrie. As Ronnie studied them, her heart sank. Her chest got tight and sore. It wasn't Floyd. It was another man, built much more solidly, his hair short and sandy colored. And the children seemed older than Kent and Carrie had been when their mother had disappeared. Ronnie studied their faces, not even sure that it was Kent and Carrie.

"I... don't understand," Ronnie said. "What's this?"

"This is Ronnie Coleman and the family that she abandoned a year ago."

Ronnie swallowed. "That's not me."

"It was a year ago. You don't look any different now."

"A year ago."

Ronnie stared down at the happy-looking family. She had a feeling of unreality whenever she looked at the pictures Adah showed her. It felt like some kind of prank. Some huge, elaborate prank to make her think that she had done the horrible things that they said. But she hadn't; she knew it in her heart. She couldn't just abandon a family like that. Those sweet-faced, innocent children.

"That's not me," she insisted. "Does that make any sense to you? Someone is playing a trick. Or I have a twin. It's not me!"

"We can check your fingerprints against Ronnie Coleman's. Just like we checked them against Ronnie Plum's."

"But if I have an identical twin…"

"Identical twins do not have identical fingerprints. No two people have the same fingerprints. If you have the same fingerprints as Ronnie Coleman, then you *are* Ronnie Coleman."

Ronnie shook her head. She felt light-headed and nauseated and the tight band around her chest was really hurting.

"How many more families like this are were going to find?" Adah demanded. "How many times have you done this?"

"I don't know what happened. I didn't do anything wrong."

"Ronnie, even if you are claiming amnesia, you still know something. You know that you set up a new identity for yourself, even if you pretend not to know who you were before that. You know that you stole the identity of the infant Ronnie Kepler. You know that's not who you are."

"I didn't *steal* it," Ronnie protested. But that argument had already failed with Adah. Adah Cruz refused to acknowledge that it was the only course of action for Ronnie to take. She couldn't work or drive with no identity. Couldn't own a credit card and pay for an apartment. She couldn't live without an identity, and that meant that she had to find one. She spent hours looking through public records to find an identity that felt right. She clearly remembered the feeling of relief that came to her when she found the name Ronalda Kepler. Ronnie. That was who she was. She had proceeded to follow the procedure she had researched on the internet to order her birth certificate and apply for a social, credit card, and driver's license.

"Why don't you explain it to me?" Adah said. Not for the first time. "Why don't you explain to me why you left your family? Two families? Normally people don't just walk away from their whole lives, Ronnie. Tell me what happened. The two of you had a fight. You were having marital problems. Did he hit you, and you decided you'd had enough? Did he threaten to do something to the children if you didn't just go quietly? Explain to me how someone decides to just walk away from everything." She tapped the table. "Not just once, but twice! Maybe more."

"Who are they?" Ronnie asked, looking at the pictures of the family.

"Dusty," Adah said, pointing to the father, "Dane, and Mandi. Now, I've answered your question, you answer mine. Explain why you left them."

"I don't remember anything about them. I don't remember ever seeing them before."

"Just like with the Plums."

"Yes," Ronnie said. "I don't know what happened. I don't remember."

"What is the earliest thing that you do remember?"

"I don't know. I don't remember, exactly... I just know... I lived here... I got a job... got this apartment... lived here..."

"You don't remember your parents or your childhood."

Ronnie remembered Carrie talking about Nana and Papa, and the anxiety she had felt over the thought of their raising the kids and talking about Ronnie grew in her chest again. It hurt to breathe. She was going to be forced to meet the people who claimed to be her parents. She might be able to put it off for a few days, but not forever.

"No. Not really."

"What does that mean?" Adah pounced. "Not really?"

"I don't remember anything clearly... like yesterday... but I know some things... like riding a bike... eating peanut butter sandwiches for lunch..."

"You remember doing those things?"

"No... I just... remember about them. Like... I watch a TV show, and I think, 'I used to wear my hair in braids.' But I don't remember braiding them... or what they felt like or looked like... I just think... I had them."

"Uh-huh." Adah's disbelief was not veiled.

Ronnie sighed. "Can you go now?" she asked. "I can't tell you anything, and you don't believe me if I do. I just want to go to bed."

Adah gathered up her pictures and stood.

"I'm sure we'll have more questions."

"I'm still not going to know the answers."

"We'll see. I'll be back."

"I don't have to meet those people, do I?" Ronnie asked, nodding at the bundled in Adah's hands.

"So far, no. It doesn't look like Dusty wants to put himself or his children through that. They've had a year to get used to the idea that you were gone, and what good would it do the children to be trauma-tized again? It's not like you're going to go back to Anchor to live with him, are you?"

"No."

Adah nodded and let herself out.

At first, they had seen Ronnie as a victim. In spite of having to put her in handcuffs to bring her in for questioning, they had believed that she was the victim of foul play or some form of traumatic amnesia. They were gentle with her and assumed that she wanted to remember.

But while Ronnie put on a facade of cooperating and wanting to help them, Adah gradually came to realize that there was something more going on. While she didn't seem to recognize her family, Ronnie wasn't telling them everything she knew or suspected. She wasn't telling them everything she remembered. Behind those dark eyes, there was some recognition of a past. She knew more than she let on.

And Adah was going to sort it out, if it took another eleven years to do so.

(III)

Ronnie could see that she was going to have to quit her job and find something else. Which was too bad, because she had enjoyed her job and the economy was not good. Finding a new job would not be easy. Everybody at work had seen her on TV, or at least heard about it. They all looked at her and whispered behind her back and asked her awkward questions. She would have to find something else.

She avoided meeting her parents, Chris and Cynthia Dare, for as long as she could. But the phone kept ringing and the police and the TV station kept insisting that she should meet them. Maybe it would trigger a memory. Maybe if she could look at pictures of when she was young, talk about things that she had done when she was young, then she'd be able to remember something. It would all start coming back, and then she would want to move back in with her ex-husband and children and they could all live happily ever after.

Except that Ronnie knew that even if she did remember anything about her childhood or her marriage, she still wasn't going to want to go back to them again. The children were very nice and she felt sorry for them. She even felt a little sorry for Floyd. But she didn't have any desire to live with them and have a relationship with them. She did want to know who they were, but that was all.

She forced herself to ring the doorbell of the big brick house. There was no media, and her parents were not standing at the door to meet her. It was a few minutes before they opened the door.

The man was heavyset. On the tall side. He was balding. The sides where he had hair, it was gray. He wore a checkered blue and gray shirt. The woman was smaller than Ronnie. Short, dark hair. Her face looked kind, but tired.

"Hi... I'm Ronnie."

The woman laughed. "We know who you are, Ronnie! Come in!"

Ronnie's face flushed. She was the one who needed introductions. Was she supposed to call them Mom and Dad? Had she had special names for them? Was she supposed to call them Nana and Papa, or was that just the grandkids? Ronnie followed them into the living room. Nothing looked familiar, but there was a TV playing, which Ronnie found soothing.

She aimed for the easy chair but her mother caught her by the arm and guided her over to the couch, where they sat uncomfortably close together. Her father sat in the easy chair with a grunt.

"So, you finally came back to us," he said.

Ronnie looked from one to the other, her stomach twisting with anxiety.

"I'm sorry... I didn't mean to..."

"What happened?" Mom asked. "Where have you been all these years?"

"I... I don't really know. I guess... I was somewhere else... That police detective, Adah Cruz, she thought I had another family, somewhere else."

Mom's jaw dropped. "You had another family? *Ronnie!*"

"Well... I didn't know! I didn't plan it that way."

"We raised you better than that," Dad said. "This whole thing..." He shook his head. "It's hard to believe a daughter of ours would behave that way."

"But I didn't know. I didn't plan to leave. I didn't remember that I had another family. It was just... a psychotic break... it wasn't something I could control."

Her parents exchanged looks that Ronnie couldn't interpret. Did they not believe her? They thought that she had rebelled? Intentionally walked away from them and her children and just started over again somewhere else?

"Show her the pictures," Dad said.

Ronnie expected Mom to get out a big photo album stuffed with memories, but she had just a small selection of pictures. A picture of a baby. A girl with braids. A group shot, with parents and some other children. A picture of Ronnie's wedding, standing beside Floyd. Ronnie holding a baby that looked very similar to the one in the first picture.

Ronnie studied them closely, waiting for a rush of recognition. They should trigger something. A memory. An emotion. Love or hate. But all she felt when she looked at them was anxiety. People she was expected to know. People that knew things about her. It just made her want to run away.

"Who is in this picture?" Ronnie pointed to the family shot.

"Those are brothers and sisters. We had foster children, so not all of them stayed with us. But we adopted Alex," Mom pointed to a red-headed boy grinning at the camera, "and Janessa." A thin, awkward-looking girl with glasses.

"The others aren't part of the family anymore?" Ronnie looked at the three other children of varying ages and races.

"No. They were just temporary. You can't keep them all, even if you wanted to."

Even if you wanted to. It was obvious from her voice that they hadn't wanted to adopt all of them. Ronnie thought about what the foster kids would have been like. Troubled homes, rough backgrounds; there had probably been a lot of behavioral problems to deal with. Ronnie was lucky to have been born into a well-off middle-class family who had been so giving.

"Do you remember anything?" Dad asked. "Anything at all?"

"No."

Mom and Dad exchanged another look.

"Something must have happened to you," Mom said. "You got hit on the head or something. You hear about that kind of thing happening."

Ronnie nodded. "That's what the psychiatrist said. He thinks I either got hit or had… a psychotic break."

Mom shook her head, frowning. "Why does he think that?"

"He thought maybe… I was under stress. Something made me… disassociate…"

"What stress could you have been under? You had a perfect life. Good stable marriage to a man who provided well for you. Two lovely children. You didn't have any stress in your life."

Ronnie stared down at the floor, pondering over this. No stress? There wasn't anybody who had no stress in their life, was there? Floyd had admitted that they had been dealing with marital issues. The police had arrested him for murder; *they* certainly hadn't thought that everything had been perfect.

"When are you going to be moving back in with your family?" Dad asked.

"I'm… I'm not. I don't know them. It's been eleven years. They don't know me either."

"Then you can move back here. Your mother has gotten the room ready for you."

Ronnie looked at him, then looked at her mother.

"I'm not… I'm not looking for somewhere else to live. I have my own apartment."

It was Mom who answered. "You need someone to look after you; you're not… well. You should come and stay with us until you're better. Who better to look after you than your own parents?"

"No. No, I'm fine. There's nothing wrong with me. I don't need anyone to take care of me."

"Your old room is ready for you."

"That's really nice of you. But I don't need it."

Ronnie looked around her apartment. Everything seemed foreign to her. She was looking for the soothing familiarity of her own place and her own stuff, anxious after dealing with her parents, but it all seemed like it belonged to someone else.

Was this what it had been like before she had left Floyd? And that other man? Had she just gotten home one day and nothing seemed right anymore? Had it happened gradually, or had she just snapped unexpectedly, herself one moment and gone the next?

She moved around her apartment like a sleepwalker, gathering together a few necessities and putting them into a suitcase. The suitcase was new. If she really had run away before, she hadn't taken it with her. She hadn't packed a bag before. Hadn't had the foresight. Before, she had just disappeared without a trace. At least, according to Adah Cruz.

It only took a few minutes to pack. She hadn't acquired much in the year that she had lived there and she didn't have space to take much with her. A couple changes of clothing. Toiletries. There was nothing of sentimental value. She was like a robot. Not a human.

In the bathroom, she saw herself in the mirror. She didn't even recognize herself. She gathered her shoulder-length hair and held it away from her face. She remembered the pictures of herself with her family before her disappearance, and those dreadful school pictures of a girl in braids and felt unaccountably furious. She bounced through the apartment, opening and closing drawers, until she found a pair of scissors. Not even bothering to look in the mirror, she grabbed hanks of hair and chopped them off at ear level. She didn't want to be that person. She couldn't ever be that person again.

When she got down to her car, she hesitated. The police could trace a car. They could put out an APB on it and track it down by its license plate. There were far too many surveillance cameras in the city to avoid detection forever. If she wanted to be untraceable, she needed to walk away without it. But if she were going to get far enough away to start a new life, she needed a car to get there.

Ronnie got into the car and sat in the driver's seat for a long time before turning the key in the ignition. Was she really going to do it intentionally? After all that they had told her about how she had hurt everyone, abandoning them as she had, was she really going to do it cold-heartedly this time? With forethought?

She wasn't leaving a family this time. There were no husband and children to abandon. It was just her, all alone. Her parents had lived without her for eleven years. She was already dead to them. They would forget all about her brief reappearance, like a ghost from the past. Their lives would go on just as they had.

She got to the highway. Red and blue lights flashed in her rear-view mirror. Ronnie pulled over a lane, slowing and waiting for the police car to pass her. It didn't; it stayed behind her, lights still flashing. Ronnie pulled over to the shoulder. Had she been speeding without realizing it? Forgotten to signal?

Ronnie watched in her mirror as she put the car into park. It was an unmarked police car. The policeman who approached the car was in a suit, not a uniform. Ronnie reluctantly rolled down the window. He held up a police badge to identify himself.

"Police, Miss Kepler," his lip curled when he said her name, like it tasted bad to him. "Get out of the car, please."

Ronnie forced her body to obey. She was shaking. They didn't have anything to arrest her on. There was nothing illegal about leaving town. It wasn't a police state where people were required to have visas in order to leave their own city. The policeman turned her around and pushed her against the car. He patted her down and pulled her hands behind her back to handcuff her.

"Wait—" Ronnie resisted.

"You're under arrest for breach of bail conditions," he said briskly. "Do you understand?"

"Bail...?" Ronnie vaguely recalled Gordon, her boss, offering to put up bail for her, tut-tutting the police accusing her of identity theft when, with no past and no identification, Ronnie had had no other option than to create a new identity for herself.

"You're outside the city limits," the officer told her. He looked in at the suitcase on the back seat. "You're obviously attempting to flee custody. So, guess what? It's back to the pokey for you."

He reeled off her rights as he strong-armed her into the back seat of his car and slammed the door. Ronnie just sat there while he talked on his phone, used his on-board computer, wrote up citations, and performed a cursory search of her car. Eventually, a tow truck arrived. The cop talked to the driver and waited until the tow truck took Ronnie's car away. Then they were on their way back to the police station.

"I knew she was going to run again," Adah Cruz said with satisfaction. "Once a runner, always a runner."

Eddie Paine nodded slowly. "But… this doesn't match her usual MO. There was no indication of planning when she left the Plums. She walked away without a vehicle. Left behind her purse with her cash and her ID."

Adah didn't look at him as she tapped a few notes into her phone.

"We didn't *find* any indication of planning," she corrected. "That doesn't mean that she didn't plan it. Just that we didn't find any evidence. She could have been planning it for months. What if she arranged her new ID, squirreled away some cash, and bought a new car before leaving? How would we know that?"

"We couldn't then, but maybe we could now," Eddie said. "We can see when her ID was issued. When her car was registered."

"It's relevant as part of the identity theft investigation." She nodded and looked up at him with a hard smile. "Good thinking."

"I'm not sure it contributes anything to the missing persons case… that file is resolved, now that she's back. There was no foul play."

"Maybe so, but I still think that Floyd Plum deserves some answers. To know whether his wife was a victim of circumstances, or whether she ran away." She cocked her head at Eddie. "I'm leaning towards running away, in case you were wondering."

He grinned. "No, really?"

Booking finished with Ronnie and an officer escorted her into the interrogation room. They watched her on the closed-circuit camera. Ronnie was obviously agitated. She initially sat down and looked expectantly at the door. But as time passed and no one came in to talk to her, she got up again and paced around the bare room. She sat back down again, jiggling her legs. Rubbing her arms. Folding her hands together in front of her and then wringing them as she was forced to sit.

"Did she ask for a lawyer?" Adah asked.

"Nope."

"Say anything in the car on the way in?"

"Just that she hadn't done anything wrong."

She studied Ronnie's slim figure, her chopped-off hair, and her pale, pinched face. Eventually, Adah decided there was nothing left to learn by observing Ronnie alone, and she went into the room and sat down across from her.

"So nice of you to come and see us again."

Ronnie scowled. "It's not like I had any choice."

"Well, you had a choice about running away or not. As usual, you took it."

"I don't have to stay here. I'm allowed to leave if I want."

"Your bail requires you to stay here. Because you haven't gone to trial yet."

"I didn't do anything wrong. So I shouldn't have to stay here."

"You're welcome to your own opinion. But you're still required to abide by the terms of your bail."

"Okay. I'll stay."

"You're going back to jail now," Adah pointed out. "This isn't a three-strikes thing. You don't get a second chance. You left the city, your bail is revoked, and you get to await your trial in jail."

"That's not fair."

"That's the law. You break it at your own risk."

Ronnie sat there looking at her, face pale and petulant. Adah wasn't sure that Ronnie really comprehended what was going on. She acted like a kid that had been grounded, rather than someone who could be incarcerated for the next several months or years. There were no tears. No indication that she realized how much she had just screwed up her life.

Ronnie was escorted to a cell. Not an open-barred jail cell like she had seen on TV. It was a small room with two bunks, one steel toilet, a writing desk and bookshelf. It was probably less than half the size of the bedroom in her apartment, and two people were expected to live there. Ronnie knew she had roomed with others before. Her foster sisters. But it would be close quarters.

The woman who was already there sitting at the desk was older than Ronnie, or looked it, anyway. Deeper lines on her face. Dry, wispy blond hair, cut short. From the tattoos all over her arms and the holes in her ears, Ronnie suspected that she was used to having a lot of product in her hair. Gel, mousse, colors, maybe she spiked it.

The limp does it was in didn't do anything for her. She had glasses, but probably used contacts when she was on the outside.

The guard locked the door behind Ronnie. She looked at the other woman and looked at the beds.

"This one?" she guessed, pointing to one of the bunks. It was stripped, the sheet and blankets folded in a pile on top, waiting to be used.

"Brilliant, yeah," the blond said.

"Thanks." Ronnie sat down. "I'm Ronnie."

"Anna Stegner. Ronnie what?"

Ronnie sighed. "Kepler. Dare. Plum. Take your pick."

Anna lowered her eyebrows at this. "Which one do you go by?"

"Kepler."

Anna nodded. "Ronnie Kepler, then. That's good enough for me."

Ronnie looked at the folded blankets. She knew that she should make the bed, in case she was too tired to do it before going to sleep. Making the bed would mean that she was going to stay there, and she wasn't ready to admit that. She kept thinking that she would get out. Go home. They wouldn't hold her in jail just because she had tried to leave town. That would be cruel.

"What are you in for?" she asked Anna.

"None of your business."

"Oh."

"You?"

Ronnie should just answer back that it wasn't any of Anna's business, but she wanted to visit, wanted to make a connection. Just one person that hadn't known her before. One person who would just take her at face value, without trying to dig down below the surface.

"Broke bail conditions."

Anna snorted. "Bail for what?"

"Uh… identity theft. But I didn't mean to do anything wrong. I just needed…" She trailed off. Anna didn't need to know that. She didn't care what Ronnie's reasons were for assuming a new identity. Ronnie didn't want to explain the whole amnesia situation.

Anna's eyes drifted away from her, back to the letter or journal she had been writing before Ronnie got there.

"Well, just stay out of my way, Kepler, and we'll be just fine."

"Sure… okay."

Ronnie stared at the blankets on the bed, still refusing to acknowledge that she was going to need them.

~

Ronnie slumped in her seat, looking down at the table instead of at the psychiatrist. She didn't want to talk to him again. He really hadn't done anything to help her out, and she didn't like the idea of someone digging around in her psyche. She pictured him bent over her brain with a fork in his hand, delicately dissecting her. How much could he really figure out without messing things up? She might not be able to remember what had happened in the past, but she was still sane. She could only imagine the damage he could do poking around in her brain.

"Your family said that you used to draw," Dr. Able said, laying down a sheaf of paper on the table, and supplying her with a box of pencil crayons of various lengths. Some of them had long scars or bite marks on them. "I think today, we'll try a little art therapy."

Ronnie looked down at the pencils. "I don't draw. What do you expect me to do?"

"It doesn't matter whether you can draw well or if all you can do is stick figures. Let's just see what you come up with. I'd like you to draw what comes to mind when I say... family."

There was a shocker. Ronnie rolled her eyes. "Can't I do something else? I already met my family and I don't want to draw them."

"You don't have to draw the people you met. You can just draw something that represents family to you. It could be someone you know, or just a picture like you might see on a cereal commercial on TV. It could be something other than people. A Christmas tree or a puppy. A warm plate of spaghetti. Really. Just draw me... family."

Ronnie frowned, staring down at the blank white paper. It was open, pristine, waiting for her to make her mark. Even though she didn't draw, she had a sudden impulse to fill it with something.

She started with some tentative lines. Her fingers seemed to know what they were doing, and the picture began to come together, even though she wasn't sure what she had in mind. She switched pencil crayons a few times, adding some color, filling in the forms. After a while, she pushed the paper away, frustrated.

"I can't do it. I can't... I can't get the details right. I can't see their faces."

Dr. Able picked up the paper and studied it. "Well, they were right about you being able to draw. This is very good."

"But it's no good if I can't get the faces. They're just... bodies. They're not right."

"Close your eyes and tell me what you see that you weren't able to get in the picture."

Ronnie closed her eyes, searching for the images. She shook her head. "I can't. That's the problem. I can't see them. Just this!" She gestured at the paper. "It's not right."

"What isn't right about it?"

"You can see it's not my family," Ronnie pointed out.

He lowered it so that they could both see it at the same time.

"It isn't Floyd and the children," Ronnie said.

"No. But it doesn't have to be."

"And it's not my mom and dad. He's tall and gray and going bald. And she's a little woman. Petite. Smaller than me. Not like these people. I saw pictures of my brothers and sisters, or foster brothers and sisters." Ronnie looked over the other shadowy forms in the picture. "These just... they aren't right. I don't get it."

"I told you that you didn't have to draw your own family. Maybe this was a picture that you saw. Or a movie. Sometimes my patients remember things from movies and think that they happened to them in real life. It's very hard to differentiate sometimes, especially if you've had a traumatic incident. Your brain tries to fill in the holes and sometimes it fills them in with things that don't actually belong."

"You think I saw this family on TV? I drew them because I don't have a family of my own?"

"It could be a family you saw on TV," he repeated.

Ronnie didn't mind that idea. She had had so many new people claiming to be family forced on her lately that she was happier with having picked a family of her own. Safe, with no real claim on her. Not anyone that she would have to meet in real life to explain why she had abandoned them. She looked at them with new eyes, thinking through the programs she liked to watch on TV. Were they from one of her sitcoms? A soap? Maybe even a reality show or one of the talk shows where they did lie detector and paternity tests.

Those always fascinated her. Or maybe they were from a movie. Something that she had gotten a happy feeling from. A classic, nuclear family.

The mother figure was large and fat. She scowled out of the picture, even if her face was only an outline. Something about her just exuded disapproval. Probably not a sitcom or family movie, then. The man was less distinct. Not the big, tall, balding man that Ronnie had met. He was smaller than the woman. His hair darks. He hugged a couple of the children close to him.

"Is this a family from TV?" she asked Dr. Able. "Do you know them from anything?"

There were five children. The two biggest blond, and the smaller ones all dark-haired. Ronnie felt a kinship with the middle child. Stuck between two older siblings and two younger siblings. Alienated. She wasn't one of the children that the father was cuddling.

"I don't recognize them," Dr. Able said. "But I don't watch a lot of TV. They could be very well-known, and I still wouldn't recognize them. Why don't you tell me something about them?"

"There are four girls and just one boy," Ronnie observed. "I wonder how he feels, being the only boy after all of those girls."

"Is he the youngest?" Able asked, his eyes intent on the picture.

"I don't know. I think so."

"What else can you tell me?"

"They're all together," Ronnie observed. "One big, happy family."

"Are they happy?"

Their faces were blank, so what made him ask that? Ronnie looked at their body language. Tried to imagine what it would be like to meet them in real life.

"The mother is angry," Ronnie said. "She screams at the kids when they act up. But this is a happy picture. Everybody's happy in this picture."

"I see. That's good. What other feelings do you get when you look at them?"

"I want to go home..." Ronnie was startled by putting the thought into words. She wanted to go home? Where was home? Back to her own apartment? With Floyd? With her parents? None of them evoked the feeling of *home*.

Able was nodding. He rubbed the stubbly growth on his chin. "What else? What do you feel about family and home?"

"I don't know. I feel like it's been a long time... and that I'll never go home. I feel... abandoned... isolated."

"Yes, yes...?"

Ronnie shook her head at him. "None of *those* people are my family. I don't feel connected to any of them. They just *say* they're my family. Why would they do that?"

"Why would you feel that way?" he countered. "That's what we're here to find out. We want to dig down into those feelings. See what's behind them."

Ronnie rubbed her eyes, feeling distant and dreamy. "What good is it to look at my feelings when I don't remember anything?"

"Because even if the memories aren't there, the feelings still are. We can learn something from them. I think this," he tapped the picture, "tells us that the memories are still there, locked up somewhere."

"You said it was from TV."

"I said that it could be. But you attach very strong emotions to it for it to be from TV or another outside source. I think that there is meaning in it, even if it came from TV."

"That's stupid," Ronnie scoffed.

Able shrugged, seeming unoffended.

"Do you want to try another one?"

Ronnie was interested in what her brain might reveal to her, but she didn't want to let him see that. So she shrugged like it made no difference to her. "If you want."

"Okay, let's try another one. How about... yourself."

"Myself?"

He nodded.

"I can look in the mirror and draw myself. What's that going to prove?"

"Why don't you just try?"

Ronnie considered, picking out a fresh sheet of paper and hovering over it with a pencil. She started to sketch her own face. At least she didn't have to concentrate to remember what that looked like. It wasn't like the blanks in the family picture. She stalled and restarted several times before pushing the picture across toward Able without a word. He picked it up.

"You're very small," he observed. "You had the whole page to use, and you are small and alone in the middle of it."

"What does that mean?"

"I guess it means you feel small and alone."

Ronnie nodded. That wasn't news to her. She couldn't see the picture the way that he was holding it, but she knew what it looked like. Not a picture of her as an adult. Not a mother and wife. Not the adult that she was now, single and apart from anyone else. But her as a child, similar to one of the pictures that her mom had shown her. Long, dark braids. A pinafore dress that came down to her knees, neat and clean. Hands joined in front of her, like she was posed for a photograph.

"Tell me about yourself here," Able suggested.

"I don't know. I don't remember."

"You drew it. What made you draw yourself that way?"

"I guess just one of the pictures that I saw. Of me when I was a little girl. I kind of thought I had braids before I saw it, so it was… like I remembered, but not really."

"Are the braids important?"

"No. They're just braids."

"Did it make you feel happy when you saw the picture? Familiar?"

"No."

"Tell me how you felt."

"I felt… anxious. Like I did when I had to meet Floyd and the kids. But… more so. I didn't want to be there."

"How do you feel toward your parents?" Able put down the picture, and his eyes drifted back to the family picture again, studying out the figures with their blank faces.

"Unreal. I feel like someone is just setting this all up, like a hoax. I don't feel like they're my parents, like I love them. I feel like they're actors in some bizarre movie. Gaslight."

"Gaslight?"

"It was a movie where this guy tried to make the girl think she was crazy—"

"I'm familiar with it. I'm just interested about the connection. This feeling of disconnection could be Depersonalization or

Derealization Disorder. You feel like you're watching yourself in a movie?"

"No…" Ronnie was frustrated. "Like everybody else is an actor, and I'm the only one who knows who I really am. Or they know, but they're trying to keep me from believing it."

He nodded slowly, mulling that over.

"If you could get out of here, what would you do? Where would you go?"

"I'd get away… go somewhere else. Where there aren't all of these people who know me, or pretend to know me. I'd go somewhere I could be myself again."

"And who are you? Who is Ronnie?"

"I don't know. Just an ordinary person. I just… I just go to work, curl up to watch TV… go to the grocery store… I'm just ordinary, maybe a little boring."

"Don't you get lonely?"

Ronnie hesitated. She teetered between wanting to have someone in her life, someone who just appreciated her for who she really was, and never wanting to get close to anyone. Never wanting to have to face another family who claimed to know who she was and where she had come from.

"A little, maybe. But I don't want a family."

Able scratched his ear and looked down at the picture. "You don't want *this* family? Or any family?"

"Well… maybe I want that family. But not any others. And… I don't know who they are."

(IV)

Ronnie tossed and turned on the hard bunk, unable to settle in and find sleep. She groaned and pressed her face into the pillow.

"Be quiet, Kepler," her cellmate growled. "Some of us are sleeping."

"I'm trying," Ronnie protested. "I can't get comfortable…"

"You ain't gonna get comfortable here. It's not possible. Just be still and shut up."

"I didn't say anything."

"You're moaning and groaning and driving me crazy. Zip it, or I'll shut you up myself."

Ronnie sighed and squeezed her eyes tightly shut. She didn't think that Anna Stegner was going to do anything about it, but it was prison—Stegner might be capable of violence. It was medium security. Not somewhere that Ronnie could walk away from, but she wasn't being housed with murderers or violent offenders. Stegner was probably guilty of theft or hacking. She was a thin blond, with short messy hair and studious-looking glasses. Ronnie wasn't particularly afraid of her.

Ronnie turned her pillow over and curled her toes and tried to find the sweet spot in the uncomfortable cot that would allow her to find sleep.

She found sleep, but her night was filled with restless dreams. Her mind roved from one problem to another, trying to sort through the questions that Able had asked her, her feelings of not belonging to the families who claimed her, how she could persuade Adah to let her out of prison.

Her head hurt, and it was dark. Ronnie became aware of a repetitive noise near her head. A *clunk-scrape*, *clunk-scrape*, over and over again. Broken by the occasional swearing or period of silence, and then it started over again. What was it? Ronnie's eyes were too heavy to open. The headache grew until it was overwhelming. She wanted to throw up, but she didn't want to wake up and move. Her body was too ponderous to even raise her head. She curled more tightly into a ball. The noise stopped.

"Ronnie? Are you awake...?" the question was soft, furtive. Whose voice was it? Floyd's? Ronnie was afraid to answer. She couldn't anyway, not with her head pounding and her body so heavy. She didn't seem to have any control over her body.

There was a hand on her. Fingers searching for a pulse on her wrist, then flinging her arm away again with a grunt.

The man was muttering something to himself, unintelligible to Ronnie. Then Ronnie felt arms under her, lifting her behind the back and the knees, and then dumping her back to the ground with a crash that sent Ronnie's head spinning so badly that she must have blacked out for a time. She awoke again later, unsure how much time had passed. The clunk-scrape continued, but at the end of each *clunk-scrape*, a patter of rain hit Ronnie's body. *Clunk-scrape-spray, clunk-scrape-spray.*

There was an increasing weight on her body, and it seemed a very long time before full awareness reached Ronnie's consciousness. It wasn't a spray of rain. It was dirt. It was piling up on her body, getting heavier and heavier. Suffocating.

Ronnie tried to escape, but the dirt was too heavy. Her body was too heavy. She couldn't use her voice, screaming in her head without a sound. He was burying her! Burying her alive!

All at once, Ronnie was screaming aloud, her limbs were her own again, and she was clawing, trying to escape, crying and gulping and taking great gasps of air before he could cover her face. His hand was on her arm, shaking her, trying to get her to stop screaming.

"Wake up!" Stegner shouted, shaking harder. "What the hell is your problem? Wake up!"

Ronnie opened her eyes. It was dark, but there was enough light from the security lights outside and in the corridor that she could see around her. See Stegner standing over her. The shapes of the cell's furniture around her. She was in prison. Not being buried alive. That was a dream.

Stegner dropped Ronnie's arm, just like Floyd had in the dream after checking for a pulse, letting it fall back to the bunk.

"Just when I get to sleep, you wake me up screaming bloody murder!" Stegner complained. "What's that all about? You keep that up and I'm going to get you moved to solitary! I need my sleep."

"Sorry," Ronnie gasped. "I'm sorry. I just had a nightmare."

"No kidding!"

"I'm sorry."

She lay there, her whole body tense, waiting to see if Stegner were going to hit her. Eventually, the other woman backed off.

"You'd better not wake me up again."

Ronnie sat up, propping herself against the concrete blocks of the wall. She cuddled her blanket close.

"I'll stay awake," she promised. "I don't want to dream anymore."

"Make sure you don't. I don't like being woken up. I need my sleep!"

"Okay, I'm sorry. It was... really scary."

Stegner climbed back into her bunk. "What was it about?" she asked, in a more conciliatory tone.

"I was..." Ronnie swallowed. "I was being buried alive."

"Yeesh. That's freaky."

"Yeah."

Stegner was quiet, going back to sleep. Ronnie lay there, thinking about the dream. Was it true? Had it really happened? Adah Cruz had told her that Floyd had been suspected of her murder. They thought that he had killed her and buried her. There was a shovel in his trunk that had recently been used, and his explanation hadn't rung true.

Was it possible that he really had buried her? He knocked her out and thought that he had killed her, but Ronnie had awakened while he was burying her? Or maybe she had woken up afterward and clawed her way up to the surface to escape? The nearly-fatal injury and the trauma of being buried could have caused her amnesia.

Wouldn't someone have reported a woman wandering around disoriented, covered with mud and blood? That wasn't normal. As soon as Ronnie reached civilization, someone would have said something. It would be reported to the police, she'd be taken to the hospital. She would need clothing and a shower, at the very least. Probably medical treatment.

Ronnie sighed. More likely, it was just something that her brain had made up, inspired by Adah's words. She was restless and entombed in prison, and her brain had just taken the idea and made a dream out of it.

It had felt so real.

～

"Visitor, Plum," a guard said curtly, motioning for Ronnie to come forward.

Ronnie approached the cell door and put her hands through the access hole for him to handcuff. "Can you not call me that?" she said. "It's not my name. Not what I go by."

"According to your booking records, that's your name."

He opened the door and Ronnie joined him in the corridor. She waited while he closed the cell door again, and then he took her by the elbow and escorted her down the hall. They worked their way through a maze of hallways that Ronnie hadn't been able to get accustomed to yet, to the open visitor room. It was mostly filled with small tables and chairs, but there were a few couches and more homey pieces of furniture around the outer perimeter. Good for families with kids.

Ronnie looked around to see who was there to visit her, expecting another cop or lawyer. Or maybe a social worker or some other kind of case worker. She couldn't keep track of all of the professionals who came to see her, claiming that they had some task or another to complete on her behalf. Mostly, they seemed to be people who were curious and just wanted to get a look at her. To say that they had talked to the woman who had disappeared for eleven years with amnesia, not even knowing that she had a family and starting another one.

But it wasn't another professional. It was Kent. Ronnie swallowed and didn't walk up to talk to him. When the guard pulled her hands toward him to uncuff her again, Ronnie resisted.

"No, just..."

"I'm taking them off, Plum. Hold still."

"No, I want to go back. I don't want to talk to him."

He stared at her. "You don't want to visit? You want to go back to your cell?"

Ronnie nodded quickly. "Yes. Please. I don't want to have to talk to him."

The guard stood there, unsure of what to do. Ronnie didn't know whether protocol was that she had to visit even if she didn't want to. Surely, they wouldn't force to meet with someone that she didn't want to. She still had some rights, didn't she?

"Mom," Kent said, when he saw that she was trying to go back to her cell without talking to him. "Mom, please. I came all the way here. Had to get special permission to come see you. Please talk to me."

"We don't have anything to talk about." Ronnie still resisted the guard removing the cuffs. But he persisted and turned the key in the locks, removing them, and gestured toward a table.

"Go sit down with your son," he said gruffly.

Ronnie gazed at him unhappily.

"Please," Kent pleaded again. "I just want to talk. Why won't you let me talk to you?"

Ronnie dragged herself over to the table that the guard had pointed to and sat down, breathing out a long sigh. Kent sat down across from her. His eyes were sharp, watching her intently, taking note of every detail. It was humiliating, having to face him like that with her orange hospital jumper. Like a murderer or rapist. She had done nothing wrong. All she had done was try to make a life for herself.

"I'm sorry," she told Kent.

"It's my turn to talk."

She stared down at the top of the table. People had scratched words and crude drawings into it. With what? Ronnie hadn't been allowed so much as a pen. They wouldn't let anyone have a knife or anything that could hold a point.

Ronnie looked at the graffiti and not at her son. The stranger that they said was her son.

"I just want you to know," Kent went on, his adolescent voice cracking. "I want you to know what you did to our family, leaving like you did."

Ronnie didn't answer. He didn't want her to say anything. He came with his own speech prepared.

"I was four when you left," he went on. "I don't remember you much. I know your face from all of the pictures. Dad and Nana always talked about you. Talked about how great you were and how they missed you. No one ever thought you would come back. We all thought you were dead."

"I didn't... I didn't abandon you on purpose." Ronnie thought about the dream. The dream of being buried. She felt that way again, short of breath, like she was suffocating. Like she wanted to scream, but couldn't get enough breath, the weight on her stomach and chest too heavy. "I don't know what happened. I didn't do it to be mean. I... don't know what happened."

"You should have come back. Or maybe you shouldn't have, I don't know. Maybe it's worse, you coming back, instead of letting us think that you were dead. I could handle having a dead mother.

People understood that. Teachers at school were nice about it. They didn't whisper behind their hands about it. Having you come back... having all of the kids say that you left because of me, because I was so horrible and you didn't want to be my mom... that *hurts*."

Ronnie nodded. "I know... but I didn't. I didn't leave because of you. I didn't mean to come back. I didn't mean to mess everything up. Twice. I just... I didn't know you were here. Didn't know what had happened. That I used to live here. I would have stayed away. I would have gone on to another town. But I didn't. I liked the sound of it here... it felt... like home."

"It's not. Not anymore. You shouldn't have stopped here."

"I didn't mean to. I didn't know all of this. I just... I thought I was settling down somewhere new. Somewhere I'd never been before. I didn't know I was going to cause any problems."

"Why did you leave us?" he demanded plaintively. "Why?"

Ronnie stared down at the table. She felt so bad for him. But there was nothing that she could do to change all that had happened to him. Or to her.

What was done was done.

Adah looked down at the stack of messages on her desk, sighing.

"What's up with the flood of pink slips?" she asked Eddie, not bothering to pick them up.

He scratched the back of his neck, pursing his lips. "Ronnie Plum."

"Plum? What about her? How can she be causing me this much trouble from inside a prison cell?"

"There have been a number of objections raised about her being incarcerated awaiting her trial. Public sympathy is on her side."

"What do I care about public sympathy?" Adah gathered up the message slips and tapped them into a neat stack, then set them to the side without reviewing them. "The woman was running. We can't keep a tail on her twenty-four hours a day to make sure she gets to trial."

Eddie could have just gone back to his desk and left her to stew about it, but instead he slipped into the visitor chair on the other side of her desk and made himself comfortable.

"People think that what she did, while it might be a technical theft of identity, shouldn't be counted as identity theft because of the extenuating circumstances."

"Because they think that she did have amnesia and that breaking the law was the only way for her to survive."

He inclined his head.

"If we allow that, we'll get a whole avalanche of people claiming to have amnesia as an excuse for ripping people off and bilking them out of their life savings."

"Except that's not what Plum did. She never took money from anyone, as far as we can tell. She lived her quiet life and used her identity just to work and survive."

"I thought you were on my side on this." Adah looked away from Eddie and tapped her login into the computer. When her email box popped up onto the screen, she saw that, as she had dreaded, it was also full of messages regarding the pain in the neck, Ronnie Plum.

"I'm not on anyone's side. I agree that what Plum did was breaking the law. She doesn't get to just walk away from it without facing justice. On the other hand... it appears that it was a victimless crime. If she does have amnesia, there is at least a defense."

"But we don't know if she really does have amnesia."

"Right."

"Are they going to release her? I can't control it if they do. But I'm not going to tie up our resources surveilling her if they do."

Eddie looked at the pile of pink messages slips. "From the volume of messages and some of the names on them, I think the scale is tipping."

[V]

Ronnie had been invited several times to the family's Sunday dinner. She had avoided it for a couple of weeks, giving excuses about having to get settled back in after getting home from jail. Getting caught up at work. Eventually, she ran out of excuses and agreed that she would go.

"We'll have the whole family together again," Mom gushed happily over the phone. "All of my babies in one place."

"Okay," Ronnie told her. "I'll see you then. What do you want me to bring?"

"Nothing. Just bring yourself. I'm cooking."

"I could bring a bottle of wine or something."

There was a sharp intake of breath. "You don't drink wine," Mom said sternly, "and neither do we."

"Oh... yeah. I forgot." Ronnie bit her lip, pondering this new piece of information. Was it a religious thing? Moral? Personal preference? The family might have lost a loved one to a DUI. She had no clue what the basis for the wine prohibition was. "Well then, dessert? Brownies?"

"I suppose, if you want to go to all of that work," Mom said, her voice doubtful.

"Okay. Great. See you then."

Ronnie wasn't going to go to any work on the brownies. She would buy a just-add-water mix. Or maybe buy them frozen or from a bakery. She wasn't a baker, but she did enjoy sweets. A family Sunday dinner wouldn't be complete without some kind of dessert. Maybe Mom had been planning on another dessert and Ronnie was insulting her by insisting on bringing something. Ronnie sighed after hanging up the phone. Navigating the waters around this family she couldn't remember was dangerous work. She had no idea what sharks lurked beneath the surface.

When Sunday rolled around, Ronnie was at the brick house at four o'clock on the dot. There was an unfamiliar car there ahead of her. A red Beetle. As Ronnie got reluctantly out of her car, a man pulled up on a noisy, exhaust-belching motorbike. He turned in behind Ronnie and cut the engine. He unstrapped his helmet and Ronnie looked at his short-cropped red hair.

"You must be Alex," she guessed.

"And you're Ronnie." He looked her over thoughtfully. "You haven't changed that much. Cut your hair, though. It was longer when you were on TV."

Ronnie nodded. She had gone to a hairdresser to get her self-inflicted bob tidied up and made to look presentable. It actually ended up looking pretty cute.

"Come on in, they'll all be waiting."

Ronnie looked at her watch. "She said four. It's just four now."

"Well, Mom expects us to be here early. If you don't get here until four, you're late. Then she starts to worry that…" He cut himself off and pursed his lips. "Well, that something has happened to you."

"Oh."

Mom started to worry that she had disappeared and was never coming back. That she'd been kidnapped or murdered or disappeared into thin air again. Ronnie hadn't meant to worry her. She thought that four meant four.

"Don't worry about it," Alex said. "If you don't give in to her paranoia, maybe she'll learn to relax about it."

"Is that why you're here at four?"

"Once I was even five minutes late," he teased. "Of course, by the time I got here, she'd already called the police."

Ronnie narrowed her eyes at him, trying to decide whether he was serious or kidding about that part.

He just raised his rusty eyebrows and grinned and Ronnie couldn't figure it out.

The woman who came to the door when Alex knocked and let himself in was gorgeous. Ronnie divested her coat and studied her surreptitiously. Surely this wasn't Janessa, the awkward girl with the glasses in the family photos? She was a willowy blond with perfect teeth and makeup. No glasses; maybe she had contacts.

"Ronnie!" she greeted in a low, rich voice. "Oh, it's so good to finally see you!" She gave Ronnie a brief hug, hands on shoulders, leaning in close and landing a kiss in the air somewhere near Ronnie's ear. She smelled of a flowery perfume. "Wow, I can't believe you're back." As she pulled back from the stiff embrace, her eyes flicked around. "I honestly assumed that you were dead. I never thought I would see you again."

"Sh," Alex hushed her.

Then Mom was there. "You finally made it! I was starting to worry. Was traffic a problem?"

413

"No, Mom, we're right on time," Alex said. He greeted her with a quick hug and kiss, and Ronnie followed suit.

"We'll just be visiting with Dad until suppertime anyway, won't we?" Alex said. "It's not ready yet, is it?"

"Of course not. I'm still slaving in the kitchen. You go see what your dad's doing."

"I already know what he's doing," Alex laughed, looking at Ronnie. "He's watching TV."

"Do you need help in the kitchen?" Ronnie offered. She'd rather watch TV, but knew she should be polite and help out if she could.

"No, no, I've got it under control. You guys go visit. Get caught up. You've got eleven years of gossip to catch up on!"

Ronnie had a lot more than that to catch up on. She had thirty years of lost memories. She looked uncertainly at Alex and Janessa. Janessa nodded and linked her arm through Ronnie's.

"Come on. We'll go see what Dad's up to and get caught up."

Ronnie let herself be pulled along to the living room, where she had visited with Mom and Dad before. Again, the TV was on and Ronnie felt soothed by its presence. Just a normal family, doing normal things, living normal lives. She could fit in there. She could be a part of that family and not mess up or feel out of place.

They all greeted their father and sat down. Ronnie turned her attention to the program on the TV, but that didn't last long.

"So... tell us all about it," Alex said. "You disappear for eleven years, then show up again. Big hoopla. You must have a pretty good story."

Ronnie glanced over at him. "Well, no. Not really. I don't remember what happened."

"Not at all?"

She shook her head. "Nothing. I just... I just remember being in town, for the last few months... a year... I don't remember anything about living here." She gestured to indicate the house around them. "Or with Floyd. I don't remember him or the kids... or anyone..."

"Not Mom or Dad?" Janessa asked in surprise. "Not us?"

"No. Sorry."

"Oh, wow!" Janessa's eyes were wide. "That's incredible. I thought... you'd remember your childhood and everything. I thought that when you met Floyd and the kids... well, you'd start to remember. That's the way it always works on TV." She gave a little shrug. "I know you can't judge real life by TV, but I thought that was the way that it worked."

"They said that familiar things might help to trigger memories, to bring it back. But so far... no, nothing has really made a difference. I don't remember any of this. Not here, not... anyone."

Janessa swore. She and Alex exchanged looks.

"You must have all kinds of questions, then," Janessa said. "Don't you? What do you want to know?"

"I'm watching TV," Dad pointed out, gesturing at the program he had on.

Janessa flapped a hand in his direction, brushing it off. "You're supposed to be visiting. This is Ronnie! Your long-lost daughter! Don't you want to talk to her? To help her?"

"She came and visited before. She can't tell us anything about what happened. Or won't. So, what's the use of asking her about it?"

Janessa rolled her eyes. She looked back at Ronnie. "Just ignore him," she said. "He's not really mad. When he's mad, you'll know it."

"Oh... okay."

"So? You must have all kinds of questions."

"I don't know. I don't know what to ask. You guys..." she considered, "are you married? Do you have families?"

"No. Yours are the only grandkids. Mom and Dad spoil them rotten. Let them do all kinds of things that we were never allowed to do," Janessa raised her voice, pointing this comment at their father. "Feed them all kinds of sweets and let them get away with murder."

"Grandparents are allowed to spoil kids," Dad said. "That's our job. It's the parents' job to raise them. Teach them how to behave. It was different when they were here... while... you know."

"While Floyd was in jail," Alex contributed. He raised an eyebrow at Ronnie. "Did you know that part? That he was in jail and Mom and Dad took the kids?"

"Yeah, I know."

"I'll bet you do," Janessa agreed with a little laugh. "Floyd's been pretty bitter about it all along. I don't suppose all is forgiven now that you're back."

"No," Ronnie shook her head slowly. "He said that I could go back there to live. In the spare room. But... it's kind of weird. I wouldn't want to. He did tell me about being in prison. I know it's no fun. But… I didn't want that to happen. I didn't leave… because I wanted him to suffer."

"Of course not," Janessa said quickly. "I don't mean that. I just know the way he is. He's been pretty miserable about it. Never let it go, all these years. Still complains about how he can't get a good job, and being in prison ruined everything for him. The injustice. He still talks about it."

If Janessa were trying to make Ronnie feel better, she wasn't doing a very good job of it. Ronnie looked at her father, who didn't appear to be listening anymore, and then back at Janessa.

"What about before I left?" she asked. "What was Floyd like then? Did we… get along?"

Janessa bit her lip and stared at the TV, but Ronnie didn't think that she was watching the show.

"You and Floyd…" Janessa sighed. "Well, you never were lovey-dovey. Over the moon. I mean, you liked each other well enough, but you were never… mushy… starry-eyed. With having kids so fast, and financial stuff… you were so young! I can't believe that we all just acted like it was normal for a seventeen-year-old to marry a twenty-five-year old right out of high school. You never had any time to find yourself, mature, or even get to know Floyd."

"What happened?" Ronnie tried to build a picture in her mind. That young bride in the pictures. Floyd, who she had met. The children were only four and two when she left. "Did we fight?"

"Sure you fought. I don't mean you didn't love each other anymore, or were threatening divorce, or anything like that. Just… it was stressful. You fought. You argued over money, over parenting, the housework, chores, how late Floyd worked… all the usual. I mean, it's perfectly normal for couples to go through tough times, especially that early in the marriage. Perfectly normal."

"I guess."

"I didn't think you'd stay together," Alex confided, his eyes on the TV. "I thought… Mom and Dad rushed you into it too fast, and once you got tired of the fighting, you would separate. Share custody or give him visitation, and he'd give you child support, and you'd be better off living in different houses."

"Really?" Janessa looked at Alex. "I never knew that."

Alex shrugged. "I just figured. What do I know? I was just a kid myself. But I didn't think it was going to last."

"You thought I got married too fast?"

Both siblings nodded immediately. Dad looked away from the TV. "You needed someone to look after you," he said. "Someone more mature, who could help you through... your issues."

"My issues?"

They were all silent, looking at each other. Dad looked back at the show. "Well, maybe issues is the wrong word... but you always had some... difficulties."

"What kind of difficulties?"

He didn't answer right away. Ronnie looked at Alex and Janessa, but they didn't jump in with any suggestions.

"You were just... immature. You needed a good, stable provider. Like Floyd. You weren't ever going to go to university or be some big executive. But you liked kids. You were good with them. Being a stay-at-home mom was a good choice for you."

"Until it got to be too much," Alex offered, brows raised.

"She didn't leave because of the kids," Dad said. "Those are good kids. It wasn't because of them. It was just..." He scowled. "I don't know. She was never good with stress."

Ronnie breathed out. *Never good with stress.* Well, that at least sounded like her. She wanted to just run away. She had already tried once to just run away. Or drive away. She wanted to veg in front of the TV, not to discuss the past or her psyche. She didn't want to have to deal with the stress. Just to leave it behind and think of more pleasant things.

"What happened when I got stressed?" she asked.

Dad rubbed a hand over his bald head. He looked toward the kitchen.

"Cynthia? Did you need any help out there?"

They all looked at him. Mom popped out of the kitchen and looked into the living room.

"I already said I don't need anything. What's wrong? Is something wrong?"

Janessa giggled. "I think Dad wants to be rescued. He's got himself into a corner."

Mom looked at her husband, puzzled. "What does she mean?"

"Nothing is wrong. I just wanted to know if you needed any help. Get you something from the storeroom or open a jar or something."

She smiled, still looking uncertain, and shook her head. "No. I'll call you if I need anything... *manly* done."

Mom retreated back to the kitchen. Dad looked back at the TV and ignored his children. Ronnie looked at him, and then at the other two.

"Was I depressed? Schizophrenic? What? I should know what my history is, shouldn't I?"

"That was a long time ago," Janessa said. "A lot has changed since then. You seem like you're really together now. Matured."

"I am thirty-three, not seventeen anymore," Ronnie pointed out, "and I've had four kids."

Janessa's jaw dropped. "Four?"

"Well, that I know of. The police investigator seems to think that I've started dozens of families everywhere I've gone. But a person can only have kids at certain intervals, right? At one per year, so I couldn't have had more than... eleven since I left."

Dad looked over, his face red and thunderous.

"You will not talk that way here! It's not a joking matter!"

Ronnie pressed her mouth closed and swallowed. She felt horrible. Her stomach clenched tightly and she watched him, worried that he was going to get out of his chair and come after her. He looked so angry. Of course, he was right. It was serious, what she had done. A horrific thing she had done to the two families that she knew about, the four children. In addition to her own parents and siblings. It wasn't funny to joke about having eleven more children after she had left Floyd. Even having just two more was devastating to her. Those poor children were now motherless and Ronnie hadn't even been legally married to their father. She wondered if he could come after her for child support, now that he was raising them alone. Garnish her wages to help to care for them. Even if he didn't, she should probably try to do something. Kids had school fees. Orthodontia. Psychiatric bills.

"I'm sorry," she said, barely able to voice the apology. "You're right. That was... inappropriate." Ronnie looked down at her hands. "I feel bad for those kids. Kent and Carrie, and the other children that I left. I never meant to hurt anybody. I don't think. I just... I don't remember what happened. I guess it was just too much."

"You *should* feel bad for what you did," Dad said. "That's not the way that you were raised. If you needed help, you should have asked for it. Running away is never the answer."

They were all silent for a while, the mood of the room subdued.

"Because this family never runs away," Janessa said suddenly, "or hides anything."

Alex looked at her. Dad scowled and stared at the TV screen, starting to flip restlessly through the channels.

"What does that mean?" Ronnie asked.

Janessa considered for a minute before answering, her eyes flicking over to Alex for support.

"It's just... the way that we've grown up in this family. We all come from different backgrounds, and the way that we deal with it is just... to forget about it. Pretend that it doesn't even exist. Live in the present. Think about what's best for the family."

"Because you're adopted," Ronnie said slowly. "You're just supposed to forget about what happened before you came to this family?"

"Yeah," Janessa nodded. "Forget everything. Cut all ties."

Alex scratched at an invisible spot on his pants. "When you become part of the Dare family, that's all you know. No contact with old family or friends. No talking about them, even. You have a new life and you live without a past."

Ronnie pondered over this. She rubbed at the frown lines in the middle of her eyebrows where a knot was forming. "But isn't that... doesn't that sound like what I've been doing?"

"Well... we're not talking *literally* forgetting," Janessa contributed.

"But that's right, isn't it? That's what I've been doing. Forgetting about the past. Starting a new family with a fresh slate, completely new. That's what I've been doing the past eleven years."

"We never told you to do that," Dad growled. "Don't you act like this is all our fault. We raised you to be better. You were married and the mother of two children. You were supposed to stay there and raise them up, not run off somewhere. You can't lay this at our feet. We tried to give you the best upbringing we could."

"No. I didn't mean that. I'm sorry. I just mean... there's sort of a parallel. Maybe... something broke in my brain and my subconscious decided to take it literally..."

"This isn't because of us," he repeated.

"No. Of course not. I was an adult. Whatever happened was all on me, not you."

He nodded.

Ronnie watched the TV for a few minutes, trying to distract herself and to let the room calm down a little. She didn't want to get her father upset. Every time that he raised his voice or expressed disapproval, she felt like a little child, waiting for the belt. Sick and frightened and guilty. Had he whipped her when she was young? Was she unconsciously afraid, reliving whatever he had done even though she couldn't remember it?

When he seemed to be fully engaged in a TV show again, Ronnie looked at Janessa.

"So... what kind of a background did you come from? You weren't a baby when they got you?"

"No. Not a baby! I was... I guess I was six, almost seven." She looked at their father. "Been here ever since."

"But you don't live here." Ronnie gestured to their surroundings.

"No!" Janessa laughed. "Little birds get kicked out of the nest. Gotta learn how to fly."

"Do you remember your family? From before? What were they like?"

Janessa cleared her throat and looked at Alex.

"Didn't you get the part about forgetting your previous family and never talking about them again?" Alex asked Ronnie. "We don't talk about it. Not at all. I don't even remember them anymore. My birth family. I've been able to completely block them out." He looked pleased with himself over this. "I was eleven when I came here. Almost a teenager!"

"You don't remember your real family at all?"

"*This* is our real family," Alex said. "This is our forever family. The families that we were with before, they were just... surrogates. That's just how we came into this family."

"That must be really weird."

He cocked an eyebrow at her. "Weirder than your situation?"

Ronnie had almost managed to forget about her own situation. Maybe that was what they all shared. The ability to forget.

"Well... of course that's weird... but I prefer to think about other people's situations."

The three of them all laughed.

"What's it like for you?" Janessa asked after a while. "I mean... we're talking about intentionally moving on. Forgetting your troubles from the past so that you can make a future for yourself. But what's it like to unintentionally forget? To come back here and meet your family again, like it was the first time? To realize what you've missed?"

Ronnie had been avoiding thinking about it as much as possible. She studied the room around her. It was completely foreign to her— other than the fact that she had been there once before—it was like she had never lived there. When she looked at the pictures over the mantel, she could pick out herself, her children, Janessa and Alex. But she didn't feel like a part of it. The books on the shelf might have been ones that she had read when she was younger. Maybe for school. But she had no memory of them. There were clay vases and crafts made by children's hands. Had she made one of them? Had Kent or Carrie?

Had any of the furniture or decorations in the living room changed since she had lived there? Or was everything still precisely the same?

"It seems like someone else's life," Ronnie confessed. "I feel like it's one big prank, and at some point everyone is going to say 'surprise' and laugh, and admit that it was all just made up. I feel like I'm an actor in a play, only I don't know my part."

"Did you just melt when you met Kent and Carrie? They're such sweet children. I bet that you loved them, even though you couldn't remember them."

Ronnie started to chew on her thumbnail. "Well, no. They're pretty mad at me. And they should be," she hurried on, "that's not saying anything against them. But it's hard to feel love toward an angry teenager you don't even know. I just feel... attacked. It's unfair. I'm not the mom that they lost. Even if I am."

[VI]

Ronnie wanted to quit her job. She wanted to find something else. Somewhere they didn't know who she was and that she'd been arrested. But she found it impossible whenever she clocked in. Everyone was so nice to her. They'd even covered her bail, which ended up being a really bad investment. Gordon hadn't even censured her when she had broken the terms of her bail and been sent back to jail. He should have. He barely knew her and certainly should never have invested money in her.

So Ronnie found herself unable to give notice. But it was getting harder and harder each day to get to the office and to check in and do her work. Harder to wake up in the morning. Harder to drag herself out of bed and to drive herself to work. She had to have the job to survive, but she could barely function. She wasn't doing well, and it would probably be better for the company if she just quit and they didn't have to carry her anymore.

Then came the morning that she couldn't get out of bed again. Ronnie turned off her alarm and went back to sleep. The phone rang and she ignored it. She managed to drag herself out of bed to make a trip to the bathroom, and made a cup of coffee that she didn't drink, just climbing back into bed again and finding it later in the evening, cold, still on the counter.

Ronnie told herself that she was just sick. She'd feel better the next morning and she'd get up and go to work. But she didn't get out of the apartment the next day, either. When her body got too sore from lying in bed all day, she got up and sat in front of the TV, eventually falling asleep there.

Day and night became a blur. The TV played constantly in the background, giving her restless dreams when she fell asleep. She unplugged the phone and let the battery run down so that it would stop ringing. There were even some knocks on her door, but Ronnie ignored them, afraid of facing the police again, having to look at more pictures of forlorn families or face more questions that she simply couldn't answer.

Adah Cruz would not normally have been part of a simple welfare check. Certainly, she wouldn't have gone on it herself, but would have simply have sent a subordinate if it were in her circle of responsibilities. But the subject of the check was Ronnie Plum. No one had seen her and they had received more than one concerned call.

Since Ronnie was no longer on bail or under charges, there had been no reason to keep her under surveillance. They couldn't just surveil random people on the chance that they might commit some crime. The crimes that Ronnie had been guilty of were not violent murders or thefts, not drugs, not anything that they could watch for to go down again. She had taken years to start a family, head to a breakdown, and to run off again. That in itself was not a crime, except maybe for failing to provide for her children. It was only taking on a false identity that they could prosecute her for, and for the time being, she had her own identity back. She had her own identification numbers and cards. They didn't have anything to charge her with, let alone any reason to keep a watch on her, which was incredibly expensive for the department.

When the welfare check came in, Adah snatched up the chance to look in on Ronnie again and see what was going on. Ronnie had probably run again, though if she had, there was nothing that Adah could do about it.

They knocked on the door. Eddie rapped it sharply. When Ronnie didn't respond, he called out her name. Still no answer. No sound from within. The sounds of a TV that was coming from a neighboring apartment. No footsteps or call for help. Eddie rapped again. Still no answer. He stepped back, nodding at Adah.

She slid the landlord's key into the lock and swung the door open, pushing it quickly and standing back out of the way. There was no movement from within. They entered cautiously, but without drawn weapons. There was no indication that Ronnie was a danger or that there was anyone else there who might be. It was just a welfare check. Look in and make sure she was okay and hadn't fallen in the tub or taken a bottle of pills.

The TV was not the neighbor's, but Ronnie's, which was the first indication that she had not run away this time. There was a litter of unwashed dishes in the kitchenette. Ronnie was not sitting in the easy chair in the living room, but there was evidence that she had spent plenty of time there lately. At least, a lot of garbage had accumulated there since the last time Adah had been in the apartment.

They moved on to the bedroom and that was where they found her. Ronnie's slim form was stretched out on the bed in the ratty t-shirt and yoga pants that served as her pajamas. She was thin, pale, and unmoving. The room stank of sweat and rank, unwashed body. Eddie moved into the room first, shaking the girl and then feeling for a pulse on her thin neck.

"She's alive," he confirmed.

Adah had dared to hope, not being able to smell any decomp.

"I'll call an ambulance." Adah glanced around the bare room. "Any sign of overdose? Illness? Injury?"

Eddie gingerly checked her wrists and pulled back the covers she clutched to her chest to get a better look at her body.

"Nothing obvious. I'll check the bathroom."

He left Adah there and ducked into the small bathroom.

"I don't see anything. No drugs or prescriptions. Tylenol is almost full."

Adah nodded at him, waiting for the emergency dispatched to pick up. As they waited for the ambulance, they took a look around the apartment. The welfare check call enabled Adah to check things like fridge and cupboards for sufficient food, and they found nothing. The place was bare. There had obviously been food there to start with, as evidence by the dirty dishes, but at some point Ronnie had run out and had not bothered to go out to buy more.

"Either she's been sick or she's a psych case," Adah said.

"We already know she's a psych case," Eddie pointed out.

"Yes, well... at this point it looks like she can't take care of herself; we'll ask them to put a hold on her."

Eddie nodded agreement. "Looks that way."

Ronnie awoke in a hospital bed, with an IV in her arm. She looked around listlessly at first, barely even taking in her surroundings. Eventually, it all started to seep back. She sighed deeply.

"You awake and alive over there?" a girlish voice asked.

Ronnie turned her head toward the sound. There was a curtain pulled between them, but somewhere beside her was another bed, with another patient in it.

"Yeah, looks like it," Ronnie admitted.

"You attempt suicide? They don't usually put suicides in this section. Not to start out with."

"No. No, I just..." Ronnie grunted as she moved her body and tried to find a comfortable position. "I guess I just... wasn't feeling well, or something. I don't really know what happened."

"Huh. I'm Faith. You?"

"Ronnie." Ronnie didn't say anything for a while, not sure how to continue the conversation, or if she wanted to. But it turned out that she was lonely and she did want to continue the conversation. "So... what are you here for?"

"Cutting."

"Cutting... your wrists? I thought you said they didn't put suicides in this section."

"No. Not attempting suicide. Just... cutting... you know, to make me feel better."

"How would cutting make you feel better?"

"Endorphins. It really does work. Makes you all calm and relaxed. But... it's self-destructive and addictive, so you get caught and they send you here."

"Right."

"You never cut?"

"No."

"Take pills? Anything?"

"No. I just..." Ronnie trailed off, not wanting to discuss her coping mechanisms.

"What?" Faith prodded.

Ronnie didn't answer. She punched at the pillow, trying to get more comfortable. She was too restless to go back to sleep, but she didn't want to be awake. There were noises from Faith's direction and in a few minutes, the sound of the curtain being pulled in the track, and Faith was peeking around at her.

"Hey, roomie," she greeted. She sat back down on her own bed, looking Ronnie over.

Ronnie also studied her. Faith wasn't at all what she had expected. With the soft voice and a name like Faith, she had expected an angelic face. Slim, willowy body. Even knowing about the cutting, Ronnie had expected someone who looked frail and vulnerable.

But Faith looked like none of that. Dyed black hair. Lots of tattoos down her arms. A hefty girl. Solidly built, like someone who would be comfortable on the back of a Harley. She didn't have on any makeup or piercings, but Ronnie was sure that when she was out in public, there were plenty of piercings and stark, dramatic makeup.

Faith had been evaluating Ronnie at the same time.

"Anorexia?" she guessed. "You look like you've lost a lot of weight recently."

Ronnie had, having given up food for the past little while. "No... I've just been sick."

"Sick with what? This is psych. Not stomach viruses."

"I don't really feel like talking about it."

"Well, they're all about the talk here. If you don't talk to me, you'll be talking to someone else. You're going to have therapists poking into every private corner. Get used to it. There's no keeping quiet around here."

"I'll walk to a psychiatrist if I have to," Ronnie said, "but I don't want to tell everybody my problems."

"Yeah. Good luck with that, all right?"

Ronnie shrugged.

Dr. Wanger looked at Ronnie over the tops of his glasses, and back down at the paper file in front of him. Ronnie could tell that he had at least the records from Dr. Able. Maybe there was more too, it seemed to be pretty thick for the file of someone who had just been admitted.

"Why don't you tell me about your history," Dr. Wanger suggested.

"Looks like you already have it all there." Ronnie folded her arms protectively in front of her, covering up the vulnerability she felt sitting there in a hospital gown having to talk about her history or innermost thoughts. "That's more than I know about myself."

He chuckled at that. "Tell me anyway," he cajoled. "I'll tell you if you get anything wrong."

Even in her melancholy mood, Ronnie found herself smiling at that.

"I mean it. I don't really know anything about myself. I have amnesia." The word always made her feel odd. She didn't like to use it. A clinical word, thrown around in budget TV movies and treated like a plot twist or a joke. Ronnie didn't feel like it really described her. She wasn't crazy or crippled. She wasn't mentally ill. She just happened not to be able to remember most of her life.

"How far back does your memory go?"

"About a year."

"Good. You've at least had a year to learn about yourself. How about before that? Your childhood?"

"No. Nothing else."

"Nothing from your childhood."

"No."

"Have you visited any old haunts to see if they would trigger memories?"

"Yeah. Nothing happened."

"Fine, fine," he assured her. "Not to worry. Your parents are here?" he asked, flipping through pages of the file.

"Yes."

"You've met them? What did you learn about your childhood?"

"Well… there's Mom and Dad and me and two adopted kids, Alex and Janessa. They were foster kids that stayed with them."

"Uh-huh. Did you meet them too?"

"Yeah."

"Wonderful! Were you adopted from foster care as well?"

"No. I was their natural daughter."

"Interesting. Were they not able to have more children after you?"

"I don't know." Ronnie thought about it. "I think they just liked having foster kids."

"Some people find it very fulfilling. Helping less fortunate children out."

"I think it's really nice. They took care of my kids when I was gone and… my ex-husband was in jail."

"That's nice of them," Dr. Wanger agreed. He didn't ask her why she had been gone and why Floyd had been in jail, and Ronnie didn't offer it.

"The kids really like them. They call them Nana and Papa. So, I guess they did a good job. They're still really close."

"What did you think of them when you met them?"

Ronnie considered. "I don't know. They seemed a little... weird. But I guess you can't judge real families by what you see on TV."

"We'd have a pretty skewed view of the world if we did. Weird in what way? Were you comfortable around them?"

"No. Not really. I felt like... they treated me like a lost dog. Something that they owned. Instead of... another person. I haven't had anyone treat me like that before." She hesitated. "That I can remember," she tacked on.

"I imagine they did feel pretty possessive about having you back again. Maybe afraid that they would lose you again. Or that you would not want to be with them."

"They acted like I did something wrong. Leaving my families behind. When I had an episode. It wasn't like it was something that I wanted to do. It wasn't like I planned it. But they acted like... that wasn't the way they raised me. Like I had done it out of anger. I don't know."

Dr. Wanger nodded. "That would feel awkward. Anything else? Something that seemed out of place?"

Ronnie shrugged. She stared at the shiny clock on Dr. Wanger's desk. It was brass and glass and she could see the inner workings spinning away. "None of it seems right," she said. "I drew pictures for Dr. Able, and the picture that I drew for family didn't look anything like my real family. It feels like they are all impostors. Just trying to trick me into thinking that they are really my family."

"Have you talked to them about these feelings?"

"No!" Ronnie was horrified. "Why would I do that?"

"It's important to have open and honest communication. Especially in a situation as difficult as this one."

"They don't seem very open to hearing what I have to say... It's like... they want to wipe out what happened in the past. We're not allowed to talk about it. We're just supposed to focus on the present."

"Focusing on the present is one thing. But I think there's a whole lot of the past that you're going to need to be reminded of. I think that you should have them come visit you here. Maybe we can have a session together. Maybe a facilitator would help."

~

Ronnie had already been through x-ray, which she had found frustrating enough, having had to wait for several hours, then been constantly repositioned for the x-ray, as if they were looking for the most uncomfortable position possible. Then she had to wait for the brain imaging that they wanted to do, and then the procedure itself, which involved lying in a coffin-like chamber until she felt like she really was going to die. She was supposed to be as still as possible, and she tried, worried that if she moved they would have to start all over again. But her breathing started to feel labored, her legs were itching like crazy, and she really had to pee.

"Are you almost done?" she called out finally, "I don't know how much longer I can do this!"

"You're doing fine," a bored voice responded. "We'll be done shortly and you'll be able to get out of there. Please don't talk. Stay as still as possible."

Ronnie focused on not moving her restless legs, though she supposed it was her head that really mattered, and maybe she could shift her legs slightly without it messing up the test.

Finally, she felt the bed start to move and she slid out of the tunnel feet first.

"You did really well," said a smiling, curly-haired nurse who smiled down at her. "You can go get dressed and there is a bathroom down the hall."

Ronnie moved stiffly. She got to her feet and shuffled quickly out into the corridor to find the toilet.

Then there was another wait for the doctor to review the test results with her.

He had introduced himself earlier, but Ronnie couldn't remember his name when she sat back down in his office again, this time to look at the big computer display on the wall where he arranged the images. Ronnie studied them, looking for cracks in the skull on the x-ray, or some kind of hole or inactive area on the colored brain scan.

What would the tests show? Were her dreams about Floyd trying to bury her, injured but still alive, true? Were they memories? Something that he'd really done? If she'd been hit over the head that hard, surely it would show up on the x-ray.

"Did you find anything?" she asked.

"Well, it turns out there's nothing in there," the doctor teased. He waited for Ronnie to laugh at his joke. "Actually, everything appears to be normal. No old fractures. No lesions or tumors in the brain, nothing that might indicate an old injury or more recent trauma. As far as we can tell, your brain is perfectly healthy."

Ronnie slumped back in her chair, disappointed.

Had she really wanted to be told that she was brain injured? That Floyd really had tried to kill her or that she'd been in a devastating car accident? Did she really want an answer that badly?

She did.

"So... nothing. What does that mean?"

"I guess that it means that your memory loss is likely psychological," he said. "It's still possible that there is some physical problem that we were not able to see, something that didn't leave any scarring or other traces. If an injury had caused your memory loss, I would expect it to be pretty severe. But there's nothing here."

"So, it's back to the drawing board. Or to the couch."

"I'm sorry I couldn't be of more help. I know this must be really difficult for you."

"Yeah. Well, thanks for doing all that."

[VII]

Sleeping at the hospital was difficult, even though they gave her something before bed to 'help her settle.' Ronnie moved around restlessly, unable to find a comfortable position. It wasn't as uncomfortable as the bunk in prison, but it was still just as hard to get to sleep. Her mind kept going back to the session with Dr. Wanger. She didn't want to have her family in to visit and dredge up the past, even though she couldn't remember the past and it would be easier to function if she at least knew something about herself. She really didn't want to remember. Maybe that was why she couldn't.

Ronnie closed her eyes and forced herself to lie still, completely unmoving. Barely even breathing. If she didn't let herself toss and turn, she would soon fall asleep and then she could forget and be oblivious again, just for a little while.

When she did fall asleep, she was still restless. Slipping in an out of consciousness, her mind racing like a hamster on a wheel, spinning but going nowhere. As night wore into early morning, she started to dream.

It wasn't a dream of being buried this time, though she had dreamed that one several times and it sometimes made her afraid to fall asleep.

The noise this time was a tap running. Not a sink, but the deeper, broader sound of a bathtub being filled. And accompanying it was a whole cadre of confusing feelings. Guilt and disgust. Anger. Her body hurt. It felt bruised and raw. There were voices, a man and a woman.

"You hurt her. She's bleeding," the woman said.

"It's nothing. She'll be fine."

"It's not just a little blood. It's too much. You were too rough!"

Ronnie groaned, trying to escape the dream. Her head was dizzy and nauseated. She wanted to wake up. Maybe she had the flu and it had triggered this bad dream. Everything seemed fuzzy and far away.

"Just shut up and get her cleaned up."

Ronnie felt herself being lowered into warm water. A spasm of pain wrenched through her, starting somewhere deep inside.

"Mommy!"

"Oh, hush, Ronnie. Let me get you cleaned up and then you can go to sleep."

Ronnie was crying. "Mommy..."

"Shhh..."

"Mommy..."

She floated in the warm water. Time seemed to be suspended as well. Ronnie continued to cry, the tears flooding her cheeks and running down her throat. Eventually, she was lifted out of the water. The cold air immediately made her shiver. When she was put down, the pain got worse. As she was toweled off, Ronnie tried to roll up into a ball, holding herself and gritting her teeth against the pain. Her sobs grew louder in her own ears. It was unbearable.

"I'm taking her to emergency," Mommy said.

~

Ronnie, Book #5 of the *Between the Cracks* series by P.D. Workman
can be purchased at pdworkman.com

~

About the Author

P.D. Workman is a USA Today Bestselling author, winner of several awards from Library Services for Youth in Custody and the InD'tale Magazine's Crowned Heart award, and has published over 100 mystery/suspense/thriller and young adult books, including stand alones and these series: Auntie Clem's Bakery cozy mysteries, Reg Rawlins Psychic Investigator paranormal mysteries, Zachary Goldman Mysteries (PI), Kenzie Kirsch Medical Thrillers, Parks Pat Mysteries (police procedural), and YA series: Tamara's Teardrops, Between the Cracks, and Breaking the Pattern.

Workman loves writing about the underdog, who the reader may love or hate. She has been praised for her realistic details, deep characterization, and sensitive handling of the serious social issues that appear in all of her stories, from light cozy mysteries through to darker, grittier young adult and mystery/suspense books.

> P. D. Workman, does not shy from probing the deep psychological scars of childhood trauma, mental illness, and addiction. Also characteristic of this author, these extremely sensitive issues are explored with extensive empathy, described with incredible clarity, and portrayed with profound insight.
>
> —KIM, GOODREADS REVIEWER

Some of Workman's titles have been translated into Spanish, French, Portuguese, German, and Italian.

Workman began writing at an early age and is a prolific reader as well as writer. She is also passionate about teaching and learning, expresses her creativity through art and cooking, and loves exploring the Calgary parks and green spaces where the Parks Pat Mysteries are set. She was a legal assistant for many years and has done extensive charitable work.

Workman was born and raised in Alberta, Canada, and is married with one adult son.

∼

Please visit P.D. Workman at pdworkman.com to see what else she is working on, to join her mailing list, and to link to her social networks.

∼

If you enjoyed this book, please take the time to recommend it to other purchasers with a review or star rating and share it with your friends!

tiktok.com/@pdworkmanauthor

facebook.com/pdworkmanauthor

x.com/pdworkmanauthor

instagram.com/pdworkmanauthor

amazon.com/author/pdworkman

bookbub.com/authors/p-d-workman

goodreads.com/pdworkman

linkedin.com/in/pdworkman

pinterest.com/pdworkmanauthor

youtube.com/pdworkman

patreon.com/pdworkmanauthor

reamstories.com/pdworkmanauthor

Find P.D. Workman's books at

PDWORKMAN.COM

Scan the QR code below

www.ingramcontent.com/pod-product-compliance
Lightning Source LLC
Chambersburg PA
CBHW031028030726
47497CB00004B/1054